THE DARKEST CHORD

DARKEST NIGHTS BOOK ONE

JENN BULLARD

The Darkest Chord

Edited by Amber Nicole

Cover Art by Teased by Antonette

Formatted by Epitaph Formatting

Published by Jenn Bullard 2023

It only takes one voice, at the right pitch, to start an avalanche. - Dianna Hardy

FOREWORD

The Darkest Chord is the first book in the series. This began as a duet, but then as the story grew, I realized Lennon and her men have more story to tell. The Darkest Nights is now planned to be a series of three books. This is a shared universe, so you may see cameos of people from The Unwritten Truths Duet. However, this The Darkest Nights books can be read as a standalone series.

If I'm not new to you, you will see this series is darker and grittier than my first duet.

This book does have some content that may be considered triggering. If you have would like the full list, please email me jennbullardwrites@gmail.com

CONTENT WARNING

The Darkest Chord is book 1 in the Darkest Nights and contains triggers of grooming, dub con, non con, kidnapping, drugging, graphic sex, history of cutting, history of child abüse , bullying. If these topics, or any other dark themes bother you, then this book may not be for you. For a complete list of triggers, please email Jenn at jennbullardwrites@gmail.com

PROLOGUE

I always wondered why my mom was so different from others. Sometimes she's super happy and excited and planning all kinds of things, and other times she's exhausted and sad. She likes to talk to herself and always thinks the neighbors are taking things that aren't theirs. I just didn't know why she was like this.

I first started noticing it more when I was about seven years old, the day my dad moved out of our small town. He told me he'd always love me, but he couldn't stay any longer. My mom stood there, muttering to herself, with her hand covering her mouth.

She shakes her head, hand dropping to her side, and says, "You can't stay because you don't love me, is what you should tell her. This behavior is selfish James, you promised to always love me."

My dad responds with something I will never forget. "Sometimes love isn't enough. Goodbye, Carrie. I love you, Lennon. Never forget this."

He turns and climbs into his truck, packed full with his

things, and drives away, dust trailing him as he leaves me. Unfortunately, I will always remember every word, thanks to how impressionable I am at this age.

I look over at my mom, and she opens her arms, then run to her and squeeze her tightly. "I'm so sorry, Mommy, I promise I'll always stay," I cry. I don't know why I'm sorry, but it seems like the right thing to say.

My mom rubs my back, softly humming as she watches the dust left behind from my dad's departure. She sighs. "I know you will, Lennon dear. You're a good girl and you love me. Men can't be trusted. They have silver tongues, telling you what you want to hear. Don't get pulled in by them. Nothing good will come from it."

We sway, half dancing, to comfort each other, my mom's humming sharing space with the frogs.

1

LENNON

Twenty-One years later

The crowd is amazing, the energy electric as I weave my way through my song of stolen moments and missed opportunities. My voice is a contralto that calls out to people, makes them ask for more, and I love giving it to them. I walk slowly back, glancing over my shoulder to see Turner, my guitarist, picking up his solo just as I stop to take a breath. I grin as I watch him toss his tawny blond hair out of his face, his eyebrows knitting as his tattooed fingers fly up the frets. My eyes catch over his washboard abs, enjoying his current shirtless state.

He is breathtaking, and I know every woman beyond the stage is drooling as they watch him, too. I bite my lip as my eyes crawl up his arms, drinking in the vine tattoos that weave up the sinew of his muscles. I know that my name is hidden in one of the vines.

"Wipe the drool, beautiful girl," Roark says behind me and I turn to grin at him, blushing. "We'll show him how much we appreciate how gorgeous he is after," he chuckles behind his drums, arms flexing as he readies himself to play.

I don't know how I got so lucky to have these two men in my life. My eyes run up Roark's form: barrel chest, broad shoulders, brown hair perfectly styled in waves, and warm caramel eyes that make me melt with the protection and love he watches me with.

I nod and turn back as Turner finishes his piece, walking forward and catching his gaze as I wink at him. We've been performing together for a long time, and it never gets old. I bring the song to a close and Roark and Turner link arms with me to bow. The crowd goes wild as Roark kisses me soundly and loses it completely when Turner pulls me from him and dips me to kiss me hard. These men are territorial with me and each other and the crowd eats it up.

"Thank you, Portland," I yell into my microphone with a grin.

The three of us run off stage, waving, and I gasp with a laugh as Turner picks me up from behind, hugging me.

"God, I'll never get tired of performing with you, beautiful. Every time you sing, you're pure magic and everyone here tonight could hear it," he says.

Our manager comes up, smiling at us as she watches us interact. "You were incredible as always, guys. Portland loved you tonight. There's a group with VIP's that you'll need to visit with before you're done for the night, and then I'll make sure you have food in your bus afterwards. The entire band shines during this part, so don't disappear yet, please?"

I love Prescott, but she worries too much. "We would never disappoint our fans. Seriously, *The Darkest Nights* will be the perfect hosts, we'll sign swag, take photos, and then go respectfully crash," I tell her with a giggle.

Roark and I share a glance, knowing that the three of us are riding a high of adrenaline and endorphins after the show. The first thing that'll happen once we get on our bus is a post show orgy. Prescott is newer to the label, so I'll have to mention to have our pizza and beer delivered at least an hour after we finish with our fans. She doesn't need to be subjected to Roark's naked ass as he rails me over the side of our couch.

I smirk as I think of how we wouldn't even flinch if it happened. It wouldn't be the first time.

Turner grabs my hand, pulling me towards the green room where the VIP group will be.

"Prescott, did you give away passes to the audience tonight? I remember you said that you might," I say over my shoulder. "Oh and you wouldn't happen to have some of my candy on you, would you?"

She blinks at me in confusion, and then explodes into motion to follow me, digging into her pocket.

"Yes! We did throw out some passes into the audience before and during the show. It was a lot of fun, so we may continue to do this in other cities. It's still an intimate group though, so you'll be able to spend time talking to everyone," she assures us, then pulls out a packet of my only vice, gummy bears, and hands it to me. I'm found with them before a show and after for the sugar high.

Our VIP passes can't be bought. It's a rule that we put in place, because we didn't want to spend time with entitled assholes that think we owe them something. I want to see my fans, people that are excited when we walk into the room. So the label gives VIP passes to local radio stations and they have people call in to win them.

It's been working well for us so far. I tear open my gummy bears with a grin, munching on them as we continue.

We walk into the room, chatting and laughing. Everyone in the room turns, and excited chatter starts up.

"Hi everyone! We are so excited to meet you. How did you like the show?" I ask with a smile, walking towards the largest group of people standing together.

One of them grins at me. "I can't believe we won passes. We brought our daughters, and you're their first concert!"

"Oh my god, really," I squeal, my enthusiasm not at all feigned.

I love that our music talks to all ages, and it has life lessons sewn in through it. Lessons of acceptance, misunderstandings that lead to hatred and fear because you're different, and most importantly love. My relationship with Roark and Turner is loud, messy, but worth every fucking moment that I get to call them mine.

"Can I just tell you how much I love you," one of the girls says wide-eyed.

"Yes, and then you can tell me something important about you that I need to know. I live with two men and I need girl time before they come find me," I joke.

I don't have any girlfriends, so sad as it may be, this is my girl time. They dish, I listen and sign merch for them, soaking every moment in.

I feel an arm wrap around me, and look down, seeing familiar vine tattoos. I lean into Turner with a happy sigh and he kisses my neck. He quietly listens as one of the teenagers asks me a question about a boy.

"I can also answer that from a guy's perspective if you'll have me," he says, his voice rumbling through his chest and through my body, straight to my clit. I'm not going to last much longer if being near him makes me this turned on.

"You don't want to answer teenager questions though, do you?" asks her mom, chewing on her lip.

Turner is thirty-six and eight years older than me. You would think this mom is right and he wouldn't have patience for a teenager, but you'd be wrong. Turner is interested in what he feels is important, and making people feel seen is his superpower.

"I most certainly do. Lennon can tell you that I have opinions on all sorts of things, some she actually agrees with," he says, leaning forward to kiss my shoulder.

I twist my body so I can also watch him and he arches his eyebrow at me. I press my lips together to hold in my answering smile before turning back to the group.

"He's right. Turner enjoys breaking apart the things that guys do and making it make sense. This boy, Jared that you're asking about, is giving you mixed signals. He's telling you he's interested, while flirting with other girls. If he wants you, he'll be completely invested in you. How do you feel when he flirts with other people?" I ask her.

"Shitty. I feel like I'm not as pretty as those girls. They do things that I'm not comfortable doing, and it makes me wonder if I should be," the girl says. I wrack my brain to remember her name, and give her a blinding smile when I remember that it's Rachelle.

"You are beautiful, Rachelle. You have these eyes that sparkle when you talk, and any boy who is flirting with other girls doesn't deserve you."

Turner frowns. "Is this boy pressuring you for more than you're willing to give?"

Rachelle bites her lip. "I go to parties and he'll hug me, telling me how pretty I look. Sometimes he'll dance with me and his hands will roam a little, but not enough that I feel like I need to move them. Then, later in the night he'll be all over another girl or girls, and takes them upstairs to have sex with them. I know that's what they're doing, because I went to an upstairs bathroom once and they didn't make it to the room. He just watched me while he fucked her against the wall," she says softly.

Her mom looks horrified, but whatever she says won't be helpful. I lean into Turner's arms, knowing he can handle this conversation. We've fielded a lot of these conversations over the last few years as we've toured. We are real people and that's how people see us after spending time with us.

"He's unfortunately manipulating you. He wants to push you into doing something that you're not ready for, something that you'll regret. He's hurting you, and this asshole doesn't deserve your light. Now, you have to decide what you want to do," Turner says with a shrug.

"You're right. Fuck him," she spits out. "Why are guys dicks?" she groans.

"We have one so we figure we need to act like one," Roark says, joining the conversation.

Turner and I separate so that Roark can lazily throw his arms around our shoulders.

"Boy problems, I see. Were Turner and Lenny any help?" he asks with a lazy smile.

Rachelle's eyes widen and she nods. I can see that she's fan girling inside and I love it. As much as we act like normal people, we are still rock stars. We each have people that we are star struck over, and I'm not going to take that away from her. I also regularly worship Roark on my knees, enjoying every moment with this gorgeous, green-eyed god.

He turns his head and whispers in my ear, "There are more people for you to see, Lenny."

I nod and excuse myself after taking a photo with all of us. I smile to myself as I walk to the next group. A man turns and I see familiar dark brown curls and piercing, almost black eyes. My breath starts to hitch as I scan his face, stomach sinking. He has a small scar over his eyebrow from a bike accident, and I gasp because I thought I would never see him again after I left our small town.

"Hey there, little bit. Fancy meeting you here," he murmurs softly, his eyes cruel and calculating as they move over me.

At five-foot-nine, nothing about me is small, though my men enjoy making me feel tiny. I have wide hips, big boobs, and I've grown to love myself over the last few years.

"Derek," I whisper in horror.

It's the boy who terrorized me when I was young and my mother was ill. A boy turned man who doesn't seem to have outgrown the cruel streak that runs deep within him.

DEREK and I became enemies when I was eleven years old. It wasn't a normal confrontation either, I didn't even do anything to him. We barely spoke to each other during the four years he was my neighbor before that day.

HE WALKS *past me and pushes me into the wall, whispering in my ear that I am the girl that no one loved, not even her daddy. I don't know how he found out about my past, but nothing is a secret here it seems. He is incredibly cruel as the days continue in my first year of junior high school, and because Derek is also gorgeous at thirteen and popular, everyone follows his lead.*

My town is small, so grades six thru twelve are housed in the same building. I see the same faces day in and day out, so unfortunately everyone knows the other's business as well. Everyone knows that Lennon O'Reilly has the mom who is unstable and a bit off.

I'm sitting in seventh grade study hall, and he throws a piece of paper at me. It hits me in the forehead and I flinch, even as I struggle not to. Paying attention to his cruelty only eggs him on. Fuck, why can't I just ignore him? I blink back tears of embarrassment as multiple other balled up pieces of paper hit me.

"Don't be a baby, little bit. Take your punishment like a good girl. No one likes you because your eyes are a weird color, and you probably dance in the woods naked under the full moon. Although," I cut my eyes over to him in time to see him bite his lip, "I'm almost tempted to see that," he says. Such a creep. I don't know how these rumors keep starting.

Study hall is held for the entire school together even though Derek is in the ninth grade. There's zero reason for him to be bothering me. He should be working on his own work, as I am trying to do.

"Shut your stupid mouth," I hiss, glancing at the teacher at the front of the large room who is chewing gum and reading a book. Study hall is a walk in the park for the teacher assigned this period.

Derek grins. "Maybe you should look at what the 'love' notes on your desk say. I wouldn't mind sticking something else in your mouth, you need to relax a little. Live a little."

Over my dead body. Never happening. My life has been complicated enough recently, and my mom's episodes are happening more often. I don't need any part of his mean boy; I'm sure it would just blow up in my face anyway.

I shake my head. "That's a fat chance in hell, devil boy," I mutter.

Derek may help others push untrue rumors that I dance under the moon and dabble in the occult, but the truth is this dark eyed, cruel boy is much too beautiful. He hides his dark and twisty parts until you're too deep to back away, and you're drowning in his sins.

I always feel like I'm off beat when I'm around him. I don't know how to navigate junior high or the older kids around me in high school. They're all so much more mature than I am, or maybe I'm just emotionally stunted.

I sigh, opening one of the papers.

Your mother is fucking the mayor, *says one piece of paper and my jaw drops. No, would she?*

My mother does things when she's in a manic state that she wouldn't normally do. Sometimes she dresses in tight dresses and leaves me at home for days. I don't know where she goes, and she takes the car so I'm forced to walk to school since the bus doesn't pass by my house. I thought it was normal to be on my own so much, since I didn't know any different.

It's possible it's not the norm, and my mom isn't a good person.

Paper after paper say unspeakable things, and finally I can't handle it anymore and grab my stuff. I rush for the teacher's desk, telling him that I feel unwell and need to go to the nurse, and then I hide there until the last bell rings.

My life in Farrelsville, Kentucky is hard, and Derek is the dark eyed devil that leads the pack in destroying my life day after day.

I BLINK HARD, taking a shaky breath as I come back to the present.

"Derek, how are you here?" I whisper.

"I won a pass. I deserve to be here, little bit," he says softly, taking his finger to tip my head back just a little.

He is taller than me at six-foot-two and muscular. My dark eyed devil played football in our town and was really good. I can see he takes good care of his body too, not letting it get to fat.

I shake my head to clear the fog of my past, as I don't

belong there. This can't touch me here. *You are a badass. Act like it.*

I push his finger away, my other hand on my leather clad hip. His eyes slide appreciatively over my breasts in my black corset and I roll my eyes. If you can't appreciate me when I'm malnourished and before I had breasts, then you don't deserve to look now.

"My eyes are up here, douche canoe. Look, I'll take a photo or sign something for you if you want, but you are not one of my favorite people. The sooner you slink back to where you belong, the better," I tell him, pursing my lips like the scum of the earth that I should think he is.

Honestly, he looks amazing, in dark washed jeans and a well worn band T-shirt. His dark curls look soft, making my fingers twitch to touch them. I don't know why I feel like this, and as he smirks, my heart skips a beat. Better to nip this in the bud, as I never plan to see him again.

"Oh good, Lennon. I see you met Derek Williams. As you may remember, we've been looking for a new social media manager since Tony is getting married. He wants to be closer to home, which I commend, so he's going to do the editing on your videos from home. However, you need someone on the road with you, and Derek has made a name for himself over the last few years. The label thinks he's perfect to work with you and the band, while being true to what you're about," Prescott says with an excited smile, bouncing on the balls of her feet.

I'm sorry, did I say that I liked her?

"Do I get a say in this?" I bite out, grinding my teeth. Derek is a fucking liar, and if he's working for the label, he'd easily have access to this room to snag a VIP pass to surprise me.

"I'm sorry, Lennon, interviews have been conducted and he really is the best choice. If you think there's a problem, I'm sure you can push past them. You're a professional," she reminds me as her smile turns slightly brittle, then turns away.

I close my eyes and take a deep breath to center myself. I'll cry into my beer or work out my anger while the guys fuck me later. Mmm, the promise of orgasms sound like a great way to get through this.

Opening my eyes, I draw on my mask that I haven't had to pull in a long time. I like being myself, but fame was hard when it first started, so I created a mask to be able to push through my insecurities and anxiety of being around so many people. I am, after all, a small town girl.

"I do have a job to do and I *am* a professional. Now, if you wouldn't mind moving so that I can do it, I'd appreciate it," I tell him with a smile that is entirely fake and I know doesn't touch my eyes.

Derek's head tilts to the side as he looks at me in confusion. "Do you have multiple personalities that I need to be aware of?"

Dick. I walk around him, pretending he doesn't exist, and move to the next group. I let my mask drop and smile genuinely as they turn to see me.

"Sorry it took me a bit to find my way over to this side of the room," I tell them.

It's a group of men and women in their thirties and they grin back at me. "Please don't apologize. This has already been an amazing Tuesday night, and you're here now," one of the men says.

I spend the remainder of the VIP meet and greet firmly ignoring the elephant in the room that walks around taking candid photos. I don't think he had his camera when I first saw him, but honestly I was too shocked to notice much else. His presence is hard to ignore but I do my best to.

Roark and Turner meet up with me at the end of the event,

with Turner firmly pulling me into his side. He kisses my forehead as he talks to Prescott, when Derek walks up to us.

"I got some really great photos, guys. It's clear your fans love you," he says with a jovial smile. He says I have different personalities, but I've never seen this smile on him before.

It's almost more sinister to me than when he's cruel. I know what to expect then. I shiver and Turner glances at me in concern. I look up at him and furrow my brows a little and he nods. We have found ways to communicate without speaking, being in the public eye as often as we are.

Derek's eyes bounce between us and Turner's attention turns back to him.

"Our fans are amazing, especially the ones that win VIP passes. We love meeting with them after the show, and it's a blast. I understand we'll be seeing more of you as our social media manager?"

"Uh, yes. I'll work with Prescott on some events in different cities that you're in, but mostly I'll be taking your photos and managing your social media accounts. Tony is supporting the band from home, answering questions, and fielding any issues. I'm excited to work with you. I'm a big fan of the band and your music," Derek says, eyes lighting on me.

I struggle not to cringe or get pulled into my memories again. Thankfully my stomach saves me by growling.

Roark pulls me out of Turner's arms with a chuckle. "Lenny, we need to feed you before you turn into a gremlin."

His hands skim down the sides of my corset, stroking the exposed skin above my tight pants. I bite my lip, starting to get lost in his gaze. I am easily distracted by my men, heat filling my eyes. He notices and smirks, but whereas Derek's smile is cruel, Roark's projects screaming orgasms and filling my mouth with something other than food. My breath hitches and his hands tighten on my waist, lifting me up and over his shoulder, which is followed by his signature spank. I bite the inside of my mouth to hold in my moan.

"Prescott, please have pizza and beer delivered to the steps of the bus in an hour. I wouldn't suggest coming in, or we may offend your eyes. We have some post show celebrating to do," Rorak says, turning his body, so I can move my hair and look up at Derek and Prescott from where I hang.

"Yes, can't scar another manager, can we," I say with a cheeky grin.

Derek's jaw drops slightly as Turner does that deep chuckle that immediately floods my panties. I pinch Roark's butt to get him moving and he yelps. "Let's get the princess to her throne, shall we," Roark says as he turns away.

"Absolutely, if you mean my face," Turner growls softly.

I almost think no one hears him when I hear, "For fucks sake are they always like that?" from Derek.

Roark's strides quickly take us down the hall and out of the stadium, so I don't hear Prescott's response. He'll learn soon though that my guys don't give a shit who hears them when it comes to loving me.

2

LENNON

I squeal as Roark puts me back onto my feet, boots hitting the pavement hard. My hair flies everywhere and he winks at me.

"Is it me or are there weird vibes between you and Derek, Lenny?" he says, pulling me into his side and continuing to talk.

I blow my purple hair out of my view and make a face. "That is a long story, baby, and I would much rather be swallowing Turner's cock while you fuck me," I tell him.

"Oh, that's happening, but on a scale of one to ten, ten being we need to start looking for a gravesite, how much do we hate that cocky dick?" Turner asks as his lip twitches.

They're both so stabby and protective, and I really do love it.

"Um, a twelve, okay? Derek is someone from my past, and he has always been mean to me. I don't know how the label didn't run their top candidates with us before hiring someone," I mutter.

Turner blows out a breath. "Lavender, honey, you know the

last year has had a lot of managerial upheaval. It's not the first time that they've cut us out of a decision that impacts us. So the question is, can we live with this one?"

My growly, blue-eyed boy calls me Lavender, after my hair, when he's frustrated or really turned on, and I give a small smile at the familiarity. He and Roark are my people and I know that Turner and my growly bear will back me up on whatever I decide.

Before I can answer, Roark growls, "I didn't like how he looked at you; like you're a puzzle that he wanted to solve."

I have my head against his barrel chest, so I feel the vibration of every word. I turn and kiss as high as I can on his chest and he chuckles. These men make me feel tiny and fragile, as big as they are.

"I meant what I said; I'm a professional and I can handle him. However, he is intent on picking at old scabs of mine that I spent a long time working on sealing over. My childhood was not easy, and he was a part of that reason. I am not in that small, bigoted town any longer, and even though I may continuously dream of stabbing him, I can try really hard to not do it in person," I say with a sigh. Yeah, that was really convincing.

"Aw Lenny, that's so big of you," Roark praises and I snort.

"Hush, love," I say, laughter heavy in my words.

"We're back at the bus, so I am willing to table this for now, since we're all a little tightly wound tonight. Should things change and we can't all live with him working with us, can we promise to circle back and talk?" Turner asks as he unlocks the door to our home away from home while we are on the road.

"Aye," Roark and I chorus and Turner blows us both a kiss.

"Now get your sweet asses on this bus so I can fuck one of them," he growls and I shudder in need. Being with these men will never get old.

"Yes sir," I say in a breathy voice, and he turns to me as Roark opens the door.

Turner grabs me under my ass as I jump, climbing him like a tree, then kisses me as he walks up the steps, tangling his fingers in my hair.

"I bet her pussy is flooded right about now," Roark says as he locks the bus back up and turns on the engine to start the air conditioner. "Check for me and make her scream before I feed her my cock. I heard my girl was hungry."

I moan as Turner kisses down my neck before biting and teasing where my neck and shoulder connect. I grind on his abs, shamelessly looking for friction.

"My Lavender is such a needy girl," he growls as he unzips my corset. He greedily takes in my breasts as they spill out. "I will never get tired of staring and kissing these," he whispers reverently as he licks my nipple before sucking hard. I gasp, arching my back, wanting him to pull more into his warm, hot mouth. The piercing on his tongue only makes me want his face buried between my thighs. He lays me back on the couch next to us and pulls my pants down to my ankles.

He grins as he trails his fingers through my folds and I whimper. "Fuck, Roark you're so right. She's sopping wet and smells delicious." He lifts my legs, settling between my thighs, my feet trapped in my pants and resting on his back.

We've spent many nights this way, and it never gets old. He licks me like his favorite dessert, and I shamelessly grind my pussy on his face.

"Turner," I groan. "I need more, baby."

"So fucking beautiful when you beg," Roark groans, unbuckling his pants and pulling out his pierced cock.

I lick my lips, imagining him pushing it between them before my back bows as Turner sucks hard on my clit, while using a little teeth. He pushes two talented fingers inside me, crooking them just right as he massages one of my special spots.

"Oh my god," I scream. My fingers sink into his hair as I ride his face, coming just for him.

Roark quickly pulls off his motorcycle boots and pants, painting my lips with his precum as I turn my face. I open wide, alternating between sucking on the head and lapping at his weeping slit.

"Fuck, Lenny, I want to let you play with my cock, but I'm so close. I need to fuck your mouth, baby."

Turner lifts my legs, slipping out from between them and flipping me onto my stomach. I scramble to my hands and knees, still half dressed, knowing that I'm about to be ruined by them.

Roark gets on his knees in front of me so that his cock is in the perfect position for me. He gently slips his hands through my hair. "Are you gonna scream for me when you come, Lenny, like the good little whore you are?"

My mouth opens slightly, already panting for his cock. They worship the ground I walk on, but here, I am whatever fantasy they want me to be. I'll be their good girl, little whore, or strap on a dildo and be their mistress to fuck them. I fucking love it all.

Turner holds my hips tightly as he slides his cock between my folds, thrusting so he's sliding between my ass cheeks. I shiver, wondering where he'll be fucking me. My eyes widen as I look up at Roark and he grins widely at me.

"She's primed and ready to be fucked. Lavender, darling, we are going to play you like our favorite instrument. Roark, gag her pretty mouth," he groans before lining his dick up with my needy hole, forcing me to take every inch.

"Turner, please," I scream, gasping as I feel him stretch my walls.

"You shouldn't still be talking," Roark chides, pushing himself between my lips as his hand gently circles my neck. He's playful, but dominant and I can't wait to see what he'll do next.

I open my mouth wide, tongue sliding down the underside of his thick cock. "Fuck yes, just like that, baby girl," Roark coos, throwing his head back.

He wraps his hand still caught in the strands of my hair until it's fisted tightly, guiding my head until my nose meets his stomach. I gag slightly before adjusting to his size, tears starting to well in my eyes. Turner pulls out and then thrusts so that he is stroking my cervix and I shudder, swallowing hard. I can't scream with my mouth around Roark. They work together as tears stream down my cheeks, Turner's hand sliding between my thighs to rub firmly on my nub.

Roark slowly drags me up his pierced member as I breathe as deeply as I can before his hand around my throat tightens. He groans and I swallow to tighten my throat even more. His cock twitches and I suck harder as he rolls his hips back and forth with a groan.

The boys work me between them as I sob as Turner fucks me from behind. I can feel my walls start to flutter, and I know I'm close. I push back against Turner and he tightens his hand on my hip almost to the point of pain. Fuck yes, give it to me, baby.

"Oh you want to play with the big boys now, baby. Game fucking on," he says, his voice becoming hoarse with need.

I hold on to the couch for dear life as Turner fucks me into Roark, and I take both of them deeper. Roark throws his head back as he starts to lose what semblance of control that he had, fucking my face. The sounds of moans, slapping of skin against skin, and sucking fill the bus as we get closer and closer to oblivion.

My stomach cramps hard with need, and I can only whimper. "So fucking beautiful and flushed, tears running down your face as you suck off our gorgeous Roark. I can feel how close you are, you're strangling my cock so well, beautiful," Turner gasps, his thrusts pushing me higher and closer to his goal of soaking his cock.

He circles my clit with his fingers before pinching hard. I wordlessly scream around Roark as I come, and Turner grunts as he follows, fucking me through my orgasm as I clench hard on his thick cock.

"Swallow every drop for me, Lenny. Be our beautiful, needy cum whore who loves my cock. I'm gonna come, baby," Roark gasps, groaning as he thrusts twice in my mouth before I taste his salty sweetness.

I eagerly swallow as much as I can, but there's always so much and I know I miss a little. Roark is breathing fast, and I know his heart is beating as hard as mine is, but he'll never let me waste a drop of cum. He gathers what I missed, pulling out of my mouth with a pop.

"Open and clean my fingers," he commands and I wouldn't dream of disobeying.

I open, his fingers entering my mouth, and I swirl my tongue and suck hard to clean his fingers.

"Your mouth is like a fucking Hoover, Lenny. Fuck, you are a gem," he says, eyes filled with heat, and I see his cock is still hard.

Turner has wrapped his arms around my waist, keeping his weight off of me, giving me open mouthed kisses along my back. "Our gorgeous, dirty girl. We are so lucky to call you ours. I love you so much," he says happily.

I smile as Roark pulls his fingers out of my mouth, replacing his fingers with his tongue as he kisses me hard.

"You taste delicious," he groans. "I love you to the ends of the earth and back. Let's clean you up before Prescott comes with our food, and then we can have round two in our bed."

As much as I love that they can't wait to undress me before making me scream again, a shower sounds heavenly.

"My body is a puddle of goo," I laugh, happily exhausted. "Turner, honey, can you help me out of the prison that are my pants?"

"Oh yeah, you're still wearing clothes. I like them better half on," he chuckles darkly.

They help me undress, and I take the first shower. Our tour bus is nicer than others, but the shower is still small. Every four stops, the label will treat us to a hotel room so that we can stretch out in a larger space, with a giant shower.

Our life is amazing, filled with adventure, but I'm glad for the breaks in between of tour life. The band has been together for seven years, with a few substitutions as band members have left for whatever reason. We love music, and we live for the music without the drama.

Unfortunately the label has left us out of key decisions over the last year, and I hope that their latest decision won't unravel everything that we've worked so hard for.

I LAY IN BED, draped over Roark. He makes the best pillow with his well-built chest, his arms wrapped loosely around me. Pizza and beer have been consumed, now we're surrounded by the sound of the bus' AC as it makes a whooshing sound. We're still awake, enjoying our downtime before we head to our next city tomorrow morning.

One of the things we asked for on our bus was a king-sized bed rather than little bunks so we could all snuggle together. We don't go to bed angry, so there's never been a need for separate spaces. We either talk or angry fuck until we figure it out. It's the healthiest way that we've been able to make things work between two very alpha men and myself. Okay, so I'm not perfect. Sometimes I can be a hot head, while I act like a brat just so I can be spanked.

Add to it all that there's not a lot of space in a bus, this allows us to have living spaces and reading nooks throughout the bus. The tour agreed when designing our bus, which means they rarely have any *behavioral issues* with us, as they call it. Really it's the other bands in the label pitching a tantrum for not getting their way, but I am not incredibly happy with Derek being hired.

Maybe it's time for me to become the diva that others think I am and throw an epic tantrum? It holds some merit, though I'll have to see how this goes.

"Penny for your thoughts, my gorgeous Valkyrie," Roark murmurs, twirling one of my drying curls around his finger.

I sigh, squeezing him to me. "I was just thinking about how much I love my bed and both of you. I'm thinking of everything and nothing, love," I half-lie to him, tilting my head back to look at him.

"Nuh-uh. You may not have realized it, but you snorted to yourself. So you were thinking about something," Turner says next to us, propping his head on his hand to look down at me.

"Um," I know my cheeks are coloring as they grin at me. "I was thinking about our newest member of our social media team, and how I'm usually a team player and rarely complain. But then my thoughts turned towards that possibly changing and my inner brat coming out if he continues his pattern of being a dick to me," I tell them.

"Baby, if he's a dick to you where I can hear him, he'll get his teeth kicked in," Turner growls. "When you were younger, you didn't have people to protect you. I know you dealt with a lot growing up in that shitty town, but nothing's the same anymore. Your mom is gone and you have us. We will burn down this whole fucking world for you, and I hope you know this." He tempers this with a roguish grin and a wink and I smile back at him. Leaning down, he kisses me hard. "You're all ours, the world just gets to borrow you," he whispers.

The guys know a little about my past, and the boy who made my life hell. I wanted them to know why I startled so easily when we all first met. Shoving and hitting happened often when I was bullied in school, and my mom could be volatile when she was depressed and angry too. This made me skittish once I left it all behind. Or, at least I tried to. It looks like a piece of my shitty past is following me now.

I love knowing that I'm theirs and they are mine. Some people would chafe at the possessive terms, but I've never had this before.

"I know, baby, and I love you for that. Seeing Derek opened up a lot of doors that I thought were firmly closed. I just have to find a way to process this," I mutter.

Roark sits up, pulling me onto his lap. His index finger drags up the column of my throat before pushing my chin upwards. My eyes meet his fierce green eyes and I drown in their depths. Apparently, this answer isn't working for him.

"What do you usually do when shit gets confusing for you," he asks. It is asked like a question but I feel like he's demanding me to be honest with myself. His soul pulls at mine to be better than I think I can be and my breath hitches.

"I write songs," I respond softly. These feelings are so raw and savage, I don't know if they'll ever be able to see the light of day if I put them to music.

"You write best when your mind is chaotic and your feelings are wild. What's the worst thing that can happen, my sweet, fierce girl? We're here to catch you, like we always will be," Roark growls.

I glance at Turner and his lips tip upwards. "Not one damn word that our man uttered is a lie, beautiful," he says. "Wanna write something with me?"

I can't deny them anything right now and I nod. Turner's voice is gorgeous, and sometimes he'll jump in and sing with me on stage. Our fans eat it up, always wanting more of his deep, growly voice. One thing that never changes, is how much he loves to compose new songs. He's often my sounding board, helping me make everything work together.

I don't have any formal musical training, but music speaks to me and grounds me when the world spirals. I take a deep breath, listening to the air conditioner of the bus, the light growl of the engine, and decide they're right. I need to work out some of these feelings that are bubbling up inside of me.

"We have to get semi dressed for this," I say shyly, blushing. Making music together is an intimate process, if I'm not wearing something, it'll lead to wandering hands.

"Lenny, you're adorable. Are you saying you can't write while warming my cock with your tight, pink pussy?" Roark teases me, burying his face in my neck before kissing it.

"Yep, that's what I'm saying, big man," I say with a giggle, getting out of bed. I grab a bra, off the shoulder crop top and panties from the dresser. This is all I really need for now.

"Let's go boys, cover your cocks so I'm not tempted," I demand, dressing quickly.

"Mmm. Half dressed Domme Lennon is just as tempting as a naked and begging one," Turner says lazily, crawling out of bed and pulling on soft joggers.

Roark groans and follows Turner's example and we walk out into one of our living spaces that has lots of pillows and is colorful. It's the perfect space for late night songwriting.

Turner opens a compartment and pulls out his guitar as Roark grabs bottles of water and a bottle of whiskey. Sometimes our muses require alcohol to talk to us, but I'm hoping it won't require much, since we have a show and interviews to give tomorrow.

I grab a notebook, thinking about how my past and present are colliding, nodding thanks to Roark as he pours me some liquid courage. I take a healthy sip, humming in appreciation at the caramel taste of it.

"You despise what you don't understand.
Can't you look beneath what the eye can see
Hate all around me and I cannot breathe
When you stand out from the crowd all they want to do is make you bleed
Lies and tricks make me sick
Falling for men that don't belong
Ripping apart someone who was never strong

It's easy to dislike what you don't understand.
A laugh that's too loud, escape that's misunderstood;
It's easy to point fingers, to want to rewrite the world you know."

I BITE my lip as I glance up from my writing, the guys are laying relaxed and drinking. This is what I would think if I didn't look deeper, noticing the twitch of Turner's fingers and the worry in Roark's eyes when he glances at me.

"I think I have a start," I confess to them. "Derek always hated my mom, and I never could get him to tell me why. Other people in town and at school disliked her, because she flirted with married men. I have this icky feeling that she may have done more too, but can't trust the rumors I heard. My mom had these wild moments where she'd climb trees with this hyperfocus, saying she *had* to, or there's the time that she went swimming in the lake naked on Derek's family property." I remember, blowing my bangs out of my face. "I just trailed after her, trying to make sure she wasn't hurt, while the town laughed behind our backs."

"Lenny, you know now she wasn't just doing these things. You told me she had fits of paranoia and depression as well," Roark reminds me gently.

"Yes, she did. I just keep waiting for something like that to happen to me. They say it's genetic," I whisper, eyes wide as my lip trembles. I don't want this to be genetic, I want to stay me.

"Baby, you haven't shown any symptoms of bipolar disorder. And, if it happens, there is treatment. I for one am not going anywhere, Lenny. Turner isn't either, okay? Can you show us what you've started writing? Maybe it'll help," Roark coaxes.

My eyes bounce between them, looking for a lie, or a look that I may be losing it. However, I see none of this, just encouraging smiles and love.

I nod, looking back down at my notebook. I can hear a melody weaving through my head: it's eerie, heartbreaking, and perfect for the story about a girl who should have been protected instead of reviled.

I glance back over at the guys and Turner picks up his instrument where it's been waiting beside him, expectant for whatever words I may grace him with. Turner and Roark have taught me that my words are a gift, my voice something to treasure. Before them, I always felt small, weak, and forgotten. I'm stronger with their love.

I take a deep breath and sing the words to the tune that exists in my head; softly at first, building confidence as I go. I refuse to look at them, staring at the pillow sitting between them, the lavender and white pattern calming to me. As I end I glance up, my eyes landing on Turner. His eyes are misty, and his mouth slightly open.

"Lavender, tell me you have more of that in you, sweet girl. Give me your pain, so we can purge it together," he rasps.

Oh my god it didn't suck. I'm always surprised when my emotional chaos creates lyrics that mean something. I chew my bottom lip, looking over at Roark.

"Lenny, you're going to destroy your lips if you keep that up. Stop, or I'll take you over my knee. This song is you, how does it feel when you sing the words?" Roark gently asks.

My gentle giant, asking the words that I'm not at all sure of.

"They feel real, the words hurt, but they also unravel other questions. I may never know what happened behind closed doors, or why people hated me in that town so much, but I'm going to find a way to deal with the aftermath here," I say with a sigh.

"Don't put too much pressure on yourself to figure it all out, Lavender. Feel what you need to, and draw the pain out and into your lyrics. It's like purging, even if you don't know what it all means yet," Turner advises.

I nod. "Okay, I can do this. I can feel the melody to this song, and I need to write some more before it's gone," I say, scrunching my nose.

I didn't see tonight going like this, but fuck it. Songwriting therapy it is.

"Let's go, Lenny-bee," Roark says with a grin, his fingers twitching, and I know that he wishes he had his drum set.

I add the next verse, humming to myself to make sure it fits. The tune is almost haunting, and I don't know if it'll mesh with the songs that we've been writing for our next album.

Smack.

I gasp, jumping in surprise. I look up and see Roark lifting a newspaper.

"Was there a bug or something? What the fuck was that about?" I shriek, shaking my head.

I had been really in the groove, not expecting such a loud noise.

"I was killing your self-doubt, my Valkyrie. I can see you questioning yourself from here and your forehead may as well be inroads on it. Stop. Worrying," he says punctuating each word with a smack of the newspaper on the table.

"Okay," I sigh. "This song just feels so sad, I don't know if it'll fit the album we're making," I mutter, raking my fingers through my hair.

"It doesn't matter if it does or doesn't. This may never leave this bus. That's not what this is about and you know it. You're sharing a piece of your beautiful soul with us, and we're going to listen and help if we can," Turner says gently, picking up for Roark.

I growl because they're right.

"Do you need a Snickers? An orgasm? That was scary shit," Roark giggles.

I snort because he's not wrong. I rarely growl, but not having a clear path is frustrating me. I also find my lips twitching because a giggle from a tattooed bear of a man like Roark is a gift.

"I love you, but I will take you up on the orgasm later," I tell him, laughing.

There's a banging on the bus door and I frown.

"It's after midnight now, who the hell could that be?" I mutter.

Shrugging, Turner grabs the bat we keep nearby. While we have security, he isn't one to be lax about keeping us safe. Knowing he can handle whoever is here, I turn back to my notebook.

The door opens, but I find myself drawn into my passion, humming as I ignore the faint drone of voices.

Scratches, punches, and bruises, they all melt into the background when faced.
Harsh words of anger and misunderstanding.
Just need to be replaced.
Faces in the crowd are blind when they see.
No one believes the sweet, kind and pure gray-eyed girl is me.

"I WAS HALF afraid Prescott was right and you'd be having an orgy with groupies," says a voice, snorting in derision.

I glance up, rolling my eyes when I find the reason that I'm writing tonight to begin with.

"Prescott has a very vivid imagination, doesn't she, boys," I murmur softly before going back to what I'm doing.

I purposely am speaking softly so he can't hear the tremor of anger his words leave behind. *Orgy. Ha!* The only people having sex on this bus are us. Prescott is a judgy bitch.

"Yes, Lenny, clearly she needs to get laid if she thinks the three of us make an orgy," Roark growls.

His growl makes my hair stand up and I look at him. Roark is staring at me, and I can see the anger in his eyes. I smile weakly to show him I'm okay. He hates that our relationship is often misunderstood, because there are people who think that we have sex with people outside of our threesome. We are committed to each other, and we've certainly never brought groupies onto the bus.

"If you're our social media manager, I would hope you follow our accounts. It's pretty clear to anyone with eyes that the boys and I are in a relationship, one that gives me everything that I need. So what can I do for you, Derek? It's a little late for you to be here, isn't it?"

I meet his eyes, which are slowly trailing down my body. It's then I remember what I'm wearing and decide to own it. I'm dressed in more than I would in a bathing suit or some of the photography sessions I've done. I refuse to balk because he's in my space.

"Yes, well, I wanted to tell you before I turned in how impressed I am with your fans. You sounded amazing tonight, and they've been blowing up the IG and Twitter feeds with photos and video clips. They're very loyal. I've been commenting on a few of them, and a few fans doubted I was you. Do you answer your fans yourselves?" he jokingly asks.

He thinks he's joking, but he's about to realize differently.

"Sometimes, yes. After a show, the band will pull up our trending hashtags and respond to fans. We spend fifteen minutes on it, and then we move on. Each of us has our own tone and signature, so I'm not surprised that someone would notice," I explain.

"Fuck, well why didn't anyone tell me this?" Derek yells and I flinch.

I fist my hand, forcing myself to breathe. *Fuck, I wasn't ready to see him again so soon.* My ears start to ring and I beg Roark for help with my eyes.

He stands, moving in front of me. "Well I have had enough

of that for one. Our bus is our home, where we enjoy our downtime, and can be ourselves. You just made yourself unwelcome. We will not tolerate being yelled at because you didn't bother to educate yourself on what we do or do not do on social media. Go do your fucking job and learn about the band that you're working with. It's late, and you're fucking up our creative mojo. Lenny is writing up a storm for a song, and I know the label would look poorly if you fuck with her muse," Roark explains.

He takes steps into Derek's space, forcing him to walk backwards. Turner gets up and steps towards me before dropping to his knees in front of me.

"I see what you meant before," he says softly, Derek and Roark are much further down the bus now. "He's vile, isn't he? We will do our best to make sure you see him the least amount possible. Derek the Douche Canoe is on our shit list, beautiful."

Turner's hands wrap around my thighs and I relax slightly. He's safety and violence wrapped up as one, the first to offer to bury a body for me, and I love it.

"He really is a douche canoe," I giggle. I focus on how warm his hands are, the pressure as he squeezes my thighs slightly, and the fierceness reflected in his pale blue eyes. "I love you," I breathe, feeling my anxiety fade.

"I love you most, baby. Now that our unwanted visitor is gone," he says as the door slams shut and Roark relocks it. "I think I'm going to need to unalive that man anyway for how he keeps looking at you," Turner says, pitching his voice louder so Roark can hear.

These men are my favorite.

"You can't kill him because he looked. I stand on stage and people stare at me for hours while I sing. I am sure that their thoughts aren't entirely pure about any of us," I admonish, though laughter echoes in my voice.

"You're saying I can't, but in my head I'm already talking to

Roark about how to best introduce him to our fists," Turner says, pouting.

I lean forward, kissing him gently. "If I haven't told you recently, thank you for being you."

Roark collapses on the couch across from me, legs sprawled open.

"This man doesn't know whether he hates you or wants to fuck you," he grouses. "You shouldn't have to worry about what you wear on the bus, though I may have hit him if you had been naked," he confesses with a chuckle.

I smirk. "Do you really think I believe you'd have let him in if I was naked, Roark? There's not a chance in hell that you would. Though, this is giving me some great fuel to keep writing if you're up for hanging out?"

Turner leans in, kissing me hard. "Baby, I live for late nights and writing sessions with you and Roark. Let's fucking do it."

I grin as he slides away from me, resuming his seat next to Roark. My earlier anxiety is pushing me to write more, and even if this song never sees the light of day, I know Roark and Turner hear my pain. They won't turn away, flinch, or wince because they need my words, my smiles, and my tears.

Life is shadows and light, and we need both to appreciate everything life has to offer.

3

LENNON

"Prescott, I can't work like this. I need to know more about their habits so that I don't damage their reputations or look like an ass," Derek complains.

We're sitting in our bus with the entire band for an 'emergency meeting' that Derek demanded after last night. Ugh, he ratted us out to Prescott. *Who's the unprofessional one now?*

"No one asked what we do or how we interact with our fans," Turner interjects. "We want organic conversations with them, so each one of us agreed to spend fifteen minutes a day on social media to talk with our fans. Honestly, man, grow a pair and communicate."

I snort, covering my mouth in embarrassment. *I didn't mean to do that!*

Derek sets his sights on me, eyes narrowing. "I obviously need to be walked through your day to day life in an effort to get to know you, so one of you should be tasked with showing me them. Don't you think, Prescott? Wouldn't Lennon be perfect for this," he gushes insincerely and my chest seizes.

Fuck no. I open my mouth to deny this manipulative

request, and my guys carefully watch me. Roark growls in anger, starting to say that I'm too busy for this.

"You're not that busy, Lennon. It wouldn't kill you to spend time with people outside of your band mates, and you and Derek need to become better acquainted. I need team players, not divas. I know this wasn't run by you all, but this is where we are at. Derek's not going anywhere," Prescott says, stomping her foot.

Gone is the shy and ditzy handler, and in her place is a twat waffle. I blink in surprise at the change. Holy shit.

"Now wait a fucking minute," Mav, our rhythm guitarist, says. "I don't care if we have a hundred new changes, we'll work through them. I get that you may be overwhelmed, but you don't get to talk to Lennon like that, Prescott. Apologize to her and then take a breather. Don't be a bitch."

My jaw drops as I stare at him. I expect this kind of outburst from my guys, but this surprises me. My body pivots to Prescott who's now stuttering. *Not so fucking mean now is she.*

"Fine, fine. I can't work in these conditions. Lennon, will you just do this for me, please? Explain to him what your days with the band looks like. Tell him about your downtime, when you're on social media, etc. Derek wants to do more posts of your songwriting, exploring cities with the band, and hanging out with the guys. Your fans adore you, and they want more candid social media content. Make it happen...please?" Prescott makes a bid to play nice.

I nod, barely holding onto my groan. I want to punch something badly, and I feel the prick of tears. Songwriting is my safe space and it feels invaded. Our bus is where I go to unwind and now *he'll* be around more. This man was my living nightmare; how the fuck am I going to spend time with Derek without having a panic attack?

Derek smiles smugly at us, and my hand twitches. *I really want to punch him, can I? Ugh, being an adult really sucks.*

"I'll see you in a half hour to get started outside the bus, Lennon. Don't make me have to come find you," he says. He turns and walks out and Prescott follows him with a flounce.

My tears that I've held so closely start to fall and I lift my hand to my mouth to hold in my sob. Nothing he said was mean, but the history binding us together colors every word he says to me.

"Will someone tell me what's going on? I've never seen Lennon fall apart like this. Some of us clearly need to be looped in about the new guy," Mav growls.

"I'll be fine in a second," I gasp, struggling to shove my feelings back in the little box named Derek Fucking Williams.

"Lenny, don't do that. Come here," Roark says, leaning forward and scooping me into his arms. He always looks larger than life in the bus, especially with how compact our living quarters are.

I snuggle into him and focus on taking shuddering breaths. "I know Derek from my hometown," I start, "and he wasn't very nice to me back then. I think he still harbors some of those feelings, based on how he says things to me or looks at me. I don't know why he'd want to be on this tour if he has issues with me," I tell them, my tears unable to be contained. "I'm aware that this isn't like me, and I sound like a baby-"

"You sound like someone who was traumatized," Atlas mutters, blowing out a breath. Atlas plays keyboard for us, and is the sweetest of our band members. "Guys, I don't like that this guy is on our tour. Lennon is our girl, we've worked together for years. There's no way I'm letting this shithead get away with being a dick to her."

My heart warms with his words, but it's useless. "Apparently the decision has been made," I hiccup. "I can probably handle it, as long as there's someone checking in on us."

Mav scowls. "I don't fucking like this, and this guy better be really good at what he does, because he's a right shit. I don't even need to know what he did in your past, you're fucking shaking, so that's enough for me. You're fucking Lennon O'Reilly! Channel the badass that I know you are and don't put up with his lip. He doesn't know this version of you," he reminds me.

I nod. He's right. I've changed. Grown up, and I don't want to be the scared little mouse that I was. I want to be Roark's Valkyrie. "Okay, you're right. I may need a drink after this, guys," I mutter, pulling myself out of the safety of Roark's arms.

"Lavender, will you tell me when I can break his legs?" Turner asks sweetly and I giggle.

"I love you," I tell my cheeky man instead as he wags his eyebrows at me.

"Text me when you're done, please. I want to know how this bullshit goes, and I'll have that drink with you. We may go back to our bus and decompress," Mav says.

"It's been a while since we've hung out, why don't you ride with us to the next venue," I suggest.

The guys grin and I know I've made the right call when they cheer. I'm the glue to this band, I need to act like it.

I head to the bathroom and wash my face, putting on makeup to conceal how blotchy it is. I can't change because he'll notice, but the air is cooler than the bus. Turning out the light in our small bathroom, I take two steps into our bedroom, then sort through some clothes in a pile and find Turner's sweatshirt. I bring it to my face and inhale his smoky scent. He wore it the other day and the smell clings to the fabric. I need a little comfort today, and Roark's clothes are too big on me. I pull it on, breathing easier because it feels like one big hug from my guy.

Unable to procrastinate any longer, I pull on my combat boots to complete my outfit of jeans, hoodie, and a tank top underneath it. I am dressed for comfort, not expecting to impress anyone. Tossing my lavender locks over my shoulder, I walk out of our bedroom.

"I'll see everyone later for that drink," I say as I walk past them, grabbing my phone to shove into my back pocket. I feel like I'm walking the gallows, rather than going to catch a team member up to speed.

"I think you're forgetting something, Lenny," Roark says, his presence making itself known against my back. His cock is also pressing against me as he loops his arm around my stomach to stop my forward progression off the bus.

I turn my head to look up at him. "What am I forgetting, gorgeous?" I ask with a lazy smile, thinking he wants a kiss.

He unknots one of his bracelets using his teeth. "You need to carry me with you too. I know you can't wear my hoodies, but I can make this fit your wrist. Hold us close, and you'll be fine. But remember when in doubt, kick his nuts in, Lenny," he says with a vicious smile as he takes my wrist.

"Holy shit, why was that so hot," I mutter, watching as he visibly claims me.

"I'm not going to comment on the fact that I know you just ruined your panties, beautiful. But I want you to know that I'll be tasting you and making you scream before our show," he growls into my ear.

I know that only I can hear him and I rub my thighs together for friction.

"Nuh-uh. That pretty wet pussy is mine, baby. Now go be a good girl and get to work," he whispers as he kisses my neck.

"Sir, I don't want to anymore," I groan softly. I'm rewarded with a crack across my ass and I yelp. "Fine! You're mean," I sass, rubbing my ass as I walk quickly away.

The guys all roar in laughter. They may not have heard what was said, but they're well acquainted with my bratty personality. Perks of being together so often while living on the road, you could say.

I love this life, and I'm determined to not let an overgrown man-child take it from me.

Derek

What is taking her so long? I bet she's complaining to her boyfriends about having to do this like the prissy bitch that she is. All the band members spent equal time glaring at me during the meeting, so I wouldn't be surprised if she's fucking them all.

I shift my weight before taking a deep breath to ground myself. I am angry at Lennon for many reasons, but I also love this band's music. I knew that I'd have to see her often when I took this job, but I've been obsessed with her ever since I saw *The Darkest Nights* perform live five years ago.

I didn't know the lead singer with the purple hair was *my* Lennon though when I bought my tickets with my friends, eager to experience their music. It wasn't until she walked out onto the stage that it clicked. I thoroughly enjoyed torturing her when she was younger. She never knew why I enjoyed stripping her of her pride and instilling fear in her, and I don't plan on telling her now.

The soft shushing sound of the bus door opening carries through the air, and I glance up. Lennon steps off the bus in boots, ripped jeans, and an oversized hoodie. She obviously didn't make an effort, but I've also seen various photos of her dressed just like this on her social media.

"I see you decided to grace me with your presence after

all," I tell her, lifting my hand holding my laptop and swinging it behind me to get her moving.

She raises her eyebrows regally, and I suddenly feel like the scum beneath her boot. My emotions are a mess, and I want to hurt her for making me feel out of control. I turn away from her, knowing she'll follow. I can't afford to lash out too much at her or I'll be fired. While Prescott is content to make the band uncomfortable with my staying on with the label, she can't afford to rock the boat too much.

I roll my eyes as I lead us towards a copse of trees and picnic tables just inside the parking lot. This is often used to tailgate before shows, but it'll work for our purposes as well.

I set up my computer as I sit, making sure my phone is face down next to me on the table. I want to delve into her life under the guise of creating original content per the label's requests. *Music Horde* loves *The Darkest Nights'* image, but wants to cater to their fans that want more intimate views of the band.

Now I just have to get Lennon on board. She doesn't have a choice though, so I'll state our next steps as a foregone conclusion.

"Okay, so the first thing I need to know is what is your pre-show ritual? I noticed there aren't any photos of you all getting ready or bantering with the team members before a show. Is there a reason for this?"

Lennon is standing by the table, assessing me. She seems to make a decision and steps up onto the bench before sitting her ass down on the table. Why can't she do anything like a normal person? She turns her body so that she can see me and leans onto the table. This gives the impression that we are more comfortable in each other's space than we are. Except...her finger twitches just a bit, and I realize there's a rhythm that she's keeping time with in her head.

"There's a few reasons for this. Roark climbs to the top of the venue before a show and gets in the zone there. No one would dare to disrupt him, so our roadies know to stay away when he disappears. Turner throws on a hoodie and disappears into the crowd for a few hours, joining in the tailgating. Somehow, no one has ever realized that it's him, and that's not something he wants publicized. You also may be wondering why I'm agreeing to tell you this, but I know that everyone who works for *Music Horde Records* signs a Non-Disclosure Agreement. So our little chat will stay between us," she says with a wink.

I shift, suddenly uncomfortable, as I feel my cock stir. Her loyalty and intelligence are a turn on, and I realize that for how much I terrorized her, I rarely heard her speak. Her voice is low and sexy, and fuck I need to think about dead bunnies or something sad before my dick betrays me.

I clear my throat to disguise how inappropriate my thoughts are. I wouldn't care if it was anyone other than her, maybe I'd even flirt a bit. But flirting with her would betray all of the reasons that I hate her.

"This explains why, and I'll make sure to relay this to the label if they ask," I say. *Newsflash: the label doesn't give a shit about this, but I do.* "What do you do before a show?"

She shrugs, looking out at the trees that surround us. "I get ready in my dressing room and then watch the crowd from the curtains backstage. The energy is electric, and it fuels my fire to perform. I share my words with our fans, show them that we acknowledge their triumphs and their pain, and that they're not alone. There's no better high than knowing that you're about to walk out on stage and share your soul with them. So you see," she says, looking back at me from beneath her lashes, "my ritual is my own in a way too."

I purse my lips and nod. I make a note in my open doc to discreetly follow her when she goes for her walk after getting ready. Rockstars don't have privacy, but she won't know that until she looks later on the band socials. This is what I was hired to do after all.

"What do you usually do after a show? I saw you for the first time in years at the VIP event last night," I lie. "Prescott told me those are every night, so I plan to walk around the room and take photos during that time. Don't worry I'll be discreet so you can connect with your fans, but what do you do afterwards, if it's not the orgy that she thinks you're having?"

Lennon huffs out a surprised laugh, shaking her head. I honestly thought I'd get a glare instead. I can't get a read on this girl, and she's very different than she was ten years ago.

"I'm going to choose not to respond to this, other than to say that Roark, Turner, and I unwind in our bus privately after a show," she murmurs, laughter still dancing in her eyes.

I nod, taking her in. There's still the twitching of her fingers and I'm dying to ask what that's about. But, I'm honestly enjoying the slightly teasing Lennon for now. *See how fucked up I am? I should be figuring out how to fuck with her, but I can't yet.*

"Fair enough," I say with a smirk. "Now tell me about how you respond to your own fans. No one does this. So why do you?"

Lennon draws herself up from her half slouch to stretch. She takes her time, under the guise of thinking. She then rubs her thighs and I bite my lip. *Baseball, dead fish, my grandma's underwear...*

"*The Darkest Nights* isn't a gimmick, and we won't sell out. *I* won't sell out. Our fans are important to us, because they are the reason we get to live out our wildest dreams. The band is a family, a team, and we follow each other's lead. One day a couple of years ago, Turner responded to a tweet from one of our fans himself, and it made a big difference in that man's life.

Turner met him at a VIP event a few months later, and he gushed about how much it meant to him. We all noticed, and now we make a point to scroll through our social media tags after our shows. This is why we don't want you to respond for us. They'll notice, because we talk the way we normally do when we respond," she explains passionately.

Well okay then. I'm officially a dingbat. I get blinders on with this girl, and I usually dismiss everything she has to say to me.

"Noted," I say, not showing her a hint of the thoughts racing through my mind. "I want to tag along a couple of times when you play tourist in between shows. Prescott mentioned that the band will disappear for hours to explore the city you're in for the day or night. Depending, of course, on the time of the show. Would you be open to that?"

I don't know why I phrased this as a question, but I feel rewarded by her intake of breath. I surprised her again, and I find myself enjoying pushing her off balance. This is a different game than the one I've played in the past, even though she didn't play by choice.

"Yeah, as long as you're not going to be a douche canoe during it. Derek," my name on her tongue makes me want to do degrading and vile things to her, "you're kind of a douche canoe. I can't name one instance in which you've been nice to me, and I want to have *fun* when we go out. You look like you wouldn't know fun if it punched you in the face."

Ouch. I can be fun...but can I be with her? *Fuck.*

"I promise to be unobtrusive," I grumble. "I'm totally fine walking a bit behind you all so I can get my photos. You don't need to try to pull me into your group of sycophants and suck ups that live to eat your pussy."

I watch as a wall comes over her gray eyes, and I almost feel bad as she flinches. I didn't come here to become her friend, and I need to remind myself of this. So as I close my laptop and walk away from this lavender-haired siren, why does my chest feel pinched? I kind of feel like this douche canoe that she mentioned, but she looks too much like her mom. Her mom was popular with men, a little too much, and I refuse to be another fool that falls at her feet.

4

LENNON

I did it. I refuse to let him see how anxious he makes me. My fingers keep in time to the rhythm of the new song that I'm working on; grounding me in the present separating me from his cruelty. I did so well until the end, when he insinuated again that I'm fucking all of my bandmates. I am not shy about my body, what I wear, or my confidence. However, consent is everything to me.

Especially since I didn't always have this growing up. Boundaries and personal space were nonexistent while living in a small town that didn't respect either.

I watch him abruptly walk away from me and take a shaky breath. That definitely sucked, and I'm not happy that I'll have to be around him more, but I've learned it can always be worse with Derek.

There was also a moment where I saw uncertainty in his eyes, and I wonder if he's seeing that he's wrong about me. My mother slept around, and there was a rumor that Derek's dad was fucking her. If that's true this would have caused various problems because Mr. Williams was still playing the dutiful, faithful husband in public. I was too young to understand it all when I was eleven, and I've since been piecing things together from remembered rumors and the whispered insults of my bullies.

I close my eyes and hum the melody that my fingers have been playing over the last forty-five minutes. It's slightly haunting, weaving its tale of sadness. This is the only way that I could keep the anxiety and remembered trauma from pulling me under. My fingers tapped to the beat as Derek's words tried to pull me under. I don't know if he noticed, and even if he did, who the fuck cares? I'm a musician as well as a singer: I live and breathe music.

My fingers itch for a keyboard, and I wonder if Atlas will let me borrow his. I'm closer to their bus than mine, and I need to work out some of these lyrics to music before we leave. This song is calling to me, begging me to tell my story, the history of those bullied by those that needed a scapegoat.

People tell you that high school doesn't matter, you'll grow up and walk away and start your life. For the most part this is true, until you walk into an interview and the girl you cruelly rejected as a prom date is about to be your new boss. History matters, and while I would love to say that poof we all become the bigger people and it disappears, this isn't true.

High school is a cautionary tale in being kind. Everyone is full of hormones, impressionable, and trying to find their way. Unkind words, bullying, and being jumped regularly is enough to make anyone unhinged, even if there isn't a history of mental health issues in their family. I held on by a thread, knowing that as soon as my mother was gone, I could leave having fulfilled my promise to her when I was seven.

It seems silly, but I clung to that promise.

I clamber off the table and walk towards my other band members' bus. Atlas and Mav live there and thankfully get along well. The band is a family, and our supporting staff were too until they started to leave. We are surrounded by strangers and enemies now as the label replaces them and it unsettles me.

Music and the stage is my happy place, and I don't want it taken from me. I knock on the door to the bus with a forced smile. Atlas opens the door with a grin.

"Hey minx, was the social media dweeb's interrogation awful?" Atlas asks, trying to keep things light.

I wrinkle my nose and shrug. "It could have been worse, but I have to get to a keyboard like I need air. Can I borrow yours for a little?"

Atlas breaks into a wide smile. "Abso-fucking-lutely. The guys told me you were writing something, but hadn't decided if it was too private to share yet," he says, grabbing my hand and pulling me up the stairs. "So is it...too personal?" He's trying to temper his excitement by being understanding, and it's adorable.

My lips purse in thought. "I've been thinking about it. Every kid deals with insecurities growing up, or bullying of some kind. This song talks about this, so I think it needs to be shared. I want people to know that they're seen, and it's like a virtual hug to our fans," I explain. "I need to write this. It's like my demons are chasing me, so maybe this will help put some of them to bed."

Atlas nods as he shuts the door behind us, pulling me deeper into the bus. I've practically lived on both buses for years, and this doesn't bother me. Their instruments are in the middle space of the bus, where they regularly set up jam sessions. These men live and breathe music, and this is the environment that I need.

"Yo Mav, Lennon is here," he says, stepping into the space as I trail behind him.

"Hi," I grin, leaning around him to wave. "I have words that need to join the world, mind helping me?"

The cool thing about the family you create for yourself, is that you don't have to translate. They just know what you mean.

"Fuck yeah, our tiny Valkyrie is back at it. Ror and Turner mentioned you were, and I need to hear it," Mav says with a vicious grin.

I know it hurts him to see me fall apart, and his grin bolsters me. I have people to fight for me now. I'm not alone, and I'm not that beaten down little girl anymore.

"It starts out sad, but I want to end it on a roar for vengeance," I muse, scooting around Atlas to face them. *This is what is missing from this song.* "I want it to be a fucking anthem by the end, for anyone that's ever been hurt or bullied, or not listened to. Ya know?"

Musicians are soulful people. Most of us haven't had an easy life, and unfortunately have been teased or bullied at least once for being different. I can see the shadow in their eyes as they stare hard at me, and we share a moment of solidarity.

Atlas breaks away first to nod to where his keyboard is set up. "Show us what you've got, where you have doubts, and where you want to smash it," he chuckles.

I throw my head back with a whoop, skipping over to his keyboard. I can feel the excitement building between us and it's electric. It's exactly the energy I need to work through this.

I begin to play and Mav sits to listen. Atlas stays standing, legs spread wide and arms crossed. He's challenging me to bring it, and I plan to. As I sing the first few notes, I can see the goosebumps on his arms grow as I continue.

By the chorus he's sitting too, pensive as his head nods to

the music. He grabs a notepad towards the end of my lyrics, scribbling notes furiously. I sigh as I finish, looking around the room. Mav looks angry, Atlas looks on in awe, both have respect written across their features.

"This is where I want to transition," I explain to them pensively. "The pain is in every word-"

"I could feel it," Atlas said softly. "I had to sit my ass down to keep myself from falling. This shit is powerful. Let's end this by burning the fucking world down, what do you say, girlie?"

My lips part in surprise. "Yes," I exclaim excitedly, bouncing in my seat. "This is the vibe I want to end on. You may be knocked around by life, but stand back up and kick back."

"Kick their fucking teeth in," Mav growls. "This is good shit, Lennon. Now bring it home. What's bouncing around in your brain?"

I chew on my lip, itching for my notebook. "Fuck, I should have brought my stuff with me. I didn't think I'd need to do this right now," I complain.

Atlas shrugs, opening a compartment with notebooks. We go through a lot of them in the band. "Gotchu. Now let's destroy this fucker," he says, eyebrows knitted.

I smile and take the notebook. Do I want to make this personal? Or do I want to say enough, so Derek sees I'm done taking this lying down?

You tore me down, destroyed my rep.
You saw my pain, and you relished in it.

Now I'm here to say, you failed.
I'm standing strong, surrounded by love.

I know my worth, and it's more than yours.

We deserve more than the memories of others.

Their lies and hits will fade, and we will come out stronger.

. . .

I AM ON A ROLL, writing frantically as I hear the drums crashing and Turner on the guitar in my head. I am breathing hard as I compose, but no one says anything. My muse is riding me now, and these men know how this feels.

My heart beats hard as I write, as I remember every time a group of girls would stop me as I went around a corner at school. Every beating, kick, and cruel word is ingrained on my heart and I release it into this song. I struggle to forgive the girl who accepted the abuse quietly so as not to make her mother's life more difficult.

My childhood was shit because I was so busy being a reverse parent. My mom had moments of lucidity and sweetness, but they were few and far between. I often felt the pangs of hunger because she would just forget to grocery shop. I take all of this anger, and channel it into my burn the world ending.

As I finish I look up and the guys are waiting, two intense pairs of eyes begging to hear it.

I smirk, power flooding my veins as my truth fills me. I lived, breathed, and bled this. It's time to change how this makes me feel, how small Derek makes me feel. *No fucking more.*

I take the song from the top, singing my heart out. The beginning makes Atlas wrap his arms around himself, while Mav grabs his guitar and follows my lead. The guitar complements the keyboard perfectly, and tears prick my eyes. *Holy shit, I can't believe this song is gaining such steam.*

The lyrics change, gathering fire, filled with piss and vinegar as it promises change. Life happens, violence occurs, but we overcome it. Atlas' deep voice joins the chorus and I grin. It feels good to not walk alone, and I dare to think about Turner singing this on stage with me. *What will it be like for our fans to sing this back?!*

I almost stumble as I blow my own damn mind before pulling it together. I need to lay this track down, and record it, before I even think about singing this live.

I let the last notes fade and there's silence. It feels wrong to break this, and I place my hand on my panting chest, tears freely falling down my cheeks.

"Fuck, I feel like we need a group hug after this," Mav says, shaking his head.

I sob a giggle because I think he's right. I stand, and there in the aisle of the bus, the three of us hug tightly.

"This song is epic," Altas rumbles as he squeezes me.

"Yeah? It's different but-"

"It works because it's raw and real," Mav interrupts. He steps away from us, rubbing his eyes. "I think your guys need to hear this and then you need to record it as soon as you can. When are we next in a studio?"

I give Atlas a reassuring pat and step back. "I think the label wanted us to start in a few weeks when we're in Maryland, but I can talk to Prescott about finding us a studio sooner."

Mav thinks, his forehead knitting. "Can you also ask her about releasing this as a single? I know we don't do that often, but this song...Fuck. People need it, Lennon."

I nod, absently chewing on my bottom lip before releasing it. "I'm gonna talk to Roark and Turner first, work on the song with them on our drive, and then bring it up to Prescott. It's just...she's been a little off I feel, right?"

"Fuck. I'm glad I'm not the only one," Atlas mutters gratefully. "She seems to have a hard on for you, minx. Constantly on you about stupid shit, that's not like her. I don't know what her deal is."

I nod, my hair flying as I do. "Ohmigod...yes. Like, what the fuck? When did I piss in her Cheerios? Ughh. To think I thought that she was nervous and finding her way. Instead she may just be a twat waffle in disguise," I grumble, blowing my bangs out of my face.

Mav snorts, shaking his head. "Your words are always just so colorful," he teases. "Now get out and make that song perfect. We'll deal with our prissy manager later. We need this song to be perfect, Lennon."

"Can I take this?" I ask, holding up the notebook now filled with my lyrics.

Atlas' lip twitches. "Of course. Our notebooks are at your disposal, girlie."

I give them a megawatt smile and happily skip down the aisle, yelling, "Bye! Thanks for the jam session boys."

"Bye sweets," they call out behind me, and my heart settles.

I was meant to spend my morning doing what I love, with the people that mean the most to me. Even if I had to take a detour to get here with Derek Fucking Williams.

Roark

I haven't heard from Lenny in hours and I'm trying not to freak out. I even texted the new dick from the label to see if she was still with him. *Where is she?*

Atlas and Mav also aren't responding to messages which is almost comforting. *Maybe she's with them?* Turner has threatened to kick my ass and then fuck it if I don't calm down, so now I'm turned on and anxious. Fucking awesome.

Our bus door opens and it's the best sound I've ever heard when I see lavender hair peeking out from the top of the stairs. I see her face next and I bite down on my anger when I see her face. I can tell something happened.

"Lenny," I whisper. "You look like you've been through hell. Did that bastard do this?"

She shakes her head sadly and lifts a notebook. I deflate, instantly knowing that her demons followed her today. I open my arms and she runs to me. I squeeze her hard, kissing the top of her head. This song is her story, intrinsically related to Derek, it makes sense that she needed to create after seeing him.

"Is she here?" Turner asks, stepping into the front of the bus. He played it cool for me, but he holed up in a corner, strumming the haunting notes of his lavender-haired girl.

"I didn't mean to worry you, I should have texted-" she starts.

"No, you don't have to do anything with us, Lavender," Turner says as I spin so he can see her. "Your muse struck, right?"

She nods, remorse making her eyes water. Lenny feels bad as it is, she doesn't need us to point out that a text would have kept us from worrying. She doesn't go off without letting us know very often, so what she needed to do was important. That's it.

"We don't make each other feel like shit over our music," Turner murmurs, wrapping his hand gently around her throat and making her look at him. "Ror and I get you, the guys knew you needed this, we live in your orbit, sweet girl. Whatever you need, you get, okay?"

Her gray eyes are filled with tears and they're so large, I'd swear she looks like one of those anime characters right now. She's so fucking gorgeous and ethereal. I hate that she thought we'd be angry. I was angry out of worry, but never at her.

"K," she whispers.

He leans down and kisses her gently, fingers tightening. She moans; I thought I couldn't get any harder, but clearly I'm wrong. I grind myself on her ass for an ounce of relief and she whimpers into Turner's mouth. Fuck, I love to see her needy and begging. Maybe I should make her crawl to us later and suck us off.

But first, we need to hear what made her disappear.

"Let's table this for now, my beautiful Valkyrie. Use how much you need to be fucked and sing for us," I growl into her ear.

Lenny shivers and Turner grins down at her. "She's so fucking hot when she's wet and needy. Lavender, your voice gets sultry and makes me want to make you sing in a different way while I eat you out."

Nice. She may stab one of us if we keep teasing her. Though...making her sing while she comes has its merits too.

Shaking my head out of my lust filled fog, I ease her away from us. Turner looks up at me in defiance. I am slightly taller than him, so I enjoy the power play in our height difference. "Punishment goes both ways, and your ass looks gorgeous red with your cock throbbing for release," I warn Turner.

His cheeks flush as he remembers other times that we've played this way. "Yes, sir," he murmurs, eyes dropping to the ground and I grin.

"Such a good boy for me," I praise.

Lenny gives a dramatic half sob as she stomps over to sit. Chuckling, I grab my drum sticks to work out a tentative beat on the tabletop. Ever since last night, Lenny's haunting words have been on my mind. I'm itching to start laying this down in a studio, but I don't know if my brave Valkyrie is ready to share this with the world. Turner shifts as he sits, harder than stone, and I smirk evilly. It's about a three hour drive to Seattle, and I know the perfect way to spend the time. Then I remember that our girl offered to spend quality time with our bandmates and curse under my breath.

Turner grabs his guitar, playing a few notes that make me shiver with desire. There's nothing sexier than my pale-eyed lover when he's in his zone. I clear my voice, deciding that our next day off will be spent playing, fucking, and sucking Turner off, while I command him to play. Missed notes will be punished. *Fuck, I missed what Lenny just said.*

"-I'll take it from the top, and you guys can do your thing. We can build the music around the song. Atlas and Mav started earlier today, and the hair on my arms is still standing up. I also think," she breaks off, chewing her bottom lip. I want to pull it from her teeth, then bite it myself to distract her.

I take a deep breath and adjust myself, telling my dick to chill the fuck out. "Take it slow, beautiful. Anything you have to tell us we'll go with," I reassure her.

And we will. She's ours, and anything important to her is important to us.

"I want to record this. I think people need to hear it, then talk to Prescott about adding it to the tour. I know we're halfway through but-"

"What did Atlas and Mav say?" Turner asks, gathering info before putting forth an opinion either way.

"They agree. I finished writing it with them today. After meeting with Derek, who was his usual sparkling dickhead self, I felt driven to write. Atlas and Mav were closer and I needed a keyboard. I had to hear it," she explains.

"Cool, then let's hear it and decide from there," he says with a shrug. Turner is explicit in not rushing things until he can see all of the story. This is one of the many parts that I love about him. As odd as our trio may seem to others, we all fit together.

Lenny nods, grateful that she doesn't have to put into words what she's feeling yet. If her emotions are this big after a jam session, then I can already tell this song is gonna destroy me.

She closes her eyes before wrinkling her nose and bending over to pull off her boots. I don't think she can be any more adorable than she is right now. Socks come off next and then she presses her feet into the cold tile of the floor.

Recognizing this as one of her grounding techniques, my lips twitch, proud of her for taking care of herself when she's overwhelmed. I don't want to bring attention to it right now, so I'll reward her in orgasms later.

Lenny keeps her eyes closed as she starts to sing. She has a photographic memory, so she just needs to see it written once and it's there forever. My eyes drink her in, skin pebbling in goosebumps as I breathe in her words. Her pitch is perfect, her voice deep and sultry. Fuck, her pain shows in every note, every word...and then it changes. Her voice gets stronger, louder, and then her eyes open.

Turner joins her with his guitar. I watch him out of the corner of my eye, and I see that he's just as mesmerized by our girl as I am. My eyes center again on Lenny, my fingers itching to draw her, as I'd bathe her in fire. I can see her changing as I watch, seeing a very different Lennon coming out. She's done taking shit, and if Prescott thought she worked with a diva before, just fucking wait.

Lenny takes a breath like if she doesn't she'll die as she finishes, her eyes wide from her expulsion of emotion.

"Fuck, baby, that was everything," I whisper. "Do you want to share this with anyone else?"

It feels like we just shared a religious experience, and I'm afraid to speak any louder for fear of spoiling it.

"Should I? I really fucking want to. Turner, I want you to sing this with me. I know it's raw and it fucking hurts, but how many other people do you think have been thrown away, bullied, and their trauma follows them like a stain on their souls? I want to tell people that I see them, and I get it. And now it's time to take back our lives," she says passionately, blowing her bangs out of her face.

I swear, I'm going to start picking up hair accessories to keep them on hand so her hair will stay contained. As if she knows I'm annoyed, she winks at me cheekily. *This girl.*

"I would be honored to duet this with you, Lavender. I agree with you: people need your words. I know we say this often, but this was fucking everything baby girl. Like fuck. I don't know if I want to cuddle you or worship between your legs and make you scream." Turner grins to show he'll be equally happy with either option.

"I'm sure Altas and Mav feel the same, but we'll back you if Prescott catches an attitude about stopping into a studio to record this. She lives by her schedules, but the label emailed me yesterday to see if we were working on anything new. I have no problems showing her it if she starts her passive aggressive bullshit," Lenny says with a grin, tossing her hair over her shoulder.

I snort in amusement. "Is there really an email?"

"Nope, but I'll make sure there is before I present it to her," she says giggling.

"Fuck you're sexy when you're devious, Lavender. How long do we have until Mav and Atlas come over for that drink?"

I stand and pull my phone out of my pocket to text Atlas. Sending it off, I throw it on the table and stalk over to Lenny. Tossing her over my shoulder, reveling in her shriek, I tell him, "We have an hour. Plenty of time to fuck her senseless."

"Fuck yeah," Turner cheers, grabbing the back of his neck and pulling his shirt over his head. His muscles ripple and I lick my lips, making sure my love knows how much I appreciate him.

Heading into our bedroom, I toss her onto the bed. "I really want to make you crawl to us like the good girl you are, but this morning I want Turner to fuck you while I fuck his ass. You in?"

She bites her lip, watching as we strip off our clothes. "Well that's just not fair, if Turner's getting his ass fucked, why can't I?"

So fucking perfect. "Oh baby, if you want my pierced cock riding your ass, you've got it. You seem to be wearing too many clothes at the moment though," Turner teases, crawling onto the bed naked.

I palm my cock as I watch his tight ass move towards her. Unable to contain myself, I crack my hand across his asscheeks. He gasps, glancing over his shoulder with heat in his eyes. I like it when he fights me a little when I fuck him.

"Make our girl scream while she chokes on my dick," I growl. Lenny opens her mouth wide, sticking her tongue out before she winks at me. The joke is on her though, because Turner is still coming for her.

She squeals, scrambling to take her clothes off. I can't wait to see what that bratty mouth can do to me in a moment. Turner flips her onto her stomach and she glances over her shoulder. Seeing me crawling towards the headboard, she gets on her hands and knees eagerly. Someone is excited to suck me off, I see.

"So eager, so fucking beautiful," I groan, coating her panting lips with the moisture collecting on the tip.

She licks her lips before opening her mouth wider to suck on the tip of my cock, lapping at my slit.

Lenny moans, back arching as Turner licks her lazily from her pussy to her puckered hole. He grabs her ass cheeks with his large hands, spreading them so he can trace his tongue along her labia before sucking on her clit.

Mouth full of cock, all she can do is moan as her eyes roll in pleasure. I grab her hair with both hands, daring her to swallow more, go deeper. With a glint in her eyes, she lowers her head, working through her gag reflex, wordlessly screaming when Turner makes her come the first time.

"Fuck, her throat tightens when she comes, and it's pure magic," I gasp.

I roll my hips, thrusting gently, using her hair to bob her head up and down my cock. The sounds of sucking, slurping, and wetness fill the air as we enjoy each other. I lift my eyes from my goddess swallowing my cock to take in Turner's efforts. He's scissoring his fingers as he twists them inside of her and Lenny whimpers. She's steadily getting wetter, and I can hear her needy pussy sucking them back into her as he finger fucks her.

"Fuck, you're taking Turner's fingers like such a good girl, baby. Come for him again, and then he can start working your ass. Would you like that?"

She sobs as she shudders, and I know she just went from a level six to a nine. She's so close to creaming on Turner's fingers, the thought of it makes my cock even harder. Her eyes widen as she feels it, and she grabs my ass, pulling herself down.

"Ugh, baby, you're gonna make me come. Please, please, fuck, you're amazing," I beg, pant, and praise her. I'm not entirely sure that I'm making much sense now either.

"You're going to make our man speak in tongues, Lavender," Turner teases before sucking and nipping at her nub.

Lenny shudders, fingers digging into my ass as she showers

Turner with her cum. I pull out of her mouth with a pop, and Turner flips Lenny onto her back.

He kisses her hard before he grabs a bottle of lube from the nightstand. "Can you taste how sweet you are, baby?" He lubes his fingers up, gently running them along her ass.

His first finger slides in as he kisses her again. She moans, her hands moving up to play with her breasts. They're gorgeous, flushed, with deep red nipples. I love their size, enjoying the privilege of fucking them regularly.

Her back arches as I watch Turner insert a second finger into her ass, slowly thrusting further and further. Watching his fingers disappear inside of her has me slowly jacking myself off. They are so beautiful together as they writhe on the bed.

Lips twitching, I move, wrapping my hand around Turner's thick, pierced cock and applying pressure to Lenny's neglected clit. She wails as his eyes roll back, blown with desire.

"Fuck," Turner whimpers, inserting a third finger and fucking her ass with them.

"I'm so close, please please don't stop," she begs, feet going flat on the bed and fucking Turner back.

"Such a demanding brat, telling us what to do," I say, clicking my tongue in reprimand. I don't stop rubbing her, instead I move my fingers so I'm barely touching around her clit instead.

Her eyes widen in denial. "No! No, I'll be a good girl. Please, sir, please," she begs and it's so perfect. I pinch her needy bud tightly. Her hips jerk in surprise before her back bows, hands wrapped in the bed sheets as she comes.

"Yes, you are a good girl," I tell her.

I move behind Turner, grabbing the lube and prepping his tight hole to take my cock. He grunts as I enter him with two well lubed fingers, but I can't wait much longer. Before long, he's taking three thick fingers like the good little bottom that he's playing today.

I pull them out, surveying my lovers before my lips part in a wide smile. I pull out a toy drawer that's built onto our headboard, discarding choices that won't work before finding a dual action vibe that is bendy enough to work. I toss it by Turner's thigh before resuming my spot behind him.

Turner slips his fingers out, grabbing the toy with the other hand. "Are you ready to feel really good, Lavender? You're such a lucky girl, you're going to scream when you cum, aren't you?"

"Yes, please, I need it," she whimpers.

We all switch in our need for dominance. Lenny had such a big break through, I know she needs to let go of everything and be well taken care of. Turner powers on the toy, pushing the bulb into her so it'll perfectly hit her g spot. He adjusts the other bulb over her clit, and Lenny gasps in pleasure.

He ramps up the speeds until she's writhing and moaning before applying lube to his cock from the bottle next to him. Turner lifts the handle out of the way, and I grin savagely, having pulled this toy for this reason. Turner lines himself against her tight hole, slowly pushing himself in. Lenny is having none of this, wrapping her legs around him and pulling him against her. They both shout as he slides in.

"Motherfucker, Lennon, fuck me," Turner yells, gasping.

"Ror is doing that today, if you ask nicely, I will after the show," she sasses.

Turner growls pushing her legs open, so her legs are wider. Leaning slightly over her, he holds onto her thighs as he thrusts.

"Fuck, I feel so full. Fuck me harder, sir. Please. I want to still feel you on stage," she begs and goads.

Turner hips snap back to give her this and I wrap my arm around his waist to stop him. "My turn now," I growl in his ear.

My cock is ready and well lubricated as I slide into him. He whimpers and gasps, taking me inch by inch until my hips hit his ass. I wrap my hand around his neck, turning his face to kiss him.

"I'm gonna fuck you into her, and it'll be merciless and fast. We're running out of time, and I want both of you to feel sore tonight," I say with a grin before pulling back slightly and then slamming my hips against him.

Lenny whimpers and Turner gasps. "Baby, Roark, you know what we need. But faster, harder, more sir," she pleads.

That was dangerously close to telling me what to do, but I want what they want. I fuck Turner into Lenny over and over. The toy makes her scream as she comes, soaking the bed sheets and I'm sure, Turner's balls.

"Roark, fuck I love your cock, it always feels like the first time," he says with a sigh.

I kiss his neck as I pound into his ass. I can do soft and sweet, but I need to reassure us all that we're alive and strong. Our Lenny is a queen, and she did hard shit this morning, for which she is owed orgasms. *Or something like that.*

As Lenny sobs as the sensations overcome her, Turner leans over her to run his tongue along her breasts. He bites, sucks, and pinches her nipples, pushing her farther over the edge. My hips begin to stutter as I feel the tingles start in my balls, and I reach over to massage a nd tug at Turner's. I want us all to fall together.

I bite and suck up his back. "Turner, I'm going to empty into your tight ass, if you don't come with me, I'll take a belt to it. Fuck, you'd look so good wearing my marks," I taunt.

Turner buries his face in Lenny's neck as he pants. "Lavender, I'm gonna blow baby. Ror's wicked tongue fucking slays me. Come with us," he pleads.

He lifts her ass slightly, pushing himself up, changing the

angle as he fucks her harder. "Oh, oh, oh yes. Turner," she screams as he fucks her through her orgasm.

I wrap my hand around his neck, other hand tightening on his hip as I pull out almost completely and then push in quickly. Turner inhales to scream and I tighten my hand around his neck. He shudders as he comes, and I mutter, "Good boy," as I follow.

The three of us can hardly breathe after exerting ourselves in the best way possible. I gently pull out, collapsing to the side. Turner has no such restraint, tossing the toy aside and collapsing on our gray-eyed girl. Lenny huffs a laugh, kissing his forehead.

"Holy shit," she whispers in awe. "Can we do this every time I write an epic song?"

I chuckle, shaking my head. "So greedy. Who am I to deny you orgasms? If I could, I'd live inside of you," I confess. "You are my happy place."

Turner moves his face from where it's buried in her tits. "Yes please. I need all of that." His words slightly slur and I smirk. He's still coming down from his high from orgasming.

I play with his hair and he gives me a silly smile. We relax together for a few minutes before I sigh. "We have to shower, guys. Lenny, do you want to go first," I offer.

"Mmmm yes please, thank you Roark," she says with a smile. "I know as soon as Turner moves, I'll have a large amount of liquid rushing out."

Turner gets an evil glint in his eye. "Unless I plug you and you have something to remember on stage," he says, winking.

"Holy shit, well, that's new," she squeaks.

We love introducing our girl to new kinks, of which there are many. She's so open, but I know there are still things that shock her. I can also see she's not against it. The gears are grinding in Lenny's head, and I can't wait to see what she decides.

She wiggles out from under Turner as soon as he pulls out and runs for the door. "I'm not saying no," she says, peeking over her shoulder, "but I don't think I'll survive a three hour drive without begging you to fuck me. Mav and Atlas will be here and they don't need to hear you railing me at the back of the bus!"

She runs off for the bathroom as we snicker, imagining it. Life with Lenny is never boring.

5

TURNER

This was a good idea. I lean back into the pillows on our couch as I watch Lavender laugh next to Atlas. I take a sip of my beer that's loosely held by the neck, reveling in the sound.

Her hair is braided tightly in two sections in anticipation for tonight. She likes to style it herself unless there's a special occasion and she needs to keep appearances. Lavender isn't fussy, she learned early on how to do her hair and makeup when we were just starting.

No one can call Lennon O'Reilly a snob or a diva, she's one of the best and sweetest people that I know. I don't know why Prescott seems to think all famous musicians are. She seemed nice, though nervous, when she first started, but I may need to keep my eye on her.

"I think we should tell Prescott today about needing studio time at our next stop," Mav grins evilly. He's disliked her from the moment he met her. I thought it was sexual tension, but Mav has better taste than that.

He just sees how odd some of the things she says are.

"Oh, fuck yeah," Roark agrees. "What are you calling it, Lenny?"

Lennon bites her bottom lip and I lean forward and gently release it. My eyebrow goes up in admonishment and she nods. Her index finger taps in the air instead and I grin. Her nervous energy needs to go somewhere, I would just prefer she not destroy her gorgeous lips to do it.

"What about *Together We Roar*? Sure this is based off of my life events, but a lot of people can relate to it. It's what gives people goosebumps, gets the blood roaring, until you just need to scream the end of the song together. Oh my god, can you imagine this played live? I want to get this in as many people's hands as possible, and then sing it live towards the end of the tour," Lennon decides, eyes sparkling in excitement.

It's a smart play, and one that even Prescott will have a hard time finding a flaw in.

Our bus door opens and we glance over. If we're here during the day, we rarely lock it. The woman in question huffs up the stairs. Lennon makes eye contact with everyone in the room and shakes her head. Agreed, this is not the time to tell our handler that we are going to fuck up her plans.

"Why is everyone on this bus? I've been looking everywhere for Atlas and Mav to ensure we don't leave them," Prescott rolls her eyes in annoyance.

Atlas lifts his phone, waving it slightly in the air. "It's called a phone, love. Use it," he says, his words clipped. He's not one for dramatics, and after Lavender cried earlier today, he's not impressed with Prescott.

"I honestly didn't think to," she admits. "Are you all riding together today then? It looks like a party," she says with a tight smile.

Mav shrugs. "We're friends, and that's what we do. We

hang out and talk. Is there anything else, Prescott?" His tone is the perfect mix of boredom and irritation.

I roll my lips inward in an effort to resist the smile his comment is prompting. I don't know if this girl is going to last very long, as we are determined to make life difficult for her now. Fuck, I wouldn't want to be her right now.

"There is, thank you for reminding me," she says, blatantly ignoring his tone. "There are reporters from different magazines that want to speak to each of you at four today. They will also want photos, so please make sure you look appropriate," she accentuates her words while staring at Lennon. Her eyes widen in disbelief.

Our girl always looks fine when she's in the public eye. It doesn't matter if we are playing tourist, getting lost in a city, or she's hanging out before a show, she's beautiful. Lennon is comfortable in leggings and a slouchy sweater right now, because this is *our* space.

"Understood, Prescott, thanks for the update. Now get the fuck off our bus so we aren't late," I demand. I'm over her shit.

Prescott startles at my words because I'm not usually like this. However, I've hit my limit with this ungrateful twat waffle who should have been booted immediately for her inexperience. We have been nothing but gracious as she's learned the ropes until she began to insult us that is. Hmm, right around the time that Dickhead Derek came onto the scene yesterday.

What interesting timing.

Prescott turns around quickly and exits the bus, all while muttering to herself.

Lennon glances at her watch and sighs. "Four o'clock, ugh. We'll be pulling in at three-thirty if we're lucky. I'll have to disappear to dress in a couple of hours, guys. Y'all can be picture perfect faster than I can," she mutters.

"You're perfect now," I tell her. "Fuck Prescott. Anyone

else notice what a twat waffle she's become almost overnight? She was really nice before. Think she's fucking our social media manager?" I grin salaciously.

Lennon giggles, shaking her head. "The man may be gorgeous, but his personality has much to be desired. No thanks. Pass."

I wonder if she ever had a crush on him, but I'm not one to pick at old wounds.

We tease, drink, and laugh over the next two hours. We're sure to not drink so much that it's obvious during our interview, and Lennon has always been an adorable lightweight, so she switches to water earlier than we do. At three she disappears into the back to get dressed and do her makeup.

When she reappears, it's in ripped jeans, a fuschia long sleeved crop top, and high heeled boots. Her makeup is flawless, and from experience, I know that it'll be different when she hits the stage tonight. Her hair is still in the cute double braids, giving her this innocent look with her wide gray eyes.

"Holy hotness, Lennon," Altas says, whistling.

I chuckle, adding my own whistle as Roark yells, "Work it, strut it!"

Mav also shakes his head at our antics before he grins, saying, "I'm pretty sure you'll destroy your interview today, tiny Valkyrie."

She looks powerful and beautiful, ready for anything. Lennon has been the belle of the music scene for the last eight years. The media knows very little about her past, and while they're intrigued, surprisingly they've left it alone. The public loves her, and while we always stop for autographs, we aren't mobbed when we disappear for the day to explore a city.

It's the same reason that I can blend into a crowd before a show. I'm sure some people recognize me, but they're content to allow me anonymity to chill with them. We take photos tailgating, have a blast, and no one calls attention to the rockstar who hung out for the night with them.

"They always ask if we're working on something new... should I tell them?" Lennon asks, a smirk appearing on her purple lips.

"You know what, fuck it, tell them. Make sure our bosses know though first. Let's not piss off the big dogs, but Prescott? Fuck her," Mav says with a dark chuckle.

"While there have been a few times where I've wanted to explore my sexuality, I'll respectfully decline Mav," Lennon says primly.

"Oh shit," I sputter, laughing. Lennon grins as she sits next to me, leaning in as she pulls out her phone to email Jordan Miles, our actual boss. "That was on point, Lavender."

"I know, right?" Her fingers fly across the screen as she writes. "Do we want to ride out Prescott's antics to act like she's a bitch in power, or nah?"

Roark sighs. "I don't want us to be the whiny bitches. Should we wait and see if it gets worse? Or even better, let our girl show her what her place is," he says, smirking.

We, the members of *The Darkest Nights* are chill people, we're cool to go with the flow. There's never been a single instance where we've acted like an entitled asshole, unless it was to right some kind of wrong. Like when I've watched a restaurant snub someone for no reason. Or to put a bitch in her place.

"I'm content to let Prescott dig her grave," Atlas growls. "She's more and more erratic in her actions, it's only a matter of time that she fucks something up. Then the label owes an apology and we are more likely to get a say in our next manager."

Lennon twists her mouth to the side in disgust as she writes. Oh yeah, she's about over her. "Prescott isn't really a manager. She's a babysitter for the label because they're restructuring. They're short handed as they grow, so they threw her at us. We aren't known to be problem children and are mostly self-sufficient. I'd be fine with it, if she wasn't fucking Jekyll and Hyde."

Roark's lips twist in amusement. "Lenny, what are you writing over there, anyway?"

"Dear Mr. Miles, I just wanted to let you know the tour is amazing, and I love the addition of the new cities. I love seeing all our fans! We also have an update regarding new songs: we have a new song! It's called *Together We Roar*, and we'd like to get into the studio soon to record. I am hoping you can get some time scheduled in one while we're on the road? I am dying to play it live, but I know there's some things to do before this can happen. Well, I'm needed for an interview! Sincerely, Lennon," she says, glancing up. "Is that okay?"

"That's amazing. It literally sounds like you're just shooting him a line from the road," I say approvingly.

"Good, everyone good with this before I send it?" Lennon asks.

Everyone consents and she hits send.

Lennon glances out the window, watching as we pull into the concert grounds. It's a large concert hall and beautiful. We look around the bus excitedly. Even though we've been doing this for a few years, it hasn't grown old. I think part of the reason for this is the label gives us creative control. We don't have to run anything creative by them: they trust us and we do what our muses fuel us to do.

As soon as we stop, the door opens and I hear heels moving quickly up the steps. Ugh, this bitch again.

"We're here! Unfortunately, we are behind schedule," Prescott says as her head pops into view. Her nose wrinkles when she sees Lennon already dressed and I wonder if she was trying to take her by surprise. "Oh, Lennon, you're ready. That, or you're trying to impress people that you're already fucking. You're first up today, please make a good impression. Chop, chop, let's go. Guys, you have forty-five minutes to make it to Hall C for interviews."

Prescott turns, and Lennon meet my eyes incredulously. *Bitch*, she mouths. I scowl back at her to show I agree.

"Lennon, you should be following me," Prescott says in a sing-song voice. "I'd hate for you to get lost on the way there."

Lennon growls under her breath, standing up and opening one of the built-in compartments. She pulls out a packet of gummy bears irritated. If she's started early on her sweet indulgence, it means she's going to be super hyper by tonight. Sugar hits her hard and gives her the zoomies.

She winks over her shoulder as if she can read my thoughts before ripping open the bag and pulling out a bear, biting his little head off. I wince in solidarity. *Rest in peace, poor little bears.*

Mav's eyes bounce between us and snorts in amusement. I lean back in my chair as she disappears and wink at him. "She's gonna be a holy terror later tonight if she's already eating gummy bears," I remind him.

Roark twists up his face in commiseration. "Fuck, I didn't think about that, I just figured it was nice she thought to bring something to help destress when she grabbed it. Ugh, the zoomies will be serious tonight," he groans.

Altas chortles. "The zoomies, is that what you call a hopped up Lennon? That's awesome, man, she definitely fits that perfectly. The crowd will love her for it and she usually will sing encore songs. Ha." He laughs harder, becoming breathless. "Prescott is gonna be so fucking pissed!"

The rest of us snicker, because she'll undoubtedly be

unamused by it. Oh well, the new mantra regarding Prescott is going to be "fuck it". We don't work for her anyway.

Lennon

I roll my eyes as I trail Prescott. She is ordering people around as she storms through and irritating the shit out of them. Seriously, I liked her better before this crazy lady came out. This crew knows what they're doing, they don't need a heavy handed touch.

I grimace before pasting on a smile for the road crew. I say hello as I walk past, and they grin and nod as they work.

"Honestly, Lennon, could you focus for two seconds," Prescott grouses.

"Is there something I need to pay attention to at this time? Are you doing tricks or giving me important information? Oh no? Then I'm good, and I'll continue on my way. Later, P," I snark, breaking away and heading to the hall where my interview is.

Did I mention that gummy bears make me hyper yet?

I walk in with a bounce in my step, noticing they aren't ready for me yet. Frowning, I grab my phone to check the time and see it's not four yet. Sigh, it would be like Prescott now to rush me to make me look bad.

What the fuck did I ever do to her?

I unlock my phone to check my emails and see Mr. Miles responded to me. I wasn't expecting him to message back so quickly.

Opening the email, I start to read :

Lennon,

I'm so glad that tour life is treating you so well. Your fans are very vocal about how much they love The Darkest Nights, and some have asked when you'll be recording new music. We'd like to release this new song as a single, and have you start to record new music while on the road. I understand it can be quite stressful to do this while on tour, do you think you could handle recording nine new songs? We would book your studio time, you'd go in and do your thing.

Also, if you see this in time, please drop a teaser about the song you told me about with the journalist.

It's so nice to work with artists whose muse is so loud, even while performing nightly for their fans.

Regards,

Jordan Miles.

. . .

OH WOW. My weight leans on my right foot as I read over every word again. Mr. Miles rarely gives out compliments, being known as a hard ass. I'm quite floored.

"Why do you look like a cross between having to take a shit and being confused?" comes a voice from beside me and I startle.

Eyes flying up, they meet Derek's calculating ones, his lips twisted in cruel amusement.

Straightening up, I tell myself I will bow down for no one. *Fuck that noise. No one can make me feel small unless I give them permission.*

Guess what...permission not fucking granted.

"Thank you for that startling and crude description of my

surprise, Derek. Now, if there's nothing more, please fuck off," I say sweetly.

His jaw drops, and I turn away when I hear my name being called, dismissing him. I start to walk away when Derek grabs my arm, squeezing hard. I show no reaction, looking over my shoulder bored.

"Uh-uh, I'm wearing a sleeveless shirt tonight, and I don't have the makeup to cover up a bruise. Lay off the manhandling there, you brute," I taunt him.

"Quite the personality change there, Lennon. It reminds me of your mother's mood swings. Have you finally cracked then? Such a shame, I always knew crazy was catching. Maybe I shouldn't get so close, yeah?"

I feel like I've been doused in cold water and force myself to breathe. "Crazy is catching", is one of the many taunts he started at school. Derek was my neighbor, so he saw more than his share of my mother's mental health struggles.

Fuck, fuck, fuck...I'll get lost in the memories later. Today, I'm untouchable.

"It's cute that you think you can still hurt me, Der," I mock him. "Now, I have work to do, and I'm sure you don't want me to have to explain how I received a bruise on my arm. I have people that'll actually listen now, unlike before. Now, off you go." I shoo him with one hand with a pleasant smile on my face that I don't feel.

He releases me slowly, hands going up. "Do your men know you have multiple personalities, or am I just special, little bit?"

"My mother had bipolar disorder with mania, she wasn't schizophrenic, you dolt. The least you could do is get it right when you try to harass me," I mutter, rolling my eyes.

I walk away, fingers slightly curled in to keep from touching my arm. It throbs slightly and I'm fair-skinned. Bruising would really suck when I'm about to be around a lot of people. Taking a deep breath, I pray that it's a delayed bruising, and walk to the journalist with a more natural smile on my lips.

"Lennon, darling, you look gorgeous. Kerrie, our makeup artist, isn't going to have to touch up a thing, will you?" she asks as she turns towards her.

Kerrie looks at me critically, head tilting to the side. "Lennon can you turn for me please?"

I oblige, slowly spinning so she can see my hair and she sees how the light plays on my features. She smiles wide, nodding in approval. "Orla, you're right. I don't have to change a thing. You are gorgeous, Lennon, and you know how to play up your attributes. I would kill for your hips," Kerrie says wistfully. "You're perfectly proportioned, and every man and woman's wet dream."

I blush at the comment, still not used to them, even after so many years of performing. This compliment was organic, she wasn't trying to suck up to me, and she has respect and attraction in her eyes as she watches me.

"Kerrie, I think that's one of the best compliments that I've ever received. I honestly will cherish it. Thank you," I tell her sincerely, my smile hitting my eyes finally.

Kerrie's eyes widen. "Holy wow," she whispers. "Your smile is incredible...I'm going to stop fangirling before this gets weird," she says with a small, shaky giggle. "Go kill it on this interview, you look like a million bucks."

With this, she turns and walks towards a group of people that I'm assuming is from one of the magazines. Prescott vaguely had told me on the way over that I was interviewing with *You* magazine.

I turn to face Orla, the journalist I'll be speaking with, and she's staring reflectively at me. "You're so nice, how are you a rockstar," she says in awe.

I will never get over how being a famous musician automatically means you get body snatched and become a dick. "I am a better version of myself than I've ever been, being able to perform for people that give a shit about my words," I tell her honestly. "I went a long time where my words didn't matter, so I will be forever grateful for this gift."

She stares a beat longer, and I wonder for a moment if I was too candid. She rocks back on her heels as if holding space for me and I release my breath. She holds her hand out to where there's two chairs set up and I follow her to them.

The interview goes smoothly, and I decide I like her. We banter, tease, and have fun during it. I ignore the lights, sound of cameras going off, and other background noise. I usually dislike interviews because they ask me a lot of questions about my childhood, but Orla skipped those questions.

She was especially excited when she asked me what plans we had for future music.

"Oh my god, so it's funny that you ask this," I gush, dishing like we're old friends. "I finished writing a song this morning, and the guys and I are very excited about it. In fact, *Music Horde* and I discussed the possibility of recording it while we're still on the road touring, and they gave us the green light. We should be recording a new album very soon," I explain with a smile.

Orla's eyes are the size of saucers. You'd think that I promised her candy on the moon.

"Seriously, I mean, this is incredible news. I love your songs and *I'm* excited about this. I love how dedicated you all are. Tours can be draining, but you all are just energized by it. You're enigmas in the music industry, and I am so pleased that you're sharing this with me," she says sighing happily.

I grin at her conspirally. "There is also a possibility that we may debut this song live on tour after the album goes live. It all depends on timing, but," I shrug with a smile, "we are going to do our damnedest to do it."

"Are you serious right now," she squeals before slapping her hand over her mouth in embarrassment.

"Oh girl, I'm stoked. You can be excited, I swear, and I hope others are too when you tell them," I say, beaming at her.

Orla bounces with enthusiasm in her seat, while making notes in her notebook. "This may be my favorite moment of the week, meeting you I mean. I do this thing, where I rate the moments of my week, so I'll never forget what makes my days brighter," Orla confesses to me.

I consider this, deciding to incorporate this into my days. "I think I'm going to start doing that too," I admit. "It's such a great way to show gratitude every day. Yep, totally doing this. Thank you, Orla for inspiring me today."

I swear this girl may pass out from the compliment but she pulls it together. "You're welcome. You're amazing, and while this is our first time talking, I can say that the rumors are true. Those that talk to you, always confess that you're so real and down to earth. I think one fan said that you helped her daughter with boy problems, is that right?" she asks.

"Honestly, yeah. Our VIP meet ups after the show are super chill and organic. We talk about everything during this time and really get to know our fans. Last night, there was a young girl who was trying to figure out how to deal with a boy that wasn't very nice to her. He kept giving her mixed signals and she felt he was pressuring her to do more with him sexually. She wasn't ready to," I explain with a shrug. "I told her to do what she felt was right, and not to be bullied into doing anything."

Orla nods so hard, her hair flies into her face. "Yes! This is such an important message, and honestly not talked about enough. Everything is highly sexualized, so everyone is in a rush to experiment."

"Experimenting is amazing, but you shouldn't feel pushed into it," I say with a wink. "It was a really great conversation, though her mom almost had a heart attack." I giggle as I remember it.

"Okay, one last question. Can you give us a hint about what this song you wrote today is about?" Orla leans forward as she asks to receive a secret.

I seriously love her. I'm not usually at such ease during an interview, and spend it dodging uncomfortable conversations about my relationship with the guys. This is refreshing.

"A hint. Yeah I can. It's a song about life experiences that shape you, try to break you down, and you come out fighting anyway. Turner is going to duet it with me and I can not freaking wait!"

Orla's eyes get bigger and bigger. "Woah, this sounds heavy but amazing. I also don't want to pry, but is this song influenced by anything specific?"

My lips twist as I think about every traumatic experience in my childhood. "I can say it's influenced by some of my experiences as a kid. I was bullied heavily from junior high through high school, and some things are hard to forget. I don't know if any of them will hear it," I lie blatantly, knowing that Derek will definitely hear it, "but the song is too powerful not to release."

"Thank you for sharing, and I just want to say that I'm sorry this was your experience. You're one of the best people that I've ever met, and you deserved better," Orla says softly.

I reach over and squeeze her hand gently. "Thankfully, I have better now, and people who protect me."

She shakes herself, pulling herself together. "Uh, are you up for some photos? Our photographer should be ready for you now. Seriously, this interview was incredible. Our readers are gonna flip out. I am so excited to hear the new album."

"Hey ladies, are we ready for some pictures?" asks a man as he walks up to us.

I smile when I see his camera. "Yes, I think we're just about done," I say, standing with Orla. "Orla, this was a pleasure, love. Please have Prescott put you on my list of preferred people to talk to, okay?"

Her eyes widen in surprise. It's not a secret I have a list of journalists and reporters and photographers that I prefer to work with. It is a secret there's also a list of people I won't work with. One tried to feel me up, and I was hard pressed not to break his finger. I mentioned it to the guys, and they started the *Lennon's Black List because You're a Douche* List. I still giggle when I think of its name.

"Perfect, I have a backdrop set up, and may I say you look gorgeous. You're gonna make my job easy," he says, talking a mile a minute.

I roll my lips inwards to hide my amusement. He has shoulder length curly hair that's tied back and pouty lips. He's adorable and I still have no idea who he is.

"I can tell we're going to have a blast," I say as I allow myself to get carried away by his energy. "Do you have a name? Because I'm about to start calling you The Adorable Photographer until I get one."

He sputters, shaking his head. "I'm sorry, that's totally my fault. I am not against you calling me that by the way, but my name is Zach. I can't get over how naturally gorgeous you are and it's throwing me right now."

I study him as a soft smile plays on my lips. He's not hitting on me, he genuinely thinks I'm pretty.

"Thank you, I really appreciate it. I did my own hair and makeup on the bus before running over here," I explain.

"Girl, it looks so natural...and this lavender hair is absolutely perfect on you. It's always this color, right? It's a whole mood with your gray eyes," Zach gushes as we walk over to the backdrop set up.

It's a green screen with a white couch. "Yes, I started coloring it six years ago. It's just part of who I am now. Where do you want me, Zach?" I tease him. I'm getting distinct vibes that he's not attracted to women.

Zach beams at me. "Yesss. I want to drape you over the couch-"

"Propositioning people already, are you Lennon?" says a voice.

Fuck me. Why is the universe punishing me today?

"No, Derek, but way to insert yourself where you're not invited," I respond, turning towards him. I wince on the inside because I see my mistaken innuendo too late.

"Sounds like a party," he says with a wink.

This is completely unprofessional. Why is he still here?

"I don't have time to entertain you, man child. I'm working," I tell him through my teeth.

I make *please save me,* eyes at Zach and he jumps into action. "Yes, working now, shoo whoever you are," he says, making an actual shooing motion.

I grin at him, and head over to the couch to lay on it the way Zach directs me to. Derek scowls, moving away from the set a few steps before stopping to watch like a creeper.

Zach asks me to arch my back and look over my shoulder. While it's an awkward position, I've learned the odder it feels, the better it looks on camera. "Yes, awesome, now sit up, lean your forearms on your legs and stare right at me," he demands.

I smirk to myself with how in his element he is. I love experiencing people's passion. Photographing people is Zach's happy place.

I get into the new position, hands relaxed, and arch my eyebrow at him. He didn't tell me how he wanted my expression, but instead he continues to take photos. I relax my face, my smirk returning to my face. I'm amused that he's going with whatever my face wants to do. I can't hide how I feel unless I regress to my mask of indifference that I used in high school often.

"Don't move, give me all the sexy Lennon smirks right now. Damn if I didn't like boys and your boys weren't so attached... just damn! You're a smoke show, babe." Zach hams it up, speaking nonsense only he understands.

I burst out laughing, throwing my head back in mirth. This is fun, and I don't always get this during this part of the tour. People rarely want to see the real Lennon in an interview and subsequent photo session. However, I'm happy with the surprise.

"Absolutely incredible. Can I just take photos of you as my job," Zach sighs.

I look at him indulgently, but notice Derek has crept in and is standing behind him. Sighing, I say, "Unfortunately, it looks like someone already has that job, otherwise I would say absolutely."

Derek rolls his eyes at me and I decide I've had enough.

"Zach, honey, do you need any other photos?" I ask with a forced smile. This isn't as fun as it was previously, now that he's spectating. I know I said I would be stronger when it comes to him, but some reactions take a bit to unlearn.

Zach checks his photos in his camera. "Ya know, these are awesome and the magazine will love them. As will everyone else. You're comfortable in your own skin, and it shows."

My smile becomes more real as I allow his words to wash over me. Derek has hit my self esteem hard, the hard work I put in to become the truest part of myself, undone. I am not the girl he knew anymore.

"Thank you so much. I'm truly honored to have you take my photos today, Zach. You're a breath of fresh air to the industry,." And I'm the one gushing now.

I walk out of the hall with my head held high, forcing myself to not rub where my arm is starting to hurt. I'm glad my sleeves cover it now, or I would have to answer a lot of questions I'm not ready to. I had pushed everything else away for the last two hours, but now it's catching up to me. I need food and then I need to start getting ready. We have someone opening for us, and they start at eight-thirty. I want to watch them from the wings, partly because I've never heard of them before. The label books our opening acts, so who is performing is always a surprise.

This is the time that I live for, when I'm in between obligations for the label, and I get a little quiet time. Turner will be joining people in the parking lot to tailgate with them, hoodie pulled over his head and a pack of beer to share. He gets to be a regular person for a few hours, enjoying the pre-show energy. Roark will be found high above the stage soon too, zoning out and preparing for tonight as well. We each have our rituals that ground us, keep us centered, and ready to rock out Seattle.

I'm so not ready when I get pushed into a wall. I can't see who is holding me, and then a door opens and I'm herded into a closet. I kick and try to get my shoe wedged for leverage, but these damn heels aren't doing me any favors. I open my mouth to scream when I hear, "Shut the fuck up, Lennon. I just want to talk to you," growled into my ear by a voice I know.

He wouldn't be this stupid, would he?

I'm stunned in my surprise, losing precious moments as he manhandles me into the stupid closet. The door is slammed close, and he turns on the overhead light with the hanging cord.

My eyes are wide, I'm sure my pupils are blown, and I'm afraid. What does he want with me?

Derek's hand grabs my throat and he shoves me into the wall. I grunt in pain, realizing he's fucking lost it. He would have these attacks of rage, but he usually channeled it into football. It's why he was the best.

"What do you want?" I squeak out as his hand tightens.

"You think you're hot shit, tossing attention at everyone in the room? Everyone bows down to the whore's daughter, the golden girl. Fucking *why?*" he screams into my face.

He's angry that I rose above being the mud under his shoe. That's rich.

I stomp my heel into his foot and he hisses. My shoes can be used as a weapon, at least. His hand releases its pressure slightly, but he shoves his pelvis into mine in an effort to keep me from running. Derek grabs my wrists and pins them over my head. His dick is rock hard and I gasp, arching to try to get away, but failing. We are pressed together from thigh to chest, and I'm unsure now if I should be turned on or pissed at him.

I settle on being both, huffing that I'm cornered. "I have never been anyone but who I am in the last ten years. The difference is I was who you decided I needed to be while you hated my mother for god knows what," I explain, refusing to yell and strain my voice.

"What?" His forehead furrows. "Your words don't make sense. Are you drinking before you're supposed to entertain all those people? You don't look drunk," he scoffs.

I sigh. "I only get drunk when I don't have commitments the following day, and only with Turner and Ror. Now fucking sod off, and get your dick away from me," I say gritting my teeth, bucking underneath him.

He chuckles. "I did hear once that you liked it rough in high school. Are you wet right now for me, Lennon?"

I freeze, any attraction I was feeling quickly dying. There was a vicious rumor spread by two football players that I was a hell cat in the sack. In reality, I fought them off when they dragged me under the bleachers while I was walking home. This is just what I want to remember when I'm pinned under a man twice my size in a janitor's closet. Awesome.

I take a deep breath, telling myself not to show fear. Derek gets off on it.

I try to channel everything I've worked so hard for, shoring up my defenses, but he knows just what to say to knock them down. The worst thing is: he doesn't know the truth. Derek hasn't a clue who I really am.

6

DEREK

Lennon O'Reilly is pinned to the wall by my hands and my pelvis. My cock is rock hard and it should sicken me. Instead, I want to know if her pussy is wet, why her eyes change emotions so quickly, and if her pupils are blown from excitement or fear. Either will do in my mood.

"Why did you leave Farrelsville when you seemed so content in your place? I have so many questions, and you never directly answer any of them," I growl, tightening the hand around her delicate wrists.

The truth is I haven't asked her many questions, since I'm all bark and bite when I do speak to her.

"You haven't asked any questions that matter," she says haughtily. "I got a letter saying my mother died the day I turned eighteen. I was waiting to see if she'd come back, or what happened to her when she left. With Mom gone, there was no reason to stay in a town that hated me. Is that enough of a straight answer for you Derek the Dick?" she asks sweetly.

She's dead? I grimace as *ding dong the witch is dead* plays rent free in my head. I'll have to process how I feel about this at another time. I dig said dick into her stomach. I'm taller than her, and the height difference is really working for me, allowing me to tower over her. "Why didn't you leave before, if your mom was gone?" I ask.

I am fascinated by all things Lennon. It's the reason I applied for this job after I realized she was the lead singer. I was obsessed with her fifteen years ago too, and it's grown in leaps and bounds. Lennon is gorgeous, but so was her mommy dearest. There has to be something wrong with her.

Carrie O'Reilly was beautiful on the outside, blonde with blue eyes, but she was dark and twisted on the inside. I knew she wasn't well, didn't take care of her daughter, and in different circumstances she'd never have kept Lennon. Our town just didn't give a shit about the O'Reillys outside of gossip fodder and a good time. I never got a taste, but apparently Lennon was quite popular with some of the guys in school. A hoe just like her mama.

I wonder if she'll let me have a taste now. She's with two men, she has to still be loose and wild, right?

Lennon's eyes reflect anger, fear, and a glint I'm not familiar with when speaking with her. "I am not a piece of meat so stop acting like I am. Back the fuck up," she bites out.

"I'm perfectly comfortable here, and the view of your tits is spectacular. Answer the question," I insist.

"Fucker," she growls. "I didn't know if my mom would come back, so I waited. As soon as I knew that I wasn't needed, I packed a bag and hitchhiked out of town. Now, if you want to go for a walk down memory lane, may I suggest a different locale than a janitor's closet?"

My face contorts in disgust as I stare at her. "You seem to think you're in charge, little girl. You're still nothing, trash, just shined up a bit-oof-" I grunt as I bend in half. The bitch somehow got enough space to knee me in the balls. "Bitch," I wheeze, quickly going to tighten my hands around her wrists and neck, but she shoves me with her full weight behind it.

She kicks me in the stomach and I fly into the cleaning supplies piled against the other wall. "I'd prefer to remain an enigma. My past should stay there, regardless of the roles you played within it, you should have remained buried there too. You may be hot as fuck, but you're a bully. I'll be carrying a knife from now on everywhere I go. It is professional courtesy that I'm warning you, can't have our social media manager bleeding like a stuck pig as he tries to get our best angles. Can we?" she asks sweetly before glaring at me.

Who could guess that tone and facial expressions could be so different? She snorts disgustedly, as she grabs the handle and pushes out of the room.

I, on the other hand, struggle to get my breathing under control after having my nuts kneed into my throat. The girl has serious power behind her kicks, it makes me wonder if someone taught her how to fight.

Slowly, I stand up, muttering curses. She apparently isn't as easy as her mother was, but I didn't imagine the attraction behind her eyes. Lennon O'Reilly has decided she has standards now, and is too good for me. I frown, gently massaging my balls. It's just me here, and they fucking hurt. If she was her mother, she would have climbed me like a tree and fucked me against the wall.

The fact that she didn't, definitely shows me she isn't her mother, but where do the similarities end? Her purple hair instead of white blonde color from the past helps differentiate the two. I've had small pangs of regret when I fuck with her, and I've been chalking it up to her hair color. However, she doesn't act like the docile girl I remember that took the bullshit given to her like she deserved it. *Am I seeing things that aren't there?*

I decide I'm going to pay special attention to how she interacts with Roark and Turner. Are they jealous of each other? Is Lennon jealous of them? I've read the rumors that Turner and Roark are also in a relationship, and I don't know how true it is. They are very private about their love lives when talking to the media, yet I know there are photos that circulate. Is it being too much of a stalker if I look them up?

Fuck, I don't think I care.

When I can stand up with only a twinge of pain, I straighten and leave the room. I am halfway down the hall, when I hear my name. Turning, I see it's the annoying woman that manages the band and keeps their schedules moving. Gah, I thought she was the nervous/anxious type, but she's been pushing my agenda without knowing by being a bitch to Lennon.

I don't know how I feel about this yet, but it's working to my advantage for now.

"Yes, Prescott?"

"Did you get any photos of the band doing interviews, by chance," she asks, her lips pressed in an annoying line. Honestly, Prescott currently looks constipated when she does this.

"Yep, I was able to get snapshots of each of them. They seem to interview well, even the grumpy ones," I say with a small chuckle.

Her lip twitches in amusement. "Yes, well, they've learned how to thrive in the public eye after years of practice. Lennon dropped a pretty big bomb to the girl interviewing her, and gave her exclusive information I didn't even know about. The girl just came and gushed all over me about how grateful she was for the interview, telling me all about it. While I'm irritated that Lennon and the guys didn't tell me, she did run it past the label and they told her to go for it. So, we need to get ahead of this from a social media perspective. I need you to find a photo of Lennon and the journalist with verbiage stating she dropped exclusive news which included a peek of their newest album coming soon. Then, be sure to tag the magazine and what issue the interview will be out in. This will ensure everyone is happy," she says with a huff. "Got it?"

"Yes ma'am," I respond with a droll, lazy smile.

Prescott nods crisply and glances at her clipboard. She starts muttering to herself and walks away. This woman is wound very tightly, and while I'd usually offer to help her relax, my attention is fully on a lavender-haired beauty.

I check my watch, deciding there's enough time for me to find the perfect photo, edit, and post it before stalking Lennon as she works through her pre-show ritual.

I walk back to a room I'm using in the stadium that is acting as a mock office for a few of us working with the tour. I pull my camera strap off of my neck before pulling the photos up on my laptop. Scrolling through, I purse my lips critically. I slowly relax them into a satisfied grin when I find a picture of Lennon leaning forward to touch the journalist's hand, her face animated.

This is perfect.

I touch up the photo a bit before loading it onto IG, Facebook, and Twitter's platforms with the caption: Lennon and Orla from *You* magazine were caught having a moment as she spoke about what to expect for their new album. Get all the details here! I make sure to add the link and tag the magazine on all socials.

Once that's done, I check the time, finding it's seven-thirty. Shit. I need to hurry. I power down my computer, leaving it here because there are other people working in the room still. I stand, shoving my phone in my back pocket and hanging my camera on my neck.

I rush out the door, heading toward the main stage, pushing my way through the doors to the back stage. I heard Prescott say Lennon sometimes dressed in the dressing room provided since she usually had interviews before a show. The guys tended to dress on the bus for the night and then disappear for their own pre-show rituals.

I hear loud music playing from her dressing room, and find the door is wide open. Lennon is jamming to the music as she does her final makeup touches. There's a jar of gummy bears she reaches into periodically for treats as she works.

Her hair is unwound from the braids she was wearing, wildly kinked down her back. She weaved flowers through the braid she created at the crown of her head, and if she wasn't Lennon fucking O'Reilly, she would look like a throwback flower child. Instead, she's wearing a leather sleeveless mini dress with a deep scoop neck. Her tits are pushed high, begging me to pull them out. I bite my lip to hold back the moan that wants to escape.

I don't know how she hasn't noticed I'm standing here, but she hasn't. This is when I noticed she is now applying makeup to her arms. Fuck, she warned me I was hurting her, and I was so driven by desire and anger, I didn't listen. Now she's forced to hide the bruises from where my fingers dug into her soft flesh. She has a full sleeve of colored tattoos, the other arm bare of ink. She's hyper focused on the naked arm, where the bruising is most noticeable.

I'm a dick. I've honestly spent most of my adolescence being cruel, impatient, jealous, and most of all violent towards her. My history with her mother colored every interaction from her freshman year on, but even before this, I wanted Lennon to pay for existing. She was always too beautiful, too innocent for our small town, so I recruited the town to destroy her. We got close a few times.

Lennon sighs, turning her arms from side to side to ensure all bruises are covered. She stands, smoothing her dress. Fuck me, she's wearing black, thigh high combat boots that climb her legs, and I bite my fist. *Get it together before she notices you...*

I lift my camera, focusing as she leans towards the mirror. I'm hidden from her view as I step in and hide behind a bunch of boxes. Lennon's so fixated on grabbing a gummy bear and popping it into her mouth before snatching up her lipstick, she never notices.

She makes an annoyed sound as she lifts the color to her lips, and I take the photo. I perfectly capture her image and her reflection as she gets ready. My camera is silent, no clicking or whirling sounds to worry about. Once done, she does a practice twirl in the mirror, making sure she won't have any wardrobe malfunctions.

This gorgeous girl then murmurs with a sardonic smile, "Not too shabby for the orphan who ran from her past." Sighing, she walks out of the room and I swear my heart seizes.

My dad might be a dick, but he's a dick who is still alive, well, and now the mayor of our childhood town. I pick up the phone whenever I want to speak to him, something that this lavender-haired siren can't.

I take one last glance around the room, wondering what it is about her and gummy bears, then leave.

True to our discussion earlier today, she is in the wings with a smile as she watches the opening band start up. I choose a curtain to peek around as I watch her, camera ready. She jumps, dances, and cheers for the band enthusiastically. Seattle's fans cheer loud and hard for these performers, so only she and the roadies hear and see her antics. One roadie in question, spins her as he walks past.

Quickly, I push the shutter button down, capturing her dancing. I glance down, checking the photos, finding I can see her joy projecting through. I refocus the camera, then wait for the next perfect shot.

Lennon peeks out the curtain to watch the band, and I move from my hiding spot to find another where I can see her face. I find one, adjusting the light exposure before taking the photo. Deciding I don't want to get caught, I slide through the curtains, exiting through a back entrance into the service hallways to take a break.

Leaning against the wall, I look at the photos. Lennon is radiant, the picture of happiness, reveling in a fellow musician's music. I doubt she knows the members of this band, but the fact they play is enough for her. There's no guile in these photos, and it makes me wonder...

Who is the real Lennon?

Roark

THE ELECTRIC ENERGY during a show is a high I will never be able to find anywhere else. Before I joined the band, I dabbled in some harder drugs, and I was an adrenaline junkie obsessed with driving cars in illegal drag races. Once I met my Valkyrie, Turner, and the band it became less necessary. I found my adrenaline rush playing drums for screaming fans, and in the very beginning there was the rush of uncertainty if we'd be booed off the stage as an unknown new sound.

Imagine my surprise when we weren't.

I swear it's because of my siren. I'm a solid drummer, but the magic happens when my girl picks up a microphone and looks out into a sea of people. She smiles her secret smile every performance, ever since our first, and says, "Thank you for listening to our words. I hope they make you feel seen." I always marveled at this, wondered, but didn't want to push.

Very soon after though, we started to tell each other that our words mattered, our emotions were important, and we would always see each other. This is why I didn't yell at her when Lenny forgot to check in when her muse hit. She was dealing with the shit storm of emotions, Derek the Dick brought with his return the only way she knew how.

I hit my groove perfectly as Lenny turns to the side to face me with a wide grin, dancing for me. The fans scream as she throws her head back in abandonment, lost in the sounds I pull from my drums. Her wide hips sway, her hair wild in curls left over from her braids. Lenny could be anywhere from worshiping the moon and dancing outside in the woods, to Woodstock with her crown of flowers weaved through her hair. She's our fucking gorgeous girl.

Lenny pulls herself out of her dance and tosses a wink at me before turning back to the crowd to perfectly sing the next note. She's masterful as she flirts with the crowd, feeding them her words, and I bare my teeth in a grin as her voice croons to our fans.

Lennon O'Reilly was born for the stage, to do this right here.

I glance over at Turner, who is also staring at her like she is the last sip of water in the whole damn world. We are obsessed with her, and I see nothing wrong with it. Her smiles light up our world, her words our balm.

I take a deep breath as we hit the last leg of our set, soaking in every moment. Mav's guitar complements us perfectly, and while he was our last addition to the band when our past member left, he is our perfect match. He defends Lenny fiercely, and I had to talk him down from beating the shit out of Derek the Dick when he made her cry. I really need the backstory on this guy soon so I can help protect my girl, but I'm not one to rush things. There's a reason Lenny is known as the girl without a past. She doesn't speak about it, and somehow the media never pushed it.

Somehow she gets to keep her secrets, and I'm grateful for it. I'll wait a thousand years for her to be ready to spill them to me. All I know is her mother wasn't the best, and apparently Derek the Dick was a bully when she was growing up.

It's enough for me to want to let Turner introduce him to his bat.

Turner and Lenny close the show with a duet about missed opportunities and regrets, and the crowd starts to scream for an encore. Lenny brings the microphone to her lips and I think, *shit Atlas fucking called this.*

"What do you think boys, is Seattle hot enough to deserve another song?" she asks, turning to face us.

We look over at each other with mirth in our eyes. She's had this incredible energy all night, and I know the combination of the music, the zoomies, and her fans are to thank for it. I shrug in acquiescence, because who am I to deny her anything.

Atlas yells, "Let's fucking go," and Mav, Turner and I whoop and howl.

"Well then, the boys say you all were fucking incredible tonight, so let's close out with *Lessons We Learn*, shall we," Lennon says as she jump turns to face the audience.

I shake my head with a chuckle. I don't know how she managed to do this in her dress and not flash the world. I swear, it's a gift she has.

Our fans of course go insane for another song, especially one that isn't performed on tour often. The instrumentals on it are wicked, and one of my favorite songs to go wild on. Lenny is definitely feeling spunky tonight, and it'll be worth Prescott having a coronary over. The label will back us as we cater to our fans though, so I'm not worried.

We lose ourselves in the magic of the night, as Lenny sings the story of our love. Everyone has questions about how our relationship works, if there's jealousy or how committed we are to each other. You have to be deaf and dumb to not understand our love when you hear this song. Our girl was skittish and broken when she met us, but all we saw was how her shattered pieces sparkled.

Even when her light sputtered in the darkness, she still shone brighter than the masses.

We all stand with a roar, carried by the energy. I stride across the stage, throwing the mic at Turner, as he's close on my heels. I pick Lenny up, squeezing her tightly and kissing her. Depositing her back on her feet, we face the crowd and wave as they cheer.

"Thank you, Seattle for being incredible, we have to go now," Turner says, breathlessly as he stares into the sea of darkness with cell phone lights flashing. "Good night!"

The crowd screams as we wave again before turning to run off the stage. Tonight will be one of my favorite nights. You'd think the nights would meld together, become monotonous, but they never do.

"How much trouble do you think we'll get into for this?" My beautiful Valkyrie is the picture of mischief as she giggles, equally breathless.

"I doubt–" I start before a roadie comes up to offer us bottles of water.

We nod in thanks, each grabbing one from him. Lenny opens it and drinks deeply. I have trained myself to listen for the crack of an unopened bottle, but fail to hear it when she opens it.

"Hey baby... " I'm again interrupted, but this time by Prescott who stomps into our view.

She blows out a breath as she looks over us like we are naughty school children. I snort softly at the picture she makes: I haven't been a child in a long damn time.

"I hope you lot are proud of yourselves, you've thrown the schedule off for tonight," she says with a sigh. "Come along, it's time for you to make the rounds now."

Lenny links her arm through mine, and looks up at me with a grin. I look down at her with an answering smile, and kiss her. She molds her body to me, and I think about how amazing it'll be to sink into her later. Her body was made for mine, and I know she feels tiny when I turn and wrap my arm around her to pull her into me. My girl deserves rewards in the form of orgasms tonight.

We start walking over to the room where we'll meet with those that won VIP passes, while Prescott gives us the silent treatment. Honestly, I would rather she stay quiet than speak anyway. Lenny smiles as we walk in and looks up at me as she slips her arm out of mine. There's an odd sheen to her eyes that wasn't there before, and I frown.

I don't get to ask her before we are pulled away from each other. Dammit, I want to scream, I just want to make sure she's okay. I didn't like that her bottle sounded like it had been opened before. I hold up my bottle curiously. It's still closed and I never had a chance to take a sip. *I wonder...*I twist it and I hear the crack of a seal being opened. I'm now more confused than before.

I track her with my eyes as we move around the room and she seems fine, chatting and smiling. I still have this growing anxiety that something is wrong though, I'm missing something, and Turner picks up on it when I shift my weight yet again. My chest is growing tighter and tighter. I want to go to her, have my eyes on her, assure myself she's okay.

"Hey, Ror, you look like you're gonna jump out of your skin. What the fuck is wrong?" he asks out of the corner of his mouth.

"Fuck, I think something is wrong with Lenny. She accepted a bottle of water, and it may sound crazy, but I didn't hear the sound of a seal being broken," I explain.

Turner's eyes meet mine in panic. "Fuck no," he leans forward as he says to the group smoothly, "Sorry, folks, Ror needs eyes on our girl. It's been too long since we've seen each other. It was really wonderful to chat with you all."

The group grins, and one of the women talks about how fun young love is. I would smile at this, if I wasn't so worried about her. We walk with purpose, not wanting to raise an alarm. I tower over most people here, but I don't fucking see her.

I do, however, see Prescott. "Hey," my voice doesn't sound like mine and is hoarse, I never did drink any water. "Have you seen Lenny? I can't find her any-"

"Ugh, the brat disappeared an hour ago. She seemed fine, but I saw her walk out with her fingers on her temples. Maybe a migraine," she mutters. "I don't know, but I'm sure she's fine. Listen, you can't leave right now. Since she's gone, you need to be here a few more minutes at least."

"I don't think so. Atlas and Mav are here. I'll start looking for her. Something just wasn't right, and I don't have a good feeling about this. Turner, text me when you're done here and I'll let you know if I've found her?" My eyes turn to his, begging him to be okay with this. I know he's gotta be affected by how agitated I am.

Turner's lips press against each other as if he's keeping his words inside by force and nods.

"Which way did she go, Prescott?"

She looks like she's sucking on a lemon as she shakes her head at me, refusing to say.

"So help me God, woman, I will make a scene if you don't fucking tell me," I growl.

She nods at the door that leads outside and I explode into motion, only wanting to find my girl. Maybe I'm overreacting. Or is she on the bus?

I just can't chase this feeling that something awful happened. I need to find her.

7

DEREK

I left the meet and greet early once I had enough photos of the band mingling. I'm wiped from the day, and decide to take a walk. My emotions are pulled from anger, to remorse, to anxiety, to blinding rage. I feel so confused, my thoughts clouded by this siren who doesn't want me.

I walk through the halls, taking the long way out to the parking lot. Lennon O'Reilly is effortlessly beautiful, and it's unfair how she haunts my thoughts.

I stood in the crowd, surrounded by fans near the stage to take photos and videos of them during their concert. I captured them between my phone and my camera, live posting throughout the show. I've always thought *The Darkest Nights* were incredible in concert, following their career and attending performances when they were near my home in Colorado.

As soon as I graduated from high school, I left to go to the University of Colorado Boulder and played football on a full scholarship. I'm two years older than Lennon, and I didn't think about her for a second after grinding her into the dirt where she belonged one last time. I didn't keep tabs on anyone from town outside of my father, I just wanted to escape.

My end game was to play professional football, and I did for a couple of years before I blew out my knee. Thank God I had a back up plan and got a degree in something I enjoyed: Communications and Mass Media. All of this led me to where I am now: really fucking confused.

I should hate her, right? Spawn of my enemy is my enemy, or something like that. Lennon has the same cutting way of speaking when she's angry as her mom: formal, clipped, and hurtful. It's not like I don't drive her to do this though: angry people show their true colors and their truths.

However, her truths seem to be clouded by fear. *Is she scared I know the real her?* I muse as I step outside into the fresh air. It's been dark for hours now, and there's a hint of rain in the air, normal for Seattle in September.

I drag my hand through my hair in frustration as I think about this enigma of a girl that tortures my thoughts now. It hasn't escaped my notice that the media doesn't know about Lennon's past. They don't know about her mom, the torture she went through by my hand and others with my encouragement in school, or how much of a whore Lennon was in high school. I never had concrete proof, she rarely came to parties, yet the rumors grew from guys who had been with her.

I scowl as I get uncomfortably hard, remembering her soft curves against me. However, she never wanted me, not that I could ever want her in public, either. Or that I should want her, after her mom fucked with my life on her many days of 'not being herself'. I doubt Carrie O'Reilly knew who she was between the mania, depression, and bouts of extreme anger.

I remember the tornado that she was, though.

Carrie started fucking my dad right around the eighth grade. I came home early from spending the night at a friend's and walked in on them messing around on our kitchen island. The island my mother made meals on, kneaded dough for bread, and I often sat after school and ate on.

Bile crawls up my throat as I watch, horrified but unable to look away. My mom's out of town for the weekend, visiting her sister. My dad isn't supposed to be breaking his vows, cheating on my mom, sucking on-

I step back on the wooden floor, which betrays me by creaking. Fuck my life. *The woman lays back, spreading open her pale legs. The morning light spills into the kitchen, cheerful and bright, so at odds with the darkness I'm watching. My father dives in like it's his last meal, and I can see everything from where I'm standing. I feel light headed as the blonde massages her breasts, then she turns her head. She isn't surprised to see me, her eyes hooded with desire, moaning and panting. My eyes widen in surprise as I realize it's the woman who lives across from us, Mrs. O'Reilly.*

It would figure that my first experience with porn would be this. She rolls her nipples between her fingers, pulling hard as she comes. She begs him to fuck her, and somehow my father never turns his head to see me as he pulls her off the counter, turns her and pushes her upper body flat on it. Her eyes continue to make contact with me, her wrists held tight at the base of her spine in his hand. He unbuttons his pants, smacking her ass hard. She cries out but begs for more, and I wonder why he's hurting her. And why she likes it.

He thrusts into her and I decide I can't stand to watch anymore. I no longer feel like puking, but even more embarrassingly, I'm rock hard. I walk quickly to my room, even though I want to run. My father can't ever know I was here. This shouldn't be possible, right? I must be sick, depraved to have watched them fuck. Yet, I push my basketball shorts off, staring at my erection.

I palm it through my boxers, my breath becoming shorter. I'm confused by these feelings of arousal and guilt. I pull my dick out, mesmerized by it as I stroke it. My head falls back as my memory replays the images I just saw, until I'm exploding into my hand.

I can never tell anyone about this. I want to beat the shit out of my father for being such a cheating asshole, but I can't. I can't tell my mother either, worried it will destroy her. Who can I take all of this black, burning ball of hatred and self-loathing and aim it at?

This is when I think of little Lennon O'Reilly who just started sixth grade at my school. She's cute, sweet, and bubbly. People love her, her teachers adore her. It's time to bring her down, make her hate her life, and she'll never know why.

Or that it's all because of her mom.

I SHAKE my head as I weave around the traffic that's trying to get out of the stadium parking. I should have really gone out another door to go directly to where the buses are, but I needed to clear my head.

I hear honking and yelling as I walk. Frowning, I wonder what's going on, outside of the normal asshole not being patient after the concert. I catch a flash of lavender hair and frown. *What the fuck?*

It can't be Lennon, right? There have to be other girls with lavender hair at this concert, fans of their favorite rock star. What is she doing on this side of the stadium? I walk faster, throwing up my hand in apology as I cross in front of cars. Who the fuck is this girl?

I see it is Lennon, wildly laughing as she dances and sings between cars. Fuck, this could be really bad if someone takes photos. I notice quickly not one phone is out, just people yelling at her to get out of the way, asking if she's alright. It's so reminiscent of her mother, I swallow thickly. The least I need to do is get her away from traffic. *Why is she out here?*

I feel distinct deja vu now that I hear her laughing. I shake my head as it threatens to send me spiraling into thoughts of *her*. Carrie doesn't belong in my present, not now that she's apparently dead.

Sighing, I watch as she twirls mindlessly in the road. I would almost think she was high, but I've never heard a murmur that she touches anything stronger than alcohol. I feel helpless, and I wonder if I should call someone. All other decisions are taken from me when someone almost hits her. Fuck.

I run towards her, grabbing her around the waist. Lenny tries to fight me and I throw her over my shoulder, my fingers cramping in an effort not to spank her. Fucking spoiled brat, what does she think she's doing right now?!

I jog away from the cars, grunting as she hits my back.

"Do you have a fucking death wish, Car-erm Lennon? Why are you in the road? What is happening," I am screaming question after question, the feelings of hysteria clawing at my throat as I lift her off my shoulder.

Lennon wiggles to get free like a fucking feral cat and I drop her on her ass. She squeals as her backside hits the pavement, flashing her panties at me.

"What the fuck, Derek? Nothing is wrong with me," she says, throwing her head back to look up at me. "I just needed to dance," she says dreamily with a dopey smile.

"Ya know, I kept seeing similarities between you and your mom, but I definitely see it now. Lennon you're fucking loopy and hyper at the same time, do you even know where you are right now? How did you get outside?"

She blinks at me, then, looks around in confusion. "I don't know. I was in the VIP meet and greet and then got a headache. It's all kind of fuzzy right now. I was just dancing..." Her head moves back to me and a huge smile crosses her face.

It's not the genuine smile I've been seeing on stage though, it's a crazed one. I have goosebumps crawling over my skin and I shiver at the sight of it.

"Hey! We should dance, wanna? Why am I on the ground, did I fall? Can you help me up?" her voice is higher pitched than usual in her confusion and makes me wince in pain. She lifts her arms up, making grabby hands for mine.

I lean down, unsure what else to do and help her to her feet.

"Thank you," she sing-songs.

"Lennon, I really think something is wrong. Do you have your phone to call someone? One of your guys maybe," I ask trailing off. I can't believe I'm trying to help her when clearly she's not completely with me right now.

She shrugs, as she looks at me. There are overhead parking lights above us, and there is an odd gleam in her eyes. Confusion also clouds her gray eyes. It's scaring me, the knowledge she really doesn't know how she got out here.

"No, I don't need them right now. They always find me. They're the fucking best, aren't they," she gushes as she throws her arms over my neck.

This is how I want Lennon O'Reilly to want me, but she never has. The experience is soured as she raves about Roark and Turner while she does it. I frown at her, and she smoothes the lines caused by it with her fingers.

"If you're not careful, you'll end up with wrinkles, old man," she says, laughing wildly.

I can't shake the feeling this isn't Lennon, but I'm becoming seriously triggered.

"Lennon," I start again. "Why don't we go inside-"

"I don't want to," she whines, stepping back and spinning. "Come spin with me!"

"Lennon, I don't think that's a good idea," I tell her. "Why don't we-"

"Get naked," she says with a laugh, coming to a stop closer to me. *What?* "Good idea, I'm so hot," she complains, starting to pull down one of the straps of her dress.

There's an odd sheen of sweat on her brow that shouldn't be there as it's cool out. "What the fuck, Lennon! No, what is wrong with you? You're not yourself, is this what crazy looks like on you? I mean, your mom did shit like this all the time, didn't she? Do you remember what I told you the day she stripped and went skinny dipping in my lake?" I am screaming now, lost in memories of the woman who took advantage of a young boy with no remorse.

She stands there with a strap hanging on her shoulder and her mouth open in shock. "Crazy is catching," she whispers, a tear slipping down her face. "Oh my god, it's happening to me too," she sobs, hand moving to her mouth.

She turns and runs from me.

"Lennon, wait," I scream. She's moving fast for someone in combat boots. She slips out the side gate of the parking lot, taking a right, disappearing into the night. "Fuck, I'm sorry," I whisper.

My hand covers my chest as it constricts. I meant to help her, not lose her. She's in a city she doesn't know, and I didn't see a phone in her hand. Fuck, I could also lose my job after this.

Fuck the job actually, I just lost a fucking *person*. I don't know what my next step should be as I stare after her in shock. I never think about my words, and typically they don't cause anyone pain outside of the emotional kind. I'm a dick, I know this, my tongue is sharp.

Anxiety starts to claw at me as the full ramifications of what just happened hits me. What do I do now? *I need to go find Roark and Turner*. I start running towards the room where the meet and greet is happening, to find them. What will I tell them? Hey, I lost your girlfriend...fuck buddy? What are they to her?

I feel a surge of jealousy too that's out of place. She's not mine, never has been, and now likely will never be after this. Fuck, anything could happen to her, and the worst starts running through my brain:

SHE COULD BE BEATEN up and hurt.

She could be raped.

She could be kidnapped.

She could be killed.

MY HEART IS POUNDING as I see a large man with anxious, hunched shoulders striding towards me yelling Lennon's name. Here comes Roark.

"Oye, is that you, Derek? Have you seen my girl? She left earlier and she's not on the bus," he says.

"Um, funny story," I tell him, rubbing the back of my neck. Fuck, why did I say it like that. "I ran into Lennon, and she was acting oddly. Her eyes were glassy, and she was dancing in between cars. She was fine, but-"

"But what, fucker? If you saw her, where is she now," he roars. I shudder at the emotion I hear in his voice. He's angry and terrified, and he's not wrong to feel these things. Lennon isn't well, she's mentally unstable, and now she's gone.

"I said some shit to her because she was out of her mind, and she ran away, okay," I yell back at him. My emotions are stretched tight, and I definitely chose violence with these words.

As I watch the fist flying at my face, I accept I deserve this and I'm an asshat.

Roark

I'M GONNA KILL HIM. I couldn't help myself and punched the bastard. Then I kicked him with my combat boot and clenched my fists as I screamed.

"If she's hurt, I'll take it out on your fucking hide. How dare you fuck with her when she's not well," I roared.

This isn't helping, she's still out there. I restrain myself from kicking him again, knowing the rational part of me is right. I need to find her. Derek is a moron, but he didn't know she was possibly drugged. Whatever he thinks isn't right in regards to my Lenny is wrong, but I don't have time to explain it to him.

"Tell me what way she went at least, ya fuckwit," I growl.

Derek takes a pained breath, pushing himself to a sitting position. "She was by the North entrance, slipped out the side gate there, and then took a right. I don't know anything else," he says.

I pull my phone out of my back pocket, forcing myself to pull air through my lungs to quiet my rage. All that matters is finding Lenny and her safety. It doesn't help that part of this anger is at myself for not seeing she left sooner.

I throw one last disdainful glance at the man at my feet, forcing myself not to pop his head like a grape. Blowing out a breath, I call Turner, turning away from Derek the Dick to stare at the now empty parking lot.

"Hey, did you find her?" Turner answers.

"No, but apparently Derek did, said some shit to her and she ran out the gate," I explain, striding away from the man who continually bullies my girl in an effort not to pound on him. It won't help outside of making me feel better for a time.

"Fuck, why would she leave? She's never been to Seattle, she wouldn't know where to go, why not come find us," Turner groans.

"I think she was drugged," I explain, my legs carrying me towards the North entrance of the stadium. "Lenny didn't look right to me after she started drinking from her water bottle, and I just wasn't able to ask her about it. Fuck, man, I feel like this is my fault," I mutter, owning part of the reason I'm so angry.

"Not again," Turner whispers. He has some experience with being drugged. He's usually the bottle police, but tonight was so crazy. We were all distracted with other shit instead.

"We just need to find her. I'm walking towards the North entrance. Grab Atlas and Mav, and we'll start canvassing the area. I already beat the shit out of Derek for his bullshit, but you're welcome to take your bat to him *after* we find our girl. Understood?"

"My Lavender always comes first," he agrees. I hear him yell, *"Yo, Mav, Altas- we gotta go! Yeah, I'll explain on the way,"* he says. Turner comes back to me on the phone, blowing out a frustrated breath. *"The room cleared out shortly after you left, but Prescott wouldn't shut the fuck up. I've never been more frustrated with a woman before,"* he growls.

I hear running sounds and his breath gets slightly more labored. I feel less alone, knowing my mates are on their way to help.

The door to my left slams open as I walk up to it, the boys spilling into the parking lot and I disconnect the call. Shoving my phone into my back pocket, I update them on what I know.

"I'm assuming Lenny doesn't have her phone, but she isn't

in the best mindset. Can someone try it anyways," I bark. Altas nods, lifting a finger as he calls her phone. "Derek says she went this way out the side gate, but initially found her dancing in traffic as cars were leaving. This isn't like her at all, which is why I'm worried-"

I stop suddenly when Atlas clears his throat. My eyes cut to him, begging him to tell me she's fine.

"Sorry man, no answer. It goes straight to voicemail. It may be dead," he says.

"Fuck a duck," I mutter. It would be funny if we weren't all so worried. "Okay, we'll keep this quiet for now. We're all going out to find her, and hope to God she's alright. Agreed?"

"Aye," the boys all say.

Fuck, I love these men. I turn sharply, walking towards the gate. Just as worried as I am, they follow, foreheads furrowed, struggling to keep their anxiety and questions at bay.

Questions I don't have the answers to.

WHY DID *you leave the meet and greet, baby?*

Why didn't you tell me you didn't feel well?

Why didn't I stop you to check your fucking water?

I STORM out the side gate, raising my hand at the guard. I'm the one people recognize from our band members faster than the rest.

"Hey man, going for a walk. We'll be back soon, don't lock us out, yeah?" I give him a tight smile that I'm sure comes off as anything but friendly.

Waves of violence and the threat of destruction are all I feel, so it's hard to be nice at the moment.

"Yeah, man. Heard it was a great show tonight. Congratulations. I'm here all night, just come back through here and I'll let you in," the guard says.

Well, at least we won't be locked out.

"I really appreciate it, man. Thanks," I say nodding.

The four of us pass him, heads on a swivel as we look for Lenny. There aren't many people out right now, which is lucky for us, but also terrifies me that the wrong kind of person might find her. I want to yell her name, but also don't want to scare her. Fuck only knows what the dickhead said to her.

I need to know more about their history, but only after I find my girl in one piece. Nothing else matters.

"Let's split up. Atlas, start checking alleyways. Mav, look to see if she is on a bench or passed out against a wall. If someone slipped something into her water tonight, I'm worried she's incapacitated somewhere and can't hear us if we call for her," I explain.

"Who the fuck would drug her," Mav explodes.

"I don't know, that'll have to be tabled until we find her. So let's move out and fucking find our Valkyrie," I growl.

"Copy that," Atlas murmurs, breaking off to hit the alleys.

Mav splits off too and I blow out a breath.

"We'll find her, Ror. Let's go. When we find she's fine and giggling, I'll toss her over my knee and punish her sweet ass," Turner teases.

"Yeah, okay," I mutter, before calling out her name. I won't be able to joke around or find any joy until I have her in my arms.

We cover ground between the four of us, checking a park, alleys, and dumpsters. I swear to God, I never want to have to do this again. I'm terrified she's scared and broken somewhere and we won't be able to find her. Opening dumpsters to check for her body is one of the lowest parts of my life, and I've had some pretty fucked up ones.

I haven't prayed since I was a boy in Ireland, attending Mass with my ma, but I do it for her. *Please, please God, let her be okay. I will do anything.*

Minutes turn to an hour, then to two hours, and the hope we'd find her quickly turns to ash. *Where is she?*

Tears prick my eyes as I sniffle and Turner throws his arm over my shoulder to squeeze me.

"Don't count her out, Ror. Fuck, please don't cry or I'll start too and we'll never find her," he begs.

I nod, unable to talk past the lump in my throat. Lenny and Turner are my *everything*. I wipe my arm across my eyes before dragging my hands through my hair.

"Lennon, where the fuck are you?" I scream.

Turner swallows hard, looking away. She's the glue holding me together, my light, and I can't survive without her.

"She can't have gone this far, let's turn around and canvas again," Turner says, his voice filled with tears.

I have to get it together for him, even if I have to fake it. *Come on baby, say something for me. Whimper, scream, let me hear your voice.*

8

LENNON

I feel like my body is floating, disconnected, yet ill at ease. I don't know where I am, but I'm surrounded by darkness. I know this isn't right, I have men who love me, but I don't see them.

I whimper as I hear my name. Who is calling me? The disconnected feeling starts to fade and I feel pain. My ankle hurts, my head throbs, and stomach roils. It's like I went on a bender but I wouldn't have before a show. My mouth tastes like ass too.

"Lenny, where are ya baby," I hear.

Roark? Only he calls me Lenny.

"Roark," I whisper, struggling to open my eyes. My lashes feel glued to my skin, my eyes dry. I also have the overwhelming scent of magnolias pricking my nose. *Where the fuck am I?*

My arms feel heavy, as if I had a million pound weight on each of them, and I struggle to raise them. I rub my eyes, and my eyes open. I'm in an alley, in a wet puddle, and I shiver.

How did I get here? This can't be anywhere near the stadium we performed in.

I cough, shuddering at how dry my throat feels. Slowly, I manage to get on my knees, feeling dizzy. I'm kneeling in dirty water, but I can't get my limbs to move the way I need them to. I have so many questions, too.

I throw my hands on the ground, wondering if I can crawl out, or even wiggle on the hard pavement. I force my right arm and knee to move forwards and then the other. *Hey look at that, I did it.*

"Lenny, if you can say anything, I need to hear your voice. Tell me where you are," Ror yells.

My thoughts are so unfocused. He wants me to do something, but this alley is so gross. Something skitters by me, making a squeaking noise, and I realize it's not something fluffy or cute.

A scream tears out of me, and it occurs to me I can use my voice. Oh my god, Roark, I wanna go home.

"Roark," I scream. "Help me," I sob. "Please, I wanna go home."

"Guys I hear her," I hear him say, the sound of feet pounding on the pavement loud. "Baby, what's around you? I'm coming. What do you see?"

"I'm in an alley, and I can't really move," I yell, head raised to project my voice.

I hear shuffling clothes and talking, and freeze in fright. Is it my guys, or someone else? I whimper, worried my screaming has brought someone that'll hurt me. I'm shivering, my body covered in goosebumps in this stupid tiny dress that wasn't supposed to leave the stadium halls.

Derek left bruises earlier in the night, and it's like every one of them is sitting up and screaming for attention. Even the bruises he left are dicks like he is.

"Fucking hurts," I mutter. "Focus, Lennon, just a little longer. We got this."

I must be losing it, talking to myself like I am. A flashback from the night breaks through. "Crazy is catching," replays over and over in my head.

What's wrong with me? Did I black out? My mom used to lose time, saying she didn't remember what had happened. Am I becoming my mom? I can't. I can't do this.

Focus. Get safe, then process.

"Lenny," a yell comes from down the alley and my head turns so quickly my hair flies.

"Roark, here," I scream.

I see the guys starting to pass the alley I'm in, and I don't blame them because a dumpster is next to me. My body is obstructed from view, outside of where I managed to crawl out of the space next to it.

I scream, "Wait, I'm here," to get their attention before gagging and coughing as I taste bile. My body is all fucked up.

Roark quickly comes into view, Turner next to him, both frantic. I feel bad I worried them, adding this to the myriad of feelings I need to process. This night has been a shit show of epic proportions.

"Where are you, I can't see you," Turner says, eyes bouncing everywhere but where I am.

One more step, you can do it. I crawl a bit more, the rough pavement and gravel digging into my skin. I pant as I push myself to go further so they'll see me. I can feel the ground tearing at my skin, my limbs starting to cooperate as the heaviness starts to lift.

Roark's eyes fall on me first, his jaw dropping open. I must look a sight. Definitely not the perfect lavender-haired beauty he tells me I am. For some reason, this makes the tears fall faster, making it harder to see.

"Bloody hell, beautiful, if you aren't a sight for sore eyes," he says softly, rushing towards me. The words are spoken like you would a prayer, the Irish brogue that rarely graces his words unless he's drunk or around other Irish men, thick.

My growly protector was scared shitless for me.

"I'm so sorry," I cry in despair and remorse for things I don't remember.

Roark shakes his head as he picks me up into arms.

"No, baby, we've died a thousand deaths looking for you. Don't apologize for things that aren't your doing. I love you so much," he whispers, burying his head in my hair.

Turner gives me a small smile as he comes closer to us, cupping my face. "Ror thinks you were drugged tonight. Something was in your water bottle," he says gently.

I blink hard. "Really? But one of the roadies gave it to me. I didn't think anything of it, which I guess was stupid," I croak, then cough hard, hiding my face in Ror's shoulder. "I need water," I explain.

Turner nods, starting to turn. "I'd prefer you wait to drink on the bus, Lavender. I really need you safe, and I only look like I'm keeping it together at the moment. The things we had to do while we looked for you are going to haunt me for a bit," he says.

I feel a pang in my chest, wondering what he means.

"Now don't go making her feel bad," I hear as much as I feel the grumble in Roark's chest and give a small smile.

This man will keep me safe, even from something as small as a hurt feeling. My feelings aren't hurt, but I do feel awful that they worried about me.

"I should have checked the cap before I drank the water," I started and Turner blows out a breath violently. I flinch because he reminds me of a dragon about to lose his shit.

Turner notices and mutters, "I'm being a fuckwit right

now." This is one of Roark's favorite insults and my lip twitches in amusement. "Lavender, honey, I'm not mad at you, I'm fucked over the situation. Let's start walking and I'll call Atlas and Mav. They've been losing it looking for you too."

He connects the call and my head drops to Ror's shoulder.

"I don't know what the fuck they gave you, honey, but I need you to stay awake for me, yeah," Roark growls as his strides eat the pavement.

"Yes sir," I murmur as I yawn hugely. "I don't know what happened tonight, but is it wrong to say I'm glad I was drugged?" Roar snorts in disbelief and I shake my head carefully. "No, obviously not like that, but I really thought I was becoming my mom. She'd lose time, do all kinds of things she normally wouldn't, and then not remember them. I sometimes wondered if she was lying, until this happened. What if I'm losing myself?" I whisper.

Roark is my confessional right now, and I'm scared for the others to hear. Turner is ahead of us, walking towards the guys. I turn my face into Ror's chest, breathing him in.

"Ugh, I probably smell super gross right now. You can put me down and I'll walk-"

"Baby, love of my life, I respectfully decline your offer," he grunts. I can't help but giggle at the formal tone. "I don't think I'll be letting your cute arse walk anywhere alone for a long while. Enjoy riding in the chariot of my arms or on my back, 'cause that's what'll be happening, love."

My face falls into a frown. I feel awful that they worried so much about me. I was somehow in a fucking alley where anything could have happened to me. My thoughts are still jumbled, and I have so many questions. I shudder as what ifs flood my mind, visions of rapists and serial killers teasing my thoughts. Breath hitching, chest tight, I tremble in Roark's arms, unable to think about grounding myself.

"Hey, woah, Lenny," Roark soothes. He puts me on my feet gently, turning me to face him with his hands on my arms.

I whimper, twisting to get away as my bruises scream at me. I'm vaguely aware we're on a sidewalk and I look a spectacle. My stomach takes this moment to also remind me it's upset, most likely due to whatever drugs I was given.

Roark releases me like I'm on fire, scrutinizing me.

"What hurts," he asks softly.

Somehow my growly teddy breaks through when nothing else does. Shit, I didn't see them after my interview, and I never told them about Derek hurting me. I wrap my arms around myself, wincing.

"I have some shit to talk to you about," I rasp, coughing hard and shuddering in pain.

"Alright, but let's table it until we can get water, and Turner's closer to his bat. I feel there may be some retribution needed from the way you flinched when I went to squeeze you. Up you go, my beautiful Valkyrie," he says gently, carefully scooping me up again into his arms.

He kisses my forehead, carefully walking so I'm not jostled. Roark loves so hard, even though it takes a while to get through the gruff exterior. *I'm so glad he found me.*

"Baby, I'll find you anywhere, even if it takes me a little longer like tonight," he growls.

I jerk in surprise, then whimper when every bruise flairs.

"I didn't realize I said that out loud," I murmur.

"Remember, I want all your words, sweet girl. I don't want you to hurt yourself, and your throat is fucked and dry right now. Anything that accidentally slips out while you're thinking, or want to tell me, is the right thing, alright?"

I blink furiously. He's just so good.

"I love you," I whisper.

"And you know you're my everything. You and Turner are

my sun, moon, and everything in between. I love you on your good days and your bad," he murmurs.

The rumble of his chest comforts me and I relax as tears stream down my face.

"You found her," Atlas calls out, running from god knows where. They really were canvassing the area for me.

Mav is close behind, features pinched. "Tiny Valkyrie, where were you? Roark says you may have had your drink spiked, the fuckers," he rages.

A small smile pulls at my lips. *I'm not alone anymore.*

Mav frowns. "Lennon, you're never alone anymore. You have all of us. We would do anything for you," he says.

Oops, I did it again.

"I'm really not feeling all that great," I whisper to prevent a coughing fit. I don't know how much longer I'll be able to hold it together as I swallow hard. It's getting harder and harder to be able to breathe through the need to puke.

Mav and Atlas nod sagely. "Got you. Unfortunately, we've all been drugged at least once, and how you're feeling is normal," Atlas says. "Does your head feel a little foggy right now?"

I nod, head lolling to the side. "I feel really shitty," I tell them. All of a sudden, I lose my battle as my stomach rebels and I don't have time to do anything but turn my head as it empties. "I'm sorry," I gasp as I heave, shuddering.

Roark just turns me to face the ground, and Altas runs forward to pull my hair out of my face. "Ugh, Lennon, I'm trying here, but you're gonna have to wash your hair," he groans.

I whimper as I puke again, focusing on a hand that's rubbing my back. I don't know who it is, or when it started, but it grounds me as my body revolts. I cry pathetically as my body tries to curl in from the pain. Each one of the guys murmurs sympathetically, none of them disturbed by how I undoubtedly resemble Regan from the *Exorcist*.

Finally over, my lungs saw in exertion. "That fucking sucked," I say through my tears.

"There she is," Mav says with a sigh.

"I feel so gross," I moan, feeling pitiful.

Roark carefully turns me in his arms. "Think you're okay for me to carry you back now," he asks, gingerly pulling me to his chest without a care of what I may have in my hair.

Atlas carefully lays the strands so it won't touch me, frowning at the lack of hair tie. *I feel the same way.* I turn to complain to Ror that I'm gross and can walk, even though I don't know if my ankle can handle it when all four guys growl. I freeze in shock.

"You're not walking, so don't open your mouth to ask, Lennon," Mav growls at me.

"Aye," the guys chorus and I roll my eyes. This is what I get for having such dominant men as lovers and besties.

"Yes, sirs," I mutter.

Turner chuckles, shaking his head and beginning to walk again. As if by design, the guys follow, protectively flanking me. Altas walks next to Roark, and Mav follows behind them. Feeling well protected, I close my eyes for a moment.

"Lenny, baby, open those beautiful gray eyes for me," Ror cajoles and I groan as I do as he asks. "We're home. Can you drink some water and then shower for me? Then, we'll talk a little if you're up to it," he says.

Nodding tiredly, I let him carry me to our kitchen area on the bus, and hand me water. I'm not surprised I passed out for the rest of the walk home. Turner follows, undoubtedly headed back to turn on the shower and grab a towel. The boys are both on a mission, and I support it since I feel like something scraped off a shoe.

There's a knock on the bus door, and Roark curses.

"Maybe it's just Mav and Atlas," I soothe as I drink deeply. Neither was at the bus doors when I woke up, so I figure it'll be them.

"Nah, they said they were going to grab tea bags from their bus for you and a bottle of whiskey. The whiskey is for us while we try to piece together what happened tonight. You also said you had some things to tell us...is it okay for them to be here?" he asks, nodding at my glass to encourage me to drink more.

I take another sip, content to play the good girl for him after tonight.

"Yeah, I don't mind because I know y'all are in my corner. My mind is all confused, and I really want to figure out what happened while I was high as a kite from the drugs. Please go check and see who it is, so at least one mystery is solved," I tell him as Turner reappears. I'm getting grumpier as the night wears on, and need to get clean.

"Up you go Lavender," he murmurs, jaw tight. He's a tightly wound ball of anger, and I breathe, reminding myself he's not mad at me.

I stand, and he gives me a gentle smile. I know he's really trying.

"I am going to be a creeper and stand by the door in case you get dizzy, okay? I fucking hate that this damn bathroom is so small," he growls and I huff in amusement.

"If you wanted to see me naked, all you had to do was ask," I tell him, lip twitching.

"I will never say no to seeing you naked," he says with a grin. "Now get moving. This is a test to see if you're even able to shower alone. I'll fucking find a way to fit if I have to."

I allow myself a full smile as I walk to the back of the bus. My ankle twinges, I somehow twisted it, but it's not awful. That's a problem for tomorrow's Lennon. I begin pulling my dress up my torso once I'm outside of the bathroom, knowing I may need help. I whimper as my bruised body complains and Turner gently stills my hands with a shake of his head. He pushes my straps down my arms, undressing me carefully.

His eyes take in my scraped knees, torn skin along my elbows and forearms, and frowns. When I'm naked he ushers me into the shower, closing the curtain behind him. I sigh as the water hits my body before I realize the makeup is going to wash off. Fuck it, I'm not covering for Derek. I spent too many years doing this when I was younger.

"You're muttering to yourself, Lavender. I couldn't help but notice you look like you're in pain, but I don't see bruises. You're a little banged up from crawling on the ground or maybe falling, so ya wanna spill? Maybe it'll help if you can't see my face when you explain," he says softly.

My teeth drag along the cracked skin of my bottom lip as a start to wash my hair. I'm filthy from the alley, but I have dried vomit in my hair. Ugh, there are no good choices on where to start. Turner is right though, it'll be easier if I can't see him, see how angry he is at the situation.

"You're right, but not because I did anything wrong," I start to say.

The curtain separating us is torn open and Turner crowds the space. His hair is getting wet, his body soaked, and I stare at him in shock.

"You are one of the most noble people I know. Please don't ever fucking speak about yourself like that again. Fuck my being at the door, you're missing spots of your hair. I'm helping you," he says, staring at me intently.

I know when not to argue with him, and this is one of those times. I don't even mention he's getting wet. He simply pulls his tank top off and throws it behind him where it squelches as it hits the ground. Next come his combat boots and socks, and he fully joins me in the shower in his tight jeans.

"Those are gonna suck to get off," I comment lightly.

"Fuck it, you're worth it. Roark can help me wrestle them off, we can play fuck the aggression out of Turner. If he gets them off, he can fuck my ass," he states tightly, unweaving the braids at the top of my head. I wasn't gonna bother, mostly because my arms are so sore.

I sigh as I enjoy his ministrations, moaning as he massages my hair, my back pulled tightly to his front.

"Don't get sidetracked, beautiful, spill the tea," he encourages.

"Ugh," I groan.

"What's this shit running down your arms..." Turner trails off as he rubs my arm gently.

The makeup I painstakingly applied is washing off now that I'm in the shower.

"That's the tea," I tell him with a sigh.

Turner growls, "We definitely have to talk, little girl."

He gently moves me into the water to rinse my hair. He's vibrating in anger as bruises in the form of fingers become more apparent as the makeup washes away in streaks. He never once turns the pent up promise of violence on me as he takes care of me. This is such a glaring difference between Turner and other men.

He hands me the body wash, and I wash my body, then wash my face next as he rewashes my hair. It's seriously so gross, and I feel miserable. My eyes prick with tears as I feel sorry for myself.

I know once I am clean and talk to Turner, I'll feel a little better. Lashes removed, face clear of makeup, with much cleaner hair, I breathe easier. He's practically on top of me due to the small space, but I feel safer with him. I'm not even irritated he pushed his way into this stupid tiny shower.

Flicking off the water, Turner opens the curtain and grabs a towel.

"I'm gonna dry you, then grab another towel for your hair, baby. I want you to go change while I get these jeans off, please. Grab a hoodie and undies, make sure you're comfy before we have this conversation, okay? Uh, make sure you grab one of my hoodies since the boys are coming over," he says with a snort.

I grin as I let him take the lead. It makes him feel better, and I really don't want to make any decisions right now. I feel adrift, confused as to who would want to hurt me, thoughts of how much worse this night could have been flooding my head.

I'm surprised out of my thoughts when Turner lifts me out of the shower.

"Out of your pretty little head, Lavender. I have no doubts as to how dark you may be going. Use it, don't get lost in there, baby," he insists.

"You're right," I agree, turning to get dressed.

Turner wraps his arm around my waist, pulling me to him.

"Hey, tell me to fuck off, fight with me, don't just take my macho bullshit," he grumbles. "I know I'm overbearing, I'm just-"

"Struggling," I finish for him.

"Yeah," he breathes out.

"I'm not taking it just to avoid my feelings. I'm feeling a little numb and confused...and hungry," I mumble the end as he chuckles.

"The last I can fix, honey, scoot and then tell me I'm a dick."

"I like your dick," I call over my shoulder as I slip out of the bathroom, warmed by his bark of surprised laughter.

The warm water helped to loosen my cramped limbs from

when I passed out in the alley. It's amazing how much a shower helps things. Throwing on Turner's sweatshirt that hits mid thigh and panties, I pass him in the aisle as he leans into our room to grab a pair of jeans. Going commando, he pulls them on and my mouth waters. There must be something wrong with me that I'm thinking about sucking his cock after this shit show of a night.

Turner palms my face, lifting it to look in my eyes. "I know this look, and you can have my cock whenever...we finish talking," he promises with a smirk.

"Cock-tease," I hiss, sticking out my tongue at him.

"You're not wearing a bra, are you," he asks, changing the subject as he buttons his jeans. His eyes are glued to my chest, which are free as a bird.

I turn away from him, firmly ignoring him, to rejoin Roark. I am amused Turner thinks I would be wearing one after they've been in boob jail all day.

"I know you know the answer to this, old man," I tell him.

"Old man?! Princess, I promise you're gonna end up spread out over my lap counting the number of spanks you've earned if you're not careful. Bruises be damned," he yells after me and I cackle.

I feel more myself every moment we're together. I don't like to feel weak, small, or scared. Tonight was a rollercoaster I'd gladly like to get off, but I am gathering my armor slowly. I am loved, cherished even. *Even warriors have bad days.*

Roark comes into view and another piece of my heart settles. "Ror, I'm hungry," I confess, knowing he won't deny me anything.

I stop suddenly, staring at him. His chest is heaving, his face red, and he wasn't like this before I went to get cleaned up

"Roark," I ask softly.

"What fucking bruises and do they have anything to do with this piece of shit?" he asks gruffly.

I am confused until I see Derek is laid out at his feet. Ror has his boot in his neck, seeming to enjoy the choking sounds coming from him.

Well shit, I didn't expect this.

9

ROARK

All I can see is red. I was pissed off at him before I went to find Lenny, but he came by the bus to ask about her. I didn't really want to let him in, but I thought maybe he genuinely felt bad since he lost her. Derek had flashes of remorse when I spoke to him in the parking lot, but finding out he's been putting his hands on her...I may commit murder tonight.

I didn't hear Lenny per se announce that Derek was responsible as she walked into the kitchen, but this dick's eyes went wide in guilt and fright and I lost it.

"Are you putting your hands on her, you motherfucker," I growl softly, holding on to the last vestiges of control I own. I push harder on his neck with my shit kickers, enjoying how red his face becomes from the inability to breathe.

"Roark, what's going on?" my beautiful Valkyrie asks softly. Her voice is worried, and I glance up. Her hair is wet, already starting to curl, and she's in one of Turner's sweatshirts.

I suddenly want her surrounded by my scent and hold an arm out to her. She rushes towards me, fitting perfectly at my side. I wrap my arm carefully around her, hating how breakable Lenny suddenly feels.

"You said you had bruises, and Derek the Dick had the nerve to look guilty. I need your words, baby girl. I need you to tell me what happened to you, as much as you can remember," I beg, my anger leaching out of me as tears fill my eyes.

"I'll tell you, Ror, but you're gonna kill him if you don't let him breathe. The parking lot doesn't have great burial spots, what with all the hard concrete," Lenny teases me.

"Fuck, you're right, and it would be annoying to carry him somewhere to get rid of the body," I say chuckling, showing her I'm coming back to her. The tension bleeds out of her as she relaxes completely into me.

I raise my boot, restraining myself from gracing him with a parting kick. Derek wheezes as he sits up, rubbing his throat. Fuckwit needs to man up, I doubt this will be the only time he'll cower under my boot.

"Start talking before Mav and Atlas get here, douchebag," I say sourly. My gaze flicks over to Turner and I roll my eyes. "No, no, if I can't kill him then you can't beat him with your bat, babe."

Turner's face is curled in a scowl, bat already lifted. He was barely holding it together earlier, now he's livid. We are both so protective of our girl, abuse is grounds for a beating and then begging for death. We may seem bloodthirsty, but Lenny deserves to feel safe.

We are both on edge with the knowledge we may have failed her.

"Derek, get off my bus, because I can't guarantee your safety right now," Lenny tells him, lips pressed together as she watches him sit up and wheeze.

"You're all fucking crazy, just like her," he says coughing.

Lenny bursts into motion, slapping him across the face.

"I am not my mother," she screams, kicking, hitting, and losing control. She's a tornado of violence and Derek the Dick gets up despite all this, finally grabbing her arms to pin them. He pulls her flush against him so Lenny still faces us as she sobs.

Derek is a huge trigger for her, I don't know how I didn't realize how much of one until right this moment. She's also already had a shit night as it is.

"Yes you are, and you need help," he spits out. "Dancing in traffic, lost in a city where anything could have happened, and uncontrollable rage are all things your mother would do."

He's fucking gas lighting her. These things happened, but not because she was manic. His understanding of what she did is so fucking skewed.

I can't bring myself to speak, shocked by Derek's actions. Part of me wants to set him straight, but the other is watching him bury himself in his hate. We have to get him off the tour.

"I'm not her," she keens and just like that, I'm done.

"Give her to me, and get out. I'll be talking to Prescott about canceling your contract and releasing you from the tour. You have no idea what you're talking about, and it's clear to me now you're not safe for Lenny to be around," I bark.

"Safe? She's a fucking menace and she kneed me in the balls earlier today-"

Lenny tries to get free, shoving her ass into him, but the angle to bruise his dick isn't right. She's not tall enough. Derek loosens his hold on her and Lenny elbows him hard. Free, she runs into my arms, gasping for breath.

"Why are you always putting your hands on things that don't belong to you," she pants. "Get off my bus, I have nothing to explain or say to you. The people who matter know what really happened tonight," she spits out.

Damn, she's pissed. And rightfully so. I bare my teeth at

Derek the Dick, biting my tongue against all the things I want to say.

"Wait, Lennon, I saw what happened. You can't convince me you're not just off your meds or something. With your family history, you can't tell me you didn't see this as a possibility-"

Lennon tenses, and I find myself ready to lose my shit again. "You're such a dick," she whispers. "I'm not on medication nor do I need to be."

"She isn't fucking bipolar," Turner roars. "I'm not responsible for the next thirty seconds if you don't fucking leave."

This night has been chaotic from the moment we walked off stage. There's so much information each of us are missing, we need to talk.

Too bad Derek is too much of a dick to speak to without wanting to fuck him up. He's not a bad looking man, but his attitude is enough to turn anyone off. I frown as I think this, it's rare for me to be attracted to men other than Turner, but his pouty red lips would look amazing wrapped around my cock. He huffs as he watches us, fierce dark eyes taking everything in. Turner sidles up next to Lenny and I, tapping his bat against the wall.

"Tick tock, asshole. Make a decision. Do I get to fuck you up with Sally here," he says, raising his bat. I fucking love that he named his bat Sally. I know there's a story there too, and he keeps promising to tell me. "Or are ya gonna run away like a little bitch. Personally, I like option A, but Lennon doesn't like it when I get blood in the bus," he grins with an evil chuckle and I smirk.

He and I look psychotic as we stare at Derek, waiting to see what he'll decide.

Derek's eyes bounce between the three of us before his shoulders sag in defeat.

"Whatever, clearly you all deserve each other. Fucking psychos," he says under his breath as he clambers off the bus.

Lenny visibly wilts in my arms. "Baby, I know you're tired, but I need you to fill in the blanks, okay," I beg.

I sweep her into my arms, walking to the comfiest couch we have on the bus, with fluffy blankets and pillows. It's Lenny's couch, and our effort to make sure she has a space all her own when she needs it. It can be rough living with two growly bastards.

"K, but I need coffee, please. I'll save the tea for when the guys get here. And I really am hungry," she whines as her stomach growls.

I don't even mind the whine because she's with me, no longer lost.

"I'll feed and caffeinate you for the rest of my life if you'd let me, baby" I tell her, turning to do just that as she gasps.

"Did you just propose to our girl, Ror, and if so, do I get one," Turner teases as he lazily stretches out next to her.

Oh shit, I kind of did, huh?

"Ummm yeah, I guess I did," I say as I flick on the coffee maker and open my phone up to order food on the delivery service app. "Okay, it may not have been the smoothest delivery," I admit, peeking up at them from underneath my lashes. "I meant it though. I lost my mind tonight, not knowing where you were or if you were hurt. You two are my everything, and I don't know if I tell you that enough."

"I love the way you love me," Lenny says with a smile. "But if that's a proposal, I need-"

"A ring," I interrupt her with a smirk as I openly stare at her now.

"Fuck no," she laughs. "I'll tattoo you on me somewhere instead, but I don't need a ring. I need to know if you meant it as a proposal so I can say yes," Lenny says with a grin, her cheeks turning pink.

I chuckle, striding towards her. *I really want her to wear my ring, though. Is that wrong?* I take her face in my hands, kissing her soundly. "I meant it. I want to marry both of you, however we can make that happen. I'm tired of people making comments about our relationship, I want to be able to introduce you as my wife or Turner as my husband. However we need to do this, I'm fucking in." I lean over and kiss Turner, loving how he melts into me. "Enough stalling, baby girl. I'm ordering Thai now, with all our favorites. Start spilling the tea. I'm dying to know everything that happened while you weren't with us."

Lenny sighs, curling up into her corner as my fingers fly over my phone screen, placing an order for food to feed my girl. Coffee finishes brewing, and I move over to it so I have something to do.

"So I had my interview with Orla from *You* magazine, and there was the most adorable photographer there," she says.

I snort as I put creamer and sugar in her coffee. The way she said this was like when you talk about a cute dog, not a person.

"Stop, Ror," she says with a giggle, undoubtedly knowing where my mind went. "He was just really excited and happy to meet me. I was super hyped up on sugar, so I had a blast, not paying attention to how I said things because I was having fun. Derek was taking behind the scenes photos, and commented on my flirting. Can you really flirt with a gay man though, when both parties aren't interested? Anyway, before this even happened, he was a dick to me. When I turned away to ignore him, he grabbed my arm, and you know I bruise easily-"

Turner and I growl and she sighs as if to say *"really"*. Neither of us can help it though.

"Show me please," I ask, gritting my teeth. As angry as I am, I will never take it out on her.

Lenny pushes up her sleeves, but there are a lot of bruises in the form of fingerprints on her arms.

"Pretty sure there's more to this story, and my patience is thin," Turner says, rolling his eyes .

Lenny bites her lip, standing to pull the sweatshirt over her body. All the windows are tinted so people can't see in as we are usually in some form of undress. I help her out of the sweater, dragging my fingers over her skin, enjoying how it pebbles in goosebumps. I have to focus, or I'll lose myself in the miracle of Lenny.

"I'm sure there's a reason you're stripping, but fuck if you aren't the most beautiful woman I've ever seen," I say reverently.

Lenny reappears as the clothing clears the top of her head and grins. She knows what this tone means. I'm close to insisting she sit on my face while Turner stuffs her pretty little mouth, but now is not the time. I shake my head, telling my cock to shut the fuck up.

She points out instead the bruises on her shoulders, back, and the fingerprints on her wrists. "I'm fucking sore, but I'm fine otherwise. He attacked me when I was walking away after the interviews. I was shoved into a wall, and then dragged into a fucking closet. He pushed me around with his hand around my neck and pinned me down. He likes to throw his weight around, so I couldn't move away since he had me trapped against the wall by my throat and wrists. Derek has anger issues, he hates me, and I was always the perfect person to use as a punching bag. Often though, he'd use the mean girls on the cheerleading squad to jump me, so he wasn't publicly hurting me. He had an image to maintain apparently," she explains with a shrug.

I drop to my knees, kissing her stomach. She flinches in pain when my fingers brush against her side and I look up in panic.

"I don't know why but my sides hurt. I must have run into something when I was drugged. I don't remember much except snippets. I do remember talking to Derek for a moment in the parking lot, loud noises, and lights all around me. I also remember him telling me what he always says: 'Crazy is catching'. I don't know if he really thinks I'm bipolar, or if he enjoys dredging up my fears," she spits out.

I frown hard, gathering Turner's hoody and covering her body. "How did you feel when you were talking to Derek in the closet? How did you get away? We've taught you a lot, but he's a big guy."

Huffing a breath, she resumes sitting in her cloud of blankets and pillows. Shaking my head, I lift her, changing positions so she's sitting on my lap now. Dragging my nose up her throat, I kiss her ear. "I'm going to be really handsy from now on, and I'm not sorry."

Turner rolls his eyes, standing to grab her coffee. I forgot about it in search of Lenny cuddles.

"Oops," I chuckle against her neck. She shivers, sighing happily as she curls around me.

Taking her coffee mug from Turner she sips carefully. "Turner, will you grab her water too, so she'll alternate between the two please? I'm worried about her throat," I explain.

He nods, busying himself while keeping a careful eye on Lenny.

"This is weird to say," she says with a small sigh. "There's something about Derek calling to me, but there's so much trauma he caused, I want to tell my stupid body to shut up. There was a moment where I was against the wall, his hard cock up against me, and I was *interested.* And then he opened up his fucking mouth and ruined it all. I know I shouldn't-"

"Shouldn't what? Look? Lavender, this is why we talk about things. I won't lie, the man is fucking hot. I watched him while he played professional ball a bit, and his ass is biteable. I don't like how he treats you though," Turner says honestly with a shrug.

"Same," I tell her. "I can think of so many ways to punish his bratty mouth, but not if he's gonna be a dick to you. You're also so fucking hot when you wear a strap-on," I whisper in her mouth, my voice vibrating through her.

She whimpers, pressing her thighs together. "You're supposed to tell me this is a bad idea, guys. I felt bad, thinking I--"

"It's not even close to cheating because nothing happened. Sorry, I didn't mean to interrupt," Turner apologizes, tossing his hair out of his face. It's getting just long enough he can start pulling it back but he refuses. "I hate that you are tying yourself up in knots over this."

"Yeah? He's always wanted me, I think? My past just is overshadowed by so much darkness I can't really remember the good. It started with pushing my books out of my arms in seventh grade when I was eleven, then escalated to spreading rumors I was a whore and getting jumped on the way home from school. We all know I wasn't a whore," Lennon says, rolling her eyes.

"I know, I remember how you felt the first time we had sex, holding you while claiming your virginity," Turner reminisces with a soft smile as he hands her a glass of water.

She takes a sip, moaning at how it feels. Knowing him, he made sure it was nice and cold.

"Anyway, I promise to rehash the past another time, now tell me what happened while I was out of it," she insists.

"Oye, open up," Atlas and Mav yell from outside and Lenny giggles.

She was saved by the boys. We will be talking about this later though, because while I initially wanted Derek gone, I may want to make him pay for his transgressions more.

Lennon

I sip my coffee as I watch Atlas and Mav climb inside our bus. Today has been a long, weird day. My thoughts are going a mile a minute, and I never thought Ror and Turner would react the way they did when I told them about Derek's actions in the closet and how I felt about it.

I have a lot to process, but first I need to get through what the guys have to tell me. I may join them in the whiskey.

"I heard someone ordered Thai," Atlas says, holding up the bag.

I grin, he must have just caught the delivery guy before they arrived.

"Yay! I'm so hungry," I groan.

Atlas snorts, shaking his head. "Whoever ordered, definitely went all in. There's so much food here."

"Good, so you can join us then," I tease back. "Grab some plates, I may threaten to eat someone if I'm not fed soon though."

"Well ya know, Lenny, I'm not against this idea, love," Roark says, chuckling darkly in my ear. I shiver, glaring over my shoulder for making me want to do exactly that.

"Later, Ror. I want to know what happened and then you can have your way with me, you horn ball."

"Aye, sweet girl, I'm gonna need exactly that. We don't have an early morning and actually have a break tomorrow, I think," he murmurs, trying to recall the schedule.

"Yeah, we are driving most of tomorrow, but don't have to do fuck all until the next day. We are headed to Cali, tiny Valkyrie," Mav says with a lazy grin, pouring himself a drink.

"Ugh, I really want a fucking drink, but I don't know if I'm allowed to," I whine.

"I'm going to veto that idea. We don't know what you were drugged with, Lavender," Turner says with a frown.

"Ugh, fine. Someone start talking then please. Not knowing is starting to fuck with me," I beg.

"Let me preface this by apologizing to you, Lenny," Roark starts to say. I turn so quickly my hair whips with me and hits him in the face. He winces, removing a piece that sticks to his lips.

"Ick, sorry I didn't mean for that to happen. What the fuck though? How is anything that happened tonight your fault?"

"I should have known the stupid cap was tampered with when I saw you open it. Turner is militant about us paying attention to our drinks, and I'm so fucking mad we didn't protect you enough," he says with a huff.

"Baby, stop. Did you put something in my drink that made me apparently dance in traffic?" I ask. He shakes his head vehemently, eyes wide. "I didn't think so, so stop blaming yourself for things that were out of your control, you sexy oaf. It wasn't your fault," I reassure him, gently cupping his face.

I kiss him, reminding him I'm here, I'm safe again. Roark relaxes into me, kissing me back with a small sigh.

"Now that we've gotten that out of the way, tell me about what I can't remember," I tell him, feeling odd having this space of time I can't account for.

"Okay, but please start eating while I explain some of this," Roar countered.

"Done," I tell him, moving to sit next to him and accepting the plate Atlas hands me.

Soon everyone has food and drinks, and we're all eating as Roark explains.

"I ran into Derek the Dick in the parking lot, and he saw I was looking for you. He said he found you acting oddly and dancing in traffic basically. Then, he told me he'd lost you because he ran his mouth to you. I was looking for you because you'd disappeared during the meet and greet and that's not normal for you. I just had a really bad feeling," Roark says with a sigh.

"Roark punched the fucker," Atlas snorts in amusement. "Derek totally deserved it too. Who taunts someone who is obviously in need of help? I don't think he went into detail though about what he said-"

"Crazy is catching-" I blurt out. This is one of the only things I remember clearly. "I don't remember very much about tonight, but this keeps replaying in my head."

"Motherfucker," Atlas mutters. "He really is a dick."

"Yep. So I guess I ran at that point?"

"Apparently," Turner murmurs, tugging on his hair. I can tell he still has a lot of pent up anger, so I may need to tease him into fucking it out of him.

"So Roark called Turner, and we met him out by the North entrance. We had no idea where to look for you, outside that you turned right at the exit. So we just walked around, trying to find you, checking all the alleys," Mav says, a weird look appearing in his eyes.

"I'm so sorry you had to go looking for me like that. I really don't know why I thought running away was the best option," I sigh, leaning into Roark for comfort.

Ror shakes his head sadly. "Baby, we checked all the dumpsters, we didn't know what to think. I'm never letting you leave my sight again, I swear it," he says as his voice cracks.

"I'm totally fine, outside of a few bumps," I reassure them.

"I don't know how I ended up in that alley, I really don't. I'm glad we aren't performing tomorrow because my ankle hurts a little," I confess. "This all could have been worse, but it wasn't. I'm safe, because you all found me."

The guys nod, thoughts of how much worse it could have been showing in their faces.

"I really wish I could punch him again," Roark laments. He sounds so wistful that it pulls a giggle from me.

"I kind of want to write now," I say, leaning up to kiss Roark's neck. I'm so blessed to have these men as my lovers and friends. I also want to distract them from killing Derek, even if the ass deserves it. "Tonight was really fucked up. I thought I was losing my sanity, guys. My mom would leave the house for days, and I'd never know where she'd go. She'd take the car and I'd have to walk to school, figure out how to pool together money for food, and worry about her. Then she'd be home without an explanation as to where she went or why."

I bite my lip as the memories wash over me. "Mom would spend the next few days depressed and angry, and I would still go to school hungry and confused. Why did she have to leave? I could have helped her, but she'd escape into her mania, leaving me behind."

I stare at the wall, lost to my memories when Roark pulls me onto his lap again. Turner takes my finished plate, and I cuddle into Ror's arms.

"I'm sorry Lennon, that's really fucked up. You were a kid, there's no way you'd be able to help her in that state," Turner says sympathetically as he puts things away.

"I know," I lament, pushing my hair out of my face, "but it was her and me against the world. The town I lived in didn't really like people who were considered different from them. My dad left us when I was seven, so the people I went to school with and their parents were constantly gossiping about us," I explain. It doesn't make it right, it's just the way things were for us.

"You knew Derek in school, right," Mav asks, eyebrows furrowed in thought.

"Yep. He was my neighbor essentially. I lived five miles outside of town, and he lived on the other side of the pasture by my house. It wasn't close by any means, not the way you see houses in neighborhoods, but I swear his family watched my house. Somehow, Derek was always around to ridicule me, and he'd drive past me laughing when I walked to school." I think back at how his face would sneer at me as he kicked up dust from his truck as he drove past.

"Can Turner help me beat him," Roark mumbles into my hair. "Five fucking miles to school, on very little food, and he laughed at you. I definitely want to introduce him to my fists again."

"You can't punch him for things that happened so long ago," I tell him, lifting my head to smile at him wistfully. "He was a staple in the *Terrorize Lennon* campaign. It started with him when he shoved my books out of my hands when I was eleven, and it only got worse. I think there was a betting pool at one point to see who could fuck me once I hit high school..."

I drift off as I replay the past. I don't know for sure, but I don't think the pool ever stated if the sex had to be consensual or not. It's super fucked up that this had to be stated, but I remember having to fight guys off on the walk home from school, and never feeling safe once I got there. I was alone way too often, and the locks never felt sturdy enough.

"Lennon?"

"Huh," I mumble, forcing myself to pay attention, searching for the person who said my name. "Sorry Atlas," I say with a sigh. "My childhood was kind of shit, and I couldn't wait to leave. As soon as I was free to get the fuck out, I did."

"I don't blame you at all for that. I don't think I would have been able to stick it out as long as you did. Do you know where your mom is now?" he asks, face flushing as he realizes how much of a loaded question that may be.

It's not though. Her death freed me from the pain of living with her choices, many I still don't know about. Her mistakes were always laid at my feet, and I get the feeling they still are based on how Derek treats me.

"Dead," I answer him. "She packed the car up when I was at school one day and bailed. I had three months left of high school, and Mom couldn't be bothered to stay. I found a note that said, "fly high, you're better than me" and that was it. I assume she must have been higher than a kite to have written that. The last few months before she left she was more erratic, and there were rumors my mom was on drugs. I couldn't tell if she was or not, she always seemed the same to me."

My voice gets deeper as I unpack some of my past, throat starting to close with unshed tears. There are a lot of reasons I don't speak about her. "Two months after I graduated high school, I got a letter telling me my mom died in a car accident. The woman writing to me was someone she had linked up with, traveling across the country. There was a photo of the accident enclosed, and I don't know, I just felt lighter. I hitch-hiked out of town the next morning."

"Holy shit," Turner says, turning towards me. "All these years, and you never told us. I knew it couldn't have been all roses, you were so skittish when you met us all."

I snort, rolling my eyes. "You all scared the shit out of me. I was so tiny when I joined the band. I was bartending under-aged at a shit bar, lived in a tiny apartment with two other people, and for some godforsaken reason, attended an open mic night. I had no idea talent scouts attended those things or what that meant. All I knew was the label promised I wouldn't have to struggle as hard to get by if I met with you. They gave me a six-hundred dollar advance just to meet with you." I shake my head as I remember. I'm sure Ror and Turner have pieced some of this together, but I have never told any of them very much about my past. I wanted to live for the present.

Atlas whistles. "They really gave you six-hundred dollars to come meet us," he asks, surprised. He's one of the original band members, and the man who asked me to meet them told me I was the key to making their dreams come true. I would have done it just for that reason.

"I haven't had the best experience with men," I say with a shrug. "What was his name...Castle? I don't think he's scouting for the label anymore-"

"Yeah, baby, I think he passed away a year ago," Turner says gently.

"Shame," I sigh. "I know he was in his fifties when I met him, but he was really nice to me," I muse. "Anyway, I panicked when Mr. Castle told me he wanted me to meet four really talented men who needed a lead singer. I was expecting big, scary, intimidating assholes. Imagine my surprise when that's the last thing I found."

I smile fondly, resting my head on Roark as I look out at them. "Y'all were excited to meet me, protective and sweet. Then when Mav joined a few years later, we felt complete. Y'all are my family."

"We love you too, tiny Valkyrie. It feels all the more fitting now," Mav says, toasting me with his drink. The boys follow, saying, "Aye," and I smile as I feel Roark's voice rumble against me.

Even if I'm not safe anywhere else, I know I am with them.

10

DEREK

I'*m a shithead.* I lay in my bunk, staring at the ceiling as the bus gently sways. I honestly would have deserved to personally meet the business end of Sally to be honest. At least I think that's what Turner called his bat, he's a bit unhinged at times.

I'm starting to second guess everything I thought was true of Lennon O'Reilly. It would be so perfect to be able to tie everything up in a bow and call her crazy like Carrie. Turner and Roark seemed really adamant about this not being the reason she was dancing in traffic.

She twirled and sang in traffic, not giving a flying fuck if she was hit or not...

It's just something her mother would do. Carrie O'Reilly was stunning, with silver-blonde hair and blue eyes. Lennon had the same color hair growing up, and when she was in high school, it hurt to look at her. Carrie was wild, free spirited, and not at all well.

I have a lot of trauma surrounding Carrie, considering I found my dad fucking her when I was fourteen, but it's not just that. It's the fact that two years later, I also lost my virginity to her. Turning, I shove my head into my pillow, wanting to scream in frustration as I think about that day, but the small bunks on this bus are close together. I don't really want anyone to hear my turmoil.

I was always really tall growing up. My dad was obsessed with excellence in both school and extracurriculars, so I started playing football at the age of eight. Funny enough, I was really good at academics as well as football, but it only pushed my father to demand more from me.

He was a powerful man in our small town, and the only thing he asked me to do was to not tarnish our family's name. This is something I later scoffed at when I found him fucking around on my mother. To this day, I don't think he knows I saw him. He would have beaten me black and blue, and then been back balls deep in Mrs. O'Reilly. No one really knew the darker side of my dad.

Mrs. O'Reilly wouldn't have said shit either way, not with secrets of her own to keep. Secrets she kept so well, some she didn't even remember.

The pressure my father put me under made for an angry teenager. I had fits of rage, but I managed to channel it into the game. My laser focus won us a lot of games, and it kept my own darkness from spilling over too often. People respected me at school, and those who didn't, found out painfully why they should.

I have always bullied my way into getting what I wanted. However, in school it was overlooked because I was a football god and popular. No wasn't a word I often had to hear, not when girls pulled me into dark corners at school to suck my dick. They threw themselves at me at parties, and someone was always on my arm. I barely had to try. So while I had some experience with girls, I hadn't lost my virginity yet.

That honor went to Carrie O'Reilly. It felt weird to be fucking her and calling her Mrs. O'Reilly, I don't have a mommy kink, but she was always larger than life. This woman was beautiful, bold, and one second on a summer night, it just happened.

I WAS LEANING *against the big cypress in my yard one night, feeling pretty pissed at the world. My dad was raging inside, and I had a black eye as a gift, courtesy of it. I wasn't planning to go back inside anytime soon, honestly I'm surprised by my dad tonight. He usually avoids my face, so now I'll have to pick a fight with someone to cover it up.*

I just started school again, so I can't use football as an excuse for a fresh black eye either. Fucking bullshit. I kick the ground, wondering if I should go for a walk. It's still warm out, not a hint of the cold that will be sneaking across Kentucky in a few months. I'm going to miss summer.

I'm deep in my thoughts, and almost miss an apparition dressed all in white walking by me. I startle, gasping at how it looks like she's floating. It's dark out, the last of the sunlight has faded from the sky, but my mom hung mason jar lights all throughout the tree I'm under. It gives this ethereal look to the woman walking past me in a white dress with blonde hair so light, it appears silver.

"Who? Wait is that you, Mrs. O'Reilly? It's really late. What are you doing here?" I ask, the last question coming out accusingly.

I haven't forgotten finding her with my dad, the images still ingrained in my brain. Sometimes, my fucked up teenage mind imagines I was the one between her creamy thighs: licking her pussy, fucking her tight hole. I smirk as I watch her creeping over for seconds or thirds. Just because I haven't caught them again, doesn't mean it hasn't happened.

Mom isn't here today, and she's been going out of town more and more often. At first I didn't realize it because it sounded legit: conferences out of town, visiting her sister, spa day with her friends a few towns over. But it's happening too frequently now to be a coincidence. Mom doesn't have to work, but went back when I started middle school, claiming she needed something to do. She never missed a game, she just made sure she didn't go home afterwards. She claimed she didn't want to miss anything important to me, but now it's like she's allergic to being home. Things are starting to add up and I'm not liking the math on this.

Mrs O'Reilly smiles and I swear the world lights up with it as she walks towards me. "Derek, Mrs. O'Reilly reminds me of my ex mother-in-law. Do I look like I'm sixty, balding, with the personality of a rock?" she asks, winking.

I blink. I didn't expect her to say that. It screws with my preconceptions of the crazy lady that fucks my dad and jumps in my lake naked because it's too damn hot in the summer. I didn't expect her to also be...charming? Huh.

"What do you suggest I call you?" I ask, deciding to bite.

She glides her hand up my chest and my eyes widen. My cock is painfully aware this dress is mostly see-through. Did she realize this when she put it on? Doesn't she own a mirror?!

She gently tweaks my nipple through my shirt and I grunt. "Hmm, you can call me Carrie when it's just us, how does that sound," she murmurs. "You play football, don't you? My daughter doesn't talk very much about school, honestly, as long as she's passing I don't care. You've just gotten so much bigger since the last time I saw you..." She trails off, blushing as she realizes when the last time she saw me was.

"So you're embarrassed you got caught," I stare, expecting this is the reason for the blush.

"Why would I be embarrassed? Your father and I are consenting adults," she says with a shrug. "You weren't really supposed to be home, so honestly it was a turn on to find you there watching. In my dreams, I imagine..." she drifts off as she leans against me, rising on to her toes so her tits push against my chest.

"What?" I ask, not recognizing my voice. It's deeper than normal, gruffer, and all I want to do is grind my cock on her softness to help with the hard-on she's causing. I swear, all the blood in my body has traveled to my dick, and I can barely think straight.

"I imagine you decided to join us, shoving your cock in my mouth and making my dirty mouth take every inch," she whispers into my ear.

I inhale sharply, asking myself if Mrs- Carrie *is really speaking to me like this. All I can smell is magnolia, which is odd because I don't have any growing in my yard. I can't help myself anymore and wrap my large hands around her tiny waist, running my nose up her neck. She's where the magnolia scent is coming from.*

"You smell incredible," I growl into her ear.

She whimpers, trailing her hands up behind my neck to play with my hair.

"Do you want to play with me, Derek? I was headed to visit your father, but I don't think that's a good idea," she says with a frown, her finger gently touching my bruised eye. "I don't like it when he hurts you, so just say the word, and I'm yours for the night instead."

"Mine?" My hands shift down to her tight ass, and I barely register picking her up.

Her small gasp makes my cock twitch, and she wraps her

legs tightly around my waist. I turn her so this time she's pressed against the tree, finally giving in and grinding against her.

"How mine *are you planning to be?" I murmur. I'm inexperienced, but I know how to play with a woman's emotions, make them do what I want. My father taught me how to be manipulative, and I've honed my skills well.*

I think having this gorgeous woman panting after me is something I very much need. Especially with her would be fuck buddy currently inside, destroying his office. He can continue to be a angry bastard, while I fuck his whore.

Deciding I need to see her tits since they're nearly bursting out of this ridiculous dress, I rip the bodice down the middle. Carrie arches her back, moaning, and I decide to follow her lead. I palm her breasts, rolling her pink nipples, wondering what kind of noises I can get from her.

She doesn't disappoint. "Yes, more, suck and bite them," she directs breathily.

I lick around where she needs me to, teasing her. I enjoy every mewl and moan. I decide that even though this woman is taking my virginity, I'm in charge of how this little homewrecker will get off tonight. My anger and libido lead me to suck her buds, and I slowly push up her dress until my hands are on her bare ass.

She's completely naked under this dress.

"Don't be so surprised, Derek. I came over to get fucked, and I have no doubt you can deliver. Girls must fall over themselves at that school to ride your dick. I may as well enjoy coming all over your cock too," she pants with a smile.

Fuck me, she doesn't have a clue. *Deciding she'll never know what a big deal this is, I pull all my knowledge from Pornhub to mind. I'm sixteen years old, so I spend a lot of time getting my cock sucked or jerking off. I also wanted to not suck when I started having sex. I'm kind of glad I put the effort into the self-taught education now as I massage Carrie's thigh, moving towards her pussy.*

"Don't tease," she whispers, thrusting her pelvis forward for friction.

I slap her ass and she squeals. Knowing no one will hear her, I let her. She can be as loud as she wants, no one is coming out to check.

"You said you were mine, remember," I say slyly. "Be a good girl and let me learn how to make you scream."

Carrie slowly licks her lips, panting faster. She's turned on, chest heaving, and I know her pussy will be dripping when I finally make my way to it. This is happening on my terms though, regardless of how it started.

"What happens if I'm a bad girl," she asks.

"I'll throw you to the ground, fuck you in the dirt, and refuse to let you come. How are you gonna play it, beautiful?"

"Fuck, both sound like fun," she laughs wildly. "Let's try it the first *time this way, and we'll see if you'll get a second ride."*

Can she know this is my first time? Am I that obvious? Needing to distract us both, I glide my hand to her weeping pussy. Sliding through her folds, I push a thick finger inside her and she arches her back like a satisfied cat. I kiss up her neck, listening to every hitch in her breath.

Beginning to finger fuck her, I also concentrate on her nub of nerve endings, her hips riding my fingers as I add another.

"Fuck, yes, just like that, baby. Curl those finger just-"

She whines as I take note of everything she says, and I quickly realize Carrie's giving me the road map to her body as she loses herself in my arms.

Any man who can't follow this map is a dick, or simply doesn't care. This woman is a gorgeous fuck toy, of course that's what she signed up for, but it doesn't mean she won't be exhausted by the time we're done.

Carrie's eyes roll as she gushes on my fingers. I don't kiss on the lips, but I want to taste her somewhere else. Her daughter has never wanted me, I don't blame her for some of the torture I've put her through, but maybe in some fucked up way, this will curb the desire.

I drop her legs from my waist, dropping to my knees. Ripping open the rest of her dress easily, I expose her to the night air.

"I hope you weren't attached to this thing," I murmur. "You'll be walking home butt naked like the pretty little whore you are."

She grins, mounting my face, legs dangling from my shoulders. This is a woman who has no problems taking what she wants.

"I don't think that's the insult you think it is for me. Now eat my pussy like a good boy and make me scream."

Who am I to say no?

I have never eaten pussy before. I always thought being on your knees was a position of weakness, but as I suck her clit hard, I decide differently as I hear her noises. Carrie gives zero fucks about being quiet, knowing no one will hear us anyway.

I finger fuck her as I suck, nip, and pinch. Making sure to coat one of my fingers I push slowly against her tight ass.

"Oh my god, yes, fuck that's good," she gasps as she takes the next finger eagerly. Thank fuck for my large hands, easily able to hold her as she rides my face.

I'm amazed by this woman who lets me do whatever I want to her. She thrusts her pelvis into me, demanding more, but I make her scream. The power lays in my licking, sucking, eating her like she's my last fucking meal. She smells incredible, she tastes like cherries, and I want to wear her on my face. I make her cream several times before standing.

I pick her up, setting her on her feet before turning her so she's facing the tree. Grinning, I stand, grabbing her hips so she bends over at the perfect angle. I rip the rest of Carrie's excuse of a dress off, dropping it to the ground.

"If you're a very good girl, I'll give you my shirt to walk home in," I tell her, my voice resembling a growl. I'll ask myself later who this cruel, controlling person is, but for now I just want to bury myself inside her.

I tangle my hand in her hair, pulling back so she arches perfectly. Her eyes roll up to meet mine and I grin. My other hand arcs down and swats her perfect ass harder than I have before. For a moment I worry I've gone too far until she moans.

"I'll need more of that, sweet boy. For now, I need you to fuck me hard, and if you do a really good job, we may do this again." Carrie gives a throaty chuckle that makes my cock twitch.

"Fucking game on," I growl. My lip switches as I embrace this confident man whose about to fuck the perfect whore.

I free my cock, slapping it on her ass. There's no sweetness living between us. We both agreed to get off and move on. I don't have a condom on me and I bite my lip as I push my hips to slide in her folds.

"Carrie," I purr in her ear.

"Yes, Derek," she pants, pushing back with her hips.

"I don't have a condom, and there's no way you did in your scrap of clothing. Is that a problem?"

"The only problem is you aren't balls- argh," she screams as I push my cock into her.

I'm done talking. I fuck her hard into the tree, kicking her legs further open. Her tits bounce as I thrust into her, and I couldn't care less if anyone saw me fucking the town crazy lady. I pull Carrie's hair harder and she whines.

I snort. "You know you like it rough," I murmur, reaching between us, rubbing her little bundle of nerves.

"Yes, I love it rough. Pinch my clit," she mewls. "Now!"

I pinch it hard and she shudders, squirting on my cock. I thought squirting only happened in pornos, my friends have certainly never had this happen to them before.

"Oh my god," I gasp in surprise, fucking her through her orgasm. Her pussy flutters and spasms on my cock, and it's strangling it. "Fuck, I don't know if I'll be able to hold out anymore."

I don't want to finish too soon, but she feels too good. I lift her leg, opening her further, pumping into her hard. I release her hair, wrapping my arm around her so she's flush against my chest. The change in position has her gasping as I'm deeper than before.

"I'm close again," she tells me, short of breath as she bounces on my cock. She's relinquished control to me, and fuck if it doesn't feel good.

I suck on her neck, licking and nipping where her ear meets her neck. She screams as she comes, and I paint her insides with my cum. Carrie signed up for me to mark her the moment she told me to fuck her bare. We stand there, breath uneven as I drop her leg, allowing myself to hold her for a moment before I pull out of her tight, wet cunt. I steady her before I step away, tucking myself back into my pants. I may be a dick, but I wasn't always.

She turns as I grab my shirt by the back of the neck and pull it off. Her jaw drops as her eyes greedily take me in. I step towards her, considering a second round when I hear my name yelled. I jump, looking over my shoulder.

"Derek, what the fuck are you doing," my dad yells from the door.

My jaw drops, trying to figure out what to say, when I look back to where Carrie was standing. She's gone, but I can hear her light feet running back to her house. It's so soft I doubt my dad would hear it.

"I was just getting some air, Dad. I was considering going for a run," *I tell him.*

"Oh, well, that's a good idea. Gotta be ready for football this year," he says as he slams the door shut.

My heart is pounding, and I gasp out a breath. I have never felt so alive or scared in my life.

My cock is rock hard as I pull away from the past. Damn woman can still affect me from the grave. Certain words she used to say or call me trigger me now. I can't have anyone call me 'sweet boy' or 'baby boy', which is why I ask people not to call me by a pet name at all. It ends up being safer for me. There's no way to explain raging out to a seemingly sweet pet name.

I also *need* to have control in the bedroom. My life still isn't entirely mine, since I'm ruled by the bullshit of my dear ol' dad, so I revel in what I can control. Forcing orgasms, denying touch, breath and sometimes some knife play. My tastes are wide, but I control every move.

Lennon O'Reilly listens to no one. She does, says, and is whatever the fuck she wants to be. I don't know how to handle a girl this wild, someone who reminds me so much of *her*. Lennon probably doesn't deserve the torture and punishments I doled out for being Carrie's daughter...but figuring out how to stop it will be difficult.

I don't know if I can.

11

LENNON

I don't quite know how I found sleep, but I drifted off to the familiar sounds of my guys chatting. I was too tired to write, but I can sense the past talking to me, and it's how I deal with things.

I feel disoriented when I open my eyes. I'm in my bed, with Ror's arm wrapped around my waist. I'm safe, Turner is next to me on his back, mouth slightly open. They're so gorgeous and I feel the urge brush his hair out of his face. I want to stay here with them, but my bladder is screaming at me.

I wiggle slowly out from under Roark's arm and he moans in discomfort.

"I'm so sorry baby, I'll be right back," I whisper.

He sighs as if he hears me, and still deep in slumber, rolls onto his back. Finally free, I carefully scramble out of bed and race for the bathroom. This was way closer to an accident, than I care to admit.

Finishing up and being sure to brush my teeth, I walk out into the aisle to see if Atlas and Mav stayed with us. The bus isn't supposed to leave until late morning, but honestly I don't know what time it is.

Humming to myself, I investigate. We have a few sofas that convert into beds for this reason. Sometimes the muse hits, and we'll brainstorm for days in between performances. One of the stipulations of our contracts for this year is to be on tour more months than not to pay for our new tour bus. We'll renegotiate next year, but the beauty of our contract is we can't be fired.

There's always the rare possibility we'll want to leave, but the reason would be to retire from music. Or the label would have to really fuck up, and we are nowhere near that point. Even though I *really* dislike Prescott.

I find Atlas and Mav deep asleep in the beds they always claim when they stay with us, and I smile as I pass them. Our fridge is filled with staple food, because I can't survive eating out every night. I need to be able to cook too, even though road life can be insane. I really think the normalcy of cooking just soothes my soul.

I smile at this thought as I pull out ingredients for eggs, bacon, and pancakes. Pancakes are a small stretch in a kitchen this small, but I can manage it. I continue humming, though I don't know the tune, or where I heard it. Trusting my muse, I decide there has to be a reason for it.

I make breakfast and coffee, and am starting to plate and set the food out on the table by the time the boys trail out. Knowing them, their noses woke them up first.

"Good morning," I say softly with a grin. I know better than to speak loudly at what is now ten in the morning, since I don't know how much they had to drink last night.

Mav sighs happily as he sees the spread of food. "Aren't you just an angel," he says, kissing my head as he reaches for coffee and slides into a chair.

Each of the guys takes a turn saying good morning in their

own way. Atlas picks me up and twirls me in the air as I giggle, and Roark kisses my neck and promises me orgasms in appreciation for me cooking. Turner kisses me soundly as he is the last to reach me and I moan softly. "Breakfast looks incredible, Lavender. I'll clean up after we eat okay? Come sit before it gets cold," he says against my lips.

I squeeze in at our table and we all dig in. All the food turned out perfectly, and my cheeks hurt by how much I'm smiling as we eat.

Mav tilts his head as watches me and I raise my eyebrow in question as I sip my coffee.

"Little Valkyrie, what were you humming earlier?" he asks.

"How did you even hear that," I ask incredulously.

"Little love, I wake easily in the morning. I was starting to stir when you walked by, and then I heard your tune. It was haunting, but familiar? I don't know how to explain it," he muses.

Oh my god. "Mav, I thought it was just me. I can't place it either and it's making me crazy. Maybe I should hum it again, and see if we can figure it out together?"

"You have the floor, babe. Show us," Turner says, staring at me intently. This man has always been intense around me, he loves hard, and gets invested in others quickly.

It's one of the things I love about him.

I hum the tune, and Roark frowns. "That face, you know it, don't you?" I ask.

"Yes and no. I don't know how you'd know it, Lenny. It's an Irish love song, and not many people outside of Ireland know it. It ended in a super fucked up way too. Mav has family in Ireland still that he visits, so it makes sense he'd know it," he says.

"Huh. I have no idea where I heard it then. I've had it in my head since I woke up," I tell him with a shrug.

Roark nods, confused as well, but willing to table it for now. We're brainstorming a time to work on another song for the album when there's a bang on our door. I frown, worried last night is about to bite us all in the ass. None of it was my fault, but the only person who bangs on the door like they're the police are Derek or Prescott.

Turner rolls his eyes and yells, "Come in!"

People rarely barge in anymore because word traveled quickly that anyone who saw me naked would lose an eye. Prescott heard the rumors and decided I was a whore that would let anyone rail her. How she jumped to this assumption is anyone's guess.

The door opens and Prescott climbs on. Her lips moue in distaste as she glances at us eating breakfast. I'm completely covered up, I don't know why she has an attitude this morning.

"This is so cozy. I'm glad you're all together at least. You dropped some pretty interesting information to *You* magazine yesterday, Lennon. I wish you had run it by me first, because I don't know how I'm going to be able to get you into a studio with your tour dates-"

"Aren't we in California for our next stop? Are you telling us there's not a studio in the area who would jump at the chance to book us some time? I find that very hard to believe," Turner drawls.

Turner's South Carolinian accent doesn't release often, but when it does it's so fucking sexy. I bite my lip, squeezing my thighs together discreetly. Ror chuckles next to me.

"Same beautiful," he mutters under his breath.

I smirk because he's always so aware of me. I blink, realizing I have completely lost track of the conversation.

"- Isn't it a little entitled to think you're big enough to warrant emergency studio time?" Prescott says, haughtily.

I don't know what she said before, but this woman seriously

dislikes people in the music industry. Why is she working for our label again?

"I don't think it's entitled," I interject. "It's seeing who we can call in a favor to. You also don't run the show here. Our *label* does, and I cleared it with them before I did the interview. I have the email with a time stamp if this will suffice, or I can just reply back to him explaining you don't want to do your job? Would you have any feelings about this?"

Prescott's mouth drops. I rarely show my claws, but that doesn't mean I don't fucking have them. I smile sweetly at her, belying my sarcastic tone. Roark squeezes my thigh gently, not to warn me to stop, but in encouragement.

"Well, how could I have known that," Prescott says with an eye roll.

"You could have asked instead of coming in hot with the snark and sarcasm. You interrupted our breakfast, and this is the band's time to unwind. We've had five back to back performances and this is our first day off, though most of it will be spent on the road. Have we complained though? No, because this is our *job* and we love it. Go talk to whoever you need to make this happen, so we can continue to record new music. By the way, that's *your* job: to support us on the tour as needed. Newsflash you're needed. So go," I tell her. I'm still tired, my body is a little sore, and I have a headache slowly building. I'm not in the mood for her shit.

Seeing I'm at the end of my patience with her, she nods curtly. "Will there be anything else then," she asks primly. This is a mix of bitchy Prescott and the nervous one. I can't help but think this may be the real one.

"Nope, for now that's it. Oh, when are we leaving?" I ask.

"In the next twenty minutes, so you can decide what bus you'll be riding on," she tells Atlas and Mav.

The guys nod, drinking the rest of their coffee hurriedly.

"The bus driver will be here shortly too, and it'll be Michael today."

The bus drivers are hired through the label, and tend to cycle out. We rarely have the same person each time for some reason. I nod and thank her. She walks off the bus and I sag against Roark.

"Kitty's got claws," Atlas murmurs appreciatively. "You've always been sassy in recent years, but I forget you can eviscerate people with that sharp tongue of yours too. It's a good look on you."

I hide my face in Roark's neck, cheeks heating. "Ugh, she just pisses me off so much," I groan. "Just do your job and stop complaining, ya know?"

Ror chuckles, arm wrapping around my waist. "I agree. Speaking of, are we asking for Derek's dismissal or holding out? It's your call, but I reserve the right to punch his stupid face if he's a dick again. The fuckwit doesn't know when to shut his pie hole, I swear," he growls.

"I vote him out, but I heard you may have some unresolved history with him, little Valkyrie," Mav says. "So, if that's the case, what's the harm in waiting a little longer? But the fucker needs to keep his hands to himself. I won't forget that part either."

I grimace. "Yeah, I'll be needing more makeup to cover these before our show," I say with a sigh. "I agree with you though. I won't step in between a man and his bat if he does it again. Y'all can fuck him up," I tell them fiercely.

Turner grins, picking up his coffee cup. "To fucking him up," he cheers.

I roll my eyes as the guys lift their own cups in agreement.

I legit can't with them.

~

THE DRIVE PASSED SLOWLY. I don't usually mind it, but it grates today for some reason. Biting my lip after the first five hours of reading, napping, and chatting with the guys, I'm over it.

Blowing out a breath, I throw my hands up in the air annoyed with myself. I have all this pent up energy and nowhere to go with it. Maybe we do need some time to get lost in a city soon.

Roark and Turner are making lunch together, and there isn't enough space to join them while they're moving around in there. They're so big, they take up a lot of space. Pulling out my phone, I realize I haven't had time to connect with our fans since everything blew up last night.

Starting with Instagram, I pull up where the band or I have been tagged. I smile at the photos of best friends having a blast at the show together, date nights, and parents taking their kids to their first concert. I love watching the experiences that were created last night.

I leave love notes of appreciation as I scroll through the posts, making sure my personality shows through. I then check the band's IG handle, looking for posts that were posted yesterday by Derek. I come across a photo of Orla and I chatting, and stop my finger from continuing. Our smiles are easy, looking as if we are sharing a secret. The caption states I am telling her about the new album we are dropping and I frown. Well, I guess I know who gave me up to Prescott.

I mutter under my breath, moving on to the next posts. There are videos of the crowd, Turner and I singing the last song of the night together, and loads of photos. I checked the comments on the video of Turner and I, pleased everyone who was there last night enjoyed it. It's rare that we perform that song, but I felt pulled towards it. I hum the melody as I scroll and find a behind the scenes photo of myself.

When did Derek take this?

I'm watching the opening act from last night and jamming out. Music fuels me, and these guys were really good. I loved listening to them, and congratulated them after their set. I'm pretty sure I surprised them, but I was impressed. I can't believe I didn't notice he was close enough to take this. I try to be aware of surroundings, but I was having fun, unwinding after his bullshit earlier.

The comments are filled with people's opinions of the photo. Several talked about how I obviously had no idea it was being taken, and loved how much I loved music. Others stated it was a cry for attention and I frown. My skin had gotten thicker over the years, but people rarely call me disingenuous.

"Why do you look like your phone has immensely offended you," Roark asks with a chuckle.

I glance up and find Ror and Turner looking at me curiously.

"Derek was spying on me," I mutter with a sigh. "When I was talking to him, he said he wanted to take more candid photos of us before the show. I explained why that wouldn't work, since you tailgate, Turner and Roark finds his zen. He must have decided I was the perfect guinea pig, and took photos of me jamming in the wings during the opening act."

I turn the photo towards the guys and they wrinkle their noses. "What are the comments like under the photo," Turner asks hesitantly.

"Fucking awful," I sigh, shaking my head.

Roark's brows furrow as he pulls out his phone, and I immediately dislike what this means.

"Babe, what are you doing? I can handle the snide comments..." I trail off as he growls.

"I have a feeling you purposely protected us and told him reasons why he shouldn't take photos of us, am I right?" he asks, glancing up. I nod and he scowls. "You gave him a reason to take candid photos of you instead of us, and put yourself in the line of fire. So now, I'm not going to sit back while my gorgeous girl is being attacked. I promise I won't be an asshole... there done," he says with a final tap.

"What did you say," I breathe, eyes wide.

He turns the phone towards me and I see:

Isn't our Lenny beautiful? She always lights up any time she hears music, and this opening act was 🔥.

"See I was nice, but no one gets to fuck with you," Ror says with a wink. "Food's ready, come join us, baby."

Turner chuckles and it's the kind that makes my thighs clench and I bite my lip in need. Ignoring my needy look or somehow becoming clueless, he says, "For the record, I would have responded very differently."

I follow them both to our sitting area and eat with them, lost in thought. I still feel out of sorts and I'm not sure why. I was powerless through much of yesterday: starting at the closet with Derek, and continuing to being drugged and lost in Seattle. I just don't know how to fix it.

"Penny for your thoughts, Lavender," Turner murmurs as he watches me.

"I feel really off," I confess with a huff. "I can't concentrate on anything, I'm annoyed at everything, and I feel out of control. I don't know how to fix these feelings."

Roark watches me, turning over my words in his mind. He and Turner are really good about taking my feelings seriously. "So, what if we gave you back some control? Last night was really shitty, so it's normal you'd feel off."

"How do I get back control? I don't think I've ever really had control over anything in my life," I huff with a sigh.

"Well, we did pick up a new dildo and harness the other day..." Turner trails off with a smirk and my jaw drops.

My eyes light up in excitement as I rub my thighs together. "This is true," I murmur, wanting to see exactly where they're going with this.

"What if you controlled everything we did today: where we fuck, who you fuck, how they get fucked? You're the mistress of everything, and we're your naughty boys to control," Roark growls.

"Oh my god," I moan softly. "Are you being serious right now? I've always wanted to do this, we just rarely have much time alone."

We often get pulled into another direction lately, less downtime, more time running. We end up with quickies, which I love, but setting up something like this takes more time.

"We have miles to go before we even think of stopping, Mistress Lavender. So what do you want," Turner asks with a smirk.

My lip twitches in response as I ask in return, "What's something we haven't done before that I've always wanted?"

Turner barks out a laugh. "You want my sweet ass, don't ya baby?"

I giggle at how he phrased it but fuck yeah, I do. "I want to fuck your sweet ass while Roark sucks your cock. May as well spoil you a bit," I tease.

Ror pouts. "What about me? I can admit my mouth is already salivating for my sweet boy's cock, but I want more fun too."

"Poor baby," I coo, rolling my lips in to hide my smile. "If you're a very good boy, you can choose any of my holes to fuck. Ror's choice, courtesy of his mistress."

Roark perks up and smiles eagerly. These men make me so happy. They can just sense when I need something. I need fun, control, and sex. All this nervous energy needs to go somewhere.

"Are you done eating then? If you are, let's make this happen," Turner says with a wink.

I also hear what he's not saying: let's do this before we get interrupted again. It's just the story of our lives lately.

I nod, jumping up and running towards our room. My ankle isn't bothering me anymore, and my excitement fuels theirs.

While the boys clean up the kitchen, I put on a lacy see-through black push up bra, cute black cheeky underwear, that's also a strap-on harness made of thicker material, and thigh high boots. The dildo is already in place, and I grin as I bounce a little with it on. I then put in a ton of beach wave spray in my hair and scrunch it. My hair is wild, and I look fucking hot.

I pull out a bullet from one of our drawers, along with leather handcuffs and other fun items, before going off to find Ror and Turner. They're both shirtless, sitting on the couches, legs splayed open with their jeans undone. Their positions seem so innocent and casual, but their smirks tell me they know they're destroying my panties right now.

"None of that now," I laugh. "I'm in charge, and we haven't played nearly enough with the hooks we had installed."

Their eyes heat as they trail over my body. This is the vibe I was going for: sexy, gorgeous, and a woman who has her shit together. A woman whose life isn't a train wreck at the moment, sharing some time with her men.

One of the specifications we had for our bus were hidden compartments for storage, hiding mirrors in strategic spaces, and hooks and eyelet holes placed throughout the bus. The label didn't blink at the request, and it made me wonder what other things they may be asked for by their artists.

"Ror, undress Turner after he stands up for me and

presents me with his wrists," I purr with a smile.

Turner's lips part, light breaths starting to pant as he stands languidly. Slow, measured steps bring him to me and my nipples peak in excitement. He's never been someone that takes orders easily. This is a man that usually craves control, being in charge, so I didn't expect this. Ror often tops him, but it's by playful force. They wrestle, destroy some shit, and then Roar fucks his tight little ass.

"Oh Mistress," Turner says softly.

"Yeah baby," I respond.

"Will you tell me what has your breath elevated and thighs rubbing together so wantonly?" His face is earnest, eyes playful, and his lips twisted in a smirk.

I bite my lip as I walk towards him, slowly strapping a leather cuff to his wrist. "I was thinking about how you don't give up control easily, and how delicious it is to see you like this." I strap the second cuff to his other wrist, never releasing his gaze as Roark undresses him.

"Lift your foot for me, love," Roark says, kissing his thigh as he kneels at Turner's feet. Mesmerized by me, Turner keeps his eyes on mine as he does as asked, and Ror strips him of his pants.

Turner likes to go commando most days, and I can feel his cock bob between us as it brushes against me.

"Such a good boy," I praise him, lifting his wrists above my head.

Roark is standing again, taking Turner's bound wrists as I glide one my hands up his chest, continuing to play with the hair along his neck as I kiss him lazily. I can't get enough of him, grasping his cock, enjoying the contrast of cool piercings with warm flesh. He moans into my mouth, not noticing as Ror pulls a sturdy hook from the ceiling, looping the connected cuffs onto it.

I sigh happily, stepping away from him. Turner moves towards me as if to follow, but his bound hands stop him. He growls at me and I raise my eyebrow at him.

"How do you apologize to your Mistress? That wasn't very nice," I coo with a teasing smile.

He pouts as he realized that he fucking growled at me. It would be adorable enough to climb him like a spider monkey and ride his face, but I have other plans for him.

"I'm sorry, Mistress, can I give you orgasms in punishment?"

I snort, breaking character and laughing. "I was just thinking of this as a possible punishment. I want to fuck your tight ass first though. If you're very sorry, I'll be gentle," I tell him as I turn a panel in the bus around to face us.

The panel is a mirror on the other side, showing my beautiful blond angel perfectly at my mercy. I grin evilly as I pick up lube, the bullet, and a crop. I doubt I'll use the last item, but I enjoy seeing his eyes widen before they heat with desire.

"Oh baby girl, please make it hurt," he tells me and I giggle.

I walk behind him and then check the mirror. I can see Roark now on his knees in front of Turner and myself behind him. I kiss and nip along his back as I drop to my knees. Laying out my goodies, I pick up the crop and bite my lip. This could be fun...

"Ror, lick Turner's cock like the delicious dessert that he is, but don't let him come," I order, glancing at the mirror as I do.

Turner's head drops back as he groans and Ror chuckles darkly. "Oh darling man, you've definitely unleashed our beautiful Valkyrie now."

"Lavender, please, oh fuck Ror," he gasps as he's licked from root to tip.

"So fucking delicious," Ror groans as his mouth devours our man's tip, pierced tongue dragging along it.

"Open your legs nice and wide for me," I command, my voice pitched just loudly enough that I know that he can hear me. His legs open quickly and I smile eagerly. I drag the crop over the back of his powerful legs, enjoying the darkness of the crop against his lighter skin. Pebbling in the wake of the cool leather, I drag it up his thighs before cracking it along his ass.

Turner's hips thrust forward, forcing more of his dick into Ror's hot mouth. "Agh, Mistress," he whines. "Please, I'll be good."

I painstakingly slowly drag the crop up the other leg. "Are you sure you'll be a good boy for me," I ask, my eyes devouring the red mark I made on his ass.

"Yes, baby, anything but this. I need more. This is torture," he pants.

"Mmm, maybe next time you'll reconsider growling at me," I say lightly, continuing to drag the crop along his flesh.

I'm going to end the torture soon because I'm greedy. My chest is heaving with desire, and I'm forcing my hand not to tremble as I move ever so slowly. I need to be inside his ass, fuck him down Ror's throat. I force my whimper down, because I can end this whenever I want to. I need to see how far his hips jerk forward this time.

Finally, after what feels like forever, but I know wasn't, I strike his ass. Turner isn't ready, and he gags Roark as he thrusts with a cry.

"Fuck, please please fuck me, Mistress," he begs and I grin. This is what I needed. He begs so pretty, but never for me.

Feeling high on power and desire, I stand, making sure he can feel the press of the dildo between his ass cheeks. "Is this what you want? You're not nearly ready yet though," I murmur.

I squeeze lube between his cheeks, determined to do this well, and slide the toy along it.

"Stop teasing, please. I swear I don't need any lead up... just fuck me," Turner moans.

"Is that true, Roark," I ask as I pour lube on the dildo too.

I glance in the mirror as he comes up for air, spit trailing from Turner's dick to his mouth. My lips part, and I find myself licking them. *Why is that so fucking hot.* Ror has the perfect pouty full lips for sucking cock and I flush as I stare at him.

"Yes, Lenny, fuck his naughty ass hard without any buildup. I don't think he deserves it," he says with a smirk. His piercing winks out as he turns to look at me. "Are you feeling a little needy, darling? I can't wait for your tits to spill out while I fuck you. I just have to decide what hole."

I gulp air, staring at him. Intentionally, I unsnap my bra, letting it fall to the floor.

"Jesus, you're so fucking perfect," he whispers.

Turner tries to turn his head towards the mirror to see, but his arms are obstructing his view. "This isn't fair," he complains and I grin.

My core tightens as I grab the bullet, slip it into the hidden pocket where it'll hit my clit, and then flick it to the highest setting. Whimpering, I know I'm going to explode as soon as I get enough friction. I push between his cheeks and Turner's back arches in need. Grabbing his hip and his shoulder, I push past the tight ring of nerve endings and he gasps.

"Such a good boy, taking her big cock," Ror soothes, his hands massaging his ass before swallowing him whole.

Head thrown back, Turner groans. "Fuck, y'all take me so perfectly. Why have we never done this before? Oh my god, more."

I slide out before pushing all the way in. I thrust and grind, moaning as my bullet rolls perfectly along my clit. "Fuck that's so good," I gasp. Shuddering, I gush, so close to coming, but not there yet.

My nipples are tight and needy and I rub them into Turner's back. "Take what you need baby girl, it's all fucking yours. Ahhh yes, I'm so close. Can I come, Mistress?" he shouts in need and I bite his shoulder hard as I fuck him.

"Yes, ahhh, I'm close too," I moan, rocking in and out of him intermittently before grinding hard with a cry.

I'm drenched, already soaking my thighs. This is by far one of the most intense things I've ever experienced. Glancing at the mirror, I watch Ror's eyes roll towards me in the mirror, as he gags and sucks our man's cock while I fuck him. Head thrown back, this image is burned behind my lids as I come.

"So fucking wet as you explode, soaking my thighs," Turner groans as he follows, hips losing their rhythm at his release. The sounds of Ror's sucking him to the last drop follows before he pops off.

"My turn," he growls and stands.

Knowing he's coming for me, I squeak as I pull the dildo out of Turner's ass carefully. I pull off the panties, letting them fall to the floor, then lean over the couch, presenting Ror with my ass as he stalks around Turner.

"I want him to watch me fuck you, knowing he can't touch you," Ror growls as his arm wraps around me and pulls me to him to pick me up.

I squeal as he brings me around, pushing me forwards to brace on the couch as he slaps my ass. I moan, eyes rolling as my body clenches on nothing. "Ror, I need your cock," I gasp.

I hear his zipper as he pulls it down, the sound of denim being pushed off of his hips and hitting the floor. I glance over my shoulder at Turner as he watches, unable to participate, so turned on again that his cock bobs against his stomach. I lick my lips and Ror chuckles.

"Do you want a taste," he asks and I nod. "Come here beautiful. Turner, you're a lucky bastard today. I was planning to be mean. So you're gonna brace your legs like a good boy because she gonna wrap her arms around you and suck your cock while I fuck her. If you lose your balance, she'll fall and that's unacceptable, understood," he growls.

Turner's eyes widen as he nods. "Loud and clear, come here, beautiful," he moans.

Scrambling, I stand and walk to him. I wrap my arms around him, hands grabbing his ass. I widen my stance to help my own balance, and then suck on his tip, tracing the piercing at the top of his cock.

"Fuck, such a hot naughty mouth. Ror, is her sweet pussy dripping?"

I hear him drop to his knees as he licks me from my pussy to my ass. "Fuck, she's flooded. She loved fucking your tight hole. We really need to remember how much she enjoys this," Roark sighs as he sucks my clit hard.

I wail, shuddering as I suck more of him down. "Oh my god, how are you, you," Turner sobs, no longer making sense, lost to sensation.

I'm not paying attention to what's happening behind me until Ror is pushing into me insistently until he bottoms out. Whimpering, I concentrate on getting used to this size. He's larger than Turner, and enjoys watching me take every inch.

"Your pussy is so beautiful, swallowing me whole. Be a good girl and take care of Turner," is all I hear before he withdraws and then slams into me.

I scream as my nose hits Turner's pelvis, struggling to breathe as I suck hard. He struggles not to thrust, but I squeeze his ass firmly. "Ugh, slap my ass if you can move," he says with a strangled cry.

My balance is solid, so I slap him hard. They use me together as I bob up and down on his cock, pulling in air before Ror fucks me back down. I feel cherished, loved, and full. *So fucking full.*

"You're strangling my cock, and I won't last long," Ror says as he squeezes my hips hard as he fucks me. I can't say I'm surprised though, since he is the only one that hasn't come yet. "You're going with me, baby. Turner's about to blow again too because your mouth is a fucking dream."

Reaching between us, he rubs my bundle of nerves and I shudder. Beyond coherent thought, my breasts are heavy and aching as they bounce with every thrust. Dragging my tongue down and around Turner's dick as I suck is all I can think of, along with that perfect spot Ror is hitting. My G spot is singing as he fucks into me and I clamp down on him as I moan.

"Fuck babe, how is a man to last at all with this magical pussy," he yells, and I'd laugh if my mouth wasn't busy.

Rubbing faster, Ror pushes me harder to come, arm wrapped around my waist so I can't escape. I'm so sensitive, so close, I can't think of anything until he pinches my clit. Wordlessly screaming, I drench his cock as I come.

"Fuck, yes," he yells as he leans back to pound into me, chasing his own release. My walls clamp and flutter as I continue to explode and I swear my eyesight whites out as my eyes roll back.

Turner shouts a warning as the first pulse of cum hits the back of my throat and I swallow greedily. I'm so deep though that some dribbles out of my mouth, and I moan in dismay as I revel in his distinctly sweet taste. Gasping for breath as I release his cock, I rest my head on his stomach.

"Ror release my hands, I wanna hold Lavender," Turner says as he struggles to control his breathing, too.

Roark pulls out of me slowly and I gasp at the loss of him. I can't stand up due to exhaustion from the orgasms, and my legs have given up the ghost. Soon, hands pull me up and I'm lifted into Turner's arms. I feel weightless as sleep pulls at me, the restlessness from earlier completely melted away.

12

ROARK

Our girl is amazing, and I love knowing how to piece together her broken shards when she feels out of control. Turner and Lenny know how to do the same for me, and we know how to help each other. Life is crazy right now, and I hate not knowing who drugged my girl. I don't remember ever having seen this roadie before, and I make a point of looking for him at our next stop.

The only issue? In the frenzy of the previous night, I barely remember what he looks like. I remember black hair over his forehead, a flash of dark brown eyes looking at me for a moment before looking back down, and medium height. He could be a thousand other assholes, and I'd never know. I growl softly, snuggling deeper into bed as I hold Lenny. *I have to protect her, and I've done a shit job of it so far.*

"Stop thinking so hard, Ror," Turner says with a small yawn.

"I'm trying," I say with a sigh.

Turner moves around Lenny and pushes me back. "Last

night wasn't your fault, baby," he murmurs as he kisses down my chest.

"I know but-"

"The but tells me you think differently," he says as he drags his tongue along my nipple.

I groan, arching my back into him. "You didn't let me get a taste, so now I want to play," he chuckles.

Kissing and sucking down my chest, I struggle to stay quiet, but all I can manage are soft cries. Turner's fingers play along my skin as he would an instrument, and I shiver as they wrap around my cock.

"Babe," I pant. "I can't stay quiet."

Turner reaches over and grabs one of Lenny's crop tops she left out. He balls it up and commands, "Open that dirty needy mouth before I fill it for you."

I almost decide to be a brat, but he's already pressing it between my lips, forcing them to open.

"Mrgh," I protest, but open wide. Our girl is tired after we had our fun together. I would rather she sleep so we can have a late night walk around the city when we arrive.

"Such a good boy," he purrs. He grabs my wrists and lifts them over my head. "Move them and I stop..."

I grab onto the pillow above my head because fuck I don't want him to stop.

Turner moves down, pumping my cock lazily. My eyes grow wide as he licks me like his favorite dessert before sucking the tip hard. Grabbing a bottle of lube, he slathers my cock, squeezing my tip hard enough to make my hips buck.

"I expect you to fuck my ass hard with those sexy hips. No hands, big boy. You're so gorgeous laid out like this, Ror," he muses as he straddles me before lining my cock up with his ass.

His eyes roll, groaning as I stretch his tight hole. My hands hold tight on the pillow, wanting to grab his hips and seat him fully. He's so warm, so fucking familiar and perfect, but I'll play by his rules. My face grows warm with the strain of not thrusting until I'm fully inside him, my teeth gritting.

"Fuck, you fill me so good, Ror," Turner groans as he drags himself slowly up my dick before dropping lower abruptly so I scream behind the gag.

Screw waking up Lennon, I am so close to flipping this cheeky boy and fucking him into the mattress. I'm breathing hard, so close to losing control completely, until finally, his tight ass meets my thighs. I pull my hips back slightly before thrusting hard. Turner's eyes roll as he gasps.

"Fuck, baby just like that. I'm gonna paint you with my cum while you're deep in my ass," Turner says breathily as he rides me. He fists his dick, and I'm mesmerized by this gorgeous man. His piercings start at the underside of his cock in a ladder, so as he smears his pre-cum around his tip and down, my mouth waters. "Like what you see?"

I nod, finding a rhythm as I fuck him, enjoying the work of art as he works himself over, too. His juices leak more the closer he gets and I groan. The tattoos of musical instruments and notes crawl up his forearms, forcing me to grunt as I fist my pillow tighter. It's officially a badge of honor now to crack, to behave as Turner sighs and moans over me. He's just enough of an asshole to not let me come if I touch him.

"Having trouble keeping your hands to yourself, love," Turner teases me as his hand tightens around my hip. He squeezes again before taking over and fucking me instead. He's so rarely this dominant with me, I almost sob at how fucking gorgeous he is as my cock slides in and out of his ass. "I bet you have the best view in the house, laying there watching me," he groans, shuddering in need.

We're both so close, and I keen around the gag as the tip of my cock twitches while deep inside of him.

"Oh fuck, what," Turner shudders as cum starts to spray all over my chest and stomach.

I win. I thrust once, twice, painting his insides as I grin around the shirt. Turner collapses on my chest and I grunt. He's lucky my cock is big enough he didn't hurt me. I'm still inside him and I lazily thrust through the rest of my orgasm as I groan. He twitches in bliss, enjoying his post orgasm glow. Fucking gorgeous.

I carefully lift him, slipping out before yanking the gag out of my mouth, wrapping my arms around him. Fuck the mess, that was amazing.

"Hmmm, thanks for the show, boys," says a sleepy voice.

Turner and I glance over, chests still heaving from exhaustion, to find Lenny biting her lip as she watches from her pillow.

"Sorry babes, we tried to be quiet, it just didn't quite work out," Turner says with a chuckle.

"Mmm. Wake me up anytime for that," she whispers with a grin.

"You're so perfect," I murmur, cupping her face.

"I don't know about perfect, but I am yours," she responds with a giggle.

"That you are, beautiful girl," I growl. "Turner and I need a shower, you feel like getting up and having a snack with us?

Lenny pushes herself into a sitting position, moving her long pale hair out of her face. "Yeah, I'm craving grilled peanut butter and banana sandwiches. Is that okay?"

My stomach chooses this moment to growl and I throw my head back laughing. "I would say I'm down with this decision, baby. Come on Turner. Oh fuck, I can't wait to stay at a hotel with a big fucking shower so we can all get clean together," I groan wistfully.

Lenny swoons. "Oh daddy, talk dirty to me!"

This fucking girl. Such a brat. My fingers twitch, but I need a shower first. His cum is starting to dry, and my skin slightly itches. We had very messy, but amazing fun. Turner stands, lips twitching as he winks at me. Oh yeah, we'll definitely be getting our beautiful Valkyrie back for this later.

I can't wait.

AS COMFORTABLE AS our bus is, thirteen hours on it is a long drive. Reading, eating, napping, fucking or writing... there's only so much you can do until you're stir crazy.

"Gah, are we there yet?" Lenny groans.

I snort, looking out at the dark roads and the headlights of cars passing us. "Almost? We've been on the road all day, so I imagine it'll be soon," I say with a sigh. "Do you want me to go ask, baby?"

"I'm just stir crazy, and we rarely do a trip this long without breaking it up. I really hate this," she huffs.

The girl isn't wrong, so I nod and walk up to the driver, being sure to close the heavy door behind me that assures our privacy. *We don't need to worry about him getting a surprise show.* "Hey, not wanting to bug you, but we wanted to see when we might be arriving?"

The driver meets my eyes in the rearview mirror and nods curtly. "We've got about twenty minutes until we're in San Francisco, Sir. Then about fifteen minutes more until we pull into the stadium parking lot. It's been a long drive, so I get it. I was asked only to stop for gas, so it's been a haul."

I nod sympathetically, wondering if this was on Prescott's orders. Why the hurry? Our show isn't until tomorrow, there's no real reason for the rush that I can see.

"Perfect, my girl will be happy to hear that, thanks man," I say with a tight smile.

The driver nods in understanding, refocusing on the road.

I sigh, because we're so close, and yet still on the damn bus for a bit. I walk back to my Valkyrie and Turner, hoping she can suck it up for just a little longer.

"So, we're close-" I start to say until I hear moans. I make sure the curtain between sections is completely closed behind me when I see Lenny's legs draped over his shoulders as he eats her out.

"I complained again," Lenny mewls, hips fucking Turner's face in return. "S-so I'm being punished... fuck me," she screams as her back bows from the force of her orgasm.

Turner's head lifts just a little, but the vibrations will still run through her when he speaks. "I figured we were still a ways off, so I threw in a distraction tactic. How do you think it's going?" he drawls with a dark chuckle.

Lenny whimpers at the sensations, and I sit across from them as he attacks her pussy. I pull out my cock, massaging and pumping it as I watch. Her tits are out of her tank top and she's writhing on the couch as she tugs on her nipples. She pants as her legs lock on his head, and Turner only grunts in return as he starts to finger fuck her as he sucks on her nub.

Poor, sweet girl may just kill our man with her magical pussy. I'm not worried though, he can hold his breath for a long time.

The live porn is loud, wet, and incredible. I start to feel close, when I notice more lights behind me. I grin, not worried about anyone seeing into the bus because of the tint we have on the window. I stand, pushing the tip against Lenny's pouty lips. She opens wide and I slide along her slick, hot tongue. Perfect, wet, and ready, I think as she swallows my cock.

"Such a good girl. The only way you get to come again is screaming around my cock, my gorgeous Valkyrie," I groan.

Turner looks up at me from the slit between her legs and winks as he eats her like it's his last meal. We both tend to devour her, she just tastes so good. He says she tastes like strawberries, but I always insist it's the sweetest vanilla cream.

Just the thought of her sweet taste has me thrusting harder down Lenny's throat. The angle isn't the best and she gags before she accommodates my size. Soon we establish a rhythm, and I revel in her sweet cries. Her back bows, hands latching around my ass, forcing me to thrust harder and faster.

"Oh fuck, baby, your mouth is so fucking perfect. You take me like the little cock queen that you are," I praise her. My words come out brokenly as my breath pants out faster. The world around me starts to blacken around the edges, and I grab the back of the couch as my thrusts lose their rhythm. "I'm so close, Lenny come with me, baby," I cry out with a gasp.

Turner growls between her legs and I look down at him, watching as he twists his fingers inside of her as he fucks her with them. Lenny wails around me and my fingers sink into her thick hair. Grounded, I resume face fucking her, knowing she doesn't have long before she's drowning him in her sweet juices.

"Such a good girl," I groan, pulling her hair gently so her head drops back a bit. This angle is amazing and my eyes roll. "Fuck, I could fuck your pouty mouth every day for the rest of my days...it would never be enough," I whimper.

I talk a good game, I am a dom when the time calls for it, but I will always be undone by Turner or Lenny's mouths as I fuck them. They know my every weakness...

"Her pussy is fluttering and pulsing on me, Ror," Turner growls.

I watch as he rubs her clit hard and her breath changes as

she sucks me down. Feeling evil I push into her until her nose is against my stomach. I rock in and out, reveling in how good she takes me. She swallows hard and I gasp. The pressure is almost too much as she sucks and licks me deliberately. I won't finish before her though, so she needs to come. It's a matter of honor, as I rock agonizingly slow in her mouth.

"You look so good," I murmur, my gaze moving back to her. Her eyes water, and then she bows her spine as she wordlessly screams. "Fuck, yes, let it all go," I yell as her throat constricts me so tightly, it's as if my cock is being aggressively hugged. I yell as I come, almost blacking out. After waiting so long, I have to hold on firmly to the couch so I won't fall.

Stepping back a bit, I let my cock slip out of her mouth before I collapse next to her.

"Shit, I think you broke me," I whisper, my hand over my chest as my heart beats wildly.

"Mmm, I can't say I'm sorry," the little brat says with a throaty chuckle. "All's fair when I suck your fat cock, darling man."

I bark out a laugh, shaking my head. "You'll be the death of me yet, little Valkyrie," I tell her, my brogue slipping heavily into my words. I'm heavily sated, content to fall asleep into a sex laden coma.

"None of that, Ror. We have a plan tonight. Late night Chinese at the least. San Fran isn't usually known for late night fare, but I found a foodie blog that suggested this place. We need to eat anyway, so we can hop in a cab and get off the damn bus. You in, Lavender?"

"You had me at foodie blog, baby," she says with a yawn. "I'm down for any adventure you're willing to go on with me. I just need to clean up a bit. Someone left me messy," she says.

She gets up with less than stable legs, and goes to take care of things just as we pull into the stadium.

"Excellent timing," I growl happily.

Turner grabs his phone to check the time, making sure the restaurant is open, and then calls them. "Hi, do you take reservations..."

I tune out as I straighten my clothes and pull up my zipper. I can't wait to get out and explore a little with them. I can feel Lenny's urge to get off this bus now that I've released my own sexual needs. I head to our room to grab my wallet, keys, and some swag items in case we run into fans while we're out. As soon as we can, we're off this fucking bus.

Turner

Lavender squeals in delight as she steps off the bus. "Freedom! It's been eighty-four years..."

I snort at the *Titanic* reference, shaking my head as I put my arms around her waist and pick her up to spin with her.

"Oh my god, Turner," she screams. "Put me down, please, argh!"

Ror snickers behind us. "Put her down before she blows chunks at ya, Turner," he says in amusement.

I place our girl on her feet, wrapping my arms around her to help her get her bearings. Knowing her, she'll be dizzy for a bit. "Are you ready to have some fun, babes?" I growl into her ear as I kiss behind it.

Lavender has so many delicious spots that make her whimper, and this is one of them. Learning her body is something Ror and I have turned into an art form, and we still find out new things all the time.

"Ravenous," she pants, biting her lip.

"If you weren't so tired of being cooped up," Ror says,

reaching out and gently pulling her lip free, "I'd be giving you something else to fill that needy mouth again."

I grind my hardness against her ass in agreement, and she flops her head against my shoulder. "It's not fucking fair when you work together to fuck with me," she complains.

There is a snort behind me and I look over my shoulder to see Derek walking past us. This man is on thin fucking ice as it is. He needs to watch his attitude. He's gotta have a death wish.

"Oye, you there," Ror yells, making a point not to use his name. He can be a dick as well when he feels like it. Gone is the happy go lucky man I typically see, replaced now by the hardened Dubliner. "Don't you be fucking with us tonight. It's been a long day, and I'll be reminding you that you're only still here because we allow it. Don't ya be forgetting that any time soon."

I wince, gently squeezing Lavender's hips, refusing to look over my shoulder at Derek even though it would be really fucking satisfying. Roark's been pushed too far in the last couple of days, his zen destroyed. I know he still blames himself for Lennon getting hurt.

"Yeah, yeah," Derek says, blowing out a breath. This attitude isn't going to make him any friends, and I wonder if I could make him disappear. I'll fuck someone up with my bat, but unaliving is a line I haven't crossed yet. I'm thinking hard about it though. "Look, I'm really sorry, okay? I don't know what happened with Lennon, but I should have tried harder to keep her from running off-"

Lavender pushes me away, whipping around me before I can pull her back. "Oh fuck, baby," I whisper after her, turning to follow.

I know better than to stop her, however she needs to express her feelings, is the right way for her. I worry more about what *he'll* do.

"You'll do what now? I am extremely tired of being spoken of as if I do not exist," she growls, getting in Derek the Dick's face and poking him. "I am right fucking here, if you have something to say then say it."

Derek blinks lazily at her, unconcerned by her poking. He scoffs as he looks down at her, leaning until they're nose to nose. "You're right. When I have something to say to you, that's what I'll do. Until then, I don't," he murmurs as he begins to turn away.

Way to make her feel small, twat waffle. My hand clenches into a fist as I grunt in anger. Roark's arm bands around my chest. "Give her a chance to make her move," he whispers into my ear.

He's right, she needs to stand on her own two feet if she's going to bring him to heel. I survey Lavender in her heeled boots, ripped jeans, band tee, and leather jacket, deciding to wait her out. Not letting me down, she stomps on his foot. Derek gasps, managing to stay upright as he looks back at her and I smirk. I really expected her to bring him down.

"Do not fuck with me or mine, little boy," she whispers angrily and it only throws fuel to the fire.

He grabs her face, forcing her up onto her toes. Something violent and wild flashes in his eyes and I don't fucking like it. I strain against Ror because fuck this.

"I'm no one's little-"

Derek made the mistake of leaving his nuts open, and she knees him hard. He crumples forward as he releases her face and she pouts in fake sympathy.

"You really need to learn to keep your hands to yourself, because if not I'll keep putting you on your ass," she says with a shrug.

Ror lets me go, and I do what any supportive boyfriend would do: I walk over and shove him on his ass.

"Thanks babe," she swoons and I roll my eyes, bending over and throwing her over my shoulder.

Swatting her perky ass, I crow, "To the Uber we go, continuing to fight bullies and injustice."

"So fucking hot, love," Ror growls, kissing me on the cheek.

Tonight is shaping up to be a pretty fantastic night if you ask me. The Uber is waiting for us at the entrance to the stadium, and I drop Lavender onto her feet.

"You good?" I ask, pushing her hair behind her ear.

"Yep, feed me and call me pretty, and I'll be even better," she responds with a grin.

Shaking my head with an answering smirk, I open the door to the Uber for her. Maybe she should kick ass more often if she looks this in control and happy afterwards. It was hot watching her push back at Derek, something she's not been able to do before. It's almost as if it's their form of foreplay, and in a controlled environment, I'd even be down for it. He's just a loose cannon at the moment, and there was something in his eyes that almost seemed like pain.

There's more to him than meets the eye, and I suddenly find myself needing to know more about Derek. Lennon grew up with the douche canoe, but she avoided him as much as possible since he terrorized her most of her adolescent years, so she's not a good source of information.

Pushing it to the back of my mind, I snuggle in next to her. "Hey, I wanted to tell you I'm proud of you and you're beautiful," I murmur into her ear.

She shivers as my voice vibrates through her body. I love how responsive she is to us.

Sighing happily, she leans into me. "It felt nice to stick up for myself, but I feel like I said something wrong when I was talking to him. There was a moment when he looked like he was gonna snap, but I don't know why." She blows out a breath as she shrugs. "I know nothing about him, because everyone spoke in whispers and rumors when it came to Derek and his dad. They had a stranglehold on the town that felt like equal parts respect and fear. Maybe he's more than just a bully? I don't know what to think, Turner."

"I think you're a really sweet woman who's way too good for the world," Roark murmurs on the other side of her. "Your heart has always been so big, but before you start reaching out, we need to learn a little more about Derek, okay? He's hurt you more often than any other man would be allowed to and live. The boys and I will be having a bit of a chat very soon, if ya don't mind, love."

I smirk because I'm so fucking in. "Am I included in this wee chat," I ask, teasing him slightly because his brogue has been leaking into his speech more and it's really sexy.

Ror rolls his eyes. "Aye, if you insist, Turner. We'll be talking, so you need to leave your beloved bat at home."

We continue to rib each other as we ride to the restaurant in Chinatown. It's one of the few open this late, so I'm glad I made a reservation. I pay the driver, and we pile out excitedly. Food, a new city, and each other's company ensures a good night.

Roark opens the door and we are instantly greeted by smells that make my stomach growl. We greet the hostess with smiles.

"Hi, we have a reservation under Turner Mason," I tell her, throwing my arm around Lennon.

She checks her list and nods in return. "Right this way Sir," she says and we follow.

Sliding into our corner booth, I grin at my partners. "So with there being a little darkness in Derek, what are you thinking, Lavender," I ask, fully aware I am grilling her.

Lennon blushes, and she pushes her hair off of her shoulders. "I think there may be something wrong with me. There are times I like being pushed around just a little. I'd be lying if I said my pu-"

"Hi, welcome, can I get drinks for you," our waitress interrupts.

Lavender's eyes grow huge and her chest flushes in embarrassment. I snort, shaking my head. None of us realized she was there. Oops.

We order water and sake, agreeing we will stick to one each. None of us know the schedule for tomorrow, as Prescott didn't tell us. I swear this woman drives me crazy in the worst ways. We also order appetizers too and she walks away.

"Oh my god," Lavender whisper-shouts and Ror and I burst out laughing.

"Come on baby, tell us all about how wet you are," he teases her.

"Stop," she whines. "It's fucking flooded, okay? He's always been sinful to look at, but we grew up in different worlds for being such a small town. I think part of him was always pissed that I never hopped on his dick. I was too busy trying to survive to ever be interested." She shrugs and I'm pretty sure there's more to unpack in that than she's letting on.

There's way more to Lennon O'Reilly than she lets on. She was a wounded bird when we met her, and trust was hard won. Even then, she isn't one to spill her guts. Nope, she does it instead in her songwriting. I can feel there's more to her story. I'm not pressing for it today, though. Tonight we are having fun.

"I mean, if he wasn't such a fuckwit, I would consider hopping on his dick," Ror teases her. "Think I'm his type?" He winks at her and she barks out a laugh before covering her mouth in embarrassment at how loud it was.

"I don't know babe, I've never once heard any rumors if he

liked guys. However, I probably wouldn't have since our town was judgemental. I think you're everyone's type though, baby. You know you're lickable and gorgeous," she coos while smiling, stroking his ego. Not that it needs it. The man knows what he's working with.

"Inevitably, he is Derek the Dick, and until he's not, the man is off the table for me," he says with a shrug. Ror dislikes bullies, and he hates anyone who is mean to our girl.

"I don't know if he would fit in with our vibe, guys," she says, shifting in her seat uncomfortably. "He's not open minded, he hates me for reasons I don't understand, and I really dislike being attracted to him. It feels like I'm thrown back into high school, getting picked on by the stupid hot popular kid."

I wrap my hand in her hair, gently tilting her face up to mine. "High school is the past, and you've come a long damn way from being the girl who jumped at her own shadow, sweet girl. You've grown so much while you've been with us, this is just another hurdle to jump over. We just need to figure out if he's worth it," I explain with a shrug. "If he's not, we explored the option, and discarded it after doing some fact finding, no harm no foul. What do you think?"

"No stone left unturned," she responds, kissing my lips. I grin as she repeats something I tell her when we write. We follow the song to the end, leaving no stone unturned. Only then do we decide if it works for us.

"That's my girl," I growl, kissing her harder, sharing each breath with her. "You're so fucking perfect."

There's a light clearing of someone's throat and I glance up to find our waitress in front of us, averting her eyes as she drops off our drinks. We are a little over the top in our affection, I guess.

I thank her and she practically runs away. "Damn, I think you scared her," Ror chuckles.

"It wouldn't be the first time it's happened," I counter with a lazy grin. "Let's play what kind of fuckery do you think Prescot planned for us," I suggest. "This woman has decided to have it in for us, so maybe we just do dinner and then head back? If she has something planned at the crack of dawn, I may lose my mind if I have to deal with it on too little sleep."

Ror and Lavender bare their teeth at me savagely at the mention of the she-devil. "To getting one up on Prescott," Lennon cheers, lifting her sake.

"Well, that's something to drink to," Ror murmurs. "And to not losing my mind when she bangs on our door like someone pissed in her Cheerios," he adds.

"Hear hear," I snicker, and I have a hard time swallowing my sake because I'm laughing so hard.

Damn if any night with these two isn't entertaining as hell.

13

LENNON

Last night was exactly what I needed: freedom, Roark and Turner, and kicking Derek's ass was just the cherry on top. There's no denying that I'm attracted to him, but I'm a little worried about myself for it. I shouldn't be drawn to a man who's spent so much of his time hating me and terrorizing me, right? I've heard of Stockholm syndrome, but that's not what this is called. What do you call being attracted to your bully?

Clearly it's madness. Or maybe I've been starved of attention and love for too long. I have it now, but there were a lot of years where I was neglected.

Sighing, I sip my coffee. Being on the road, days start to meld together. I still have a hard time believing we are playing a Friday night show tonight. The boys are working on something, so I'm enjoying a moment of quiet. I don't get many of them funny enough while on tour, so it's nice to hold on to it while I can-

Bang bang bang.

And there it goes. I roll my eyes with a sigh, hitting the button in the kitchen to open the door. Ror and Turner usually walk up to the front to see who it is, but only one person knocks like that.

The sounds of heels lead to Prescott's pinched features appearing and I school my own. Fucking called that shit.

"Good morning, Prescott. Isn't it the start of a beautiful day in sunny California," I ask with an equally bright smile.

Let's be clear, I don't *do* sunny, not this early. I need at least another cup of coffee before eight am to be anywhere near a cheerful human. I'm an excitable chihuahua on the best of days, but that is entirely different from being a morning person.

Prescott looks like she's smelled shit and doesn't know where it's coming from. I bite the inside of my lip to keep myself from snickering. I can't help myself from fucking with her now that I've come to the understanding she is just a sour, awful person. She's not shy, just unhappy.

"I'm unsure what's so great about it. Just another day on tour," she says with a tight smile. "Where is everyone-"

A moan sounds and I lose it and laugh. When I said Turner and Ror had to do something, I meant each other. Am I jealous? No, the boys had a fight about whether soccer or football was the better sport, and decided whoever lost would get fucked. How this solves the mystery of which sport is better? I'll never know, but it does provide some damage control.

"They're in the back," I say nonchalantly. "What's on the schedule for today?"

"Fuck, your ass is so tight. Take my cock like a good sport, no one likes a sore loser," Ror groans and I release a snort.

Well, I guess I know who won. I'm not surprised, Roark tends to win their arguments. I swear Turner puts a good amount of effort in, but part of me wonders if this is exactly the outcome he wanted. He did start the fight after all.

I arch my eyebrow, waiting for her to explain what is planned for us. Poor girl just isn't a match for us.

"Well, since they're apparently *very* busy," she says, pitching her voice higher when the sounds of skin slapping gets louder. "You asked for recording time, so you've got it. Today. All day from eight am until six. You go on at nine tonight, so you'll have time to get dressed and come straight on stage. I hope you have a few songs ready to go, because the label is very excited to get a new album out," she simpers.

What the fuck. This wasn't what we asked for and she knows it. It's also going to mess with everyone's pre-show routines. And more than one song? Can I just scream?

"Yes," I say sweetly, because I refuse to show her how irate I am. "I have been working on some songs, and I'll be able to work out any kinks in the studio."

I don't want to do that, but I have no choice. It's a good thing the guys and I are very in tune with each other. Atlas pushes me to dig deeper when I write, Mav helps me find the purpose behind my words, Roark is my zen, and Turner my passion.

"Perfect, whenever they're done-"

"Fuck, yes, take my cum like a good boy," Roark roars and I lose it cackling.

"For fuck's sake, it's like a brothel. Just do your fucking jobs. Here, take the address," Prescott explodes, throwing a piece of paper in my face. She turns to leave before mentioning over her shoulder, "You'll have a shadow today, so maybe tell the boys to keep it in their pants. Derek will be taking photos and recording video for social media and to send back to the label. They want to make sure you're not full of shit."

She then stalks off the bus and I sigh, taking another sip of my now cold coffee. I grimace, knowing Turner and Ror will be joining me soon. Standing, I pour out the rest of my cup, annoyed that Prescott managed to ruin my quiet time. I hope the rest of the day improves, because apparently I have a longer day than planned.

"Baby, why are you staring at the sink like it wronged you," Turner asks, an arm wrapping around my waist.

"It ate my cold coffee," I pout, aware I'm not making sense.

"Okay, I need a little more than that, Lenny. How about you start from the top, and I'll make you breakfast," Roark cajoles.

I want to cry because we don't have time for it. We have to go right now, or we'll be late.

"I wish we could," I say, blowing out a breath, "but we don't have time. We have to be at a recording studio in the next forty minutes, so we have to get moving."

I turn to face them and check the corner of my mouth for drool. They're in low slung jeans and nothing else, and as much as I'd love to drag them back to bed, since it's just after seven, I can't. I explain my conversation as I walk to our bedroom to change into an off the shoulder black sweater dress and heeled combat boots. I'm reflecting on my need to kick ass today in my clothing choices.

Roark sighs as he grabs a long-sleeved shirt, covering the muscles I'd much rather be licking. Fuck, my raging libido is gonna be a problem after their performance earlier.

"I vote to pick up snacks, coffee, and food on our way over then. Our muse needs to be fed," he says, wrapping his hand in my hair before pulling it back to kiss me.

I whimper, *no fucking fair*. My panties are ruined, and there's no time for either of them to fill me.

Turner chuckles as he throws on a long-sleeved tee and puts on his own combat boots. "Admit it, baby, you always work better when you're riding the edge of neediness. If you're very good, maybe we'll fuck you in studio while you sing."

I groan, pressing my thighs together as Roark snorts and shoves his feet into some shoes.

"That's so wrong, dude. You know Derek doesn't deserve that kind of show, and he'll be skulking around the studio today, Turner," he says, rolling his eyes.

"Shit, that's right. Baby, I didn't mean to be cruel," Turner croons and I pout, flouncing out of the room and towards the bus exit. "Lavender," he says, laughter flowing through his voice as he follows.

I'm being a brat, but I'm also hungry and in need of more food. "Will one of you text Atlas and Mav the change of plan please," I ask with a sigh as I stomp down the stairs towards the car I expect will be waiting.

"Yep, texting now," Turner murmurs, his fingers flying along the screen.

I blink as I realize there's not a car. "...and an Uber too because apparently we're on our own today."

"Not used to doing things on your own, princess," says Derek as he walks up next to me with his equipment.

I twist my lips as I look over at him. *Zen, zen zen...*

"It appears we are on our own, boys. I'm going to call the studio and see if they have instruments, because Mav's travel drum kit is still too heavy to bring in," I turn to tell Roark and Turner as the boys walk up. Our buses are pretty close together today.

"I thought we were supposed to go to the studio today," Mav says. "Where the fuck is the car?"

"This isn't being entitled, Derek," I explain, throwing my hand out in Mav's direction. "We have plans today, and it is up to Prescott as our handler to *handle* it so we aren't behind schedule. The fact that we do not have transport to the studio is really shitty."

I stride away angrily, because I can't control my actions

right now. I call the studio and find out they were well-equipped and waiting for us. I glance over my shoulder to see if I need to call an Uber as well and Turner shakes his head. I rarely need words when we are all in sync like this. We are of one mind to get to the studio on time now, regardless of the hurdles Prescott seems intent on throwing our way.

The issue is if I report this to the label, it seems petty, even though this is her job. I'll have to wait until she does something really big in front of someone she can't explain away. I close my eyes and breathe. Anger I can use, I just need to control it so my breath control as I'm singing is also on point.

Realizing I'm missing my notebook, I roll my eyes. *Get it together girl.* I take a deep breath, practice inhaling and exhaling as I walk back to the bus.

"I am going back in to grab my bag, does anyone else need anything?"

Turner and Roark track me as I walk and I nod that I'm fine. I'm apparently a fucking basket case, but otherwise good to go. I just need to get through today in one piece.

I unlock the bus and climb on: all I brought was my key and phone, everything else is laying haphazardly around the bus. Grabbing a tote bag, I toss in the two notebooks I've been writing in, several pencils, my phone and a wristlet with my cards and identification. I don't remember if the guys grabbed their wallets, and apparently we are fending for ourselves today.

I can't remember if I'm missing anything. I close my eyes and go through my checklist. *Gummy bears*. I pull out an unopened bag of them from the kitchen and toss them in. Now I'm ready. I step off the bus and lock back up, meeting them just as the Uber pulls up.

"Oh look, perfect timing," I say with a grin.

Turner throws his arm around my waist and shakes his head. "Better now?"

"Yes," I say, with relief in my voice. "I have what I need now."

Turner peeks into my bag and snickers. "Yeah, we are going to Ubereats ourselves some necessities on the way there, Lavender. None of us will survive if you eat gummy bears all day."

"Ooh you brought gummy bears," Mav says and Roark's eyes light up. I would swear we all bonded over our favorite writing treats late one night right after he joined the band. After that, Mav became one of us forever.

"I can't write music without them," I counter with a grin.

We climb into the SUV, making sure Derek sits up front. He's not one of us, and while I want to give him a chance, I have to protect my peace. There's a lot riding on today, if I'm reading Prescott's actions correctly, and we need to prove ourselves. You'd think being in the music industry for the past ten years would mean our place is won, but nothing is set in stone.

While the label can't fire us, they could decide we need to be taken under their wing. I like our freedom, creative license, and we are damn good artists. Time to show them.

Mav throws his arm over my shoulder and pulls me to him. "Little Valkyrie, I can hear you stewing from here. What's wrong," he murmurs.

We are at the back of the car, and I relax a little, knowing Derek can't hear us.

"I don't like how this was thrown at us, Mav. It feels like a test, and I don't want to fail."

"I'm feeling the same way. We work well under pressure, though, don't we girl," he chuckles.

"Fuck yeah we do," I respond. "I know we've got this, I just don't like it."

"Understood. Turner ordered all our favorites to the studio. You won't be hangry, and turn into a Gremlin, you'll be the perfect bratty muse," Mav teases me.

Slowly my body is uncoiling from the pressure I was feeling and I blow out a breath in relief.

"We got this Lennon," Atlas murmurs.

The Uber pulls up to the studio and we pile out. It's a pretty brownstone and I feel the rest of the tension bleed from me. I honestly thought she'd have us in a terrible part of town. I don't trust that woman farther than I can throw her.

"Alright fam, let's do this," I yell.

I'm met with cheers of "aye" and "fuck yeah" and I know we'll be fine. Striding to the door, I walk up to the second floor where it says *Crosstown studios*. Knocking on the door, I wait for someone to come answer.

"Yo, need a special invitation, come on in," is what I'm met with instead and I snort in amusement.

The door turns easily and I find the studio is larger than I anticipated. It's half the second floor, airy, and beautiful. "Hello?"

"You found us, I see," says a bear of a man as he stands from his desk.

"Ah, yes. Thanks so much for fitting us in so last minute. We really appreciate it," I tell him with a bright smile.

As shitty as Prescott is for giving us so little notice, I am not taking it out on the man in front of me.

"Seriously, not a problem. Let me walk you back to where you'll be recording. I'm just here to hit record in the booth and make you comfortable. My name is Zach Stewart, and I'm the co-owner here," he says with a bright smile.

"Thanks Zach. That's amazing. We ordered in food and beverages to keep us going, so once that arrives, we will be mostly good to go. Hanger doesn't lead to great music for us, and we try not to unleash it on others." Zach is sweet, and very accommodating. It's nice to find someone not trying to throw our day off.

He ushers us into the room, and the instruments are exactly what we need. I let a genuine smile out. Today is going to be amazing. It will not suck. I refuse to let it.

"Okay boys, shall we take a practice run at *Together We Roar*?" I ask, baring my teeth.

I glance at Derek who is setting up his equipment, and then ignore him. My focus is now the music, how he perceives my lyrics is not my concern.

"Let's do it," rumbles Roark and I stride into the recording booth with the boys. They set themselves up and I glance at Zach.

"We're going to run through it once, just to hear it," I explain. He nods and leans back to listen.

I put on my headphones and count down. The boys nail it as we start. We have practiced this a few times together, but practice and perfection are very different. I let my frustration and anger slip out in my voice, dressing the chorus in darkness as Turner sings with me. This entire week has taken its toll on me, and now I'm ready to unleash it. His voice coils around mine, urging me to join him in the light, where hope lives. My eyes drift shut as the rush of this song pulls me along, away from everyone who has ever hurt me. Away from everyone who should have protected me but didn't, pushing me to rise.

Derek

Lennon O'Reilly's voice is fire, magic, and tragedy all wrapped into one. What the fuck happened to her to be able to sing like this? I take photos as they record, in awe of how they all work seamlessly. I know this is a newer song, but you'd never know it otherwise. Turner and Lennon push and pull as they sing: Lennon's voice is full of anger, while his feels lighter. It feels like acceptance. My eyes prick with tears I don't understand as I listen and blink them away before someone notices.

I don't understand these feelings, or how these people are pulling them from me. I've always loved music, but I've never felt as much as I do when I listen to *The Darkest Nights*. Zach patiently hits record each time they restart, listening carefully to each note, also in awe of how this song builds. After the third run, he nods and hits stop, before grinning at them.

He hits the microphone so they can hear him and says, "This sounds incredible. Unless you have concerns, I think you can break for a bit before heading to the next song. What do you think?"

Lennon sends him an excited smile as she takes off her headphones. "Yeah, it sounded exactly the way I envisioned it that time. I'm good for a break," she says happily.

"I'm starving," Mav murmurs and everyone nods.

"I'll bring you your favorites if you want to keep working on some lyrics, Lenny," Roark says easily.

She rewards him with a giant hug, nodding. "Oh my goodness, please. And coffee?"

He snorts, shaking his head. "I should cut you off, but I know you weren't able to drink your requisite cups of coffee this morning. I'll be right back, beautiful girl."

Roark lumbers off, and I sit just out of sight to go through the photos. I'm not hiding, just processing. My lips part as I catch a picture of Lennon singing, completely immersed in the music. She's talented, and I saw the flak on Instagram she received for my photo posted of her listening to the opening act the other day. Lennon has a true appreciation for all good music, all styles, and I remember a past rumor that her father was a musician. I never cared enough to ask though.

I blink as I realize how much of Lennon's life is caught up in rumors because of how small our town was. No one cared enough to chase down the truth because it was more fun to pull at the threads of the little we did know.

I hear a moan and instantly harden. It can't be anyone else's breathy voice but Lennon.

"Turner, they'll be back soon," she says.

"Mmhmm, so give me a lyric as you grind on my cock, Lavender," Turner growls.

Lavender, that's cute. She didn't always have this light purple hair, but it's easier not to think of *her* now.

"THE WORLD KEEPS SPINNING, *even when it hurts.*
People keep breathing, even as they bleed.
The quiet is deafening, and-"

"OH FUCK," she whimpers, and she's so wet I can hear his fingers sliding through her cream.

"There's a good girl, take my fingers and give me more, baby," he says.

Fuck me, I mouth as my head drops back. I want to pull myself out and stroke my cock as I listen, but it'll be even more awkward if I'm caught. I make sure I can't be seen and tune back in to my new favorite live porn.

"Turner, I can't concentrate," she mewls. I can hear the sound of skin shifting against him as she wiggles.

Smack

She squeals and I smirk. So she does like the odd spanking here and there.

"I can stop what I'm doing if you don't want to play-"

"No, fuck, I wanna come," she whines. "Fine," she groans and I struggle to contain a chuckle. She's such a brat.

"The quiet is deafening but no one can hear your screams.

Don't trust kindness when you've only known cruelty, and everything is upside down."

The sound of a belt coming undone has my eyes widening. Fucking her in the recording studio with his fingers is one thing, but is he going to make her ride his cock?

"Lavender, you always do your best writing when you're bouncing on my cock, come climb onto your throne," he murmurs with a dark chuckle.

He rips off her panties and she laughs. I know the exact moment he pushes inside of her. She's so wet I can hear his cock sliding in. She sighs as she moves until he's completely sheathed inside. I've never been so jealous in my life, and I wish I could see her. I'm clearly not worthy of her, so I'd settle for watching.

"Fuck, your pussy is always so tight, beautiful. It always feels like the first time with you," he groans.

I scowl as I hear this. Lennon was the high school's whore according to my football buddies. There was a pool that was split weekly among those that fucked her, and it was always paid out. He must just be saying this so he can continue to keep getting his dick wet.

Lennon gasps as Turner sucks on her tits. "Uhh, yes, don't stop, baby... please-"

"Please what, baby? You know what you need to do so I'll grind you on my cock. Until then, I'll tease you with my piercings," he chuckles.

My lips twist as he says this. Of course the fucker is pierced. I always thought about it, but never went through with it.

Lennon gasps, and her voice trembles with need as she

continues to string together lyrics. I don't know how she's able to concentrate right now.

"*FUCK the world that's treated you so harshly, baby girl.*
Come join those that understand you.
We know what it's like to be forgotten-"

"TURNER... I... ugh. I can't, please," she screams in frustration and he kisses her hard.

I CAN HEAR the moment he takes control as he fucks her from below. I lean around the wall and can see them through the window into the booth. I don't care about being caught anymore, and clearly they don't either. Turner's corded arm is wrapped around her waist as he fucks her, his other hand tangled in her hair as he controls the kiss.

She's also completely bare. At some point, her clothes must have been thrown off, and she's in her heeled boots. Lennon looks incredible as she writhes, eyes closed as she moans. Her nipples are flushed a dark pink, and there's a tattoo of a vine along her outside thigh that trails up her hip. I've never seen it in any of her outfits, and it looks a lot like Turner's. *Did they get matching tattoos?*

I feel a rush of jealousy as I watch them. Part of me thought she was just a hole for them to fill, but people don't panic the way Roark and Turner did when they found out she was lost. They've actually built something together.

Turner grinds Lennon on him, and there must be a piercing at the base of his cock, because she comes apart beautifully for him. He follows her with a roar, and she collapses onto his chest. I withdraw before they can see me peeping through the damn window.

"You're so perfect for me, Lavender," Turner says as he tries to regulate his breath. "It would have been even better if Roark was filling your pretty mouth too."

He chuckles and Lennon mewls. "I just came, and you're gonna make me a needy mess again. We should recreate my first time one day though. Only I would lose my virginity to two men while writing lyrics," she laughs as my entire world comes to a stop.

She couldn't have been a virgin for them. Travis and Patrick fucked her the second week of her freshman year of high school, and Iris swore she watched them. It's what started the rumors about how easy she was, and I was so pissed at her that I exploited them.

Maybe I was all wrong? Fuck. I creep out of the room like the shitstain that I am, and head to the bathroom. I don't want to run into anyone. Letting myself in, I flick on the light and lock the door. Staring in the mirror, I see my wide brown almost black eyes staring back at me.

I'm drowning in memories, wondering what was real, and how much of a villain I actually am in Lennon O'Reilly's story.

14

TURNER

Lennon is one of the most incredible people that I've ever met. Not only can she create music while riding me, she has the biggest heart, even though it's obvious she's been hurt before. You can't have as much rage when you write as she does if you haven't been. Her anger is palpable, and I feel it gather power as she sings.

I glance over at her as she completes the song we just finished writing together and smirk, knowing my cum is still painting her insides. I will never get enough of her.

"So writing went well I see," Roark murmurs under his breath, humor coloring his voice.

"Mmhmm, the muse is on fire, and filled with inspiration," I tell him absentmindedly, my eyes still on our girl.

He snorts, and I realize what I just said and smirk. Oops. I didn't mean it like that.

"Got it! Ready to hear it?" Lavender looks up with a wide grin.

"Let's hear it," Atlas challenges her. He always pushes her to be her best, and Lennon loves it. I think anyone else would grate on her nerves, but they just mesh. She feeds off his competitive spirit, and uses it to feed the music.

We work on lyrics, practice and record for several more hours until it's time to head back to the stadium. Fuck, Prescott is a twat waffle for scheduling this right before a show. We've all played ball with her, been patient as we worked through the kinks of a new handler, but her lack of professionalism is showing.

"This was amazing," Lavender grins. I swear she's vibrating with energy, and between the coffee and gummy bears, I'm not surprised.

"You're amazing," Mav says, shaking his head. "You were on fire today. I swear, little Valkyrie, you make us better every day. This album... people aren't fucking ready for it."

"Aye, I second that, Lenny. Fuck, I think I need a nap, baby girl. Will you snuggle with me," Roark asks, looking pathetic and pouting.

I roll my lips inwards because I know this is the only way he'll get her to nap before our show. Roark knows exactly how to get Lennon to cater to his needs, the added benefit is it takes care of hers too.

"Is the old man sleepy," she teases, eyes sparkling in mirth. Lennon squeals and laughs as he comes for her. She runs past as he tears after her.

"Old my ass! You better run little girl, cause I'll have you over my knee for that."

I snicker as I shake my head, grabbing her notebooks and packing her bag. I'm not surprised she forgot it again. She rarely takes a bag with her anywhere these days, so the practice of remembering to grab one is now lost.

"Are they always like that?" I hear a soft voice ask.

I glance up and see Derek staring after them in surprise. I'm well aware that Ror, Lavender, and I don't make sense to everyone. We recognized each other's souls the moment we all met. Roark and I were dating when we met Lennon, and she just fit with us.

"Lennon reminds Roark to be silly," I respond. "So she often teases him. She's one of the only people who can." Do I need to explain jack shit to this man? No, but Lennon makes me want to try. "Why are you such a shit to my girl?"

I said it made me want to try, not that I had a personality transplant. I'm not that good of a person, but I'm a work in progress for Lennon.

"What?" he asks, surprised I even asked. And then he blows out a breath and sags against the door. I'm glad he decided to get his head somewhat out of his ass because he knows he's a fuckwit. "Lennon O'Reilly and I have a lot of history together, so I've always been a dick to her. But I'm starting to realize I may have been letting the wrong people influence me. Was she really a virgin when she met you?"

That's a really personal question. I scowl and he holds his hand up. "One of the reasons I was a dick to Lennon surrounds her not being a virgin in high school," he explains. "It doesn't have to make sense, but if that's true, then maybe a lot of the shit I think I know about her isn't."

My forehead scrunches as I think about this and then I shrug. I'll apologize to Lavender for this on the bus. "The only people she's ever had sex with is Roark and I. She had a passing interest in girls we entertained at one point in our relationship, but it wasn't serious. Does that help?"

Derek sighs. "Well fuck. Yeah, it kinda does. The rest I'll figure out, thanks."

He pushes off the wall and walks away and I stare after him. We were the only ones left in the room, but I still feel unsettled. I feel like there's a lot of Lennon's past I don't know. I won't push her for answers, but as soon as we have some kind of break, I'll be asking for them. I can't protect her as well if I'm in the dark.

I check the room and find I've picked up everything we came in with. I walk out with her bag and find Zach cleaning up the break room.

"Hey, we didn't mean to leave you with that," I tell him with a sigh.

He shakes his head with a smile. "You're on a ridiculously tight schedule. You weren't messy at all. This is an easy clean up for me, and you put down some insane tracks today. I can't believe I was a part of it in any way, so I don't mind it at all. Your label had me upload it and send it to them already, so there's nothing else you need to worry about today," he says with a smile.

"Thank you. Today started off weird, but this was a really great experience. You have a card? I'll rec' you to the label in case there are other bands in the area needing studio time," I tell him.

"Now that I'll take you up on," he grins and hands me a card.

"Cool, thanks man."

I walk out of the studio and find Roark has already called transport and is waiting for me with a grin.

"To fucking amazing music being made today and naps," I cheer.

Lennon and the guys cheer while Derek gives us a small smile. This man really is wound too tight. He has a certain charm and I think he's been a little fucked up by his own demons. Now that I've gotten past some of my own anger at him, I can recognize some of the signs: the defensiveness, the anger he exhibits towards Lennon, and the shadows in his eyes. It makes me want to dig a little more.

I wonder if Roark and I should tag team him. Oh shit! I

really didn't mean it in a dirty way, but now I'm hard as fucking stone thinking about taking his bratty mouth while Ror takes his ass. Derek is built like a linebacker, all hard muscles. I wonder if he has that stupid hot pelvic V too.

Fuck. I discreetly adjust myself behind Lavender as I kiss her neck. These aren't images I currently need to be having played rent free in my head right now.

"You were incredible today, but we need to talk soon," I growl into her ear. She shivers and nods as the Uber arrives. If Lennon thinks all the rage she expelled while songwriting went unnoticed, she's dead wrong. "Promise me."

She takes a shaky breath and whispers, "I promise, Sir."

Minx. My hand clenches into a fist as my lip twitches. Lavender enjoys pushing me, and I wouldn't have it any other way, but damn is this ride going to be uncomfortable. My chest rumbles in a frustrated growl and she has the nerve to giggle as she climbs in the Uber.

"Sounds like our girl is having a bit of fun with you," Roark chuckles as he gets into the car behind me.

"Isn't she always though," I snort, settling back for a difficult ride back to the bus.

I'M in the middle of the best snuggle pile ever. Lavender's back is against me, and I resist the urge to grind on her luscious ass. Roark's arm is thrown over both of us as he sleeps.

I bury my face in her hair, breathing deeply. The other reason I call her my Lavender is because she always smells like lavender and vanilla. My body slowly relaxes again and I can't tell you what woke me up. We've been napping for the last hour, and we seriously needed it.

Roark and I gladly gave up our pre-performance rituals to

sleep off our recording hangover. We worked so hard today, my brain is numb from throwing down. Prescott is an idiot for goading us into today. Fuck, we are too for letting her.

"Baby, you're thinking too hard," Roark sighs behind me.

"I hate Prescott," I mumble sleepily into Lennon's hair.

He chuckles and it rumbles through my body. I smile in return, because his amusement always sparks my own. "That's awfully random. Do you wanna do something about it, or go back to sleep?"

Ooh, Roark is in revenge mode. Fuck yeah. "What are you thinking? Whatever it is, I'm in," I tell him as I turn his way.

"I expect Jordan Miles will check in with Lenny soon, and she can tell him how Prescott has been treating us. She has a way of getting her feelings across without being whiny when she wants to," Ror says with a sly smile. "Jordan Miles also seems to have a soft spot for our girl."

I nod. "Agreed, I just don't know if she will," I sigh. "She's so used to just taking shit, she won't speak up about it. We'll have to see-"

Lavender takes a deep breath before she sighs as she stirs.

"Fuck," I whisper. "What time is it?"

"It's seven-thirty," he sighs. "Can you start waking her up, and I'll make something to eat before we play."

"Okay," I murmur and he lopes off to the kitchen. Our schedule is definitely fucked, but we need to eat something.

"Baby," I say as I kiss her shoulder, knowing she's slowly starting to wake up on her own as her breathing changes. "Do you want to grab a shower first? It'll help you wake up."

"Is this your nice way of saying I smell," she asks with a smile. Her eyes are scrunched up and she's refusing to open them. *Yeah... a shower is necessary.*

"No, brat," I laugh as I tear off the covers and scoop her into my arms, causing her to squeal. "But I know you need a shower to clear the cobwebs and then some food that isn't a gummy bear."

"Why do you enjoy hating on gummy bears so much?" she whines.

"Because," I huff as I walk with her in my arms towards the showers. "You would try to exist on gummies alone if you could and make it an important food group in the pyramid."

I deposit her in front of the bathroom and smack her ass. "Scoot. Do whatever you need to do so you're ready. It's seven-thirty and you'll miss the entire opening act if you don't move your ass."

Her jaw drops scandalized and she dashes into the bathroom. Called that shit. She hates missing any bands that open for us.

I head to the kitchen with a smile and grab a bottle of water. "She's in the shower now, you need help with anything?"

"No, no. It's nothing fancy, but I know she was craving a rice bowl the other day. We had frozen chicken, I grabbed a can of black beans, and some microwaveable rice. I threw it all together with some seasoning, made a simple sauce, and it should be ready in a few minutes," he says happily.

"Holy shit. I've never met anyone who can cook with such few ingredients and turn it into a gourmet meal. Lennon is going to flip. This is awesome," I tell him incredulously.

He shrugs. "I can get by without much, but Lennon needs something in her belly before she sings her heart out there. So that's what she'll get."

The food simmers as Lavender finishes her shower and bangs out of the bathroom. I smirk as I hear her opening and closing compartments in our bedroom. "You doing okay in there," I tease her.

"Yeah, yeah... just bloody fine," I hear and Ror and I snort.

"Oh she's in fine spirits," he mutters, his lips twitching.

"She like a gremlin, she got wet and now she's-"

I can't even finish my sentence because he and I fall into each other laughing.

"Whatever you're saying, you suck," she yells petulantly and I guffaw.

I walk to the doorway of our room and see she's in leather pants, and a purple crop top that shows off her toned belly. Lennon is methodically curling her hair as she mutters to herself.

"Stop grumbling and warm up, little girl," I command, more to see what she'll do. She doesn't disappoint as I watch her reflection roll her eyes..

I grab my guitar and strum a chord. A keyboard would be better to run a scale, but my girl just needs to hear a proper note and she's off and running. She sits up, pushes back her shoulders to open up her chest, takes a deep breath... and lets loose.

My own stress levels over this day continue to dissipate as I listen to her. I don't know if I'll be singing much tonight, because we didn't run a set list beforehand, so I join her mid-through in my own lower octave. Lennon continues to curl her hair as she runs scales, winding and releasing as she moves through them.

Soon we're warmed up, and she pulls the front of her hair back and braids the top before winding a silver hair vine through it. The effect makes her look regal, even in the leather. She then uses different shades of purple shadows to do her eyes. I don't know much about makeup, but the play of dark and light colors makes her look like a dark enchantress. She is definitely bringing out the big guns tonight and I frown as I realize I need to change.

I compliment her beauty with low slung ripped up jeans, black mesh tank top, and combat boots. I snag one of her eye liners and quickly line my eyes. I pick and choose the nights I wear makeup, but it's a whole vibe when I do.

"'Mmm, you look amazing," Lavender compliments, opening her mouth to line her lips and then add a dark maroon shade to it.

"No you do," I counter, dumbfounded by how beautiful she is.

"No take backs," she says, being silly. She slides vine earrings into her ears and I start to understand her theme. I've always thought vines were strong. They grow where you least expect them, and they're a pain in the ass to rip out once they gain roots.

Vines are also beautiful as fuck as they blossom. They've always held a special place for us, which is why we all have a vine tattooed somewhere on our bodies. I have them twining around my fingers before they crawl up my arms, with a few purple blooms. Lennon's name is on one of the petals. It isn't noticeable unless you're really close, and only Lennon or Roark ever are.

Lennon has her vine crawling on the outside of her thigh and up her hip. It's gorgeous, with small purple and red flowers, a part of Roark and I hidden within. It also hides small scars that she doesn't talk about. It's never seen unless she's in a bikini, and those moments are private. The only people outside of Roark and I who have seen her in a bikini are Mav and Atlas, and they see her as a sibling anyways. Roark has one tattoo funny enough, and it's on his wrist. It's intricate, and circles around it.

Roark is six-four and muscular, so his arms are a thing of beauty. There are days I feel small next to him, and I'm only two inches shorter. Therefore, his tattoo is a statement since it's the only one he has. He doesn't answer questions about it, and he refuses to entertain them. He simply smiles and says the secret gives him an air of mystery. The media loves him, and backed off asking about it.

In truth, the vine looks like a cuff, thick and lush with leaves. There's a single red flower that blooms, and there isn't a name on it. He told me one night when he was drunk off his ass those nights are much fewer now–that he was reserving the rose for the person he married. Roark was very vague about this statement and he never mentioned it again. The rose is definitely large enough for two names, and I smirk. I like the idea of my name sitting beside Lennon's on his wrist.

"Come eat, darlin'," I say with a smile.

She nods, giving herself a hard stare before rising to head to the kitchen. I trail after her, enjoying how her ass bounces as her hips swing. She's a fucking vision, and I can't wait to undress her later tonight.

"Roark, this smells amazing," she says with a genuine smile. If she gets too hungry, Lennon gets grouchy. It's why we try to keep snacks around for her.

We eat together before Roark disappears to get dressed. He comes out in ripped jeans, a black tank top that strains across his shoulders, and combat boots. Ror has a leather cuff on the wrist opposite his tattoo, his hair is in messy waves that my fingers itch to play in, and I swear my cock twitches with need.

This show is gonna be hell, I can already tell. Fuck it, I'll lust after them both all night, my playing will show off the edge I'll be riding tonight.

We're ready to go, but first I have to tell her something. Shit. I chew my lip as I turn to her. "We don't have a lot of time, but I want to tell you about something that happened at the recording studio with Derek today. I'm a little worried you'll be mad," I sigh.

Lavender's head tilts in the cutest way as she shakes her

head in confusion. "What could I possibly be angry about, Turner?"

I love that she has so much faith in me. "Derek asked me something at the studio, and I was so surprised by it, I answered. He said he thought you slept around in high school, and even if you did, it's your body and slut shaming is gross but-"

"But I didn't," she says with a shrug. "You both know I was a virgin when you met me, but no one knew I was back home. I was worried it would bring me even more unwanted attention, as if it was a prize to win. High school was a rough and pretty unsafe place for me, especially with Derek leading the pack of popular kids. Things were already bad within the first few weeks of my freshman year, and I could barely go anywhere without some stupid jock trying to pull me under the bleachers or into an empty classroom. Everyone thought I was a whore, so I let them believe it."

"Fuck," Roark mutters. "I really want to hit things now."

"You have the drums you can hit tonight," I soothe. "Lennon, he asked me if you were a virgin when we met, and he said it was important for him to know even if it was presumptuous as fuck for him to ask. So, I told him the truth, because I think a lot of the things he bullied you about were over dumb shit that wasn't true. Derek needs to let go of all that, because ten years is a fucking long time to hold onto grudges."

Lennon scrunches her nose, and being unable to help myself, I lean forward to kiss it. "Why would he care if I was a virgin or not?" she asks with a sigh, sounding weary already of the conversation. I hate that I brought this up now, when she's already had such a full day. She wraps her arms around stomach as if to protect herself as she thinks. "Guys, I don't understand. Derek is the one who set up the football team's bet to see who would be the first one to sleep with me. I didn't know until later when I heard the cheerleaders talking about it, but I could never trust anyone at my school after the bet was made. A lot of fucked up shit went down that I don't have time to go into, but Farrelsville is not a nice town. As soon as I could get out, I did." She shivers as she says this, and I suddenly want to burn the town she grew up in to the ground. I need a list with names and addresses of people to fuck up. Lennon was a kid, and didn't deserve any of this.

Lennon is definitely too good to deal with this shit. "Did I make a mistake telling him?" I ask, suddenly feeling even more shitty.

Her eyes had drifted to stare down at the table, but fly back up to me as I say this. "No," she says, shaking her head violently. "If it's really as big of a deal as you're saying it is, then I don't think it was a mistake. My virginity is not any of his business, but it sounds like a lot of his shit is wrapped up around if I was or not. At some point, I need to hash this out with him, and hopefully knowing the truth about my virginity will chill out his dickishness."

I snort at her choice in words. "Are we making up new words today, Lavender," I tease.

She looks smug as she smirks. "Yes, feel free to sprinkle that shit around like confetti."

Roark pulls her up from the table and gently pushes her towards the door. "Let's go before you miss the entire opening act. It's been awhile since I've enjoyed watching you dance in the wings of a show, and I suddenly find myself needing to see it."

I smile, knowing exactly what he means. Everything she does is without guile, even when she's a brat, she's not manipulative about it. Lavender lives in the moment, soaking life in, and it's a joy to witness it.

Content she isn't upset with me, I follow them out. Today may have started a little stressful, but at least I'm spending it with my people.

Lennon

Roark turns me as I dance in the wings of the stage with him. I giggle as he pulls me into him, moving with me to the music. As tall as he is, Ror easily bends his knees to be closer to my height, knowing when to turn me and when to hold me close. This opening act is so amazing, I couldn't stay still, and Roark is always an amazing dance partner. I need to make it a habit to dance more often with him.

Turner watches indulgently with a lazy grin, his fingers twitching to the music. Tonight the three of us are riding so many emotions as we process the day. Frustration with Prescott, who's currently MIA, confusion as to why my virginity matters to Derek, and the aftermath of a recording hangover. I managed to snag some gummy bears before I left the bus, and the sugar is helping me from feeling too tired. The emotional rollercoaster is something I could have done without, but we know how to fuel our music with what we're feeling.

I am catching the second half of this act, but I'm so happy I made it. Their lyrics are sarcastic, the lead guitarist incredible, and their lead singer's voice is a deep contralto. I think I'd enjoy listening to her order coffee at this rate.

Velvet Escape's set ends, and they walk off the stage, passing us as they do. I cheer for them, because I do every band that plays for us. I don't care if it seems odd, but it takes guts to open for a well known band, knowing the audience probably isn't there for you. It also costs nothing for me to be supportive.

"Woah, you're actually for real," one of them says, amused.

"I think you sounded amazing out there and I wanted to

tell you. Take it as you will, but your lead singer is absolute perfection. I loved listening to you tonight," I tell them, refusing to take his tone to heart. I'm determined to be a happy unicorn tonight, regardless of the attitudes of those around me.

"Albert, stop, she's being serious," the lead singer says as she pushes past him. I smile brightly at her, though it's a little less shiny than before. Turner growls beside me, and I know he noticed. "I'm Layla, and I really appreciate your sweet words," she says with an answering smile. "Ignore Albert, I do."

I snort and her smile widens. "I just believe in telling it like it is," I sigh with a shrug. "I'll always remember getting on stage and not knowing if we'd get booed off or cheered for. This is a different arena and they wouldn't do that, but it still takes moxie to perform the way you did." All of a sudden I feel super emotional and I push it away. I won't let a bully fuck up my night, despite being low on armor. I'm always a little more sensitive after a long day.

I step away, turning my back on them, no longer in the mood to be friendly.

"Hey wait," Layla says, but I'm done.

I struggle to push my shoulders down from where they're hitched around my ears, forcing myself to relax my jaw, and stretching my neck. The tears starting to prick behind my eyelids just piss me off, and I widen my eyes, willing them to dry. I understand few people in this industry are kind just because and it's weird for them, but I refuse to lash out. I also refuse to cry over such a little thing when I've survived much worse. This may seem like an overreaction to some, but I'm tired of getting back up each time I'm swatted down. Derek being here is bringing up shitty memories I never bothered to deal with, because I ran and never stopped.

"Hey you good, or do I need to fuck someone up," Turner

asks and my lip twitches. I'm half tempted to let him, but it's not Albert's fault I'm having a rough week.

"I will be good," I promise him before I feel his warmth behind me. Muscled arms wrap around me and I relax against his chest.

I hear raised voices behind me, but whatever it is, doesn't matter. Turner is my happy place, my safe space, and he's my port in the storm. Nothing else matters right now but him and the show. The roadies are changing out the equipment on stage and Turner gently sways me back and forth to a tune he can only hear. He doesn't often dance, but he always has music playing in his head.

"If you could sing one song tonight, what would it be, Lavender?" he asks softly. It gives the appearance that we exist in our own bubble, where the bullshit stays out, and it's just us. I take a calming breath, my tears drying before they fall and I smile.

"Easy choice. *Rising Stars* hands down," I tell him.

"Fuck yeah, tonight's a good night for it," he growls and I shiver. His growl speaks of promises, safety, heat, and future orgasms. I'm so in.

"Can I just talk to her," I hear burst in through my bubble, making me begin to turn.

"No time for fuckery, darlin girl, it's showtime. If it's important, it'll still be there later. Roark will make sure of it," Turner promises, pressing gently on the base of my spine.

Knowing he's right, I walk forward as the lights go completely dark on stage. Trusting the hand guiding me forward, I walk confidently. Everything else falls away, the stress of this week doesn't matter, and questions I have over who drugged me don't matter. I concentrate on the swing of my hips as my heels hit the ground, the smell of the slightly stale recycled air on stage with a hint of sweat, and the roar of the crowd. My lips curve into a savage smile as the adrenaline of anticipation starts to hit my blood. This is a high I'll gladly chase.

Turner squeezes my hip, signaling we are at my mic. His eyesight has always acclimated faster than mine, and I made the mistake of looking out at the stage before the lights went completely out. I'm slightly off my game, but I'm ready to slide seamlessly into my role. I grab the mic and take a deep breath before the lights switch on, and my smile splits my face as I pull it out to greet the crowd.

"Hey San Francisco, wasn't *Velvet Escape* incredible tonight?" I yell into the crowd. I can be petty too by killing people with kindness. I couldn't give two shits what those people think of me anymore, I can keep it classy. "I hope you're ready for us tonight, because we have been looking forward to playing for you all fucking day." I internally wince, because I rarely curse outside of lyrics while I'm on stage and then shrug as the crowd screams in excitement.

I glance behind me at the faces of my band members. Turner's eyebrow raises as he hides a smile behind long fingers, Mav outright roars in laughter, and Atlas shrugs it off. Roark winks at me and I nod as I tell them what song to start off with.

"This song, loves," I say as I turn back to the crowd, "is a melody that I need to sing tonight. I'm driven by my moods when I listen to music, much like anyone else. Am I right," I ask indulgently as I hear 'hell yes!' in the crowd.

I step back and music surrounds me. I feel the room swim for a moment and I dig my nails into my hand to focus. *I ate, why am I feeling like this*? I push past it, widening my stance to feel more secure: I'm not fucking falling on my own damn stage.

Thank goodness it's a longer instrumental opening, and I hit my part perfectly. Every annoyance, angry word spoken to me by Prescott or Derek... it all pushes out into this song. I'm no longer the girl who cries in the dark because her mom fucked off for the week and left without stocking the fridge. I'm no longer the person who has to stay small so people ignore her. I'm Lennon O'Fucking'Reilly, and I have people who love me, and music to keep me sane.

I used to cut myself to feel this weightlessness, but I haven't in a long time. It's my private secret, and I covered it as soon as I could by the trailing vine on the outside of my leg and hip. Roark and Turner have never made a big deal about it, never asked, but I have a feeling they may soon. Roark asked me to marry him for fuck's sake.

The song ends and my mood needs to improve. I switch gears and prep the guys for the next one. It's a duet with Turner, which I know he can handle because we warmed up together. I need to sing a song about love, stare into his eyes, and know that it's all worth it.

Not too much to ask for right?

15

LENNON

I still feel shaky and off when we step from the stage. Usually I feel energized and excited, but today I just feel weird. Turning to find Roark, I see the girl from the band that played earlier. I can't remember her name or that of the band right now, and my head is starting to pound. She walks over to me, and I know instantly I can't talk to her. My meter of niceness is empty currently.

I don't know why I can't find the guys, they were right behind me. I feel confused and just *wrong*.

"Little Valkyrie, you okay?"

I turn quickly and see Mav. I shake my head, and his face turns thunderous. He doesn't know why I don't feel well, but he's out for blood. He scoops me up and I lay my head on his shoulder.

"The room is swimming, and I feel shaky. I just don't feel right, Mav," I say softly.

"Did you drink anything from anyone," he asks harshly and I don't even flinch because he's smart to ask.

"Nuh-uh, but water would be nice. Where are the guys," I ask, coughing as my throat feels really dry all of a sudden.

"Ror, Turner, get your arses over here," Mav yells, and I love his face even more. He knew exactly who I meant.

Talking less sounds great right now, and mind readers are cool. I feel disjointed, my head is killing me, and I'd really love to know why.

"Lenny, what's wrong, my girl," Roark growls and I moan softly.

"When I was on stage, I started to feel off and now it's worse. Maybe I just did too much today," I ask, confused. "I'm not dehydrated, I drank my water and got my good girl stars," I snark.

Turner snorts in amusement. "You're adorable even when you don't feel well darlin."

"Meh, I feel like I'm mean and petty, so agree to disagree."

"We have a schedule to keep, can the princess not walk today?" I hear a nasally voice say and I swallow a whimper. I so can't deal with Prescott right now.

"The princess," Mav stresses, "had a long ass day in the studio, and will not be addressing her subjects. The rest of us will be greeting the VIP guests, but Lennon's out."

"She's the one who wanted the studio time, she should be able to suck it up. How hard is it to record and then come perform?"

"Wait, you can't be serious," says a voice. "You're shitting me right? No wonder she doesn't feel good. There's no way y'all should be recording and performing on the same day." Prescott's nose wrinkles as if she's smelling something foul and as she turns, I see it's the girl from earlier.

She has light brown hair, a tattoo on her shoulder, and I still can't fucking remember her name. The girl seems young, and I swear I can see steam coming out of her ears with how angry she is. I vaguely wonder how old she is. Dammit, I really don't feel great. I growl under my breath, and Mav decides to get moving.

"Thanks for the sentiment, girlie, but we weren't really given a choice. Turner, grab our girl some water, would you, and gummy bears. I have a feeling her sugar is a wee bit low," Mav says as he starts walking towards the VIP room. I don't know why he is, but I decide to just go with it. "And Roark, can you grab a seat please, as Lennon will be sitting her ass in a chair until we're done."

Roark grunts and heads off as well, while Prescott screeches about how unprofessional I'm being. *Yes, because I chose to push myself too hard.*

"Dying cats would sound better than whatever Prescott is doing," I mutter under my breath, but Mav still hears me and chuckles.

"You're so right. We are gonna have to do something about her. The girl has gotta go," he murmurs.

"Yes please," I sigh. My skin feels like it's too tight and I feel warm. I feel too tired yet too hyper all at the same time. *What the fuck is wrong with me?*

A whisper of fear threads through my veins as I think about my mother. Did she have any of these symptoms before she descended into her mania? Am I becoming her?

"Eyes on me, Lenny. What's going through that pretty little head of yours," Roark asks gruffly as he sets a chair down next to the door. Mav gently sets me in it and crouches next to me as he cracks open the bottle of water Turner hands him.

"I... Something is wrong. I feel hyper and tired, but that doesn't make sense. It makes me try to remember what my mother was like when she wasn't herself," I tell him, speaking carefully because we aren't alone.

"That's not what this is," says a deep voice and I look up to see the most unlikely person. Derek is looking at me like he actually gives a shit.

I clear my throat, realizing how dry it is and look back at Mav to grab the now opened bottle from him. Taking a sip, I wrinkle my nose at Derek. I don't think I have it in me to be nice, and frankly he can fuck off.

"Go away please," I say instead, closing my eyes against the lights that now feel too bright.

"Listen, Lennon. Just for one fucking second. We aren't each other's favorite people, and that's fine. I just think you're exhausted and burned out, and you're experiencing the effects of it. Nothing nefarious, no jokes, my asshole is checked at the door," he says earnestly.

I say back his last words in my head and giggle as I open my eyes to stare at him in surprise. *Did he really just say that?*

The giggle helps release some of the tightness that started to settle in my chest, and allows me to take a deep breath. "Yeah, today was busy, and I wouldn't usually push myself this hard. I couldn't really help it this time though. It wasn't my call," I explain with a sigh.

"Yeah," he drawls, his brows knitting together, "if you were mine, that's something we would be talking about. This tour's pace is insane."

I can't handle this Derek, because I've never seen him before. I've only dealt with the asshole who made bets about my vagina, commanded the cheer team to stalk me, and laughed every time I was slammed into the lockers. The Derek who still taunts me with the threat of turning out just like my mother. And, if I was his? At this moment in time, there's no way that would ever happen. He has too much to make up for.

"Who are you," I ask, shaking my head. "Have you been kidnapped and turned into a pod person?"

Derek snorts and Turner rolls his eyes. "There's my Lenny.

If you can joke, I know you're not gonna be keeling over on me," Ror sighs gratefully. "Please don't go anywhere, okay? The boys and I will be back right quick, we won't be lollygagging tonight, no matter what the Prescott bitch wants. Also, as much of a fuckwit as he is, Derek the Dick is not wrong. We will be having words with the label about our pace lately, understand?"

"Yes, Daddy," I say without thinking and then my eyes widen and Roark and Turner roar with laughter as Atlas and Mav shake their heads in mirth.

They step away and walk into the VIP room while I sit outside it. Derek follows after giving me a hard stare. I know he wants to say more, but I petulantly kick my feet out and cross them at my ankles before slouching back as I drink more water. I know he'll be back to be a pest again, because the man is stubborn about everything, but I don't care. My ears are slightly ringing and my eyes are buzzing. I didn't even know they could do that, but I swear mine are.

My thoughts drift as I try to figure out why I feel like this, and I wish I had my phone so I could google my symptoms.

"Hey Layla, just leave the girl alone, would ya," I hear and I glance up with a startled breath.

She pushes past the guy who was a dick to me and walks up to me.

"Look, I'm sorry to bother you, but I really want to make sure you are okay. It's totally none of my business, but Albert was a dick to you and you didn't deserve it. We aren't used to meeting nice people in the music industry, and he reacted badly. So are you?" she asks and I can't track what she's asking about as she bounces from topic to topic.

"Am I what," I ask slowly, feeling super dumb right now. My brain is moving way slower than normal and I sigh as I lift the cold bottle to my face. It helps to jar me out of my stupor a little.

"Are you okay?" she asks, blowing out a breath impatiently and I giggle at how cute she is. Layla's hair is done in big ringlets to frame her face, which makes her look even tinier than she is. Her blue eyes are wide as she stares at me worriedly and I give her a small smile.

"Honestly, not in the slightest, but I'm sure I'll get there," I tell her, not bothering to explain. My head is starting to hurt more than before and I wince slightly. *Okay body, I hear you. I'm not superwoman. Check.*

Layla's lips twist to the side and she sits on the floor in front of me. I raise my eyebrow in surprise, wondering what she's about. I don't mean to be paranoid, but I've already been drugged once this week. I don't need to add another traumatic experience to the weekly tally.

"I get the feeling your band members didn't really want to leave you alone, so I'm going to sit right here. I don't care if you don't say a word to me, but you don't look so hot. I mean, don't get me wrong, you're gorgeous with all that purple hair. You look flushed but sick somehow. How the fuck did you record and come here and bang out a performance the way you did?!" She doesn't take a breath as she talks and I blink at her.

She apparently doesn't know the meaning of quiet. I'm going to have to speak to her, or she's going to clobber me with her words. Fuck my life. *Don't be a dick.*

I take a deep breath as I lean my head on the cool bottle. Somehow, it helps how warm I feel. "Our manager is kind of a twatapotamus," I tell her with a straight face as she snorts. "She thinks the best way to control us is to make things as hard as possible, and I pushed a little too hard today. I recorded four songs today with the guys, and wrote three of them while I was there." My face warms a little as I remember exactly how I wrote one of them with Turner, but I'm not ashamed. Instead I'm very horny.

I uncross my ankles and cross my legs, struggling not to rub my thighs together. *Ugh, what are the chances Turner or Ror will give me orgasms?* If they're too worried about me, they may deny me. Shit.

"Wait a damn minute. You wrote three fucking songs today?! How, I'm sorry that's not normal. You are a mother-fucking machine," Layla says incredulously.

"Layla, are you talking this girl's ear off," a man asks in ripped jeans as he walks over to us. The sides of his head are shaved and it's styled in a faux mohawk. I semi recognize him as the band's drummer, but she's not bothering me, and it's nice to talk to someone outside of the boys.

Not having a girlfriend can get a little lonely.

I smile wanly at the man who is now looming over us nervously. "She's fine. She was worried I overdid it a wee bit tonight," I drawl, picking up some of Roark's accident without meaning to. I'm really tired, and I've always had issues pulling in the accents of those I'm with the most, since I don't have one at all.

"You're the girl who was cheering for us," the man says surprised. "I watched you for a bit tonight. You're kind of amazing," he says grudgingly.

"Thank you. Unfortunately you caught me on a slightly off night," I explain, starting to feel really exhausted. I lean forward to brace my elbows on my lap before cradling my head in my hands. "Hmm," I moan, rubbing my temples. "Gah, I feel like shit. I really hope the boys are done soon."

"Are you sick or something," the man asks worriedly. I realize I don't know his name, never thought to ask, and berate myself in my head for being so rude.

"She recorded four freaking songs today and then performed an incredible set, Leo. She's exhausted, and it's disgusting that her manager isn't watching out for her because she's a... what did you call her, Lennon?" Layla asks with a small thread of amusement in her voice.

"A twatapotamus," I groan.

"What's going on here?" asks a voice that sounds strangely like Derek.

My eyes had closed on their own because they hurt so much and I squint up at him from behind my hands. Yep, it's him.

"I'm being a good girl and surviving until the guys come back," I sass.

Derek snorts. "Honey, you couldn't be good if it bit you in the ass. Why are you all hunched like that?"

My eyes drift closed as I feel a stabbing pain behind my eyes. "Hurts," I whimper. "Light bad. Talking bad. It's all fucked."

Derek growls under his breath. "I'm gonna fucking kill Prescott."

"I thought you were secretly fucking the twatapotamus," I ask because I kind of want to know and I have lost my filter. I don't have any fucks left.

They all flew away when I hit my wall of exhaustion.

"Oooh, this is getting good," I hear Layla say under her breath and I swear if my brain didn't have little people drilling holes in it, I'd think she was adorable.

Sadly, I don't get to gab with her because my entire world is slowly constricting to a small pinpoint of pain.

"Lennon, why is it any of your business who I—ewww. Prescott is the twatapotamus? Nope, definitely not fucking her. I have much better taste in women, thank you very much," Derek grouses.

I smile tightly through my pain. I love that I was able to get a straight answer out of him, even though his knee jerk reaction was to be a dick.

"I don't care where you stick your fuckstick, Derek," I insist. I kind of care to be honest, but I am going to be a brat and die on this hill. "Someone as unhappy as Prescott has to have some serious issues. A UTI, herpes, hemorrhoids, the list could go on for ages, but I don't have the energy," I chuckle softly.

"God, when did you get to be such a brat," he groans.

"My girl has always been a brat," Roark says and I smile a little larger. *Finally, I get to go home. Maybe he'll carry me.* "You don't know Lenny any more, and I doubt you ever did. It's up to her if she decides that'll change, but for now, it's time to go home."

"Yay," I cheer softly, slowly sitting up and carefully opening my eyes.

Roark stares at me intently, lips pressed together angrily. If it was anyone else, or before I really knew him, I would think he was mad at me. I know better though, and I know he's pissed at the situation.

"Little girl, I am very unhappy with the state I'm finding you in," he growls.

"Wait, are you mad because she doesn't feel good," Layla asks, jumping to her feet. She however does not know Roark. Shit, there's about to be a tiny chihuahua nipping at Ror.

"Ummm, why do I feel like there's a story here, Lenny? You know what, fuck it. You don't feel good, you don't have to explain. You, whoever you are, your little boy band person was very rude to my girl. Just because you sing well doesn't mean you get to be assholes," he growls and I sigh. That went exactly as well as I thought it would.

"Roark, Layla. Take it down a notch friends," I shout, but it's not a shout, it's a whisper. I feel myself start to slide to the right and know I'm going to hit the ground hard.

"Shit," mutters Leo, who is closest to me as I throw up my hands to catch myself with a yelp. He walks forward quickly and scoops me into his arms. "For the record, this is completely platonic, girlie. I figured you'd rather not fall on your ass."

"Good instincts," I croak, still surprised.

"Please don't punch me," Leo says tiredly. "Layla is like a dog with a bone when she gets excited, and she's apparently decided to be very protective of your girl... *Lenny* you said?"

"Only I call her that," Ror says begrudgingly. "You can call her Lennon," he sighs. "Are you okay, love?"

"Yeah, I just wanna lie down though, if you don't mind."

"Whatever you want, darlin'," Turner agrees, before turning to the other band. "Look, I'm rarely the peacekeeper, so cherish this moment. Lennon needs to relax, if you want to come talk while we take care of her, I'm okay with it. But you will be *nice* to her. It's been a really fucking long week, especially for her, and she's one of the best goddamn people I know. Also, you'll have to leave your phones in a basket at the front door of the bus. If that's an issue, you're welcome to fuck off."

Turner nods at Leo and jerks his head to signal they walk.

"Wait, why do we have to surrender our phones-" Albert starts to ask.

"Shut up and do it, Albert," Layla yells exasperatedly at him.

I would high-five her if I didn't feel like such shit. Thankfully we don't run into Prescott, because I wouldn't be able to curb my tongue. We escape the stadium as if we were being chased by demons, but honestly that's the kind of day today was.

We created incredible music, but it would have been nice to have more time in between.

Leo is very careful as he carries me, making sure not to jostle me, and super respectful about where his hands are. I saw the daggers the guys are sending his way, but it would have hurt my head more to move me into someone else's arms. I need pain relievers stat.

Turner unlocks the bus and we all pile in, *Velvet Escape* making sure to drop their electronics in a basket at the front door. I doubt they'd record us and sell the information, but our privacy is really important to us. I don't want the media to get wind that there may be disharmony between us and *Music Horde Records* before I can address what happened today with them. I need my phone so I can talk to Mr. Miles.

Leo puts me down in my cloud of pillows on my side of the couch as directed by Turner. Roark grabs drinks, water for me, and pain relievers for my head. I gratefully take it and swallow the pills.

"I can get up if I need to but-"

"No," says everyone in the room and my eyes widen.

"Okay moms and dads. Can someone grab me my phone then since I'm relegated to the couch to grow roots," I snark.

Albert snorts, shaking his head. "I thought you shit rainbows and sunshine," he mocks. "It's nice to see the princess isn't all about unicorns."

If I hadn't glanced over when I did I would have missed Derek smacking him over the head.

"Good man," Mav says approvingly. "Maybe you're not such a dick. We've had a disgustingly long day, and I don't think any of us have the energy to deal with churlish behavior."

"Unless it comes from me," I say with a wide smile. My head is starting to feel better and I can feel my body start to relax slowly.

I hadn't noticed Roark leaving the room until he hands me the phone. "It was ringing when I grabbed it, love. Mr. Miles is waiting for you."

My eyes widen and I mouth *'like right now on the phone?!"*

Roark nods sagely. "The very one, love. Now don't make the man wait."

I take a deep breath, and for some reason my hand shakes a little as I bring the phone to my ear. I had planned to call him, but not right at this second.

"Hello, Mr. Miles. What can I do for you," I ask with hardly a tremor in my voice. One of the things he's always liked about me is that I treat him like a normal person. I don't know why I'm so nervous right now, it's not like I've done anything wrong.

"I understand you didn't participate in the VIP meet and greet tonight, Miss O'Reilly. Care to tell me why?"

Fuck. I wonder if there were posts on social media or if the twatapotamus told him. *May as well be honest.* Bye filter.

"I would love to," I tell him, sitting a little straighter. "I almost passed out from exhaustion tonight, Sir, because Prescott Jones thought it would be a good idea to schedule a recording session today. We recorded four songs, and I wrote three of them in studio. You may be used to that level of commitment from me, and expect it. However, I have never had to perform right after recording tracks, and Prescott insisted on it."

The breathing on the other end of the line changes, and I bite my lip. I glance around the room, and see pride in the faces of my band mates. Layla and her guys look on in awe. I'm taking no prisoners today, and as I said earlier, my fucks are gone.

"We have been keeping a really intense pace on this tour, with only a few days off. We acclimated to this change well, however my water bottle was drugged a couple of days ago, and I had to recover from that, too Sir," I continue. He sputters in surprise, and I hum. "Oh no, Sir. You asked, you'll get your full answer. Frankly, what you're asking for is inhumane, and you're about to have very burned out, unhappy performers if you continue to have us work like this. We *want* to create new music, I asked for studio time, but not the same day we perform!"

My voice raised without my meaning to and I sigh. Shit. I really am off my game.

"May I interject now, Lennon, or do you want to continue to detail your grievances? Which, apparently you have quite a few, and they seem well warranted. What the hell has been happening on this tour?" Mr. Miles growls.

"It wasn't my intention to raise my voice, Sir," I start to explain.

"Meh, fucking yell. I couldn't give two shits if you do, Lennon. You're one of the few people that aren't afraid of me, and we've talked about how much I enjoy that. I didn't know things were this bad, what the fuck is Prescott doing?" he asks.

"Being a twatapotamus," I blurt. Ugh not the best time to have this talk when my filter has left the building. He coughs out a surprised laugh and I continue, "Honestly, I think she has some kind of personal problem with musical performers. She's rude to us, petty, and pushes us harder than is necessary. I was drugged and disappeared, not because I wanted to, I assure you. She forced Atlas, Mav, Turner, and Roark to stay at the VIP event until the end. Anything could have happened to me, and she thought I was being a brat. She doesn't care about what happens to us, and frankly I don't believe Prescott is the right person to be managing our tour," I tell him.

I lean back into my pillows and get comfortable, swinging my feet underneath me. I glance to my right and meet Derek's eyes, which are wide and surprised. *Does he think I'm going to complain about him?* I may have if the guys and I hadn't decided to collectively give him a chance. We'll see how it goes. He's still on a trial basis.

"I think you're right," Mr. Miles murmurs. "Am I safe to go on speaker? Are you around a lot of people?"

I look over at Layla and she mimes locking her lips and throwing away the key. Her guys nod that they'll follow her lead and I shrug. No reason not to then.

"We're back on the bus, sir, so it's safe," I tell him with a small sigh. This conversation is necessary, but I'm annoyed it has to happen right now. I click the speaker, wondering what he has to say. "You're on speaker now, Sir."

"Thank you, Lennon. Boys, I assume you're all here with our girl, yes?"

Our girl? The moniker feels odd, but not in a bad way.

"Aye."

"Yep."

"Present."

Answers in various forms echo from the guys and I lean forward to start to take my shoes off. Turner gives me an apologetic smile and walks over to drop to the floor to remove them for me. The heels were hot as fuck for the stage, but only comfortable up to a point. They officially hurt my feet now.

"Perfect. I rarely ask this, because I usually have a better view inside the inner workings of a tour than I currently have for The Darkest Nights. *Roadies, other support staff, etc usually will report to the label to tell us how things are going. However, we have had so much turnover in staff this year as we've been expanding and moving trusted staff, that I'm flying blind here. So, dare I ask, what the fuck is happening?"*

"Prescott is a twatapotamus," Turner says candidly, copying my statement, as he massages my feet after removing my boots. My eyes roll as I melt further into my nest of pillows with a soft moan. Mr. Miles snorts at this and Turner smirks. "You can thank our beautiful Lennon for that, but she's incompetent and negligent with our safety. She pushes our drivers to drive longer hours than they should for God only knows what reason, and she berates us about how we're spoiled. Mr. M., you know our roots and how we started," he says passionately.

"Yeah," I murmur in agreement. "It's not like we snapped our fingers and suddenly became wildly popular. We worked hard for it, we paid our dues, and toured our asses off. We still are touring hard. I don't know why she keeps calling us whiny. Okay," I counter, "here's my disclaimer for the night because I am going to complain more than I usually would, Mr. Miles, because I feel kind of shitty right now."

Roark grimaces and digs into a drawer before tossing me a bag of gummy bears. I smirk because he knows the way to my heart. I tear into the bag and bite the head off one because I'm feeling a little savage tonight. Leo chokes back a laugh and I wink at him. He did carry my ass back to the bus. The sugar slowly hits me and I sigh happily.

"I want to know the truth, so list your grievances, Lennon. What was that noise I just heard," he asks.

Shit. This man has the sharpest hearing. "My bag of gummy bears, Sir. You know I'm kind of addicted to them," I explain. The label has a folder on everyone they manage, and I know he has to be aware of my favorite candy.

Mr. Miles chuckles. *"Yes, I have seen many photos over the years showing your love for this treat. How is your stash right now? Do you need anymore?"*

Is he fucking offering to buy me gummy bears right now?! My eyebrows draw down in confusion.

"Um, I'm good at the moment, but thank you, Mr. Miles. I have hiding spots all over the bus to make them easily accessible, and when Prescott isn't being a twat, she has them on her. Lately though, she has been less than helpful. The way she speaks to us is disgraceful and unprofessional. She told me I asked for studio time so I had to suck it up today and make it work. I don't mind working hard-"

Roark cuts me off. "But this was fucking ridiculous, with all due respect, Sir. Lenny almost passed out on stage tonight, and she still looks pale. The label has invested a lot of time and money into all of us, so how are we to work without our muse? She wrote three songs in that recording studio today, coordinated music, and then laid the tracks down. Her talent isn't something you can find just anywhere. Help us protect our fooking girl," he roars.

I don't even feel bad. He's completely right; tonight shouldn't have happened. I also know he's riding the edge of his anger right now as his Irish curses are pushing into his speech.

"Ror, honey, come here. My head doesn't hurt as much as it did earlier. A good night's sleep, and I'll be back to normal," I tell him. I don't mean to coddle him, but I also don't want to lose Mr. Miles as an ally and piss him off. We need him to push out Prescott.

Roark growls before he scoops me up to sit in my spot. I snuggle into him happily, leaning up to kiss his chin.

"It sounds as if you're more comfortable now, Lennon," Mr. Miles chuckles. *"You're also right, Roark. It's clear Prescott is not the right person to manage your band, or any musical group at this time. Her disdain for the music community will not be overlooked in this. Can one of you put all instances where she's been less than professional or helpful into an email for me, please?"*

I open my mouth to offer but Turner beats me to it. "I know Lennon wants to do it, but I would prefer she spend tonight relaxing. I'll get it to you myself, Sir," he says.

"Excellent, now my next course of business is to ask if you all have eaten tonight," Mr. Miles asks, surprising me yet again. I wouldn't think he'd have the time to ask, especially since it's

such a late hour for this call. I glance down at my phone and see it's nearing eleven thirty. *"If you have had such an exciting night, this may have been overlooked."*

I bite my lip as I digest that. "You're right, they were so worried about me, we kind of skipped it. We'll get on ordering something now, Sir. Thank you for the reminder."

"No, Lennon. I'll take care of it. I started out in this company managing bands just like yourselves. I assure you, I may be a bit out of practice, but can manage it. What are you all in the mood for?"

I look up at Turner and mouth, *'what the fuck,'* and he struggles not to snort out loud. He covers his mouth with his hand to keep it in, and I realize he won't be able to answer.

"I could personally really go for some pizza with garlic knots," I confess. "Since my head feels better, I'm just really fucking hungry."

My stomach chooses that moment to growl and Layla covers her mouth to contain her own giggle. Turner's face turns to horror, and he's right to worry, even though he's overreacting. I'm only slightly gremlin-like when I'm hungry.

"Oh, fuck," Roark groans. "We most definitely need pizza then, Sir. Lenny is a fucking bear when she's hungry."

Mr. Miles chuckles. *"I'm not exactly a picnic when I am either, so I understand. How many and what toppings, kids?"*

While we are far from children, he is in his late fifties and a legend in the music industry, so no one questions it.

We give him our orders and I hear him typing over the phone. Layla mouths that she and the guys want a cheese and one pepperoni and I include that in our order.

"I have pizza being delivered to the bus for you all. Turner, be a good man and send over those grievances, and I'll be relieving Prescott of her duties as early as tomorrow if possible," he explains. *"Have a good night, and we will be in touch."*

The call drops and I release the breath I was unconsciously holding.

"Holy fucking shit," I mutter. "I didn't think he'd call or that he would move so fast!"

"Can I talk now," Layla asks so softly that I giggle and nod that the coast is clear. "That was *insane*. One of the heads of your freaking label was just catering to your every need. I've never heard of anything like that happening."

"Layla, no one can know this happened, either," Leo says seriously. "I will say though, that I think it was really badass. You didn't back down from what you needed, and pushed to be heard. I'm glad you did, because I can tell you guys love to be on stage. Anyone with eyes can see it. It would be a shame for y'all to burn out."

"We live to sing, perform, and connect with people through music," Turner says with a sigh. "But it's not worth it if we are sacrificing Lavender for it. Mr. Miles knows she's our person, and he's always had a soft spot for her." He snorts, shaking his head. "She's never been afraid of him, even back when she was scared of everything. And if she was, no one ever saw it."

I smile, thinking back to when I first met him after a gig. He wanted to make sure we were worthy of being signed after we were discovered. "I've lived through worse," I tell them with a shrug, forgetting who is in the room. "Mr. Miles didn't seem so bad after everything."

"Were we really all that bad?" I hear a hoarse voice ask. *Fuck.* My eyes fly over to see Derek looking at me in pain. I don't know what to tell him. They were honestly worse than he could ever imagine.

"You don't know everything," I say with a shrug. "This isn't the time to discuss it though." I try to shut it down, because I don't want to talk about it in front of Layla and her band. He and I have too much history for an audience honestly.

"I really feel like we need to discuss some things though, Lennon," he says, straightening and rubbing the back of his neck. "I may have misunderstood some things."

I blink owlishly at him, but not because of the almost apologetic tone. I am flabbergasted that he has the right to treat someone so badly because he 'misunderstood some things'.

"You're such a fucking dick," I breathe. "The things you're responsible for... Dude. You don't even know." I sputter a laugh because he's responsible for so much pain in my life.

I move to stand up and Roark's hands squeeze my waist and I shake my head. I don't want to deal with this right now. I know I said I would, but today is not that day. I'm fucking hangry now, and adding tears to this would be explosive.

"Wait, love," Roark murmurs in my ear. "You can't storm out right now. Look, Turner's handling it now with Sally."

Oh fuck. I turn my head towards Turner and he does have Sally in his hands. "No more heavy talk today, Derek, okay? We can all agree Lennon can't and shouldn't deal with it today. Let's table this conversation for tonight, and I'll make sure you get it another time, alright?"

Derek blows out a breath as he looks at Turner and then the bat, and then glances at me. Whatever he sees on my face makes him nod slowly.

"Soon though, Lennon O'Reilly, you and I have some shit to clear up. I may have some shit to apologize for," he demands.

I snort. "Oh my god. Are you going to apologize for my entire adolescence? Please don't try to talk about things you don't understand right now. Gah, I think I need a drink," I mutter.

Mav stands and goes over to the bar. He knows where everything is, since we are all in and out of each other's buses so often. "What's your poison, Lennon?"

"Do we have a show tomorrow," I ask. That'll make the difference in what I want.

"Yes. We're in Los Angeles tomorrow, so it'll be a much shorter drive. We are there for three nights," Roark says as he pulls up the schedule on his phone.

"Margarita on the rocks please," I tell Mav. It'll be just enough to chill me out, without giving me a headache tomorrow. Feeling as if a weight is off my shoulders despite Derek still being in the room, I turn to throw my legs over Roark's so I can snuggle better.

Mav takes drink requests and I raise my glass. "To the demise of the twatapotamus and new friends," I toast.

Everyone shakes their heads as they snicker and cheer back. "I get the feeling life is definitely not going to be boring with you as a friend," Layla says with a giggle.

I smile as I sip my drink. She's definitely not wrong.

16

DEREK

I lean against the wall as I drink my beer, listening to the easy chatter around me. No one asked, but I like Layla and her bandmates. They bicker, tease, and laugh as they chat. They're *normal*, and don't seem at all toxic. I'll reserve judgment on how safe Layla's budding friendship is, but I'm realizing Lennon doesn't have female friends. Her support system all have cocks, and while it seems to work for her, the testosterone has to be stifling after a while.

I remember her face when she was talking to the interviewer from *You* magazine and how animated she seemed. She was excited, engaged, and happy when she spoke to her. I don't know much about it since I don't have many female friends either, but I wonder if she misses interaction with women. I don't remember her having any friends back home, and feel a strange pang in my chest as I think about this. *Am I completely responsible for her solitary existence?*

The pain and acceptance in her voice when she said she had survived worse than the presence of an intimidating authority figure like Jordan Miles was a shot to the heart. I was such a shit while I was in school with her, but she looks so much like her mother it hurts. I told her if she was mine things would be different, and I meant it. But, making her mine when there's a trail of pranks, bullying, and fucked up betting pools to fuck her... how can she ever forgive me for it?

I don't even think I can forgive myself for it right now, and I have mixed feelings about our past history. *What's real and what has been twisted?*

I'm pulled out of my thoughts as I hear a knock at the bus door. I catch Turner's eye and jerk my head towards it to ask if I should answer. He nods, flicking his tongue to wet his lips, and I can't help but wonder about the tongue ring that catches the light. I never noticed he had one, and my cock stirs. I don't think he meant to turn me on, and I have a feeling I don't understand the dynamics of his relationship with Lennon and Roark at all. Shaking my head, I decide that's a thought for another day. I've never been attracted to other men until I took this job.

Answering the door, I find the welcome view of the delivery guy, but the unwelcome arrival of Prescott Jones as well. I smile at the former because it's late and I'm reminded that I don't need to be an asshole to people when I'm angry at others. Check me out, being nice consciously. *Kind of weird.*

"Derek, are you fraternizing with the band? I am disappointed in you, and thought you didn't like the little brat," Prescott mocks.

God, I can't wait for her to be fired. I stood back and let Prescott get her hooks into Lennon, but no one deserves to have this vitriol sent their way. I have a lot to figure out over my conflicting feelings for Lennon, because it's causing me to make poor decisions.

"I'm doing no such thing, but I had business to take care of after the show. I'm doing my job," I lie baldly, keeping my intentions vague on purpose. My interest in Lennon and the band have nothing to do with my job currently. "I'm also fairly certain you're not welcome here tonight, so go breathe fire somewhere else. Whatever you have to say will keep."

I plant my feet wide as I take the pizza boxes from the delivery guy, intent on showing Prescott I mean business.

She huffs, and I swear if she stomps her foot I'm going to lose my shit.

"Yo, Derek, hurry up," Turner yells. "Lavender is about to turn into a gremlin and needs something in her-"

His voice sounds closer than before and I turn to see him leaning over me as he holds the rails to stairs.

"What is she doing here," Turner groans.

My lip twitches as I turn back to Prescott because my feelings are the same.

"No idea, I just told her whatever she has to say can wait till morning," I explain.

"Yep, Derek is right for once. You can go back to exercising your tyranny tomorrow, Prescott. Good night! Dude, I need the food and your ass back on this bus. Just throw a roll at her, and Lavender will go back to being normal," Turner is slightly hysterical as he says this. I guess Lennon is a terror when she hasn't eaten. I don't remember this at all from school. I guess I never really paid attention.

I climb back on the bus, and Turner shuts the door in Prescott's face with a smirk. He turns the lock and herds me back to the others, while we both ignore the woman's cursing.

Sorry about your luck.

"I understand there's hanger happening," I snort as I put the pizza boxes down on a table.

"My tummy is eating itself, and gummy bears have stopped working," Lennon whimpers miserably.

"Ummm, even I feel bad for you right now," I mutter. "Which pizza is hers?"

Turner waves me aside and piles two pepperoni and meat slices on a plate with a giant garlic roll and hands it to Lennon, kissing her forehead.

"Feel better, baby," he murmurs with a chuckle.

Food is handed out to everyone and I sit down to dig in. Lennon perches on Roark's lap, and the man easily eats one handed as his other arm wraps around her. While he could have her sit properly, I get the feeling he doesn't want to.

If she were mine... yeah I did say that to her, didn't I? Fuck it. If she were mine, I wouldn't want to let her go too far either. She's had a rough few days.

We spend the rest of the time laughing and talking, and Lennon's mood improves considerably after eating.

"Lennon," Layla says. The girl has moved closer and closer until she's sitting right next to her. I cover my mouth with my fingers as I watch. She's just excited to talk to Lennon, and I think it's adorable.

Lennon curls to the side to face her with a drowsy smile. Her eyelids are getting heavy and I wonder how long she'll hold out until she falls asleep. "Mmhmm."

"Why do you let the awful woman that was outside earlier treat you like shit? I could be wrong, because I just met you, but you don't seem like a pushover. I mean, you put Albert in his place, and he usually just intimidates people," Layla says with snort.

Lennon giggles. "No offense but I live with burly, intimidating men. Albert, sorry, but you don't scare me," she calls over to him.

He shrugs lazily, taking a sip of his beer. "My manhood can survive that, Lennon," he says with a wink and the girls laugh harder.

"Honestly, Prescott recently became a twat, and I kept waiting for it to get better and it didn't. She's with the label, and I didn't want to make any waves. However, I can't let her push me into doing things that are dangerous to my health. I'm just glad I get to sleep in tomorrow," Lennon groans, covering her mouth as she yawns.

I frown worried. We should all get out and let her sleep.

Roark kisses her forehead. "Hey there, sleepy head. Why don't we call it a night, huh?"

Lennon scrunches her nose, but nods.

Layla bites her lip. "Why don't you take my number, and we can keep in touch. I know what it's like being surrounded by testosterone, and this way we can chat. I feel like I need to get to know you, and I know that sounds odd, but-"

Lennon shakes her head weakly, yawning again. "No, it's really not. I feel drawn to you too, and can't explain why. I remember thinking I could totally listen to you order coffee, and how pretty your voice was," she says, cheeks going pink in embarrassment.

Layla grins. "Yay we can be weirdos together."

Leo and Albert snort, and the third male band member rolls his eyes at their antics. I never managed to get his name, but I'm also exhausted and can't bring myself to care. Layla enters her number into Lennon's phone and they say goodbye to each other. *Velvet Escape* leaves the bus, and I stand to follow.

"Hey Derek, got a minute for me," Turner asks as Roark stands with Lennon in his arms. The man is built, all corded muscle that barely shows any effort as Lennon curls into his arms, struggling hard to stay conscious.

"Yeah, I do. Good night, Lennon. Get some rest," I emphasize and she nods with a small sigh.

"Don't you worry your pretty heads about us," Roark coos

and I don't know how to feel about this. "We are headed straight to bed. Our girl is three steps into dreamland already."

Well, he's got that right. Lennon's eyes droop, head bobbing as Roark walks her back to their bedroom.

"Look," Turner says, and my attention turns towards him. "I don't know what your feelings are for Lennon, but don't think I missed your claim of what you would do if she was yours. You've got a long way to go between the two of you, but Roark and I are giving you the space to figure your shit out."

"Wait, what does that mean? Pretend I'm dumb, because I feel as if I am right now," I tell him. Is he giving me permission to see where things go with Lennon? Fuck, can I even see past my issues to be able to? *First she and I need to talk about this being a virgin through high school thing.*

"I'm saying, Lennon is attracted to you, but you're a dick. I know a thing or two about what it looks like to have broken pieces that don't fit quite right. It chafes a bit, and it catches you off guard when you least expect it. You're not safe for my girl yet, you hurt her, and only some of those bruises are skin deep. Someone hurt you, but I can guaran-fucking-tee it wasn't Lavender. She's too pure to knowingly hurt a soul," he growls and I shiver.

My breath hitches and he smirks. "Don't wait too long to figure it out, though. Ror and I have our own questions, and we'll come for you when you least expect it."

I swallow thickly, shifting my balance. I am hard as a rock, and a portion of this is because of Turner. I'm definitely attracted to him, his shrewd pale blue eyes feel as if they can see through me. "Yeah, I just bet you will," I murmur, chewing on my bottom lip.

"Oh, have we graduated to flirting now, you may be moving too fast for me," he teases and I snort, shaking my head.

"I was doing no such thing," I assure him. "I'm not really

into men." I don't know why I'm lying right now. I blow out a breath, annoyed with myself as my eyes move to stare at the ground.

"So why can I see your cock straining in your pants? I suggest for you to be honest with how you feel. Life is just too fucking short to be anything less. Thanks for your help tonight, now off you go. I'm exhausted too, and ready to make Lavender, the meat in my sandwich."

I shake my head, beginning to wish I could join that sandwich as my eyes trail up Turner's body. Okay, so sue me, who wouldn't be turned the fuck on by this attractive man. His long fingers are tattooed, but I can't make out what it says. I imagine what they would look like buried inside Lennon's tight cunt and my breathing becomes strained. Fuck, I have to leave before I come in my pants. This man shouldn't be allowed to be this gorgeous. My fingers twitch, and I want to see if his hair is as soft as it looks.

"Uhm," I mutter. "Fuck, sorry I have to go, and I'm just not ready for whatever this is. It was good to hang out though," I mutter lamely.

I turn and practically run down the aisle, my fingers tearing through my hair. *What the fuck was that?*

How did I go from Turner threatening me with the business end of his bat, to teasing me with his gorgeous lips. I fucking swear every time I saw his tongue slip out tonight I wanted to do naughty things to him. I bite my own fist in frustration. It should be a crime for him to be this hot. I step off the bus with a frustrated sigh, seriously confused. Lennon, Turner, and even Roark have me tied up in knots.

"Yo, Derek," I hear, and I drop my hands to my sides, gently shaking them to release some tension.

I turn to see Turner leaning against the stairs with a self-satisfied smirk. *Fuck that smile too.* I'm feeling really petulant right now, and even that is a new emotion for me.

"Yeah," I say, pitching my voice so he can hear me and I'm not yelling.

"Look, try not to overthink it, okay? Nothing will happen until you fix some shit with my girl, either. Enjoy your hand tonight," he says with a cheeky wink before closing the door. I hear the distinct sound of a lock and I chuckle.

"Fuck," I mutter. My hand and I are definitely spending some time in the shower before bed tonight. There's not a chance in hell that I want someone to hear me come with Lennon or Turner's name on my lips.

My life has definitely become weird, I think as I walk to what is now home during the tour.

~

Lennon

I barely remember falling asleep, but this is definitely a dream. There's a foreboding presence in the air, and I am not in charge of what's happening. I'm back in Farrelsville, walking past the school on my way. I feel as if I've been thrown into the past.

I USUALLY MAKE *sure not to go this way, not after the last time Patrick and Travis tried to drag me under the bleachers. My clothes were torn, my hair pulled, my mascara ran from my muffled screams as I cried, but I got away. The story the next day at school, though, was that they tag teamed that afternoon. One of the cheerleaders corroborated the story, and the lie that Lennon would fuck anyone was born.*

Fucking pricks. I rub my arms in my tank top as I attempt

to walk faster, but to my horror my legs continue at the same pace. It's not safe for me here, all school year I swear there was a target on my back. My clothes were stolen after I showered in the locker room, drinks dropped over my head, my own stalker cheerleaders intent on hitting, stomping and hurting me. No one ever says anything, my principal told me to stop being so antagonistic towards my classmates. I swear, I can't with this town.

Travis and Patrick cross the street from where they were chatting with wide smiles.

"Hey, beautiful. Lennon, I don't usually do seconds, but you're looking mighty fine today," Travis grins lasciviously as he licks his lips.

I open my mouth to call him a liar, but my body refuses to work for me. Instead I keen, backing quickly away until I hit a hard chest. My breath quickens, but not out of pent up passion. My skin is crawling in disgust, and I just want to be left alone. I don't like male attention, I always feel dirty after the leers, dirty talk, and unwanted touches.

"Please leave me alone," I whisper. I twist to see who is holding me, but I can't. All I know is he's bigger than I am, and his arm is banded around me, trapping my limbs. His other hand trails slowly up my body before wrapping around my throat.

A voice I can't place growls, "You're gonna be a good girl and suck Patrick's cock while one of us fucks your ass. Your used up pussy is probably so loose, you won't be able to feel our cocks, and I want you to feel us for a very long time. I want your screams as we hurt you, for being our own little whore, is that understood?"

Tears cloud my eyesight as I blink rapidly to clear them. I have to get away, this can't be happening, I'm not what they think I am. Finally, a scream releases as I plead for help, even as I know it won't be coming. This is what my life has come down to, being raped just outside of school because of a stupid bet Derek made with his—

"LENNON!"

GASPING as I open my eyes, arms flailing as a scream rips through me. It feels so good not to be silent, to have my fucking voice again. I sob in relief, only to stiffen as arms come around me.

"Please, no," I shriek, my mind having a hard time staying in the present. It's as if I'm straddling the line between awareness and the dream world. I feel disoriented, and my body bows, trying to get away from the unknown person holding me.

"Hey, Lavender, you're safe," says a voice I recognize to be Turner's and I sag in relief. Only one person in the entire world calls me this, and no one can take it from me.

"I'm sorry-" I start to say and Roark turns on the light.

"No apologies needed. You were thrashing in your sleep and crying," Roark says softly, trying to look as non threatening as possible.

I'm not afraid of them though, I couldn't possibly be. I fist my hands, the slight bite of my nails digging into my skin reminding me where I am. "My demons came to visit," I whisper, taking a shuddering breath. The night has been broken enough by my screams, I'm hesitant to interrupt it anymore than I already have. I relax my hands as Roark gently touches one of them, a reminder not to hurt myself. Instead, I lift my hands, my fingers shaking as they touch the wetness left behind on my face.

Fuck. It's been years since I've had a nightmare about Farrelsville. It's been ages since what happened there has affected me, but Derek's presence is bringing up old shit from my past.

"Wanna come crawl in my lap, and we can just sit with your demons together for a while?" Roark asks, opening his arms to me.

God, I love this man so much. He didn't offer to fight them off for me, though I'm sure he would if I asked him to. Roark also didn't ask me to talk about it right away, though I expect it'll happen tonight. Right now, I'm spinning out from how helpless this dream makes me feel. I remember the heaviness I felt, the inability to say what I wanted, and my decisions ripped away from me.

Shuddering, I crawl into his lap and wrap myself around his strong body. *Thump thump thump.* The sound of his heartbeat is grounding to me, with his arms wrapped around me. Instead of feeling triggered or trapped, I feel treasured. Safe. I was taken off guard when Turner touched me earlier, still stuck in the terror of my nightmare.

Turner is sitting up against the built-in headboard, watching me carefully. There's no anger or jealousy that I'm pulling comfort from Roark, but I do see a storm of worry clouding his pale blue eyes.

I close my eyes against the image, focusing on slowing my breathing to match Ror's. *I'm safe, I'm with my loves.* I inhale deeply, enjoying the scent of spices and caramel which uniquely belongs to him. I open my eyes and release Roark, slowly pulling back.

"You're back with us, little Valkyrie," his voice rumbles in askance, and I know this is his way of reminding me I'm a badass in a small package.

I smile at him, surprised it's way less forced than I thought it would be after my nighttime trauma.

"Yeah," I tell him, breath blowing out, releasing some of the stress from the experience. "I'm better now. Really shitty dream, though."

"Can you tell us about it," Turner asks softly. I know he hates asking, but my past is moving into my present more and more, and it's time to shine a light on it.

"Yeah, I can. I may need something strong to drink to accompany my memories though," I tell him.

"You got it, love. Whiskey work?"

I sigh gratefully. "Yeah, that'll be perfect."

Turner leaves the room to grab glasses and our drinks and I lean into my rock. Ror is immovable, while Turner's my gatekeeper. No one has access to me without his approval. The only person to get around this is Derek, and I know it chafes the fuck out of him. Though, tonight they almost got along. Weird.

He's back before I can think more about this, and I wonder if I'm more affected by my nightmare than I'm willing to admit. Time feels pliable, moving too fast, but I'm also lost in my thoughts.

I wrap my hands around the glass Turner hands me and take a careful sip. It's exactly as strong as I asked for and my eyes water a bit. It's perfect for this conversation. He sits next to me, not touching, simply sending me support with his presence. It's exactly what I need.

I should sit up, but my head is comfortable on Roark. I turn so my feet are next to Turner and he lets his pinky drag slowly down one. I need just a small bit of contact to keep me in the moment.

I'm safe now damnit.

"My mom started getting kind of flaky when I turned ten. I had been walking to school since the year I turned nine, and while it was a long walk, my stomach was always full then," I begin, my voice soft yet strong. "I always had a bottle my mom filled with ice cold water, and she kissed my forehead and told me to make good choices. I could feel her love, you know?"

"But," I continued, "when I turned ten, she started disappearing for periods of time. I would wake up to an empty house, having to pack my own lunch and fill my own water bottle. These are things I could handle, but it was the beginning of everything." My eyes drop to the blanket as I remember how it felt to wake up to an empty house at such a young age. I really thought she had been hurt, and went days with knots in my stomach as I pretended to the world I was okay.

"When she was home before the first time she disappeared, she started acting differently. She insisted everything was dirty and had to be cleaned. We then spent the next two days cleaning, washing clothes, and my mom somehow made more of a mess as she tore through the house. Then, on the third day, she was gone, leaving the house a wreck. Coincidentally, she also forgot to stock the fridge. I didn't have anything to pack for lunch, I didn't have money for the cafeteria, and my pants for school were still damp because she didn't change over the laundry. After panicking and running around the house calling her name and searching the woods behind our house the first time it happened, I walked to school hungry and uncomfortable."

My eyes drift back up and I watch their eyes carefully to find them banked with anger, but there's no pity. They're eager to hear more, certain it's the beginning of worse things to come, and wanting to learn more about my childhood.

They are right to think this.

"I told you some of this before, but this is the unvarnished truth. I was eleven when my mom disappeared for three weeks. It was the longest she'd ever been gone. She walked into the house afterwards stark naked, no explanation of where she was. I had no idea what to think. I asked if she was hurt, if she needed me to call for help. That was the first time she ever hit me," I remember, my chest constricting.

My mom was my best friend, and when she hit me, I wondered what I did to deserve it. "My mom was always my safe space, and I still believed she was until then. Derek also started to bully me right around the time she disappeared. I don't know if they are related, but Mom had a lot of secrets. I stayed quiet because I told her I would always be there for her, but she stopped showing up for me."

"Fucking bitch," Turner mutters, shaking his head. "How the hell were you eating while she was gone?"

"I had a neighbor way down the road from me who realized he and his wife hadn't seen my mom in a while. I told him I didn't know where she was right now, but I was a big girl, and I could manage," I explain with a shrug. It took me a long time to realize I shouldn't have had to cover for her. She was supposed to be the fucking grown up.

"It's the first time his eyes filled with pity, and food started appearing on my porch once a day. I made it last for at least two meals, but I couldn't figure out how to keep it warm for lunch, so I stopped eating entirely while at school. My dad sent child support I found out as I got older, and this is the reason the lights and water were never cut off. I was mostly okay while I was left alone, outside of when I had to start dressing out for my physical education class. All the exercise made me crabby, my stomach would grumble through my last class, and it was hard to cover up my hunger."

Roark sighs as his thumb rubs my hip slowly. "When and how did Derek start to fuck with you at school, Lenny?"

"He started when I was in sixth grade, so not only did I have to deal with my mom's shit, but also his. Derek would knock my books out of my hands daily, shove me into my locker, and drop my folders into puddles regularly," I sigh.

Fuck, I was so mad that time my research paper was in my notebook.

"Not to mention, he would call me the crazy lady's spawn as I walked home from school. I knew there was something wrong with my mom, but didn't know what at first. I went to the library after school after the first time he called me that, and started running a search. I inputted all the shit my mom had been doing as key words, and pieced together that she probably was bipolar."

Turner frowns as he takes a sip of his drink. "Okay, yes all this is super shitty, but I have to ask what else he did. Your nightmare was really intense for low level bullying. It sucks, but why do I feel like there was more?"

I wrinkle my nose as I drink deeply. "Maybe because he set up the perfect recipe in my fucked up high school for the jocks to pressure me into having sex? And no doesn't always mean no to these guys, even when you're kicking and screaming," I reply.

"I need more words than that, Lenny O'Reilly," Roark full name growls at me. I wince because I definitely dropped a bomb without explanation.

"Okay, look. I don't know all the details on how this happened. You need to ask Derek-"

"You bet your sweet ass we will be. Fuck, I actually thought the dick was kinda cute," Turner grouses.

I giggle, despite the heaviness of the conversation because he's adorable. "I never said Derek isn't cute or doesn't have abs I want to follow with my tongue," I tease him. "I always thought he was ridiculously hot, but it wasn't worth going there with him. He was too cruel, too calculating in his bets with his teammates, which funny enough revolved around me."

I remember the sly look he gave me the day everything started. It was after football practice, and I was tutoring for extra money. I quickly realized I could make sure I ate during school hours if I had the funds. I didn't qualify for free lunch ironically enough, which you can bet your ass I looked up the needed qualifications for it on the second day of school. I didn't know free lunch was even a thing.

"During my sophomore year of high school, gossip started that no one had ever seen me on a date. I don't know how I even ended up on the gossip mill, but Charity hated that guys would stop to talk to me between classes," I sneer. God, I hate insecure women, though high school girls are the worst. "The girls in my school all started dating early, mostly group dates in middle school, and I was never interested."

I stare off into space at this. I wanted to be interested, but couldn't afford to be. Dates also cost money I didn't have. "I was too busy surviving my day to day, honestly, and around eighth grade, my mom started popping into conversations. People usually overlooked me when I was around, since I was tiny from not eating well. They said my mom was dating married men, and how happy they were that their husbands were on lock down," I continue as I roll my eyes.

"Honestly, it takes two people to fuck, even if she initiated. I couldn't ask my mom if this was true, but people started wondering if I was a whore too. If I was, they felt they should cash in on this, so I guess the bet was born. I only know any of this because I overheard one of the cheerleaders say this weeks after I started being propositioned." I frown as I remember how surprised I was that all of this was happening because of a bet. Especially because two of the football players couldn't understand that *no* is a full statement.

"The Friday this bet supposedly started, my mom was actually home and suggested I go to a football game. I was shocked, because why would I want to? I kept to myself on purpose, but she refused to let me stay home. Mom said it would be good for me, made me get dressed for it, and dropped me off at the field. She also asked beforehand if I was gay, and if I was, I should make sure to try getting under a cock before I decided this. I remember how shocked I was over this whole conversation, and let her strong arm me into it. I kind of blame her for being the reason I was even there in the first place," I confess. What kind of person am I to blame almost getting raped on my mother?

As tears prick my eyes, I start to worry my bottom lip with my teeth. Turner's eyes latch onto it but he doesn't say anything. Forcing my lungs to inhale, I push out my words. "Girls at school threw popcorn at me during the game, and I narrowly escaped wearing a full cup of cola. I got up in time, moving out of the way and finding another seat. I only stayed because my mom drove me, but also told me I'd have to find my way home. She said I needed to make the effort, and refused for me to be the odd kid people gossiped about," I explain, grimacing. This is the most backwards logic I've ever heard. "She had this weird glint in her eyes, and she kept muttering to herself. Knowing what I do now, I think she was in a manic state. Sometimes it was easier when she was away."

People usually want their moms around more, right?

"I made it through the game, and decided to use the restroom before walking home. It wouldn't be the first time I had to pop a squat to pee, but with so many people on the roads, it was smarter just to go before I left. I mean, it sounded logical to me at the time." Knowing what comes next, tears start to move slowly down my cheeks, and I drop my eyes. Rubbing the blanket, I watch my fingers move back and forth. *I'm on the tour bus, no one can hurt me.*

I'm chanting to myself, forcing myself not to travel back to the first of many scary encounters. It's ridiculous that I never felt truly safe after this.

"By the time," a sob escapes as I say this. My eyes close, and

I will myself to bite back the rest. If I don't, getting through the rest of this won't happen. I clear my throat and swallow, slowly reopening my eyes. "When I left the bathrooms," I begin again, "most people had left. I didn't think everyone would clear out so quickly, and I hustled out to the exit. For some reason, the exit I went to use was near the bleachers, and Travis and Patrick sidled up to me on either side. Travis played with my hair and gave me a creepy smile. I was so confused, these guys had never been interested in me before, outside of helping Derek push me around."

I take another shaky breath, refusing to make eye contact. I won't make it through my story without it. Even though I escaped without being raped, I still lost my innocence that night. I never felt safe again at school, walking home, or my damn home.

"Patrick asked me how I liked the game, and I congratulated them on their win. I didn't say I didn't even want to come, and I was forced to. They started herding me away from the exit and I said I needed to get home. Travis snorted and asked how I was getting home, because everyone saw my mom drop me off. These damn small towns notice everything," I sigh. "I never had a chance of getting away, but I still tried. All of a sudden most of the lights on the football field went out and they laughed at me. He said, 'I hope you're ready to get really friendly with us, because I'm getting a taste of your tight pussy.' I flinched as if I had been slapped and screamed for help. One of the cheerleaders walked over with a smile, drinking from a flask and asked if she was getting an aftershow now that she had turned off the lights," I shudder as I remember the past, holding back my sobs still. Tears and fury color my words, but that's okay. I am furious with these people for violating my innocence, Iris for not wanting to protect me, and Derek for somehow being responsible for it all.

"Bitch cheered them on as I screamed," my voice finally breaking. My breaths are shorter, almost painful as I cry.

Roark finally lets himself hug me, his tight squeeze grounding me in a way nothing else could. "Little Valkyrie, you got away, and you're safe with us," he whispers as he kisses my forehead. "You're so much stronger than you even know."

"I fought them off," I cry. "But, Iris grabbed me and threw me back at them. I dick punched Patrick, and ran for the exit. Travis roared in anger, calling me a cunt, and told me I owed him his nut. He grabbed me by my shirt as I screamed *no*, and ripped it off of me. They were so fucking big, and I was so tiny. I ran faster than I ever had back home," I remember, trapped in my memories.

"When they tried to run me down with their car, I hid in the woods in the dark as I heard them roaring my name. It was awful, and they said it didn't matter, they still won. They drove off, and I didn't know until much later what they meant. I don't know if Derek knew what he set in motion, but it colored my entire high school career after that."

"Motherfucker," Turner growls. He releases himself from whatever leash he mentally gave himself, and places his head on my lap. His arms wrap around my waist, and he mutters into my stomach, "This will never happen to you again. Please start carrying your knife with you everywhere, and don't hesitate if you're ever in that kind of situation again. Promise me you'll fuck 'em up. You're so fucking precious to us, you have to stay safe."

Roark sighs as he breathes in my hair. "Luckily I speak Turner," he says heavily. "I don't like that you've been drugged while on tour. Tomorrow also can't come soon enough because it means Prescott will be gone, and it's one more way we can keep you safe. You are so loved," he swears, "but it's clear we can't be with you every second of the day. I will fuck up anyone who comes near you with the intent to harm you-"

"But I have to be able to keep myself safe too," I finish. My chest saws from so many emotions releasing, but I did it. I told Turner and Roark, and I'm okay. "I love you guys, you know that right? You are my everything," I breathe.

"Aye, you're mine, Lenny. You're so damn strong, a real warrior with all the shite life has thrown at you," he growls. Every word is heavily mired with his Irish accent, and it feels amazing as they roll through my body. Somehow, the words feel like home, and make me feel safer.

"Hmmm. All that. You are my gorgeous girl who fucks up people with your sharp words, but you're also one of the sweetest people I know. You're not alone, Lavender. Never again," Turner swears.

My eyes feel heavy as my breathing evens out, and Roark takes my glass from me. The sound of his heart steadily beating under my ear is the best lullaby a girl could ask for, and I drift off to sleep again.

Never again.

17

ROARK

I'm still reeling as I look down at Lenny, thinking about what she told us. The strength it must have taken to go to school every day with the bullying, feeling unsafe, and the threat of being raped over a stupid bet... I have no words. My blood is boiling as I process.

"Turner," I rasp, tears clear in my voice as I speak to him.

"Yeah," he says, his head still in her lap as he sighs.

"We need to talk to Derek. Something's not jiving with the boy she talked about and the man that was on my bus tonight. How can he sleep at night if he knows what he did to Lenny—" My voice breaks as I think about it. "His bet cost her her innocence. She was a shadow of who she is now when she met us, and now we know why. Well, some of it. I have this sick feeling in the pit of my stomach that there's more."

"I'm sure there's more. We just got a snippet of her past, but it's enough to know her childhood was shit. I want to surround her in snuggles and love, and protect her from the world and it kills me that I can't," Turner mutters, rubbing his face against Lenny's stomach like a cat.

Despite the heavy conversation, my lip twitches at the image. I let my hand drift to his hair to play with it.

"Mmm, feels good," he murmurs.

"Good, baby boy. Close your eyes for me and go back to sleep. We'll figure out how we can help Lenny tomorrow, yeah?"

Turner's eyes drift closed and soon he's breathing deeply. Thank goodness.

I know I won't be able to take my own advice, dimming the lights and getting comfortable. I focus on the weight of my loves on me, their breathing, reminding myself they are here with me now. I won't ever take for granted having them in my life.

Once I am reassured both are sleeping restfully, I begin to plot out a much needed conversation with Derek the Dick.

I PASSED out around seven in the morning, and managed to sleep for about an hour before someone calls me. I frown as I open my eyes and snatch up my phone. I'm definitely grumpy this morning. I answer quickly when I see Mr. Miles' name across the screen.

"Hello, Sir? I mean, Mr. Miles, what can I do for you?" I ask, clearing my throat.

"I'm so sorry for the early Saturday morning call, Roark. I know you all had a rough day yesterday. I wanted to let you know I'm pulling into the stadium in the next few minutes, and didn't want to take you by surprise this morning," he says.

I blink owlishly as I struggle to process what he said.

"Wait, you're here? Why? I thought we'd see you maybe when we hit Los Angeles today."

"I was going to wait, but honestly I'm a little bored and

wanted to see Prescott's face when I fired her," he chuckles. *"Give an old man a break here,"* he teases.

"You're so not old," I roll my eyes with a smile.

"Glad to hear it, because I'm taking over as your new manager for a while. I'll see you in a few." The man shows his reputation for cutting straight to the point as the line goes dead.

"Shit!" My head drops back with a groan.

"Shit where," Turner moans from Lennon's lap, head slowly lifting.

"Who was that on the phone?" Lenny asks softly, yawning.

I kiss her forehead because she's so damn cute. They both look ruffled and delicious. Her hair is in her face, cheeks slightly flushed with warmth from being snuggled. Turner sits up, scratching his chest as he yawns, trying to wake up. I roll my lips inwards to hide a smile, knowing my words will do the trick just fine.

"Jordan Miles is on his way here," I tell them. "He—"

"What?" they yell together.

"How far away is he—" Turner asks at the same time Lenny scrambles from my lap and takes off for the bathroom.

"Dibs on a shower," she yells.

Absolute chaos. I burst out laughing at them, shaking my head. I seriously adore these two.

"He wanted to see Prescott's face when he fired her," I explain, making sure I speak loudly enough for Lenny to hear too.

"Oh, that's gonna be fucking epic," Turner chuckles as he rolls onto his back and stretches. "Ugh, I'm gonna go brush my teeth while Lavender is showering. I would hop in with her to conserve water, but it's too small. I would fucking kill for a hotel room soon," he groans.

"Yeah, I'll bring it up to Mr. Miles when we see him," I promise. "He's apparently also going to be our new manager."

At Turner's yell, I smirk. "I promise I have now told you everything I know. He hung up right after telling me that."

"Fuck, I'm regretting that I refuse to start the morning with whiskey," he grumbles as he gets off the bed to brush his teeth.

Drama king. Feeling the need to do something, I drag on jeans and a T-shirt and walk out of our room. My stomach grumbles, and I figure I may as well make breakfast. Since Mr. Miles traveled in, I doubt he's eaten yet.

Pancakes, bacon, and eggs I decide are the perfect way to start the day. I start working on it, listening as the bathroom door opens and closes several times. Fifteen minutes later, both Turner and Lenny come out dressed and ready. His hair is wet, so I expect he jumped in after her.

"Turner, can you finish watching the last of my pancakes cook, please? I want to brush my teeth at least before Mr. Miles hits our door, too," I explain.

"Absolutely, gorgeous. This smells amazing. I can cover this while you get ready," he assures me.

Knowing he can handle it from here, I head to the bathroom. I make quick work of going to the bathroom, brushing my teeth and such. Hustling, I finish up just as I hear Turner greeting someone.

Since he's not yelling nor sounds hostile, I figure it's Mr. Miles. I smile as I see I was right. He glances up and grins. My smile grows as I notice he's dressed down today: dark jeans, long-sleeved button down rolled up to his elbows, and I even see he has some ink. I'm already learning new things about the man who makes the music industry quake. He's a legend, and has discovered so many artists.

"Good morning, Sir. How was your flight in?" I ask respectfully.

"It was productive," he smirks. "It was nice to get things done without people calling me all the time. I've moved things around that I usually handle into capable hands, so I'm considering this time a much needed vacation," he jokes.

Our ideas of a vacation are very different, but I'll take it.

"I was going to call Prescott over here, but I see I've interrupted your breakfast," Mr. Miles laments.

"I made breakfast for all of us, figuring you may also be hungry," I explain. "If you haven't called her yet, will you eat with us? And then we can watch as you deliver your epic come to Jesus moment," I chuckle.

The man rewards me with an ungentlemanly snort and I internally fist pump. I didn't know he knew how to make that noise. I'm already intrigued by our new manager.

We load up our plates, and sit down with our coffee and food. Lenny gives a small yawn, covering her mouth apologetically.

"I'm so sorry," she murmurs. "I didn't sleep very well last night. Coffee and a nap later should help."

Mr. Miles stares at her for a beat before fixing his coffee with cream and two sugars. As he takes a sip, Lenny struggles not to squirm under his gaze.

"I'm assuming Roark told you all I'm your new manager as soon as we finish firing Prescott, right?" We all murmur yes or nod. "Excellent. I know Music Horde Records has you working an accelerated tour schedule with a lot of shows—"

"Which we agreed to, Mr. M., in exchange for our new tour bus," Turner hurriedly explains.

He nods patiently. "Absolutely, and it looks as if this bus suits your needs well. However, there is the small problem that you're running yourself into the ground. This needs to stop."

Lenny takes a sip of coffee and moans happily. Turner and I snicker as caffeine hurtles through her veins. She huffs softly as she processes what he said. "That's great and all, but I won't cancel tour dates, sir."

"No, that's not what I'm suggesting. I do think we should reign in how much interviewing you do pre-show, so you have more down time. During days you have the morning or afternoon free, disappear into the city you're in. Have fun, experience it. You used to do this so much more before this tour," he says sagely. *Wow, he really does pay attention even from afar.*

"We haven't recently because we've been so busy. Even before Prescott joined us three months ago, we've been booked solid. Turner would cry for a hotel room with a hot tub and huge shower, though," I say with a shrug.

Turner hides his grin behind his own coffee cup, but I can see the slight blush gracing his cheeks. I told him I would discuss it with Mr. Miles, and I keep my promises.

"Oh, I'm sure I can get that arranged. I'll look for when your next day off is, and get it set up. As nice as your bus is, having the ability to stretch out, and have a change of scenery is necessary," Mr. Miles states with a firm nod before taking a bite of food. He hums with pleasure and a small smile. "Roark, this is wonderful, thank you for including me in your meal."

I grin, happy he's enjoying it. I enjoy feeding people, even in such a small space. This is why we made sure our kitchen would be functional, even if it is tiny.

The rest of the breakfast is spent to the sounds of happy food noises, each of us in our own world as we eat. It's oddly not uncomfortable, and I'm surprised to see how well Mr. Miles fits in with us without trying. Having him as our manager may be a really great thing. *Though, anything is better than Prescott.*

Once we're done, Turner and I start clearing the table, and Mr. Miles grabs his phone.

"What are the odds that she takes this gracefully, and doesn't cause a fuss," he asks absently.

"Very low," Lenny answers honestly. "The woman is a train wreck. Even when she first started, Prescott was all over the place. I thought she was just naturally anxious, but maybe she was covering up her nasty streak."

"Well, my dear, her reign is over as of now," he says as he calls her. "Miss Jones, Jordan Miles here. I wish I could say good morning, but it's already been a long one. I'm on property right now, and am in Bus One. Could you meet me here in the next ten minutes, please? Excellent," he bites out, ignoring her shriek. "We'll see you soon."

Mr. Miles then calls someone else, but I'm washing the dishes and can't see from this angle. "Mav, good morning. I just finished having breakfast with Lennon and the boys. Could you and Atlas meet us on their bus in the next few minutes please? I expect you'll enjoy watching your soon to be ex-manager be fired."

He smirks as I hear Mav whoop and I snicker. We are all going to enjoy this way too much. If she wasn't such a bitch, I may be able to find it in myself to feel bad for her. Unfortunately, that's not the case here.

A few minutes later, the dishes are finished and put away, and the bus is filled with people.

"Mr. Miles, I, ah didn't expect you today. Is there a problem?" Prescott asks.

Lenny pops a gummy bear in her mouth as she eats, and I roll my lips inwards to keep my smile hidden. She's so cute, this is the equivalent of someone eating popcorn for her. I don't bother teasing her for eating candy so early, choosing instead to sit next to her, kissing her temple.

"Yes, there is unfortunately a problem," Mr. Miles states with a severe frown. The man is standing up, arms folded, and looks fucking scary. I don't envy Prescott right now.

"With the band right? I'm so sorry I tried to keep them in line, but—"

"*Stop* right there, dear," he says with a shake of his head, his eyes flashing with barely veiled annoyance. "There is nothing wrong with the band, the problem lies with your negligence. You are incapable of serving their needs, and that's what you were paid to do. You've been rude and let this color your ability to do your duties, therefore you are being relieved of this as of," dramatically he looks at his watch, "right now. Please pack your things, and be on the first flight home. You are also no longer employed by *Music Horde Records*. Good day."

I watch as Prescott's face turns colors as she processes. She goes from ghostly pale to the blood rushing to her face as she embraces her anger.

"You can't do that, old man!" she screams.

"Just did," he says with a shrug as he fires off a text. The man is definitely efficient as two men in black suits board the bus. I'm suitably impressed as they each quietly take one of her arms, picking up Prescott as she screams obscenities. The moment the doors shut, we all breathe a sigh of relief.

"Thank fuck," Atlas mutters. "I've never wanted to swat someone more than I have her. She's absolutely delusional if she thinks we're the problem." He shakes his head in disgust.

"I have no doubt there's something wrong with her, but hopefully we don't have to deal with her again," Mr. Miles murmurs.

He lifts his phone and hums to himself. "You have three shows in Los Angeles in different venues, so as a show of good faith as your new manager—"

"Wait, hold on there a damn minute, Sir. I didn't think you worked in the field anymore," Atlas grills. He and Mav weren't on the bus when Mr. Miles had announced this to us, so they are in the dark.

"You're absolutely correct, but honestly, I need a change of pace, and it was either retire or do this. I'm bored," he confesses, "but not ready for retirement. I'm too damn young for that, and I love music. I miss being in the thick of it, helping bands, all of it. It also seems as if you're being run into the ground, approaching burnout. It would be a damn shame, and I won't let it happen. So, will you have me as your manager?"

There are resounding, "a yes" and "fuck yeses" and Mr. Miles chuckles.

"Excellent. So I want to offer you a change of sleeping quarters, if you're open to it. You'll have a car drive you into stadium property whenever you're ready beginning tomorrow, and a bathroom larger than a hall closet," Mr. Miles says with a shrug. "I want to break up your schedule in order to avoid burnout, which also means less media spotlights while you're on the road. They're exhausting, and unnecessary in the excess you've been having them."

I sigh happily. "Yes, to all this, please. I love our bus, but it's tight quarters day in and day out. It would be nice to spread out a bit," I confess.

"Agreed. Turner is begging for a bigger shower," Lenny giggles as Turner pulls her into a playful headlock.

"Excellent. I apologize for arriving so early, but I really wanted to get Prescott out of your lives as quickly as possible. The label decided not to retain her after what we talked about, and it was not just my decision. However, it was the right thing to do. Do you have any questions for me that I need to answer right away?" our new manager asks.

"Just one. Do we continue calling you Mr. Miles, Sir?" Mav asks with a small frown.

"No, that's simply too formal as we'll be seeing a lot more of each other. Jordan will do just fine, please. I really want to make this an environment that'll foster your creativity, and make you more comfortable. I didn't realize your pace was so intense until recently," he laments. I honestly think he regrets the speed we've been working at, and it makes me look forward to a marked change. "The buses will be leaving soon, as I want you to be able to relax before the show tonight. Any objections?"

I love that he asked, honestly Prescott would have told us to suck it up.

"None here, Jordan," I try out his name to see how it feels. Surprisingly it's not as weird as I thought it would be. I've just never thought of using it before.

Everyone else agrees with me and we split up, ready to head out.

"Is it wrong if we take a nap," Lenny groans adorably.

"No it's not beautiful. It sounds like a great plan," I say in agreement. I never bothered to put on shoes, and now I unbutton my jeans as well. "First one back in bed gets to be the filling in our sandwich," I tease her.

I roar with laughter as she and Turner fight for that honor, turning around and tearing down the aisle for the bedroom. I wish I could say I didn't see that coming, but I totally suspected it might.

Life with these two will never be boring, and I love it. I whistle the song Lenny was humming to herself the other day, absently wondering again where she heard it from.

18

DEREK

I was ready to move to Los Angeles for the next show, but was surprised when the supporting staff and roadies were called into the parking lot before we left. Mr. Miles looks out at all of us, looking casual in rolled up sleeves and jeans. Prescott must be toast, did he really come all the way out here to do it though?

"Good morning, everyone. Before we continue forward with the tour, I wanted to make an announcement. Prescott Jones has been removed from her position as acting manager as of this morning, and I will be taking over for her," he says.

I struggle to keep my face neutral as I process this. I didn't expect him to take over for her, since he's been working behind the scenes for years. At least with Mr. Miles in charge, the band will work less intense hours.

"Now, here's some housekeeping I wanted to take care of. We will be staying on track for our tour dates, but will be taking a more relaxed pace in driving between venues. I understand things have felt rushed, and this is how mistakes happen," he explains. I must not be the only one who has noticed because there's an audible sigh of relief from everyone. Mr. Miles smirks. "I trust everyone is alright with this?"

We all audibly agree and a roadie raises his hand.

"Yes," Mr. Miles says with a nod.

"This tour has moved harder than any other I've worked on. I don't know how the band is able to perform still between their interviews and performances, Sir," the man airs his concerns.

"That's another thing that'll change. We will have one interview day a month carrying forward. I wasn't aware *The Darkest Nights* were being pushed this hard before yesterday. I don't want there to be rumors that anyone complained, but—"

"Prescott was the worst," the roadie mutters.

Mr. Miles snorts in amusement. "Yes, she was. I needed to know what was going on. We are a team, and work together for the safety of all the band members we work for. If something is happening I need to know of, please don't hesitate to tell me. Also, please call me Jordan as we will be working closely together. I won't be staying on the bus for longer drives, but I'll be training a junior manager who will be capable of this."

I feel a curl of unease as I listen to him. He won't accept bullshit, and I've been a dick to Lennon. She and I have a lot to discuss, but cross my fingers no one will rat me out about my behavior before I can. *Fuck.* Things are more complicated than they previously were, but also safer now for Lennon. She scared me when she almost collapsed last night.

Jordan–*it's just weird to call him this*–closes out the meeting and we head back into the bus. I get comfortable on one of the sofas, when my phone buzzes in my pocket. My discomfort grows when I pull it out and find my father calling me.

"How long do I have before we leave?" I ask without looking up.

"Fifteen minutes, Derek," says one of the roadies.

Nodding, I chew on my lip, standing up. "I'll be back before then, man," I promise.

I don't know why he's calling me, and I don't want witnesses when I find out. Fuck me.

I hustle off the bus, answering on the last ring. "Hello, Sir. I apologize for the delay in picking up," I say formally. We don't have the best relationship, so I try my best to show respect, even if I don't feel it.

"Son, I'll let it slide today, but I dislike waiting. I have news for you, and need you to come home soon. It's been ages that you've been gallivanting on the road, panting after rockstars, and you're needed at home. Your mother is unwell, and is in the hospital also," he explains.

My stomach drops. My father never stopped fucking around on my mother, and she stayed married to him. However, she negotiated terms to live with her sister, only coming to stay with him for special events. I always wonder how Farrelsville residents don't question this when my father ran for mayor on the family first platform.

He doesn't generally need me at home, because my mom is his arm candy. She somehow always knows the right thing to say, and is tuned into everyone's lives. My mother is seen in town, has lunch there and meets with her friends, but usually leaves the moment her business is finished. She insists my aunt needs her as she lives alone. My uncle passed away a couple of years ago after being ill. It all fits well with her cover, and for now I guess it's worked.

Then there's the added fact that my mother has never been ill a day in her life. *What the fuck is my dad playing at?*

"Dad, what do you mean, she's sick?" I ask, forgetting myself in my worry.

"Don't question me boy," he roars and I wince. I am thirty

years old, and he still scares the shit out of me. It's been years since he's hit me, so that's not my worry. I could wipe the floor with him now, there's just always been this darkness hovering beneath the surface. No one whispers against him, there's not a single rumor, and fuck if I know why.

"Yeah, alright, I'm sorry," I murmur. I just want to finish this conversation, and then find out what's wrong with my mother. It's been a few years since I've seen her, but she usually texts or calls me. I last spoke to her right before I took this job, so whatever is wrong with her now has happened suddenly.

Or she was keeping it from me.

Unsettled by this thought, I swallow hard. "When do you want me home?" I ask.

"Three days from today. I understand you have commitments there, so I won't force you to attend sooner to me. However, understand I will not bend on this. Have I made myself clear," he barks.

I nod even though he can't see me and then clear my throat. "Yes, crystal, Sir."

He hangs up without saying goodbye and I release the breath I was holding. I stare at my phone, wanting to text my mother, but worried my father is monitoring her phone.

Shit.

Hey Mom, I'm coming home soon, hope to see you.

I climb back onto the bus, waiting for a message from her. I wait, lost in thought as I watch the world fly by, the bus eating up the miles. It's not until hours later that I look down and see I've lost three hours, and my mom hasn't answered.

Something isn't right, and now I'm officially worried.

~

SOONER THAN I'M READY, we arrive at the stadium. We have about five hours before the show begins, and the road crew scurry off to unload things. At a more leisurely pace, I start walking towards the stadium to find a place to hook up to the wifi and distract myself with work.

"Derek," yells a voice that makes the muscles in my stomach contract with desire. *My hormones are out of control.*

I turn slowly, watching as Roark and Turner walk towards me, faces grim. We were on much better footing yesterday, I swear it reminds me of that song, *One step forward, 3 steps back*, by Olivia Rodrigo. Sighing, I wait for them to catch up to me.

"Why do I get the feeling something happened," I ask, feeling a slight comfort that Sally the bat isn't accompanying them. My life has gotten absurdly weird lately.

Roark huffs out a breath, frowning. "Let the record show I'm trying really hard not to beat your face in for past things you're responsible for," he growls.

Turner winces as I look between the two of them wildly. The last thing I need is an altercation with them and Jordan finding out about it. I don't want to get fired. What the fuck did I do now?

"Let's take a walk, man," Turner says. "We need to talk, and Lennon is on the bus chatting with Layla on the phone. I want us to have this conversation without her, but only because I'm hoping you didn't know. If you did, understand I'll beat the shit out of you with Roark, and won't break a sweat."

"I have no idea what you think I did—"

"Walk," Roark commands, and my feet obey. I need to know what's going on.

"Lennon has nightmares," Turner begins, and I remember her words about how I didn't know how bad things were for her. *What could be giving her nightmares*? I really feel as if I'm missing something. "She had one last night, and she was screaming in her sleep. She begged people to let her go, to not drag her away, but I couldn't make out the names. The terror was real though, and I managed to wake her up."

"She didn't realize it was Turner when she woke up, her mind still wrapped deeply in her nightmare," Roark continues. I feel like an asshat, because I'm unsure how I'm responsible for a nightmare like that. I bullied her in school, but up until earlier this week, had never dragged her anywhere. "I'm gonna cut right to the heart of it, Dick. Did you have some kind of sick bet to see who could sleep with Lennon first?"

I feel the blood drain from my face as I process that. "Yeah, but I thought she was already having sex at the time, which I obviously was incorrect in that assumption," I yell in panic, jumping back as Roark jumps in my face. Fuck, this man is scary. I'm as large as he is, but angry, he's a damn bull.

"How the fuck did this bet start," Turner asks, holding his hand up.

I sigh. "Lennon's mother had sex with a lot of the men in our town," I begin, not saying anything about my personal experience with Carrie. "Mrs. O'Reilly didn't have the best reputation, and she was also sleeping with my father. Look, I was fucking angry about this. Damn woman weaved her spell around him, and I wanted to punish someone. So, yes that's when the bullying started in middle school. Lennon doesn't know this about her mother, though" I state, scuffing my foot along the pavement as I walk. I cross my arms as I speak, struggling not to let my anger bleed through too much.

"The rumors started spreading that the apple didn't fall far from the tree; which is why I also would taunt her about her own mental health."

I wince, realizing the guys won't wait much longer for their answers. Roark is already cracking his knuckles with impatience. "So one day, maliciously in the football locker room her freshman year, I started the bet. It was more of a pool: whoever fucked her, won the money. We all threw in fifty bucks and there were ten of us that agreed to the bet. I figured it would out her as the whore I thought her to be—"

"Yeah, well you didn't. Our girl was a virgin, not that the status mattered to Turner and I," Roark says in a deadly voice.

"Someone was winning the pool each week," I say with a shrug, "and there was an outside witness or two. I was kind of salty about it, which is why I asked Turner if she was a virgin. Why would she sleep with everyone else that treated her like shit, and never give me the time of day. I really didn't know! And it makes me wonder what else I got wrong," I mutter. *Fuck, if she was a virgin all this time, why were they saying they were fucking her?!*

"Why do I feel like I'm missing something? Lennon hinted at dark shit happening to her, but I didn't think we were that bad," I say with a groan.

"They all tried to rape her," Roark screams brokenly at me.

What?

"What the fuck. Why? It was just a fucking bet, it wasn't that serious," I lament. "Why take it that fucking far?"

"She was the outcast's daughter, right?" Turner states as he pulls in a deep breath and I nod. I don't trust the calmness in his voice and brace myself for the storm. "You all belittled and bullied her. She was less than a person to you all, so *no* didn't mean shit to your little friends. They wanted to see the crazy woman's daughter break. But she didn't. She fought off boys twice her size regularly. She survived, though, no thanks to you."

There's a weight in my chest and I can't breathe. Fuck. She walked home from school alone. Every day, I yelled at her as I drove past. I remember her pale face as I whipped past. I should have offered her a ride home. I could have been less of a dick. I could have... fuck. I close my eyes as my ears start to ring, and I wheeze. Fuck, I think I'm officially dying. I'd deserve it. I got it all so wrong with her.

"Derek," Turner yells, squeezing my arm. "Relax man, you didn't know. I can tell you didn't know. Breathe for me, okay?"

"Fuck, now I feel kind of bad for the little shite," Roark mutters as my eyes open. He pushes my head between my legs and I manage to gasp a breath or two.

"I didn't know," I rasp. "I looked the other way when the cheerleaders fucked with her, but the idea that they teamed up with those guys to... Fuck, I can't."

My stomach rebels and I choke on bile. I take a few steps forward, and puke. I gag, unable to feel sorry for myself as images of what Lennon could have gone through play through my head. "God, Lennon," I groan, dry heaving and shuddering.

Two sets of boots enter my field of vision and I glance up, shuddering in disgust. I wipe my mouth with my sleeve, wondering if they're gonna beat the shit out of me now. I won't even put up a fight, fuck I'd welcome it. I brace my hands on my knees as I struggle to get my breath under control.

"Lennon was a shell of a person when she finally got out of that damn town. I have half a mind to remove digits and cocks from every fuckwit that ever tried to take what wasn't theirs," Roark says in a measured voice. He's reigning himself in hard, but I would welcome his punishment. I consider myself one of the fuckwits, or whatever he said.

"We needed to know if you knew what you started," Turner says, his own growl escaping.

"No, never. I have never forced a woman to fuck me," I deny. "I went too far and was a dick a few days ago. I don't think I was ready to see her again, even though I told myself I was. She still looks so much like—"

Fuck. I can't talk about that. *Back in the vault. Lock it up tight.* "I just got carried away and was too rough," I say instead. Turner's forehead furrows. I'm Spiraling.

I was so wrong for so long about Lennon. I created a breeding ground for predators. Shit, I wonder what else happened to her during high school, and then hit a roadblock. I don't deserve to ask if I refuse to share. Relationships are two way streets, but even that is premature. The three of them may not want me at all after this. *I'm not worthy.* I'm the fucking scum beneath their shoes. I'm so fucked up.

I'm breathing heavy again and stand up, taking a shaky step back.

"Woah, Derek, where are you going?" Roark asks with concern coloring his words.

How can he feel anything for me after this? Let alone concern. How can he not hate me? I *hate* myself. My father tells me I don't think things through, I'm a fuck up, and I can finally see how right he is.

I don't deserve to see Lennon again. I need to quit.

"I need to talk to Mr. Miles," I rasp, tears I don't deserve to shed, riding me hard. "I can't stay on the tour. I'll just keep hurting her. There's no way we can get past this. I fucking traumatized her," I gasp, shaking my head.

Images of how sad she looked flood my mind. Lennon typically looked resigned to her fate, never complained, went home with the black eyes the cheerleaders gave her when they jumped her for some unknown infraction. It's like she lost her voice. I turn, walking quickly away.

"Wait, you can't go," Turner calls out. "Roark, wait!"

I almost turn when he says that, but instead a solid tank pile drives into me, and the world goes dark.

19

LENNON

The guys took a walk while I chatted with Layla, and said something about stretching their legs after the long drive.

"I'm not sure when we'll be back in that area, but we can always fly you in to open for us," I tell her. I don't know why, but I already miss her. She and I clicked so quickly, and we are finding we have a lot in common. "Prescott is also gone for good now, so I expect some things to change for the better."

"Thank God," Layla exclaims. "She's one of the most vile people I've ever met. I don't like how many stops you have on this tour. You know you're one of the only musical groups that has this many shows this year, right?" I swear she barely breathed while she said this.

"I know, but we also agreed to this in exchange for our new bus. The guys and I knew it would be hard, but we still had time for ourselves, until Prescott took over. Jordan says—"

"Jordan?" Layla asks in disbelief. "Did you just call a legend in music management by his first name?!"

My new friend has officially managed to find a new octave.

Her voice is usually so mellow and low, I didn't know she had it in her.

"He told me to," I defend with a laugh. "Jordan Miles is also officially now *The Darkest Nights'* handler. Jordan said he was uncomfortable with our pace as well, so we are staying at a hotel the next few nights while we are playing in Los Angeles. Honestly, it'll be nice," I confess, snuggling deeper on the couch in my pile of blankets. "I love our bus, but it'll be nice to shower with the guys."

"*Lalalala,*" Layla squeals, and I can only imagine her covering her ears. I giggle as I listen to her theatrics. *"Honestly, I'm still somehow surprised you're with both Roark and Turner. I had a feeling from what I've seen of your IG posts, but you're living every girl's dream,"* she teases me.

Smirking, I shake my head, even though I know she can't see me. "They are my people. Ror and Turner were already dating when they met me, and we just fit together. I dealt with a lot of bullshit growing up, but they remind me every day of my purpose." I'm not sure why I told her that, I don't speak about my past outside of my songs. I bite my lip, letting it sit for a second.

Layla doesn't say anything and I almost cut the call short. *Too much information for a call to a girl you barely know, Lennon.*

"I—"

"Is that why—"

We both snort with laughter as we stop speaking.

"You go first," I encourage with an embarrassed smile.

"*Ok, first, I have this weird feeling you're a super private person. You're so genuine it's easy to miss it, but the media says next to nothing about where you're from, your childhood, etc. My hat's off to whoever makes that happen, because they can be vicious. But, I wanted to ask, is your past what you talk about in your songs? They're so powerful, they always give me goose-bumps,"* Layla says.

I'm so happy she didn't dig more. "Yeah, my lyrics are pulled from my childhood. It kind of sucked," I said with a shrug, not elaborating. "Some people have a great childhood, sometimes it is just something you survive. So I did."

"One day, I hope you tell me about it. I'm not pressing now though—"

"Layla, who are you talking to?" I hear one of her guys say and I smile. It's crazy, but I already miss their chaos.

"I'm talking to Lennon," she says.

"Hi Lennon, it's Leo. I gotta steal her back for a bit, but be sure to call her later, okay? I think you're good for each other," he teases.

I didn't realize my shoulders had started to rise in anxiety, until I heard that and relaxed completely into my pillows. If they didn't approve, they may not let me talk to her anymore.

"Thanks Leo, I will. Bye guys," I say as I hang up.

I hear the woosh of the bus door opening and I sit up with a smile on my face. Now that Prescott is gone, I doubt anyone else would invite themselves into our space.

"Hey Lenny, are you done with your call?" Roark's voice filters through and my smile disappears.

He sounds... off. I scramble up and take a couple steps towards the front of the bus.

"Yeah, I'm done, is everything okay?"

"Umm, maybe? I need your help for a second though—"

I don't wait for him to finish his sentence, my legs running towards him. I yank aside curtains that section off the bus for privacy and notice he's holding someone bridal style in his arms. I see a huge bulk, but I can't see the person's face.

My head tilts in askance, and Roark looks sheepish.

"What did you do?" I ask. It's obvious something

happened, or he wouldn't have that look on his face. I bite my lip as I approach them and glance at Turner.

He crosses his arms across his chest and rocks back on his heels. He's fidgeting. Hmmm.

"Someone better start talking," I bark. I'm not accusing them, but they look guilty as shit.

Roark's full lips twist to the side. I want to tell him it'll be okay, no matter what he did or what happened, but I need to know first.

"Let's lay him down, and I'll tell you, yeah?" Roark grumbles and I turn with a nod. Rushing towards my blankets I start moving things. I can't even tell who is in his arms because his face is turned away, and I take a deep breath and stop.

I reach out and turn his face, brushing the hair off and see it's Derek. His neck is scraped and he has what looks like road rash on his forehead.

"So it doesn't look like you beat the shit out of him this time," I state stoically, stepping back so Ror can lay Derek down. "What happened?"

I refuse to freak out until I know the full story. I knew they were angry after hearing my story after the nightmare I had, so I expected some fall out.

Roark wrinkles his nose. "Let me tell you outside? You may decide to hit me. I swear, I wasn't thinking, I just didn't want him to quit..."

"Quit?" I shake my head. This is the last thing I expected to hear. "That's it! Off the bus. I need the full story," I shout, shooing them with my hands.

"Lavender, don't be mad," Turner says as he starts walking for the exit. "We needed to hear his side of the story. It ripped me apart to hear yours last night."

"I know, sweet boy. I just need to hear the truth. Let's go and you can tell me everything."

I hear a noise behind me and glance over my shoulder. Derek looks like he's getting more comfortable and I sigh. I expect we are going to have to talk too once he's awake.

Derek

Everything is dark, but I remember Roark tackled me. Fuck, for someone who has never played American football, he took me to the ground like a pro. I wasn't expecting it, and went down like a fucking sack of potatoes.

A light touch skims my forehead, and the broken skin from my fall burns. I want to lean into the touch, thank her for worrying about me.

I'm laid out somewhere that's super soft, and I hear footfalls walking away from me.

"I know, sweet boy," I hear and I flinch. I will never be anyone's sweet boy again. I moan softly before settling.

I drift in the cool darkness for a bit before I smell magnolias. Where is it coming from? I despise the smell of it, and when I go home, the scent surrounds me. It makes me a moody bastard, and goosebumps cover my skin. Another touch glances off my forehead, but it's less gentle.

I force my eyes open, but there's no one here. Sitting up too quickly, I moan as my head hurts. "What the fuck," I mutter. I take a breath, and the lingering smell of magnolias still coats the air.

I'm alone, and I can't stand it. I begin to push myself upright, when I hear the soft sound of the bus. Heavy footsteps follow softer ones and I wince at the sound. I wonder if I have a concussion. Fuck.

"Derek, are you awake," Lennon asks softly just before she walks into the area.

"Yeah," I groan. "I don't think I want to be though."

She hums in sympathy. "Let me get you cleaned up."

"You don't have to," I protest, shaking my head and then wincing in pain.

Turner and Roark also wince in sympathy as they sit across from her.

"Lenny is one of the most beautiful, frustrating, and stubborn women you'll ever meet," Roark chuckles. "In case you don't know those facets about her, keep your ass down before you fall down."

"Solid advice," I mutter, leaning back into the cushions.

Lennon grabs the first aid kit and opens it. "The boys told me what happened," she starts by saying.

I bite my lip as I huff out a breath. "I swear I didn't know any of that was happening," I start by saying. "I was a dick to you in school, but I was all fucked up by some things."

Lennon stops, staring at her hands, unable to meet my eyes. *How did I fuck up again?* "If I asked you something, would you tell me the truth?"

Confident there's no way in hell one of those questions will be 'did you ever fuck my mom', I agree. "Yes, whatever you want. Will you look at me when you ask, please?"

A slight blush graces her cheeks as she looks up. "Yeah, I will." She starts to worry her lip again and struggles to maintain eye contact.

What's she struggling with? "Come sit with me. Seriously, what do you want to ask me?"

Lennon picks up the kit and collapses next to me. "Did my mother sleep with your dad? I heard rumors of her sleeping around with married men, but honestly I was just trying to survive my day to day. The rumors were always just talk for me, because she was never around and even just eating was a struggle at times," she rushes out and I start seeing red.

Cats are better mothers than this woman, I swear. I growl softly and reach out to take her hand. She jumps, and I promise to all I hold dear that I'll make up being such a shithead to her.

"Take a deep breath for me," I say in almost a whisper.

Her breath sounds like a sob and my eyes fly to the guys in panic. Turner rolls his lips to keep from smiling at my reaction. He motions for me to keep talking to her and I mouth 'oh my God' at him. I swear, I never had a sister, so tears are something I flounder with. Turner covers his mouth with his hand and I give him my middle finger. He uncovers his mouth and licks his lips. Fucking *flirt.*

Lennon is oblivious to our hilarity and I reign in my amusement. "Lennon, my dad was having sex with your mom. I walked in on them once when I had just turned fourteen."

Her gasp is audible as her eyes rise to meet mine. There's a light sheen of unshed tears and I press my lips together at them. *I really don't want to fuck this up.* "I handled it really badly," I explain. "I had this irrational anger, and honestly sometimes it still gets the best of me. Car- uh Mrs. O'Reilly was always a wild card. You never knew if she would be happy, manic, depressed, or half dressed from what I understand." Lennon seems to crumble at this and my hands fist. I really want her in my lap, but the truth is she isn't mine, and she may never be. Thank goodness she didn't catch my slip up of almost using her mother's first name.

I glance over at the guys, and Turner's eyes sharpen. Fuck, I can see the wheels turning. Roark's eyes are glued to Lennon, and doesn't say anything.

"Anyway, I took out my anger on seeing them together with you, and I shouldn't have." I say as my skull throbs. I let my head fall back on the cushions and she turns to face me. "I get the feeling you got a raw deal when it came to your mom as well. Did she disappear a lot?"

She steels herself, forcing the emerging tears back. "Aye," she says and my eyebrows rise in surprise. Maybe she uses this term because Mav and Roark do? I don't believe Carrie was Irish, and I never met her father. Her last name is O'Reilly, but I'm unaware of her true roots.

"Let's have a look at your head," she murmurs and gently cleans up my scrapes. "I don't know if you have a concussion, but you did lose consciousness for a little while. Do you want to go to the hospital?"

"Nah, erm, no I don't. I'll take it easy at the show tonight, but I should be fine. I've honestly taken harder hits playing ball, but didn't expect Roark to take me down the way he did," I admit.

Roark looks sheepish and the blood rises to his face. He looks embarrassed, and I chuckle because it's adorable. These three are quickly bypassing my guard, and I don't know how it happened, or how I feel about it. Especially with them, when I saw Lennon as my enemy for so many years.

Lennon adds ointment to my scrapes and frowns. "What's with the long face?" I ask gently. I still have my secrets, but I don't want to hurt her, so I'd much rather hide them. Carrie's dead now, the truth would just cause more harm to tell her now.

"I don't want to keep doing this," she confesses. "You taunt me and tell me I'm becoming crazy like my mother... It fucks with me, Derek. I don't want to be her. The night I woke up after I was drugged and didn't remember anything. I really did think I was losing it. Bipolar disorder is genetic for some and I don't want to be *her*," she growls, pulling in a breath. *Fuck me.* I wanted to fuck with her before, but it was also a legitimate warning. I didn't want a Carrie 2.0 unleashed on the world.

Except... Lennon is so far from being her mom it's ridiculous. She was always kind in school, despite everything. God, I'm so stupid. I've even watched her talk to teens and offer advice during her VIP chats with her fans. I have to do something to repair the damage I've caused to Lennon.

"You're not," I sigh. My own eyes prick with tears, remembering how Carrie took advantage of me as a teen. Sure every time we had sex it was consensual, but it never should have been offered to me at sixteen by her. And, it didn't only happen once. "You're a far cry from being Carrie O'Reilly, I swear it. She was selfish, impulsive, and didn't give a flying shit about a single soul."

"She wasn't always like that," she whispers. I see the girl who aches for the mom she remembers. I don't know if Carrie actually was better when Lennon was younger, or if she hid her bouts of mania and depression better. "She was home, she cooked, she drove me to school—"

I'm almost scared to ask. "When did that all stop?" The things she's listing are the base-line things every parent should provide and my blood runs cold as I realize what she was going through just across the yard from me. Our yards were huge, but Jesus if I had just opened my eyes...

"I was nine when I started walking to school, but I didn't really mind," she begins.

"Lennon, it snows in Kentucky," I remind her. "It was a thirty to forty minute walk to school."

She shrugs. "It was a nicer walk when I had breakfast."

Turner slides forward until his head is in his hands. "I swear if that woman was alive today, I would be tempted to kill her," he snarls.

"Same," Roark mutters and I echo it in my head. I'm just a witness to Lennon's words. I don't deserve to yell, or commiserate, because there were parts I let happen.

"What happened after that, Lennon," I ask, terrified to know, because once I do, the guilt will lay so much heavier. It's one thing to suspect, it's another to have it laid bare right in front of me.

"Ah, Mom started disappearing when I was ten. She wouldn't leave food, didn't tell me where she was going, so I just kind of made do." I can tell she's altering the truth so it seems better than it was when Turner looks up and shakes his head.

"Lavender," he begs. "The truth or not at all. Please. She doesn't deserve your misplaced loyalty."

"I need to know," I agree. "I had a feeling she wasn't the best mother at times, and I noticed that your clothes didn't always fit, but I didn't realize she was starving you." My hands keep fisting and relaxing in an exercise of restraint, because I can't do what I desperately want to. Hold Lennon in my arms.

Lennon throws herself into her pillows with a sigh. "I learned how to go out without food, how to wash my own clothes, and cover for my mom. A neighbor realized my mom was gone at one point, and dropped a covered dish once a day in the mornings. I just figured out how to make it stretch for at least two meals," she explains with a shrug. "My dad, who I haven't seen since he left when I was really little, apparently paid the bills as part of alimony and child support. My mom didn't work at all, and if he didn't pay it, I wouldn't have had water or electricity either. Things just were rough at home."

I can tell she doesn't want to say anything else when she crosses her arms defensively across her chest. I have a feeling Turner and Roark found this out yesterday, so she must still be feeling raw.

"God, I feel like even more of a dick now," I groan, closing my eyes. I remember how dismissive Carrie was when she talked about Lennon the night we had sex for the first time, and start to drift in my memories.

A banging starts and I wince and reopen them.

"No sleeping," Turner barks and I nod. He's right. I'm so tired, I'm struggling to stay awake.

"Sorry, I'm really tired all of a sudden."

"So keep talking. You can't sleep if there are words coming out of your mouth," Turner sasses.

"Oh my God," I laugh. "Fine, brat. What am I talking about," I sass, almost forgetting my secrets. I sober as I wait to see what he may have seen in my face. I don't have many tells, but he's so damn observant.

"Lennon was talking to you the other day, and you seemed fine one second, and then the next your eyes got all dark. You got really mean then too. Even if you don't want to explain why it's a trigger for you, which I accept, I need to know what triggers you. Is there a word you dislike or do you not like certain touches," he hazards. My jaw drops and he sits up and he throws his hand up. "I knew there was something, I watch you—"

"Do you now," my voice goes deep and flirty. I didn't expect to flirt, and it's not a deflection. I can tell Turner won't let me get away with it.

His eyes heat and he smirks. "You know I do. Don't go there unless you're totally ready. I play for keeps, mister."

I bite my lip and my eyes grow hooded. Fuck, why is he so damn sexy.

Lennon giggles as she watches and I cover my face. Fuck, I'm hard as steel, and I shift uncomfortably.

"Gah, that wasn't nice, Turner," I complain.

"Maybe not, but I needed to see if your attraction was a fluke. I haven't played with a 'I think I'm straight, but maybe not' guy before. I'm moving into the box that this may be something," Turner says. I uncover my face in time to see him shrug and swipe his tongue along his lips.

"The word mister also doesn't seem to be a trigger for you," Roark observes. "I can see your cock straining from here," he says with a wicked grin. I am finding that his brogue gets heavier when he's very angry or turned on. I breathe heavily, arousal singing through my veins.

"No, that word is fine. It's only certain—" I scowl, seeing the trap laid bare. "Fuuuuck," I groan.

"Derek," Lennon says softly, gently and carefully placing her hand on my arm. I glance over and see how hard she's staring at me, and I see a touch of fear. It guts me to wonder if she thinks I'll strike her because I feel cornered.

"Yeah," I say just as softly. It's almost funny how careful she is with me. I desperately don't want her to be afraid of me anymore. I have so much to make up for.

"I don't want to hurt you, and I feel like I have been," she explains. I hate that she thinks this. It's not her fault, it's Carrie's. My pulse starts to race, but I focus on Lennon's gorgeous gray eyes. They're so different from *hers*. My nails dig into my palms, teeth tearing my bottom lip.

Fuck, I've never told anyone any of this. I don't date anymore because I can't deal with any pet names that may be too close to what she used either. I fuck girls I meet when I'm out at a club, or on the music scene to scratch the itch. It's just that lately it hasn't been enough, so I stopped bothering to try.

"I try not to encourage the use of any pet names or nicknames at all because I have a real problem with them, but I noticed you all use them," I start.

"Not all the time," Roark says with a nod, "but yes. I call Lennon, Lenny often. The three of us also use names of affection, especially in a passionate moment."

I shake out my hands and lean on my forearms as I think.

"My trigger words are: sweet boy, little boy, or baby boy," I say as I shudder. "It brings out the worst in me, and I tend to lash out. After everything I've learned today, I want to work on not hurting you ever again. I know it's selfish to say work on it and not never do it, but I'm broken when it comes to you."

Lennon watches me for a beat. "We've been doing this dance for a long fucking time, Derek. I'm so used to it, it almost doesn't register to me how messed up it all is."

"Oh my God, I'm your mother," I say in agony, standing up. "I heard how you stood up for her even with her bullshit, and you're doing it with me too, Lennon. I don't want to be the person you brush aside abuse with. The person who gets a pass to be a shithead to you. That's not okay." I weave for a second, and the world tilts. Roark quickly stands and braces my body by grabbing my bicep.

"Woah there, take it slow," he says softly. I feel out of control, and his tone shows I am. I struggle to bring it down a notch or two, but the truth is, I'm horrified. I doubt my body can take another Roark-special takedown today though.

Lennon scrambles up and stands in front of me. "You can easily get around me if you need to. I don't want to trap you, but please hear me out," she says, throwing up her hands in frustration. "It's obvious you saw me as an extension of my mother for a while," she says, not knowing how close to the truth she really is. I stiffen further, worried she'll figure out my past, though there's no way anyone could unless I told them. The truth will die with me if I have my way.

"Is that why the bullying started? Knocking my books out of my hands, ruining my notes, recruiting people to fuck with me? My mom fucked your dad, and you wanted to get even," she states as if it's the most normal thing in the world.

"That's how it started, and then it spiraled. I couldn't stop messing with you, and then I wanted you to notice me. When you didn't, I wanted you not to notice anyone else and everything escalated," I confess. I don't think I've ever allowed myself to look at it very closely.

Once I left Farrelsville, I pushed it all away, and by the time I went to visit, Lennon had moved away.

I made her life hell, on top of her mom's fuckery, and it guts me. I shudder, knowing my actions are responsible for unleashing hormone ridden monsters. Roark puts his other arm around me and squeezes. I could feel embarrassed that he can feel my visceral reactions, but I can't. He should be beating the shit out of me. *Why isn't he?!*

"Hey, stay with me, yeah," Lennon steps towards me and slowly reaches out to touch my face. I flinch, still expecting the three of them to turn on me.

"How do you not hate me right now," I whisper brokenly. "I am responsible for stripping you of a normal childhood. Lennon, I hate myself."

"Nah, our Lenny isn't like that," Roark says. "She's a forgiving lass, and believes in second chances. The question is, do you want it?"

"Yeah, I really do. But I could fuck it up. I mean, God. I'm probably going to fuck it up," I groan dropping my chin to my chest.

"So you fuck it up," this beautiful angel says as she gently presses on my chin so I'll lift my face. "I'm not asking you to be perfect—" she bites her lip, and I wonder what she was going to say. She shudders and suddenly blinks as her eyes fill with tears. "The 'no affectionate names' is gonna be hard for me to remember," she says apologetically.

"Hey, you're okay," I murmur. She must have started to say something she thought would trigger me. God, why am I like this? The last thing I want is for her to sensor herself.

She visibly shakes herself and forces a smile. "It just makes me wonder why, who hurt you, and who I need to stab for it?" she confesses.

God, that's a minefield.

"I love that you want to protect me," I tell her honestly. "I never really dealt with what happened to me, but it's not your responsibility to change everything because of it."

A part of me sincerely thinks I'm just too broken and dark for these three amazing people.

"Hold on a minute," Turner says, standing. "I have a question for you. How you answer may make everything else a moot point."

Roark squeezes me and lets go, stepping back. It feels as if he's helping me bolster my courage, because Turner is really fucking intense. He should be: I'm essentially considering dating them all. I turn to face Turner and cross my arms as if to brace myself for his words.

"Do you want to try and see where this goes with all of us? Roark, Lennon, and I are all interested. There's something about you that continually draws me to you for one."

"Aye, it's the tight ass and smart mouth, isn't it, Turner," Roark teases.

I swear my ass clenches at his sinful words, surprising me. Fuck, I've never been spoken to by a man like this. Not only that, they're all so fucking gorgeous, it's just unfair.

Roark is fiercely protective, but also has this huge heart. I've certainly never met anyone like him. God, I think I may be crazy, but I really do want to see where this could go.

"Yeah, I do want to pursue this, but frankly I don't want to hurt anyone. The three of you have been together for years, what if I fuck something up?" I ask hoarsely.

"How would you do that? We've weathered a lot together over the last ten or so years. We talk a lot, we work things out, and we've already started doing this with you. You can't fuck it up," Turner says with a shrug. "Make an effort to not be a dick, explain when you need space, and let us be there for you. The rest will fall into place, if you want it that is."

I let my arms drop with a nod. "Silly me," I tease. "Why did I overcomplicate this?"

Lennon leans into me and stands on her tiptoes to get to my ear. She's woefully short, but it makes me smirk at how adorable she is. "Turner likes to simplify things to the point where you feel dumb if you try to argue to get his way," she stage-whispers and I laugh.

I wrap my arm around her easily and she grins up at me. I don't think I've ever had a happy, pliant Lennon in my arms. I *really* like it. "Mission accomplished," I grin.

"Now that this is all figured out," Turner says with a wink, "it's just about time to get ready."

I nod. "I'm gonna go in and find a quiet place to work inside," I explain.

"Couldn't you hook up to the wifi and work here?" Lennon asks.

"Yeah, but I don't want to intrude," I start to say and then realize I don't need to.

Roark shakes his head with a grin. "You're not. Seriously, Derek, you shouldn't be by yourself anyway. Hang out, and one of us will check in on you to make sure you stay awake," he reassures me.

"It'll probably end up being me," Lennon says with a shrug. "Roark will disappear soon to do his thing, and Turner will go hang out with our fans."

"Not tonight, beautiful," Turner says, shaking his head. "I'm still not comfortable leaving you after Seattle, and we've had a lot of excitement lately. Ror and I plan to stick nearby for now."

Without meaning to, a grunt of my approval escapes.

Lennon sighs. "Cavemen one, two, and now the third has entered the game," she mutters.

I press my lips together to keep myself from laughing. As hard as this conversation was to have, I also don't think I've ever allowed myself to enjoy the people I'm with as much as I have today.

"Derek, I have your stuff at the front of the bus. I don't think anything got messed up. I'll grab it for you," Turner says, bursting into motion.

The man is always absurdly still, or exploding with energy, there's no happy medium.

Lennon directs me to sit down, Roark offers me painkillers, coffee, and water. I watch in awe as they work around each other. It's been a long time, if ever, since someone has taken care of me. I don't think my own mother has ever been this attentive of me. I feel warm at the realization that my childhood affections were mechanical in the Williams home. I had my needs covered and my extracurriculars–which were for my father's benefit as well–: food, clothes, rides to school, and football.

But someone to take care of me because of a possible concussion? That's never happened. They were to be expected since I played football.

"If you need anything else, please let us know," Roark says with a grin. "I'm going to shower, because my morning got a little hijacked with Jordan's arrival. Stay for dinner, I'll throw something together for us all, yeah?"

Lennon smiles almost shyly as she leaves for the back of the bus with Turner and Roark. *I hope she takes a nap if she didn't sleep well earlier.* My chest twinges as I watch her leave, and I force myself to open my laptop. It surprisingly escaped Roark's tackle unscathed.

I really do want to see where this goes, despite how

disturbingly broken my insides are. Carrie's influence has left long lasting scars across my soul. She found me several times after that first encounter, and each time dug her place inside my soul. Maybe a little lightness can chase away the darkness finally.

20

TURNER

I didn't expect today to go the way it did at all, but I'm glad. He thinks he's broken, it's obvious, maybe too broken for us. He's wrong though, each of us has trauma, but we all mesh together. Lennon, Roark, and I fit effortlessly within each other because like calls to like.

I wrap my arms around Lennon and kiss her shoulder as we walk to our bedroom. I'm going to convince her to nap for a little before she has to get dressed.

"How are you feeling about everything that happened today?" I ask her.

Roark groans as he stops at the bathroom. "Fuck, I wanna hear this, but I want to scrub the damn day off me too," he complains.

Mmm, I would love to scrub the day off of him myself. I'm so glad we are calling a nice, special hotel room home for the next few days. Huh... should I invite Derek? Is that weird?

"Go shower," I command. "Wash your ass thoroughly, I may want it tonight."

His lips part and he begins to pant. "Fuck you, Turner, ya don't play fair."

He slams into the bathroom and I snicker into Lennon's lavender scented hair.

"So mean," she giggles. A yawn follows and I direct our footsteps to the bedroom.

"Why don't you nap with me, Lavender? In one word though, how are you feeling? Today was kind of heavy," I murmur, keeping my voice down.

"Honestly? It was enlightening," she says as her forehead furrows in thought. "I really thought he hated me, that somehow I had offended him. It all started so abruptly, I never thought it would have nothing to do with me after all. Some of it makes sense now though, the digs on my mental health, the taunting." She sighs. "There's more, though. He's not ready to tell us, but I know there's more," she whispers furtively.

My lips purse as I nod. "Yeah, I have no doubt in my mind there's a lot more, but trauma isn't all uncovered in a day. We both know this."

"We'll follow the song to the end," she murmurs and I grin. It fits, even adding a new string of notes to our song, it fits.

Stripping, I climb into bed naked. Lennon drops onto the bed in her panties and snuggles into me. Turning down the lights, it's our very own dark, quiet cave. Knowing she'll need help quieting her thoughts, I hum softly as I play with her hair. Her breathing deepens, and while listening to her sleep, I quickly follow.

~

"HEY, guys it's time to get up now," Roark says softly.

I groan as I bury my face into Lenny's hair. "Okay. Did you

check on Derek, make sure he didn't fall asleep," I ask. I hadn't meant to sleep as deeply as I did, and now I feel bad.

"Yes, he's fine," he chuckles. "He'll be out of the window for a concussion soon, and he's built like a tank. I only managed to tackle him because I surprised him."

"Ror, you're the pot calling the kettle black here. Lavender, wake up now love. Do you want the shower first?"

She moans and flops over onto her back. "Yes please. Did anyone check on Derek?"

I smirk at how quickly we all started taking that man into consideration. Lavender has a huge heart, but there's something vulnerable about Derek that pulls me to him as well.

"Yes, why don't you check on him before you shower?"

This perks her up, just as I expected it to. She stands up and starts walking towards the door and I snort.

"What," she asks, turning. She's still only in her panties. I turn up the lighting and prop myself up on my elbows as I drink her in.

"Derek's going to get more than he bargained for if you go out like that," I tease, my tongue swiping across my bottom lip as I imagine drawing her taut nipple into my mouth.

She glances down and giggles. "Oops."

Roark rolls his eyes and grabs a long sleeved hoodie. Now that I'm sitting up, the air is kind of cool.

"Arms up, Lenny my girl. Let's work up to strutting around naked around Derek, shall we?" His lips pull up as he says this, covering our girl, and I feel my cock stir. Derek really does have gorgeous, thick corded muscles and yummy abs.

"Mmm. Anyone else ever think about licking up his abs, or is that just me? There are times where his shirt rides up when he stretches that just makes me hard as fuck," I chuckle darkly.

Roark smirks and nods. "Aye, the man is yummy. I just

don't want to move too fast, scare him off. I think you and I pull feelings and desires from Derek that he isn't used to."

"Aye, the man was straight as an arrow before he met us," I tease back, then stand up and stretch.

"Unfair," Lennon whines. "I have to leave a warm bed and a naked boyfriend. Rude." She flounces off and I sputter with laughter. Living with her will never get old.

"You should probably work on upgrading yourself from boyfriend to fiancé," Roark drops before he follows her out.

My jaw drops in surprise. Fucker. He really is right. I almost forgot about his epic proposal to Lavender and I.

~

Roark

I should have grabbed a larger hoodie, I realize, when I see Lenny's cute butt cheeks peeking out from the bottom. Oh well, if Derek is going to be hanging out on the bus, he'll have to get used to us in various states of undress.

"Did you get much work done," she asks him as she walks through the curtain dividing the kitchen area from the rest of the bus.

Derek glances up and a ghost of a smile graces his lips as he sees her. I checked on him just enough to not be annoying, even quietly watching him like a creeper from around the curtain to make sure he didn't fall asleep. The man is beautiful, without a doubt. I find myself staring at his dark eyes, wanting to comb my fingers through his curly hair. Turner isn't the only one that's got it bad right now.

"Yeah, I did actually," he says. "You even have a TikTok now."

I snicker. "Nah, for real? I don't know how to use that app at all. Seems like a bunch of thirst traps to me."

Derek looks over at me and winks. *Gah, he fucking winked at me, people.* "I know. That's why I made *The Darkest Nights* one."

Lenny carefully climbs onto the cushions, and I know she's restraining herself since she'd usually just jump up on them. "Are you flirting right now? Cause it's really fucking hot," she says, leaning into him with a teasing smile.

She's pulling off the kid gloves, and I'm glad. Her talk with Derek helped open communication between them, and a door that'll hopefully lead him to join us. No one is completely whole, and no one escapes life without trauma. It's obvious he feels like he'll break us, he even said as much, but that's not possible. The three of us are perfectly imperfect, and I think he would fit within our broken pieces well.

My little Valkyrie puts a hand on his bicep as she teases him and I hide my smile as I start making dinner, my hands going through the motions of preheating the oven and turning on the stove.

"I may be flirting just a little, Lennon," Derek responds, hiding his mouth behind his hand, with an answering smile. Freaking adorable.

"So what are your plans for this TikTok account, then," I ask to shift the focus off of him as I pull out ground meat, butternut squash, and vegetables. We have a support assistant on the tour that shops for us thankfully and keeps our fridge stocked. This is the same person in charge of making sure Lenny has gummy bears and Turner has his favorite brand of guitar picks. I haven't spent much time chatting with the gal, but she's efficient, and texts me every few days for an updated grocery list.

"I want to do videos of concerts, maybe a few live feeds in

the form of Q and A with you guys as the platform grows, and zoomed in videos of you guys playing," he explains.

Lenny continues to grin, and I can tell she's feeling mischievous as she draws up her legs to her chest. I can see the perfect view of her ass in her thong as I watch her and I bite my fist as I stir the meat on the stove. Fuck, she's so gorgeous, and her hair is tussled from her nap. She pushes a curl out of her face as she listens to Derek.

He was on his phone as he spoke to us about his TikTok plans. As he looks over at Lenny, I can tell the exact moment he catches a glimpse of her ass. Her body shifts just a bit to face him and his eyes drink her in.

"What were we talking about," he rumbles as he puts his phone down and I swear the sexual tension may just kill me. *Don't burn the food.*

I season the butternut squash and then put the casserole dish into the preheated oven, quietly working on automatic pilot as I watch their dance unfold. And it absolutely is a carefully crafted one. He moves slowly, carefully, as if he's afraid she may stop him. If I could bring myself to say something and not break the moment, I'd tell him Lenny isn't going to stop him. Not after today.

Derek reaches out and slowly drags his finger down the outside of her thigh. I can see the goosebumps rise along her skin, as her breath quickens, and her lips part. I shift my weight in the effort it'll magically ease the pressure on my cock. *Nope, no such luck.*

She whimpers as her eyes widen with need, her pupils blowing out as he gets closer to her sweet pussy. Her hips involuntarily thrust towards him and her chest heaves. Lenny wakes up needy on the best of days, but Derek is calculating as he plays with her. I may be wrong, but I think he's someone who needs control in the bedroom. He'll be fun to play with.

He leans forward and growls into her ear, "Need something, Lennon?"

She shivers as he palms her thigh. "Derek," she breathes and he hums lazily under his breath.

"You're so soft, warm—"

"And I guarantee our girl is dripping too," Turner chuckles.

Derek jerks away and Lenny squeals and jumps up. "I need a shower," she gasps, but not before I catch a glimpse of a wet patch on her panties. Mmm, she was definitely into everything he was giving her. I bet it'll be a cold shower too.

Lenny practically runs away and my lips twitch as I turn back to the food. The next few days will definitely be interesting. Speaking of...

"We're getting a hotel room for the next few nights," I begin and Turner whoops in excitement. I chuckle at how long he's been waiting for this. "I have a feeling Jordan will spring for rooms for the entire support team. If so, would you like me to request an adjoining room? We could say we've been working closely on revamping our social media platforms. Atlas and Mav always stay in an adjoining suite as well, since they sleep better near us, and the new environment often means our muse's creativity is sparked," I explain.

"You mean Lennon," he states with a nod. "I've never seen anyone create lyrics and music the way she did at the studio," Derek says in awe, his hand curling on his thigh at the loss of Lenny's soft skin. I don't miss how he resolutely ignores my question for now.

I press my lips together in mirth as I finish cooking dinner. "Lenny is one of the most incredible people that I've ever met. Emotions, events, people all drive the need to write for the lass. We've gotten used to running to find her when she texts that she's writing, because it often leads to a jam session."

"I vaguely remember hearing her dad was a musician, but

the man never visited that I know of. She never played in the school band or sang in the choir at school either, but that's not a surprise to me now that I think of it. She wanted to fade into the background, not shine." He shakes his head as he remembers her formative years. "She did always have some kind of notebook with her, I wonder if she wrote even then," he muses.

"Lennon was discovered singing at an open mic night that she attended on a dare," I tell him, still surprised at the turn in our interactions between earlier today and now. I only hated him before because he was a threat to Lenny. Now we are having that odd getting to know you period, even with our rough start. "She was then bribed by Mr. Castle, who introduced himself to her after she sang, to meet us. Lenny impressed him, and in turn this too skinny, gray-eyed girl wrapped us around her finger."

"Bribe how," he asks.

"Like Mr. Castle told me he would give me six-hundred bucks if I would just meet these four huge men," Lenny says. She's wrapped in a towel, her hair wet, and must have taken the fastest shower ever. "I need to get dressed, but don't want to keep you waiting, Ror. When did you want to sit down to dinner?"

I check the butternut squash in the oven and grunt. "Fifteen minutes, Lenny. What are you doing with your hair tonight?" I want to suggest she leave her hair wet to eat if it's going to take awhile to do.

"Something complicated," she laughs. "I'm going to get dressed and then do hair and makeup after." Lenny heads back to our room to dress like the mini tornado she is before a show.

"Oh! Hold off on the gummy bears till after dinner!" I yell after her. She raises her arm to show she heard me and I roll my eyes. "Minx," I mutter, shaking my head.

Derek chuckles under his breath as he starts to put his things away. "I'll get out of your way, guys. You're about to eat."

Turner snorts and shakes his head, sitting at the table. "No offense, Derek, but you're a little dense. Ror made dinner for all of us, and you're included now. He makes the most amazing food in our tiny kitchen, and I have no idea how. I swear it's magic," he says, arching his brow at me.

I shake my head as I walk over to Turner and kiss him. I nip his lower lip, run my tongue along his and suck on his tongue ring. "I know nothing about magic, gorgeous, but you're wonderful to say differently."

I blink as I realize I forgot myself and peek over at Derek. His lips are parted, his tongue just barely visible, and he's panting softly. "Holy fuck, why was that so hot," he gasps.

I smirk, happy he's quite alright with public displays of affection, and that the word 'gorgeous' doesn't affect him. I assume it's not a word that was used by whoever was fucking him over. I get childhood predator vibes, probably because of the words that trigger him.

Shaking off my suspicions, I enjoy the glow that Derek is definitely attracted to us. "Feel free to join in whenever you're ready," I growl. He whimpers softly, hands fisted at his sides as he squirms. *Very nice.*

"I have to finish making dinner, or I'd enjoy this more," I murmur. My hand cradles his face and I stare into his eyes. "Aye, very soon, you will be ours. Say you'll stay with us."

"You were serious about that," he breathes, his eyes wide. It's easy to forget he's a touch younger than Turner and I, but I see it now in his surprise.

I nod. "Aye, Derek, I absolutely was." I make a point to say his name as I let the pad of my finger drift across his face. He skipped shaving today and there's a bit of scruff that makes my mouth water. "Stay," I rasp, breathing in his scent of citrus. "Please."

"For the record, I would have stayed before the please," he says.

Turner chuckles darkly and I lean to touch my lips on the shell of his ear. "Noted. I also see you have a touch of brattiness, just like our Lenny."

I straighten and he shivers. "You good," I ask, checking before I go back to start plating our food.

"Surprisingly so," he says. His eyes are clear, heartbeat elevated from where my hand still lies on his face, and lips parted. God, his mouth is going to drive me to distraction.

"Good, because those pouty lips will look gorgeous wrapped around my cock sometime soon, and I'd hate to spook you." My lips curl into a suppressed smile as I turn.

"Oh my fuck," he whispers.

"Isn't his dirty talk delicious," Turner growls.

"It really is," he murmurs. Derek's hands shake slightly as he puts them on the table, but it's more from being insanely turned on, then hesitation. He's not in charge here, but I'm hoping he'll learn to trust us enough to let go.

I keep an eye on him as I plate the food, making sure he's not a flight risk. Turner relaxes next to him, pulling him into conversation. I feel better knowing we didn't spook him, not yet.

"Lenny," I yell. "You're cutting it close, my girl."

"Shit," I hear and I snort, placing dishes on the table. "I didn't mean to get distracted," she says as she swoops into the kitchen. I turn and watch her stride in. "I started talking to Layla as I was getting dressed, and time ran away from me."

She's wearing a blue crop top tonight that skims the top of her stomach. It's paired with low waisted blue pants that taper at the ankles. Four inch peep toe ankle boots finish off the outfit and I shake my head in awe. It shouldn't work, but damn it's perfect.

"You're fucking beautiful, little Valkyrie," I breath. "Damn, you even look comfortable somehow. How the hell do you manage it?"

"I overheard something about magic," she says with a wink, and I wonder how much she heard. I hope she heard it all, and that her panties are fucking flooded. "I'm gonna go with I'm magic."

"That you are. I wouldn't *dream* of debunking this," I say with a bark of laughter. "Come eat before a gust of wind blows you away." I say this regularly because when I first met her, I swear it would have.

"Not with your incredible cooking," Lenny sasses, slapping her own ass. She sits down next to Derek and I sit across from him.

"Dig in, and please feel free to tip the chef in sexual favors."

Derek takes a sip as I say this and sputters. I struggle not to snicker, rubbing his back as he coughs. "Sorry there, mate," I say, losing my battle and laughing.

He turns a little red as he gets his breath back and shakes his head. "Note to self, Roark is not safe to drink around," he says, shaking his head. There's mirth crinkling the corners of his eyes though, so I shrug. *Oops.*

Dinner is fun, lighthearted, and unfortunately there were no sexual favors.

21

DEREK

I don't think I've ever laughed this hard in years. It feels so odd to cycle through so many emotions in such a short period of time, when I've been so angry for most of my life. Lust, playfulness, amusement. They're foreign concepts for me when I've been going through the motions for years.

Roark is also so different from what I expected. He has been in protection mode for much of the time I've known him, so it makes sense. I still feel a little sick as I think about the responsibility I played in Lennon's past. I took part in ripping away her innocence, the chance to have a haven at school when her mom was a train wreck.

Twenty minutes earlier, she walked over with me into the stadium. Roark and Turner had things to take care of, so I sat sentry outside the dressing room to answer emails from the label. I feel like this is a test from the guys, a trial to see if I can be trusted alone with Lennon. I don't completely trust myself, so I don't blame them.

I sigh heavily as I stand outside of Lennon's room. Today I actually have permission to take shots of her in the final moments leading up to the show. I still feel as if I'm disturbing her though, interrupting her private moments, as I quietly open the door and look in to make sure she's fully dressed.

She looks incredible in her blue outfit. Like damn, she's so beautiful. I lean against the door frame and let my eyes drink her in. Earlier, she told Roark she was doing something complicated to her hair. I don't know what this is called, but it's worth the effort.

Lennon is adding large curls to her lavender hair, but my eyes are drawn to the crown of complicated braids she's created. It would be over the top for anyone else, but it makes her large gray eyes pop since her hair is out of her face now. The last time she did braids like this, she added flowers as well, but they're absent today. She's singing a song under her breath, and I vaguely recognize the artist as RaeLynn.

Lifting the camera, I finally pull myself from my fascination. I have a job to do, even if she is the most gorgeous creature that I've ever seen. Her creamy arms are toned, her bruises fading quickly. The last time I watched her, I didn't pay close enough attention to her tattoos, and I realize they are musical notes that flow up her arm. I wonder if it's a song, or random notes. As I take a photo of her staring at herself in the mirror, teasing a curl to lay differently, I decide they probably have meaning.

That's the kind of girl Lennon is.

"Are you coming in, or are you going to stare at me a bit longer," she asks, her eyes meeting mine in the mirror. "For the record, I'm fine with either at the moment."

I chuckle as I push myself out of my slouch and step in. "I'm gonna sit over there and stare if it's all the same to you, Lennon."

"I'm good with that, though you should know my gummy

bear consumption is up, so I'm mostly made of sugar right now."

I sit on a chair off to the side where I can continue to shoot her and grin. "You're adorable when you're bouncing off the walls... and a bit sassy."

She sticks her tongue out at me and I wish I was faster on the draw to take a photo. Playfulness looks good on her.

Pulling a deep red lipstick from her makeup bag, she paints her lips. I force myself to take a picture, and not think about what it would look like painted around my cock. It's like my blood is set on fire, and I can only think with my little head today. I know who's responsible for it too, but damn there's not enough room in my pants for this.

She fiddles with her makeup for another minute and then nods. Walking over to me, she straddles me as she sits. My hands wrap around her waist, rocking her over me. Her eyes roll slightly in pleasure and she sighs.

"What are you up to, little minx," I growl.

"Pushing limits," she says breathily. "You'll learn I'm a brat soon, and it's something I'm adept at."

I rock up into her and sigh. "Lennon, you're a temptress. You're so fucking sexy, all I want to do is—"

Fuck it.

I kiss up her chest, and lick up her neck. "You taste delicious here, and now all I can think of is tasting your sweet pussy. I need to earn your honeyed cream though, but we can play," I breathe.

I roll her against my hardness again and she whimpers.

"This outfit won't cover up if I come," she gasps. "I don't have time to change. But fuck if I don't want to," she sighs.

My breath hitches as I process that. All I can think of is how much of a mess she'll make when that sweet pussy gushes for me.

"God, Lennon," I groan. "Are you telling me you make a mess when you come?"

"Yeah," she breathes, leaning forward to kiss up my neck. It's light and airy, just a tease, and all I want to do is fuck up her lipstick. Damn, it's too close to the show for her to have to redo it. I also know how much she won't want to miss the opening act. Goddammit, I can't be selfish.

Her tongue drags up the column of my throat and I shudder in need. "Fuck, you're testing my restraint here." My hands squeeze tightly against her waist and then I release quickly. I can't mark her up again. Fuck, maybe this isn't a good idea. I can't always be soft.

Her hands cup my face and her eyes start to clear of lust. "Where'd you go," she murmurs with a soft smile. "I'm not gonna break because you squeezed too hard. I promise. A bruise in passion is way different from anger. You should see what Ror, Turner, and I get up to," she giggles. "Ropes, spreaders, floggers, oh my."

She kisses the side of my mouth and I melt against her with a sigh. "Lennon, love. I don't wanna hurt you," I breathe.

"You won't. And if you do, we'll talk about it and get through it. I'll tell you what I don't like, and you'll definitely fucking know what I do."

Soft lips tease and gently press against my lips. Mine part of their own accord and I slowly let her in. I don't typically kiss women, I honestly avoid it. It's why I usually kiss necks, ears, everywhere else because kissing on the lips feels too intimate.

Kissing Lennon... it's so different from anything else. She's warm, soft, and her lips are firm, but pliant. It's hard to describe, but I swipe my tongue slowly across her bottom lip and know I need more of this. Whimpering, she grinds down for friction and I wrap my arms around her, pushing my tongue between her lips. I demand access and she opens like the goddess she is.

If I thought she'd continue to be soft, I'm mistaken. Our tongues wage war, her body arching over me. "Fuck," I groan, coming up for air.

My hands travel up her back, thumbs rubbing her nipples. She shivers, eyes rolling as her head drops back. I hear something bang outside the door and realize I left it open. I'm an idiot.

I glance over but no one's there. Weird.

"You're gonna miss the opening band," I remind her with a smile.

"Dammit," she sighs. Standing, she double checks her makeup, fixes her clothes and grins at me as she starts for the door.

Her lipstick didn't budge. *Why is that so hot?* Scrambling, I curse as I stand and follow her. I'm stuck like glue to her until she goes on stage tonight. I don't like that she's been drugged this tour. That shouldn't have happened.

Yes, I can finally admit that I don't think she's off her medication. Lennon doesn't show any signs of mania, not like Carrie did. Even when her emotions run high, they're normal reactions to what's happening around her. *If this is growth, it's fucking painful.*

I WATCH from the audience as *The Darkest Nights* walks onto the darkened stage. Every show, I've noticed Turner walks Lennon out with his hand on the base of her back. It's easy to trip, and he sees her safely to her mic before heading to his guitar that's set up, waiting.

Every step is in consideration of the other in this band.

They care about each other, they protect each other… they're a family. I've never seen a band so cohesive and balanced, and I've been a social media photographer for the last four years.

I've worked with a lot of bands, and this one is simply magic. I could be biased because I'm seriously drawn to three of the members, but I doubt it. I can see by how they interact that they work well together. And when the lights come on…

Holy hell. Lennon looks larger than life as she takes the mic with a huge smile. "Hey LA! It's been awhile, and we're so excited to stay awhile and play in different venues here in your amazing city over the next few days. But, we came to play, to have fun, and make some memories!"

The crowd goes wild and I grin as I work with different devices to video or take photos throughout the show. Turner always seems to know Lennon's mind before she does, and I don't think they decide the set list before a show. Lennon seems like she enjoys winging things and studying the crowd's mood. There's so many things I want to ask them later as I watch them.

My plan is to show different content on different platforms, so fans connect with the band on each one. I also know from some research that people use one social media outlet over another. There are some who prefer Instagram over Facebook, or Twitter over the former. I want *The Darkest Nights* to have as wide a social media base as possible, and make a note to give each of them the password to the new TikTok account.

Turner stands with a smirk, abs standing out proudly as he walks over to Lennon with his guitar.

"Lavender," he says with a smile. "We've been working on a new song or two together, haven't we?"

She smirks. "Yes, we have. I don't know if they've even had a chance to hear it yet…"

The power of the label and their ability to push new music

is amazing as the crowd goes wild. They yell the names of new songs, begging to hear certain ones live.

I grab my phone, and go live on TikTok. Since I started posting and advertising the new account, followers have flocked to follow it. People join quickly, the live filling with chatter as I title the video with 'New Music Live from LA.'

Mav opens the song with a keyboard intro as Lennon leans over and grabs her guitar. She's played off and on throughout the concert effortlessly. She's completely comfortable on stage, music being what she obviously was born to do. Man, I'm completely obsessed with her, my eyes drinking her in as she strums the beginning notes.

Widely grinning, she turns to face Turner. Their words twine around each other, a dance of give and take, even when they are angry. The lyrics speak of the forgotten, those that are different, and how it feels to be different.

I've heard this song before as I heard them record it, but really knowing how wrong I was as a kid as I lashed out... Every word cuts deep. I blink furiously as I hear the terror, the anger that she couldn't just live her life long enough to get through a day, and the sadness. I lose the battle, and the tears spill. Every one of us who belittled, terrorized her, and refused to listen to the word *no* as she screamed it, deserve to feel like shit when we hear her words. Lennon O'Reily refuses to be silent anymore.

Good for her.

I wish I had been able to get my head out of my own ass for two seconds to see the marked differences between Lennon and Carrie back then. Carrie was coy, flirty, and at times cruel. She was cruel in her marked disinterest in how her daughter was doing at school.

Lennon was sweet, quiet, and wanted to blend into the background. Looking back, this was probably a coping mechanism so her mom wouldn't notice her too much, and neither would anyone else.

I missed so many things as a sixteen year old boy. I was pulled in by Carrie because of her beauty and most of all to fuck with my father. It didn't matter to me that he would never find out, nor did I intend for him to. He may have killed us both if he had.

Shaking myself out of memories, I allow myself to be swept away by the last lyrics:

"Now I'm here to say, you failed.
I'm standing strong, surrounded by love.
I know what I'm worth, and it's more than yours.

We are more than the memories of others.
Their lies and hits will fade.
Through it all we will persevere."

I roar with the crowd, uncaring that I'm streaming live on TikTok. The comments are wild with how they are buying tickets to the next show right now, and how raw this song is. I end the video and pocket the device. I wipe my face, unashamed of them. Instead, I am ashamed I'm the one who caused these lyrics to be created.

I have no doubt anyone who has danced to the beat of their own drum will resonate with this song. A positive result of Lennon's past, for sure it is. However, there's this guilt that lives in the pit of my stomach because I'm still keeping secrets from her. No one wants to know that the man they want to sleep with has slept with their now dead mother. They would rather turn away than face the truth that it wasn't just one time. I'm pretty sure I fucked Carrie O'Reily in the alley off Main Street because she goaded me into it.

The woman told me I couldn't handle a little danger, and then insulted my cock and told me she didn't think I could get it up. Gah, I can tell my then seventeen year old self that I was an idiot. Carrie learned quickly that the way to get me to do something, almost anything, was to call me a coward or call my virility as a male into question. *Damn bitch.*

Lennon and *The Darkest Nights* play one more song before ending the concert. I leave just before they finish, making sure to beat the crowd. I'm waiting backstage as they walk off stage, and Roark picks her up and kisses her.

"Lenny, you sounded amazing tonight," he praises her. It's adorable how her cheeks pink from the compliment and I chuckle softly. "Did you get what you needed for your videos and such, Derek?" Roark asks and I didn't expect him to say anything to me.

My eyes snap up to his in surprise. "Uh, yes, actually I did. I went live on your TikTok account during *Together We Roar*. It blew up, but the song was really powerful, so I knew it would. I will say, this song live, the lyrics blew me away." That's as close to talking about my feelings as I am able to right now. I'm still a little raw afterwards, as if the words are embedded into my skin.

Lennon bites her lip. "I wrote the song right after you arrived. I was really angry, and my memories kept bubbling up with your presence back in my life."

I shrug, understanding where she's coming from. "I get it, I'm an asshole."

"I mean you can be?" she says with her hands thrown up. She speaks in these sweeping gestures, and I wonder if she's ever knocked something over when she talks. "If it helps, I think you're working on it, and I'm reassessing things that occurred back then." She's purposefully cryptic because there are people bustling around us, and I appreciate it.

"Hey guys," Jordan comes up to us with a wide smile. "You were amazing, and while you have people that are excited to meet you, I want you to take a breather. Go hang together in the room Lennon used to get ready before the show. Take twenty minutes, hydrate, and then head in. Sound good?"

My jaw drops in surprise as does the band. "Wow, are you serious right now," Atlas asks, shaking his head. "You're like the fairy godfather of managers right now. Prescott always herded us like cattle."

Jordan purses his lips, crossing his arms as he widens his stance. I worry he's offended until he shakes his head. "The VIP ticket campaign started right around the time she started her position as your manager. She's unfortunately related to one of the executives at the label, and Prescott was given too much freedom. We also didn't know what she was doing because so many people transferred off your tour for various reasons. I would never have pushed you from performing to immediately meeting with people. You need to come down a little from the high of the show and decompress."

Lennon sighs dramatically. "Holy shit, I think I love you."

Jordan snorts. "If you think that's something, wait until you spend the night in your new home for the next few days. Your previous manager should have kept you more comfortable than you have been the last few months, and that's about to change. If you're happy, you'll feel better, and then you'll be more likely to write more incredible music. You have tomorrow off during the day, go play in the city, please. Enjoy your free time. Anyway, twenty minutes!"

He spins away, muttering to himself about incompetent managers, new hires, and how there needs to be a review of how everyone is performing in the company. I press my lips together in amusement as I watch his fit of anger. It's kind of adorable to watch him stomp away. I've always heard him described as calm, collected, and having an epic poker face. I think he cares about this band more than he lets on.

"God, I swear this is the best day ever," Mav shakes his head with a surprised laugh. "Thank God for Jordan Miles. I'm honestly worried we'll wake up and realize this was all a dream."

I snort. "That's a little dark, don't you think?"

Roark throws his arms around my shoulders, his body pulling me into motion as he keeps walking. "Nah, not even a little bit. Turner has also been dreaming about a bigger shower to fuck our girl in," he purrs in my ear.

My gaze widens as I turn to look at him. His caramel eyes remind me of the color of whiskey, his lips a whisper away from mine. Roark bites his lip and I flush as I realize I'm staring. I go back to watching where I'm going, though he's maneuvering us both just fine.

"I'll be tasting those pouty lips soon, Derek. I am a bit less forward than Turner, but I'm an impatient man," he growls.

"Holy fuck," I gasp, eyes widening, and cock twitching. It makes me shiver and his lips twist into a smile.

"You're gonna be fun, aren't you? We'll be seeing you later tonight. Jordan approved the adjacent room request as well. He said it was a smart use of our time."

An inappropriate giggle slips out, and I cover my mouth in embarrassment.

"Stop teasing, Ror," Lennon says, amusement clear in her voice. She walks by me, fingers lightly trailing down my arm. I can feel the goosebumps she leaves there as well, my eyes heating at how beautiful she looks. How is it possible to be this attracted to three people?

"Aye, stop teasing our photographer unless you're planning

to do something with the boner he's sporting," Mav roars with laughter.

"For fuck's sake," I mutter, untangling myself from Roark carefully and walking away. I swear, this group is trouble together. *I could never do anything with them with an audience, right?*

22

LENNON

Derek's blush makes my body tingle. How is that possible, when it's such a simple thing? I love how affected he is by the three of us, and it gives me hope we may be able to go somewhere. He was careful with me before the show as he hung out with me, almost too much so.

Derek is a hard man, and I wish I knew what made him this way. He is worried about hurting me... Almost as if he fucks hard, loves harder, and it makes me wonder what his cock would feel like inside of me. I shiver, not because there's something wrong with me, but because I'm so turned on. Roark, Turner, and I can get carried away, and I've worn my spankings and hand prints with pride.

I've learned there's nothing wrong with your kinks when everyone is on board. Maybe his reticence is because he's hurt me in the past, and in some ways I understand what was going on in his head. High school is such a hard time as it's a breeding ground of hormones, teenage angst, and misunderstandings.

My lips twist as I think about this all as I walk into the room allocated as my dressing room. *It's all so complicated.*

"Little Valkyrie, I can hear you thinking from here," Mav grunts as he throws himself onto a sofa in the corner.

I smirk, shrugging. These boys all know me so well. Straddling a chair, I face them, leaning on the back of it.

"So I take it that things have changed a bit with Derek the Dick? Do we still want to pummel him, or not?" Atlas asks.

"Does it count if I want to pummel him with my cock?" Turner responds as his lip twitches. He drops to the floor to sit next to me, his arm draping over my leg.

I giggle, suddenly feeling really warm and squirm. This line of questioning is just making me wanton, remembering everything I wish had happened when I was on Derek's lap.

"Oh it's like that, I see," Atlas says slyly. "I mean he's a good looking man if you're into cock with that much attitude." Atlas is bi-sexual, but hasn't been in a relationship in years. Our schedule is so hectic, it's hard to find someone willing to put up with it.

The only reason it could remotely work with Derek, is because he's on the road with us.

"I mean, we have some work to get there, but we're interested," I explain as I bite my lip. There's so much to wade through, what if he decides we're too much work?

Turner leans into me and bites my side. "Stop destroying your mouth, baby."

My back arches as I gasp. He accomplished his mission, as I'm no longer biting my lip, but my pussy is painted with my arousal.

"So not fair," I groan.

Mav chuckles darkly. "Keep it in your pants little Lennon, we have work to attend."

Work is rude.

I sigh as a roadie appears at the door and knocks outside it. "It's time, guys. Jordan asked me to remind you."

I swear we just sat down. I yawn, eyes rolling as I do. Maybe it was a mistake to sit. I pop up, turning and grabbing some gummy bears. My ass is slapped and I squeal, almost dropping my precious treat.

"That'll wake you up, my dear," Roark chuckles, propped across the room.

When I turned, I put my ass in Turner's face and he couldn't help himself. "I do love your ass in my face, but I prefer when you sit on it."

I roll my lips in because if I laugh, it'll only encourage him. "Alright, boys. Let's get to work, and then we get to sleep in fluffy beds."

"Fuck yeah," they cheer together and I do giggle. They're so in sync, it's ridiculous.

Let's fucking do this indeed.

THE VIP MEET up went off without a hitch, and we had a blast chatting with everyone. Jordan also made check-in seamless. His assistant was in the lobby handing out key cards to our rooms, and fuck if it doesn't feel good to have something go right.

Prescott is the perfect example of someone who should never work in the music industry. We throw everything into our work, it's not too much to ask for attention to detail.

"Thanks Benji," I say gratefully as I take my room card from him. Our suite has three doors, but they all open to the same common rooms. Alex and Mav have rooms that interconnect with our suite as well as Derek. So together we take over half a floor of rooms. A bit excessive? Maybe, but we are here for three nights, so it feels like a slice of heaven, and I haven't even seen the rooms yet. I stumble a little, and Derek catches me.

"Tired," he asks, surprising me by looping his arm through mine.

"A bit, but it was such a great night," I gush. "Our fans were incredible, and having *Together We Roar* sung back to us was everything. I still have goosebumps as I think about it. The road to get here was hard," I explain, almost to reassure him of something, "but to be able to create this made it worth it."

"I could feel the power behind every word," Derek murmurs, kissing my temple. I'm in shock at the gentle, sweet gesture that I blink at him. He hums under his breath as he looks at me. "I'm not so great at the dating thing. I never have been, but there's so many things I allow myself to want when I look at you, Roark, and Turner. I don't know what to do with it all yet though."

I lean into him, impressed by the honesty behind his words. "We need to talk about some things soon, but I do believe I've been teased all night."

We walk through the open doors of the elevator, where Roark and Turner are waiting. "Atlas and Mav wanted to beat the shit out of each other in video games," Ror explains. "Apparently the suites have game consoles."

I smirk. Leave it to the boys to find their fun. "Hmm, I'm glad they're winding down and enjoying all of this."

The doors start to close, but a shoe is shoved into the opening. These elevators have great sensors, because they immediately open. Jordan looks at me apologetically.

"Slight problem, and then I'm letting you take the rest of the night off. I would just fill the slot myself, but figured I'd ask—"

"Jordan, you're fine," I laugh. I'm used to plans changing abruptly, and it doesn't bother me a bit. "What's up?"

"Your opening act for your next two Los Angeles shows got into a car wreck. They're at the hospital, and out of commission. We were using the same band as the one who played tonight."

I frown. They were amazing. "That's a shame. Can you make sure to send flowers on our behalf, please?" He nods, impressed by the suggestion and makes a note in his phone. "So we basically need a band for the next couple of nights, is that right?"

Jordan nods emphatically, and I smile. He has so much energy and passion, I love it.

I grab my phone from my pocket, with a smile "What about *Velvet Escape*. They opened for us in San Francisco, and they're phenomenal. Would you like their number?"

A secret smile graces his lips and he shakes his head. "I'll call Layla and the guys, I'm sure they'll be excited for the opportunity. I'll get them on the next plane. Thanks Lennon!"

I open my mouth to ask how he knows Layla, my brow furrowing, but the doors are already closing. *What the hell.* Layla never mentioned knowing him, almost acting a bit overwhelmed by his name.

"Was that weird to anyone else?" I ask.

Turner barks a laugh. "When is our life normal anymore, Lavender?"

"Fuck if you aren't right," I mutter, laying my head on Derek's shoulder.

"I'll go straight to my room if you're tired," Derek starts to beg off for the night.

"I'm not that tired," I shrug. I am, but I want to stay up a little bit longer. I'm like the child who has F.O.M.O.

"Is your sweet pussy needy, baby girl," Turner purrs and my eyes glaze over with lust at the sound. It's like my body is primed for their dominant, growly sex voices.

My lips part and my breath quickens. Derek looks down with a smile that's all male. It says he knows I'm wet, needy, and wanton.

He runs his finger down my neck, slowly dipping under the neckline of my top. My lace bra hides nothing as he rubs along it. "Please," I gasp.

"Fuck, you're so damn pretty when you beg," he groans. Derek pulls down my shirt, angling himself in front of me so any cameras would be blocked by his body. Sucking on my needy bud through the lace, I hide my face in his neck.

"She's even prettier when she screams your name, but that ya have to earn," Roark drawls, and I swear my vagina clamps on nothing. I'm empty, and I need to be filled. Like right fucking now.

The elevator opens and Derek covers me, whisking me into his arms and striding out. My shocked face looks up at him and he winks at me. "I need to make you scream my name now. I have something to prove," he teases.

I wish I could tell him my thighs are covered in my cream, and all I can think about is his face between them. I don't know how far he'll allow things to go, but I know the boys will test his strength. Their dirty talk always does delicious things to me.

We stop at room 1007, and Ror opens the door for us. I swear the fires of Hell are following us, we run so quickly into our rooms.

"Lenny," Roark says and I shiver at the dark tone. It's the one he uses when he's gonna dominate and destroy me, and my chest heaves in anticipation.

"Yes, Sir," I whimper and Derek's lips pop open. I never 'Sir' anyone outside of the bedroom or an authority figure. I'm built to be a brat, and Ror and Turner do a wonderful job of bringing it out of me. We can all switch easily, depending on what the other needs.

It's fun blowing Derek's fucking mind though. Ror pulls off his shirt, tossing it onto a chair. "Ask Derek to put you down, because you're gonna do something for me. You asked for this punishment, and good girls who accept this get rewarded, don't they?"

"Oh fuck," I writhe in Derek's arms in anticipation.

"So pretty," he murmurs reverently.

"Derek," I say, almost a whine.

"Yes, Len," he growls, his eyes trained on mine. It almost escapes my notice that he shortened my name. *Holy shit.*

"Can you put me down please," I rasp, my words running together as I push them out as quickly as I can.

"Oh, I can't do things I don't understand," he grins evilly. "Ask me nicely, slower, and clearer. Are you a good girl or a bad girl?"

"God, not you too," I whisper.

"I don't know what you mean. Two seconds, and then I'll put you over my own knee, deny you an orgasm, and still have you screaming my name—"

"No, please," I shriek. I repeat Ror's request, one of my masters, the man who is running the show tonight. I'm rewarded with a true smile.

"That wasn't so hard, was it," Derek asks as he puts me down slowly. My nipples brush against his hard chest, and my breath hitches. Derek smirks as he steps away from me.

"I want you to take off all your clothes, Lennon," Roark growls as he steps in front of me. He drags his finger up the column of my throat and I stand very still. I won't move until he's given me all the directions needed to complete my task. I plan to be a very good girl. I *need* to come. Roark pushes the pad of his finger so my eyes rise to his. When I'm submissive to him, I won't meet his eyes without permission. "So gorgeous, such a good girl for me, aren't you?" he growls.

"Yes Sir," I whisper.

Roark swallows, clearly affected by me. He's very dominant and enjoys playing this way, but won't do it for long. I know his control won't last. "I want you to do what I asked right now, please, lass," he demands.

I nod as he steps away. Slowly undressing, my shirt comes off, boots, and then pants. Soon, I'm in my lace bra and thong, knowing my master will have another demand for me.

"Turn around slowly for me, Lennon," Roark growls.

I turn until my back is to them, hands running down my skin. My body feels warm, despite not wearing much. Blood singing, I throw my inhibitions into the wind. I don't want to make a single decision, I trust Roark to make them for me right now anyways.

"Remove your tiny thong," he demands. "I don't know why you bother with panties, since they cover exactly nothing."

I smirk, knowing he can't see me. I can be a brat to the wall. Little does he know, I only wear these because they're pretty. Hooking my thumbs through, I pull them down, being sure to bend all the way over.

"Oh my God," I hear Derek whisper reverently. Just those words give me hope this is a step in the right direction. That I won't regret this. Fully exposed, I take my time dragging them down to my ankles.

Large hands grab my ass, spreading them. I whimper as I feel his thumbs slide through my folds.

"Perfect pink, wet pussy, spread for us to see," Roark mutters. His control is ready to snap, but I want to see how long he can hold it. It's his show tonight after all, he's made this quite clear.

His thick tongue glides from my needy hole up to my ass. I pant, caught between wanting to beg for more, and knowing I need to accept what he gives me. He slowly rims my puckered hole and a cry is desperate to escape. I bite it back, not wanting to show my hand yet.

My knees are weak, so I grab my ankles to keep myself bent in the perfect position to show me just what his magic tongue can do.

"You taste so good," he groans. "Are you watching how responsive Lenny is, Derek?"

I almost forgot he was here for a moment and I gasp. Roark dives into eating my pussy like his favorite treat, not allowing me to get into my head. He pushes two fingers into me and my eyes roll back as I moan.

"Mmm, you're so fucking wet for us, aren't you lass? Our perfect little whore, waiting for our cocks," he praises and I mewl.

"Holy fuck," Derek grunts. It's different when Roark calls me his little whore from when he does. Roark loves me, reveres me, and loves how easily I give myself to him and Turner. I want him to see the difference.

"Roark," I mewl. "I'll always be your perfect little whore. Please, please, Sir. You know what I need."

Roark cracks his hand across my ass and I cry out and shudder. His arm holds me up around my waist, knowing my knees almost buckled under me. "We talked about punishment, didn't we? Did you tease Derek earlier today?"

Shit, I've been teasing him all night. "Yes, Sir," I tell him, gasping as I wait for what's coming.

"You don't get to come until I tell you," he growls. "And you'll count as I deliver your punishment. Start from one."

Son of a bitch... that means the first one was gratuitous. *Rude.* "Understood, Sir," I pant.

"So fucking perfect for me," he murmurs.

Smack.

Fuck me. My pussy clamps down on air and my fingers

spasm where they're holding my ankles. "One," I scream, remembering almost too late that I'm supposed to be counting.

"Four more," he reassures me. I know he's going easy on me, because Ror likes to tease me too. Our control is tenuous at best, a sticky elastic thing, but his hand is steady as he cracks his palm along my other cheek.

A warmth travels along my skin and I shiver. "Lennon, your ass is starting to glow so perfectly," Turner growls. I can't see him bent over as I am, my hair obstructing my view.

But... I can hear him spit, and then the sound of his hand stroking his cock. I can't handle it. "Oh my God," I whimper as my mouth waters. I want to suck on his fat cock, let him choke me with it.

"Mmm, Turner is so fucking sexy fucking his hand, Lennon," Roark groans as he drops to his knees to blow on my exposed folds. I struggle not to squirm, and hear an intake of breath. It's unfamiliar to me, since I know all the noises my guys make.

Feeling Ror's lips curve into a wicked smile as he kisses my ass, I know it's Derek. "See something you like, Derek?" he purrs.

"God, none of you play fair," Derek breathes. "Yes, I see a lot of things I like, Sir. Lennon's a fucking goddess, all that creamy skin, and *Jesus* that perfect pink pussy."

"Fuck your hand with me, Derek," Turner groans and my skin breaks in goosebumps. I want to see them so fucking bad. "I want to see your cock," he says.

Crack.

I sob, my feelings heightened. "Three, holy shit," I shriek.

"So good. What do you say, boys? Lenny is dying to turn and watch. Should I let the first one count? Your ass is so warm and pretty already, little Valkyrie. It's almost perfect," Roark admires.

Please, please let the first one count.

A moan breaks the quiet of the room. "Yes, I personally vote that it should count," Derek rasps. God, I think he's stroking his cock, I want to see it so bad.

I lick my lips, ready to beg Ror, but depending on his mood it may not matter. His fingers drag through my folds, and I'm so wet, my cream is audible as he plays. My skin is warm, my body languid from the spankings, and yet I crave more.

"One more it is, then," he murmurs. Ror gives me zero warning as he delivers one last spanking.

His arms go around my waist to catch me as my legs fail. "Five," he whispers into my ear as he draws me up. "Be a good girl and say it."

My chest is heaving as I pull in my breaths, and I force the words past my lips. "Five," I whisper.

Roark kisses me hard, an arm around my waist, and his other hand fisted in my hair to pull my head back. It may have not been a long period of time, but my body is tingling, and my core aches.

"Want to go see the boys," he whispers against my lips. "Derek's cock is thick and gorgeous, and his tip is weeping for you." He grins wickedly, and I know my eyes are blown with lust.

I nod eagerly and he lets go of me, stepping away. I whirl to face him, knowing it won't be that easy. "Crawl to them, and you can swallow their cocks or make them play together. It's whatever you want, little Valkyrie. Go take it."

With that, I'm in control of what happens next. I turn, dropping to my hands and knees. Derek's dark brown eyes are hooded, his face still a bit scraped, but it just makes me want him more. I crawl, knowing Ror is getting the perfect view of my backside. I roll my hips as I cross the short expanse, smirking as I hear his pants hit the floor.

Now we are all on even ground.

Derek is still wearing his boxers, but they're shoved down, the tip of his cock weeping, red and angry. He slowly rubs the palm of his hand along the tip, gathering his own arousal, before pumping his hand lazily along himself.

Fuck, this man has a gorgeous cock. I want to stare longer, but Turner groans. I glance over and he pants, his breaths uneven.

"Lavender, your tits will be the death of me. They're so perfect, I need to fuck them soon," he sighs.

Yes, he does, but that's not what I want right now.

"Derek, what do you think of when you see Turner?" I ask as I kneel at their feet, thighs spread wide.

"Fuck, Len, I can barely look away from you when you're staring at me like that," Derek grinds out. His teeth are clenched, and I know he's struggling after the show Roark and I gave him.

I want to come on one of their faces today, even if nothing else happens tonight.

"Derek, I want you to taste me, you promised to make me scream," I remind him.

His toes dig into the carpet. "Oh fuck me," he mutters.

His eyes drag over to Turner, where he's met with a smile. "One day, your ass will be mine," Turner promises. Derek whimpers, shivering.

"Words, Derek," I whisper, my fingers slowly dragging up his legs.

"I see a beautiful man, stroking his cock," Derek says honestly.

"Fuck, it does something to me to hear you say that," Turner gasps, his head dropping back. "One day, you'll drop to your knees for me, and suck every last drop of cream I allow you," he says, hand twisting at the tip of his cock.

"You're so close, love. If he won't let you fuck his face, I will... unless you want to make a mess for me to clean along those perfect abs," Roark teases Turner.

Derek mewls, and I take pity on him. I lick his swollen head, lapping at his slit. His fingers tangle into my hair and he draws my eyes up to his. A string of his pre-cum hangs off my tongue, and I lick my lips.

"Shit, fuck, why?" he mutters unintelligently.

I made Derek Williams incoherent. *Fuck yes.*

"Words," I breathe insistently. "Give them to me."

"Tell me you want this," he begs. "I need to hear you say it for me, Len."

"I want it so badly. I want you. I know we started badly, but let's see where this goes."

Shadows hang in his eyes, and I want to dispel them. He fights me for a moment when I move my head, and then I have that thick cock in between my lips again. Swirling my tongue, I slide him into my mouth, down my throat, sucking and swallowing as I do.

"Fuck," he cries out. "You're so perfect, please don't stop," Derek begs.

It's said to be degrading to be on your knees, giving head, but I don't feel that way. I am empowered, enjoying every gasp, groan, and sound he makes. I moan as I reach his base, massaging and gently tugging his balls. Derek pulls my hair just enough to feel the sting of pain before he shudders, coming down my throat.

I look over as I swallow, seeing Turner is watching. He loses control then, coming all over himself.

"Mine," Roark chuckles darkly, licking up the mess left behind.

Derek pulls me up, laying down on the sofa so I can straddle his face.

"Ride me. Suffocate me, and I'll die a happy man as long as my name is on your lips," he demands.

Holy fuck.

"Yes Sir," I gasp, enjoying the answering growl as his hands grab my ass like handles to keep me centered over his face. I don't even have a chance to worry about what he'll think about the roughness on my hip and thigh.

Jesus, this man's tongue. He licks me as if I'm his favorite treat, shoving his tongue into my hole to drag all my cream onto it.

"Derek, uhhh God," I cry out. I wasn't prepared for this level of dedication. My hand skims my skin of its own accord to massage my breasts.

Roark licks the last of Turner's cum off him, and I want to be in several places at once. I never want to stop riding Derek's face, I want to be fucked by Ror, and I want to clean Turner up, savoring his perfect salty sweet flavor. Roark stands, gently rubbing his hand along his piercings. My eyes roll back as I feel a warmth begin to build.

"Lenny," he says teasingly.

"Please, I want to come," I whine, chasing my orgasm.

I open my eyes, and he's in front of me. His fingers push through my hair as he kisses me. Our tongues entwine, and Turner's cum bursts along my tastebuds. I grind on Derek's face, desperately wanting to come.

Three fingers push into my hole and I squeal. "Mmm, Derek, I need to take her ass more than I need my next breath. Make our girl scream first, yeah?"

Derek's fingers twist and thrust, robbing me of my next breath. I throw my arms around Roark's neck, and he holds me tightly, just in time for me to explode. I've been teased for too long, and my hearing shorts out, white lights exploding behind my eyelids, eyes having closed of their own volition. I shudder and groan, making noises that would scare any neighbors we thankfully don't have.

Derek's arm also supporting my weight is the first thing I notice as I come back to myself. I would be embarrassed if Roark's face wasn't the first thing I saw.

"You're back," he murmurs reverently. "I'm gonna fuck your tight ass while you ride his face some more. Are you comfortable with that," he asks.

Fucking hell, Roark in my ass and Derek tongue fucking me? I may die. *I'm so in.*

"Yes, fucking please," I say with a savage grin.

"That's my girl," he praises and my pussy clamps on Derek's fingers that are still inside of me.

"Oh my God," Derek gasps and I smile.

"You're about to get up close and personal with my dick, Derek. I won't take offense if you decide to give me the same treatment you've been giving Lenny," Roark teases as he straddles Derek's chest.

I would grin, but I'm too busy shivering in anticipation from the lube Roark pours along my crack. He pours a bit more on his cock, thrusting between my ass.

Derek continues his ministrations, and Ror kisses down my shoulder. He bites me hard before he lines up against my ass, slowly pushing himself in.

I would usually need more lead up, but I'm so turned on from everything before this, I'm ready. I force myself to breathe, eyes rolling at the sensations of being filled.

"Fuck me, why is your cock so pretty," I hear Derek's muffled voice and I can't help myself. I laugh, clamping down on Roark's cock.

"Baby, fuck, you're so tight. I want to enjoy your ass before I explode, don't make me look bad here," Roark complains, blowing out a strangled breath.

Derek sucks on his fingers noisily and I moan. He's refusing to let any bit of my cream go to waste. "Roark, man, I'm getting the world's best view right now. You couldn't look bad if you tried. Damn, why do you look like you'd taste good?" he groans.

"Because he's delicious," Turner says. "I would suck him down for every meal, and it would never be enough. He loves to have his balls played with, so don't make me come over and help you," Turner threatens.

Derek's hips buck without meaning to and I roll my lips inward to hide a smile he can't see. He's just as turned on by Turner's dirty mouth as I am.

"Are you feeling needy, Derek," Roark's deep voice rumbles as he thrusts further into me.

His arms hug me from behind, a hand finding my pebbled nipple to roll it between his fingers.

"Should I play with Derek's cock if he decides to be brave, Lenny?"

My head falls back on his shoulder as Derek growls and sucks my clit into his mouth. I'm thrown forward suddenly as Roark slides in balls deep. "Argh, God," I scream.

Sucking fills the air and Ror buries his head in my neck. "Feels good," he mumbles. "His mouth is fucking sinful, God. Lenn, Derek pulled me the rest of the way inside of you. I have to move, can I? Baby, please tell me you're good," he begs. Roark is losing his ability to speak, and I squirm with need in his arms.

Fuck, Derek is sucking Ror's balls, while paying special attention to my clit with the pad of his thumb. His other hand caresses my tattoo-covered thigh without hesitation.

"I need you to move, fuck me please. God, this is so hot, I wish I could see it," I gasp.

As Ror's hips piston as he fucks my ass, my eyesight blackens around the edges.

"Lavender, I can see everything, and this will live in my spank bank forever," Turner growls, catching my nipple in his mouth. "I want to reward Derek for doing such a good job, should I?"

Everything in me clenches, and Roak curses. "Yes, yes, trust me she wants you to, you fucking tease."

Turner walks behind us and Derek groans. "Tell me no, and this all stops," Turner says.

"Don't stop, please. I'm sick of fighting this," Derek says, words strangled.

Sounds of Turner sucking Derek's cock begin, and Derek groans. His mouth splits time between Ror and I, and Ror's hips stutter.

"Fuck, I need you to come on his face. I'm not gonna last, the man's tongue is sinful," he pants.

I'm climbing higher and higher, and I'd be afraid of the fall, if I didn't know Roark would catch me. Derek is an enigma, but I hope we'll be able to figure things out. "Stop thinking," Roark commands, spanking my ass. I scream as three fingers enter my pussy.

"God love ya, Derek, you're gonna kill me," comes a gasp by my ear. *Baby, same.* I know Roark can feel Derek's fingers against the small membrane that's separating them, and I clench around them.

Expertly, Derek plays my body, seeming to know the exact moment I'm about to explode, pinching my clit. Shuddering, I give into my life-shattering orgasm, feeling the man behind me tremble as he finishes inside of me. Finally, Derek groans, "God, yes, fuck, you're so good at that. *Fuck.*"

We are a mess, gasping for air, my body limp between them. "The three of you are so beautiful," Turner says as he steps back to watch us.

He licks his lips, his tongue ring flicking out, and I wonder how he wielded it on Derek's cock. We definitely need to do this again, and I want to be able to watch next time. Roark slowly slips out of me and my breath gasps. "Roark," I whine, shivering.

"I know, I'm sorry. Let's get you cleaned up, okay? I want to snuggle you to sleep," he says as he scoops me into his arms.

"Derek, come shower with me?" Turner asks. "We've been up close and personal, you can shower with me and save water."

I know that excuse is thin at best, but my eyes are already closing. The shower may have to wait.

23

DEREK

Holy shit. I don't want to look too closely at what just happened, partially because I think I want it to occur again. Is that crazy? At first I worried I would be the fourth wheel, these three are so damn attuned to the other.

But, it wasn't like that. They let me in, held space for me, and encouraged me to join in. *And it was so fucking hot...*

"Derek, I can hear you thinking from here. Come on, let's shower. Lavender looks like she's gonna fall asleep in Roark's arms, we wore the poor girl out. Maybe you can tell me about what's going on behind those pretty eyes of yours, yeah?" Turner asks with a smirk.

Part of me is surprised he thinks any of me is 'pretty'. I've always been called attractive, all hard angles and muscles, almost brutish... but pretty? I don't think anyone has ever called me this before.

I nod, letting him lead me to a bathroom. My jaw drops, taking in the size of the shower. It's fucking huge, has two shower heads and a rainfall shower head. Damn.

Turner chuckles. "Showers like these have been giving me

wet dreams for days. It's all I could think about after that damn tiny stall on our bus. I don't usually mind it, but it's so nice to stretch out a bit, and not have to worry about knocking my arm against something."

I smirk with a nod. "Yeah, the bus showers are no picnic. This bathroom is amazing. I'm surprised you don't get more breaks between shows. This whole schedule is insane to me," I tell him honestly.

Turner turns the shower on to warm with a shrug. I thought it would be weirder than it is to chat with my dick out. "To tell you the truth, we agreed to more shows to help pay for the new bus initially, but we were still supposed to get breaks like this one. If Prescott was still our manager, she never would have thought to book us a hotel while we are in the same city," he says with a shrug.

"Jordan was livid when he saw that we aren't getting breaks at all. We have interviews, photo shoots, and we haven't stopped. So he's put a hold on the press ops for now until further notice. I love touring, singing, performing... but the pace is starting to hit Lennon's health. I won't stand for that."

I'm in complete agreement as I step into the shower with him. There's an array of toiletry bottles, and the hotel has thought of everything. My muscles start to relax in the heat, even as the water finds all my cuts and bruises. My skin stings where Lennon came on my face, but I wasn't going to make her stop for anything.

"I am concerned about how tired she was yesterday," I say tentatively. I blow out a breath, because I don't usually have a careful bone in my body. I'm a bull in a china shop, but I don't want to offend Turner either. I grab soap for something to do and start to lather it.

"Uh-huh... I don't fuck around, Derek. Say what you mean," he orders, grabbing my hands to stop my movements.

He's way closer to me than I expected, his chest a hair's breadth away from me, and my breath catches. Talking about gorgeous men, Turner is definitely beautiful. His hair is blond with brown highlights, and the tattoos over all that corded lean muscle make him appear to be a work of art. *Fuck.* Turner smirks, slowly licking his bottom lip, and I shiver remembering how the piercing felt as he sucked my cock.

"Anyone can lose time when they're too tired, not because their mental health is being called into question, but because they're just surviving the day. No one can sustain this pace, no matter how talented they are, and Lennon's ability to create music is incredible," I admit.

Turner takes a step closer to me, and his hardening cock brushes against my thigh. Surprisingly, it doesn't bother me. I still have Roark's heady taste across my tongue, and I find I'm eager for more. I'm slowly falling under their spell, even if I don't understand all of my feelings.

He telegraphs his motions, hand slowly cupping my cheek. "And how do you feel about my girl, huh? You're worried about her burning out, wanting to take care of her. Soo, what else do you want?"

Ever so slowly, he licks up my neck and my hips buck. "Fuck," I groan.

"Only if you're a very good boy" he growls, kissing the shell of my ear. Turner grinds his cock against me and my chest starts to heave. "Why does that feel so good," I mutter.

He chuckles softly. "Well that answers another question I have. Do you want me?"

I force myself to be honest, and not just because I've had his boyfriend's balls in my mouth and my cock in his. My relationship with sex is very entangled, complicated, and I'm in very unknown territory. "I do, but this is kinda left field for me.

I've never been attracted to another man before, so you and Roark surprised me. I most definitely wasn't expecting—"

"Expecting for me to suck your cock and drink down every drop," he purrs against me. He angles his hips and my dick rubs against his. My eyes roll back and I wonder if it's possible to come just from rocking against him. "Or you weren't expecting to be seriously attracted to Ror and I?"

I sigh heavily, struggling to think. "You're way too fucking sexy for your own good," I confess. I drop the soap in my hands, ignoring where it may have gone and grab his hips. Pulling them closer, I rock him into me.

"You're not so bad yourself," Turner groans. "Fuck, yeah, just like that."

I chuckle darkly with a small smirk that quickly disappears as he nips down my neck.

"We can keep doing this, come all over one another, and then clean each other up for bed," he growls in my ear. *Why is the growl so sexy*?! "But, we have to talk too. Can you multitask or are we going to bed with blue balls," he challenges.

"God, I'll talk if I can also keep doing this," I murmur, rubbing his cock against mine, squeezing his perky ass in my hands. Wanting to taste him, I give in and kiss his neck. He tastes like salt and sin.

"Talk, big man," Turner reminds me, but pushes his hands into my hair. "I want to kiss you, though. Can I? Your lips are fucking bitable, and the way you keep staring at my piercing is driving me wild," he says, breathlessly.

He's staring at me like he needs to kiss me more than his next breath. My eyes bounce between his eyes and lips. I'm fucking dickmatized by this man. What the fuck is wrong with me? God help me but...

"Yes," I rasp out. "I need it. I want to know how your tongue feels against mine right fucking—"

Turner slams his mouth against mine, and it's a teeth clashing war. Kissing a man is so different from a woman... from Len. Turner's lips are firm, his tongue stroking mine with that piercing, goddamn. I moan into his mouth, thrusting against him, needing the friction as I push him against the wall.

"Words, fuck, give them to me, Derek," he yells.

"What," I can't fucking think. "What's the question again," I whine.

Turner sucks on the base of my neck, and says, "Do you want the three of us? We're a packaged deal."

"Yeah," I sigh. "I can't think of a single reason why I shouldn't right now, but I swear there was something."

He snickers, wrapping a leg around my waist so he can thrust harder against my cock. The water allows us to slide just enough as the rainfall falls over us. The warmth of the water fogs the air, and it feels like it's our private space. I don't know if this is a good idea, hell if I know my own name right now, but I want a chance.

"Do you think you're good enough for Lennon," he whispers. The words cut like knives and I flinch. Solidly remembering why this isn't a good idea, why I was going to allow this for a night and no more, I draw back. "No," he roars. The volume difference startles me and my eyes fly to his. "No running. Fucking ask yourself if you're good for her. You care about her, you question the sanity of this damn tour, so— "

"I want to be," I scream back at him, chest heaving as I realize how damn much I want to be. "I fucking do. I want to be good enough for her. For Roark... for you. The truth is though, that I'm really fucked up and I just don't know if I can be," I say, finishing in a whisper.

Turner rocks against my cock again, and though wildly inappropriate thoughts are flooding my mind, we need to have this conversation.

"I really want to be, but what if I get triggered over... something," I stumble, not dickmatized enough to spill my secrets yet to Turner. "What if I hurt Len?"

"Len, huh?" he teases as he nips my lips. "Our Lavender is already changing you. She doesn't hold grudges, and she's the brightest light I've ever seen. You won't dull it, and she likes it rough. There are places you can bruise her, and she'll scream in pleasure," Turner whispers as he licks my neck.

Fuck, how messed up is it that my cock jumped at that. "I don't want to hurt her, but I don't know how to do soft," I sigh. "I'm always in control, it's always what I want, when I want it."

"Did I bother you when I took control earlier? Or now," he growls.

"No," I say simply. "I want more, and that's out of my comfort zone too."

"Fuck the comfort zone," he chuckles. "And fuck your past. Look, Ror, Lennon, and I are all broken. What if we see if your broken pieces recognize ours?"

I blink, my eyes smarting with tears. "I don't know," I rasp. I want this so fucking bad, but I'm afraid to hope. Bad things usually happen when I do. It's just easier to go through life being an uncaring asshole.

"Figure it out," he whispers back. "And don't hide from us. If you're upset, say it. If you're feeling off, it's fucking fine. Give us your best and your worst. We can handle it, yeah?"

I nod, and that's the end of the heavy conversation.

Turner drops his leg, pushing me into the cold tile. Gasping, I shiver as he smirks at me. He scrapes his teeth along my chin before sucking on my lip.

"Gah, why does that feel so good," I groan.

"I want to fucking mark you with my cum while I jerk you off. Tell me I can, trust me to be in control?" He kisses me hard again, swiping that damn tongue against mine.

Fuck if I don't want to say yes.

But... "I'm not ready for penetration yet," I say tentatively. My emotions have evened out, and now I want to get wrapped up completely in Turner. I just need to make sure my boundaries are set.

"Derek, you'll have to beg me for that," he says with a smirk, and I allow him to turn me to face the wall.

Turner kicks my legs apart and I gasp. "Just like that," he praises.

"Holy fuck," I moan.

He pushes his cock between my ass cheeks, coating me in his growing arousal. I hear him spit, and shiver when I feel it drip between my ass.

"Much better," Turner murmurs as he grabs my hair, pulling my lips to meet his. "Hands on the wall for me. This is going to be hard, dirty, and really fucking satisfying. I'm going to paint you with my cum." I moan as his cock finds itself between my cheeks, and I never thought it could feel so good to be used as a fuck tool.

The positions are flipped, but it doesn't bother me the way I thought it would. Because...

"One word and it ends," he murmurs against my lips. "You're in control even in this. And fuck if your ass doesn't feel amazing." Turner thrusts again and I whimper. "So fucking good," he growls.

The shower fills with sounds of kissing, teeth clashing, and Turner's thighs meeting my ass. The hand not tangled in my hair snakes around and grasps my cock. My hips jerk into his hand and Turner hums in approval. I want to preen with pride because he's happy with me, but I don't want to look too closely at what I'm feeling.

"Your ass squeezes my cock every time you thrust into my hand, Derek," he groans. "Fuck, I can just imagine all the fun we could have together." Turner sucks on my neck, teeth gently scraping and nipping. "Roark wants you so badly, and that's unusual for him. You fit with us, you just have to let yourself go."

His voice gets the growl that makes me crazy when he performs. Dark, hard, and filled with the most decadent of promises. Turner expertly fucks my cock with his hand, and my head drops back onto his shoulder. The hand that was in my hair gently wraps around my throat and then squeezes.

Continuing to brace one hand on the wall, I grab his ass and squeeze it back.

"God, you're so fucking perfect," Turner groans.

Accepting this as the consent I intended it to be, his hand squeezes tighter around my throat as the hand fucking my cock moves up to play with my swollen head. I came earlier twice, but I swear I can never get enough of the three of them. Eating Lennon's perfect pussy, sucking on the base of Roark's cock as he fucked her, and Turner sliding between my ass cheeks is just the tip of the iceburg of what I want from them.

A tingling begins at the base of back, and I writhe against Turner.

Smack.

"Such a brat," he whispers darkly into my ear. *I can't believe he spanked me!*

Fuck if my body doesn't bow in pleasure, and he tightens his hand a bit more on my throat in response.

"You'll take what I deign to give you and you'll fucking love it, won't you," he continues.

My cock jerks hard in his hand, and my balls start to draw up. *I want to come with him.*

As if hearing my thoughts his thrusts against me quicken. "I can't wait to be in your tight little hole, I bet it'll suck me in like an eager little cock slut. Fuck," he groans, releasing my throat to grab my chin so he can lift it to kiss me again.

I am surprisingly good with being his little cock slut. I'd be a good one. Fuck, why do I want this so much? I've never been interested in men before... but these men? Yeah, I have butterflies and shit when I talk to them. They don't mess with my head, fuck with my emotions, everything is laid out.

Moaning into his mouth, I shiver, struggling to breathe.

"I'm gonna come, stop holding back Derek," Turner pants against my lips. "Come for me."

Just like that, I roar, hips jerking, rhythm lost as I paint Turner's fist and the wall with my cum.

"So fucking beautiful," he praises, and then I feel the wetness as he fucks my ass crack, coming all over me.

Chest heaving, legs weak, I chuckle softly. "Holy shit," I gasp.

Turner smiles against my lips, his piercing blue eyes watching mine. "You good?"

"Way good. Fucking," I turn my face as a yawn tears out of me, "perfect."

"Good. Let's clean up and go crawl into bed with Roark and Lennon before he comes looking for us."

"Would he?" I ask, my cock jumping at the thought. Fuck, down boy.

Turner chuckles. "You're so fun. Yeah, he would. So unless you're ready for another round, we should get washed up."

My face heats as I think about that and Turner shakes his head. "When's the last time you had sex, Derek?"

As Turner talks, he leans over to grab the forgotten soap bar, offering me a spectacular view of his powerful thighs and ass. "Fuck me," I mutter.

Turner snorts. "Soon, I promise."

I shake my head, but not because I'm against it. I didn't

mean to say that out loud. Remembering he asked me a question, I bite my lip.

"Uh, like eight months at least? I've been busy working, and usually I hook up at a club or something, but even those quickies were getting stale. They were no longer satisfying, so I stopped bothering," I say truthfully.

Turner nods as he hands me the soap. "If I help you, we'll end up getting dirty again," he says truthfully with a shrug. "You're too damn edible. It should be a damn crime to walk around looking the way you do."

I shake my head. "I think you may be delusional," I tell him, dragging the soap along said muscles. I love the heated stare he gives me as his eyes follow my movements. Maybe I really am a tease. Oops.

"Do you really not see it? You're an ex-football player, and I don't know how you've managed to keep all those damn muscles," he says, shaking his head. I don't mention the late night runs around the parking lot that help me sleep at night, nor the early morning push ups in the aisle of the bus.

Damn, I really like the attention he gives me.

Shrugging, I sigh as I step into the water to wash off. "There were always the jersey chasers when I was playing football, but when I got hurt and quit, that eventually ended. I'm aware I'm tall, and I take care of myself, but the compliments started feeling hollow after a while. I kept things casual on purpose, but they never wanted to scratch more than the surface."

Turner licks his lips as he sidles up to me. Bracing his hand on the shower wall, his other hand cups the back of my head. "Believe me when I say we want to do much more than just scratch the surface. We love hard, fuck harder, and ask for everything in your own time. There's zero pressure, just give us your best effort, yeah? Lavender didn't tell us her story for years, and despite her nightmares, we didn't push for it."

I flinch as I think about how many of those nightmares I'm responsible for.

"Uh-uh, Derek. No," Turner barks and my eyes fly back to his. "Don't go there. I didn't say it to make you feel badly, but rather to show you we aren't going to push. You're already putting her first, and your presumed guilt shows that. You're not responsible for other peoples' actions. She'll accept orgasms as penance though."

The last is growled before he claims my lips. It's definitely much later before we make it to bed.

24

TURNER

Thank god for giant king-sized beds. The master in this suite has what they call a California King, and it's fucking huge. I smile happily as I watch the sleeping people in bed with me. I'm next to Roark, who has his back to me and his arm wrapped around Lavender's middle. Derek crawled into bed sleepily after our shower and collapsed behind her, hiking her leg over his leg. They look amazing entwined together.

I feel like a creeper as I watch, but honestly I'm also processing what happened tonight. It was all amazing, and the chemistry between us would scorch the earth. Holy fuck, I'm rock hard again just thinking about it. I know we may have some road bumps as we go, but there were some when Ror and I started dating our Lavender, too.

As long as he works every day to be good to Lennon, then Derek and I are square. It seems fucked up that I have to say 'work at being good to her', instead of just *be*, but the truth is Derek has a fucked up history with our girl. He's dark, twisty, and I expect there is some trauma living behind those gorgeous dark eyes as well.

My lips press together as I drink in Derek and how wrapped up in Lennon he is. He needs her, and is emotionally stunted enough to not understand what he's feeling. I can't say I completely understand it either, but their souls need each other, and their chemistry is volcanic. The vitriol they shared before feels like a form of foreplay now that I think about it, and I remember her telling me about their closet wrestling.

Mmm. Lavender and Derek wrestling has its merits. I know she can take care of herself, as she's been doing it for years, but anytime she'll allow Roark and I to battle for her, we will. It makes me wonder if it was a question of dominance between Derek and Lavender, if she would win. The man is a tank, but she uses her thick thighs and curves to her advantage. I get the feeling he would gladly die suffocated between them.

I chuckle to myself when I get swatted at by Roark. "Ow," I whisper furtively. He hit dangerously close to my dick, not bothering to look before he swung. I want to push him back, but he's too close to Lavender for me to be able to. "Dick!"

"Yes I have one," he rumbles. "Do you need mine?"

I drop back onto my pillow, rolling my eyes. "Always, I was just having trouble sleeping," I sigh.

Roark turns, content in knowing Lennon's being well snuggled by Derek and opens his arms. "I'll help you sleep," he says with a yawn. "We're spending the day in LA doing whatever the fuck we want, so I want to be sure we are well rested. Get your cute ass in here."

Fuck yes. It is zero hardship to snuggle Ror. "Will you do that thing I like," I tease, laying on his chest and hooking my leg over his waist. I'm a barnacle, but he's a furnace and will keep me warm. The air conditioner is blowing and I'm shivering.

"Yeah, yeah. I swear, you're so much work," he teases, scraping his nails along my scalp. If I was a cat, I would be purring right now. Instead my muscles go liquid, and I melt into him. "I know all the things you like, love, and all the secret ways to help you sleep. Settle and I'll take care of you."

Trusting that he will, my eyes get heavier and soon my breath evens out.

~

I YAWN, snuggling into the warm teddy bear I'm wrapped around.

"Does he always sleep like that," says an amused voice and my lip twitches. There's my favorite asshole now.

Glancing up, I see Derek peeking over Lennon's shoulder, waiting for my reaction.

"Sometimes I sleep with my head in her tits," I say with a chuckle.

"God, that sounds nice," he says with an answering grin.

Lennon rolls her eyes, and the ball is in her court. I don't have to wait for long before she turns and shoves his face into her breasts. She slept naked last night, and I don't miss the fact that Derek took a breath before he went all in. She squirms for a different reason, her grip on the back of his neck starting to release, and takes full advantage. His tongue drags around her nipple and her moans are delicious. Teeth gently pull on them, his eyes trained on her face, using it as his road map to her body. My lips roll inwards as I keep my words back. *Job well fucking done.*

"Derek," she breathes in a whine.

"Yeah, Len. What'cha need?" he asks as he continues to nip and worship her tits.

"Can you always wake me up like this," she asks as her back bows.

His eyes cut to us, wide and panicked. Derek looks like he's afraid of what his next words will be, should be, and Roark and

I just nod. Whatever he wants them to be, better fucking be the right ones. He has to decide what those will be for himself.

"Yeah, baby, you can suffocate me with your gorgeous tits every damn day," he growls before claiming her lips.

I take an inaudible shaky breath and bury my face in Roark's shoulder in relief. Lennon is too busy making out with Derek to notice, but I have to admit that could have ruined the morning. I wonder what he was thinking. Was he worried about making a claim? Or if we would disapprove of how he responded?

I make a mental note to ask him, because his brain is still an enigma at times. Roark's fingers dive into my hair, pulling until I lift my head to meet his warm, caramel eyes. The sharp pain grounds me and I take a breath.

"Everything is fine," he whispers against my lips, and then he's devouring my mouth.

These are the kisses I live for: wild, all encompassing passion.

"Boys, should I order breakfast or...?" Lennon asks amused.

I lift my head, looking over at her with my eyebrow lifted. If there's a choice to order in and a stocked kitchen, chances are Ror will choose to cook.

"Shower and then food?" he suggests, his pouty lips swollen and perfect.

"Done, and our plan today?"

"Hop in a cab and get lost in the city," I say eagerly.

Lennon fist pumps as she sits up, "Fuck yes! Derek, you'll join us, won't you?"

His lips curve in amusement and respect for being included. "I'm not going to ask if you're sure, because you wouldn't bother including me if you weren't. So, yes I would love to join you. I just have to get some work in later this afternoon."

"Sweet," I murmur with a lazy grin. "Group shower?"

Derek's eyes heat as his eyes travel over me and my only partly covered cock. "We would never leave," he groans, his voice getting louder as he speaks.

I bark out a laugh and shrug. "Can't blame a man for trying!"

"Separate showers or he's right and we will *never* leave," my beautiful Lavender demands and I shrug in acquiesce.

"If you insist."

Showers happen quickly, and Roark actually agrees to try a boozy breakfast joint called *The Brunch Lab* for Sunday brunch with bottomless mimosas and brunch drinks. I can only imagine the adventures we'll have with some champagne in our systems and all of what Los Angeles has to offer.

Jordan called twenty minutes before we walked out the door to inform us we have a private car for any shenanigans we had planned today. I snorted when I heard him say this, because of course Lennon had him on speaker.

"*I also would like your itinerary if you have one for today, or if you're going to flit around to your hearts' content that's also fine, but please be back at the hotel by six this evening so you'll be ready for the bus to pick you up by seven. Is Derek headed out with you this morning?*" he asks and my eyebrows rise.

Derek clears his throat, cheeks flushing with color as he adjusts the strap to his camera bag. "Yes, sir, I am. Did you need something from me today?"

"*No, no. I'm glad you're going with them. Can you take a few casual photos for their social media of them enjoying the city, but otherwise unplug and have fun,*" he directs and I smile.

Even if he did have questions, I don't think he would ask them over the phone. It doesn't seem like his style.

"Got it, boss man," says my sassy girl and I smirk.

Jordan sounds like he's choking on his own spit and I release the bubble of laughter that's been wanting out.

"Bye Jordan, we're headed out. Thanks for the car and the check in. That's shit Prescott would forget to do, or didn't care about," I tell him as I open the front door.

"Gah, that woman was fucking useless. The label is pulling all new hires over the last two years and making sure they're not a waste of space. Sorry Derek," Jordan says as Derek winces, *"you're included in that list, but I have no doubts that you'll be fine. It's just making sure you're doing your duties."*

Derek still looks slightly green and I say goodbye to our manager and hang up the call.

"Why do you look like you're gonna be sick?" I ask as we walk to the elevators.

"I'm honestly trying to remember if there's a 'no fraternization' policy in my contract right now," Derek says as he swallows.

Ahh. Fuck. "Nah, and if there is, we'll get it sorted and redrawn," I reassure him.

Lennon chews on her lip, thinking about this. "I don't think there is, honestly. I think the label would tell us if there was, because it's meant to be a deterrent for us as much as other employees," she says with a shrug.

Derek's shoulders relax a little as he nods. I swear his shoulders were making themselves real comfy around his ears.

"Oh, what are Mav and Atlas up to today?" Roark asks. "I usually get a text when we're going to hit a new city with jokes about being left behind."

I snort. They would never let us leave them.

"They're checking out Santa Monica Pier," Lennon says with a smile. "I got a text this morning about it, and then forgot to mention it. They left an hour ago and Jordan I'm sure set a car up for them as well. Derek," she continues, "when I said the other day I expected Prescott to set up our transport, it wasn't because I couldn't arrange our own. It's because we don't often have a lot of time in between gigs or activities. So it's nice not to have to deal with ride shares, especially because of how visible we sometimes are. It can be unsafe to use public transport."

Derek blows out a breath and looks shamed. "Yeah, Len, I get it. I was being a dick, I'm sorry."

Lennon's face lights up and she barrels into his side, hugging him tightly. His arms slowly go around her, his eyes wide with wonder. Lennon gives affection freely with those in her circle, and up until recently, she didn't want to touch him with a ten foot pole. I know it was because his mouth and brain couldn't figure out how to be pleasant. An apology from him is amazing to Lennon.

Slowly, he relaxes, even letting his lips brush against her temple. Pride blooms in my chest, lips twitching as Roark squeezes my elbow before directing me into the elevator. Derek sweeps her protectively through the open doors as well, shoving his foot in the door to stop them from shutting.

Roark nods appreciatively at the little things Derek is doing, but honestly, the man looks at a loss as he stares down at Lennon. He's wanted her and hated her for a long time. The two feelings always worked off each other, creating a toxic as fuck environment. As much as Roark and I want to give them a chance to see where their chemistry goes, my first priority is Lennon.

The ride out to breakfast passes quickly, and we joke about how hungry we are. Sex in the middle of the night burns some serious calories, and I swear my stomach is eating itself. As if to make itself known, my stomach growls and I wince.

"Who's the gremlin now," Lavender giggles.

"I'm afraid that may be me very soon. Fuck, I'm starving," I groan.

The cab arrives at *The Brunch Lab* quickly, and I practically roll out of the car in my haste to get a table. The jerks behind me laugh, but I don't care. They'll thank me when we're seated even sooner. Gah, I really am starving. I sweet talk the hostess into giving us a corner booth, and don't feel the slightest bit badly about it.

A few groups ahead of us have already been seated, so I wasn't cutting in front of anyone. See? I'm not completely gone if I can notice these things.

"Darling man," Lennon coos, laughter in her voice before she hugs me. A second later she flinches as she remembers too late and I glance over my shoulder at Derek to see if it bothered him.

Derek shakes his head with a grin. "I'm good, guys. I promise, Len, you're fine," he says, slightly raising his voice for her benefit.

She relaxes and nods. "Fuck," she mutters to herself and I smile against her hair.

Lavender cares about this man, even if it's new. Derek comes with baggage, and she wants to be aware of it, but it's difficult when he's not ready to tell us the full story.

We'll make do until he is, and figure out the inevitable issues that may rise along the way.

Wrapping my hand around her hip, I squeeze it tight enough that she'll look up. On cue she does, keeping eye contact with me as I expertly maneuver around tables as I follow our hostess.

"He's fine, Lavender, and you did nothing wrong," I say firmly.

I can see the shadows in Lavender's eyes, telling her she should have remembered, tried harder. She's beating herself up, and that's unacceptable to me, especially this early in the day.

Lavender bites her lip, refusing to respond. "I need a drink," she murmurs.

"Hmmm, it just so happens I can do that," I tease her, struggling to get her mood back.

The booth is perfect for us to pile into, and it's in a corner. We have some privacy to enjoy ourselves, and hopefully get back our happy Lennon.

Derek makes certain to sit on the other side of her and kisses her neck. "You're doing all the right things," he murmurs.

"I feel like I'm fucking it up," she sighs.

The waitress comes by and Lavender orders a mimosa margarita. I roll my lips inwards, because apparently it's going to be that kind of day. She won't drink too much since we have our show tonight, but Lennon's drinking her feelings at the moment.

Derek, Roark, and I will keep her safe, so Lennon is free to work up a light buzz to restore her good mood, relax her, and not overthink every little thing. She isn't typically someone who agonizes over decisions, but Derek's revelations struck a chord in her.

"Turner, what are you ordering," Roark says to change the subject for the moment.

Shit, food. I look over the menu and decide on a breakfast burrito with toast. Fuck, my stomach twists with hunger and I wince.

I really need to make sure I have a snack before bed from now on, especially after a show. We usually order in on the bus and stay up, so I'm never in this predicament.

Drinks come and Lennon's face lights up. Her drink does look amazing, and I wish I had ordered it instead of a Bloody Mary.

Taking a sip, her body starts to relax. Smiling, she looks around the table. "Let's do a toast to new beginnings? We have a new manager that actually cares about us, we have Derek," Lennon grins, winking at him, "and *Velvet Escape* is opening for us."

She wiggles and gives a little squeal in happiness and Derek sputters out a laugh. He's never seen Lavender just be herself, no inhibitions. It's fucking beautiful. He wasn't in love with her yet, it's a foregone conclusion.

"Yeah, Lenny, let's do a toast," Roark grins.

The four of us raise our glasses. "Cheers," we chorus.

Lennon takes another sip and moans happily. "I have a two drink limit, boys. I'm stating this now before I get carried away."

Throwing my arm around her, I press her against me. "You can count on it," I growl into her ear and she whimpers.

Derek's eyes widen a bit and he gulps his drink. Yeah, Lennon tends to get horny when she drinks too. This'll be a blast.

A hand trails over my leg, gently squeezing my dick through my pants. Eyes flying next to me, Roark smirks as he sips his mimosa. People would say it looks ridiculous for a man his size to be drinking this, but he is very comfortable with the delicate flute.

"Hey, I'm going to get a few candid shots of you guys," Derek says moving from the table. "Then I can tag the restaurant, give them some good press as well."

My head tilts as I stare at him. As much as we joked that he was a dick, he really isn't. Derek is methodical in his actions too when it comes to good press and marketing. We aren't new here, and tease and joke with each other as Derek takes photos.

Knowing he's snapping away can make it difficult to ignore, but my trick is to get thoroughly wrapped up with the people around me.

"These are amazing," he says with a nod as he slides back

into the booth. "I'll take some food porn shots, too and then I'll call it."

"You're really good at this," Roark blurts out. I haven't known this man to be a lightweight a day in my life. I'm surprised by his outburst and my eyebrow raises. "What made you decide to go into social media marketing for the music industry?"

Our gorgeous Scotsman is prying. I bite my lip to hold back my smile. My jaw hurts from how much fun I've been having. I'm pretty grouchy usually, but today has already been a great day. Derek brings out hidden smiles in me, even if they never see the light of day, I know they're there.

Derek's ears turn red, and I can't help myself. Snickering, I hide my face in Roark's shoulder. He grins, but refuses to back down. I get the feeling Derek isn't used to compliments, and it makes me want to give him more.

"I, ah, took a photography class in college as an elective. It was supposed to be a bullshit easy course, but I found I really enjoyed it. I wanted to play professional ball since I loved the game, but my father also pushed me hard in that direction. I insisted on going to school first, because I always heard stories about washed up football players who got hurt. If that's the way my career went, fine, but I wanted a Plan B. I chose Mass Communications because it checked a lot of the boxes of what I was interested in," he explains with a shrug. The food arrives and Derek looks apologetically at me.

What did I do? Oh shit, he wanted to take photos.

"Keep talking, and I'll forget all about the food, Derek," I murmur in a smooth voice as I sit up to watch him. It feels like he's finally sharing another piece of himself and I can't bring myself to look away.

Nodding, he begins to arrange plates and drinks as the waitress stares on, confused.

"Do you need anything else?"

"No, no. This all looks amazing, thank you..." Derek looks up, his brow pinched as he looks for her name tag. "Erica! We're good, thanks."

She nods with a small smile, and walks away.

He looks back at what he's doing, thoroughly ignoring us. It's okay though, because it's not the easiest for Derek to talk about himself.

"My father thought I was a fool for not going professional right away, but I decided to push for what I wanted. Honestly, he's not the easiest man to get along with," he says as his lips purse. Derek picks up his camera and takes a photo, and I have a feeling there's more to this story. "He got over it though, and the media applauded my decision to put school first. As soon as this happened, my dad changed his tune. He has been talking about running for a bigger position than the mayor of our little town for years, but it hasn't happened yet. Everything I do reflects on him."

Derek sounds like he's repeating the dregs of an old argument as his shoulders bunch. He takes a few more pictures and then passes out our plates. Taking a deep sip of his own vodka infused drink, he scowls. "I found out I enjoyed music in college when I bar hopped in Colorado. It spoke to me in a way only photography did. I dabbled in some social media blogging for a newspaper in college, but left it all behind when I got drafted after I graduated."

Derek takes a savage bite of his breakfast potatoes as if they offend him, but I can tell the topic is. He really dislikes talking about himself.

"Anyway, after my football career ended two years ago, I was offered a position as a football commentator, but my heart wasn't in it. I love the game, I always will, but I knew I wanted to go back to photographing and working in the music industry.

One of my contacts from school emailed me after hearing about my injury, and asked if I had ever thought about social media marketing."

Derek shrugs as if this email isn't the entire reason he's eating breakfast with us now. "I worked a couple of years doing this, and during that time, I heard you play again. My mind was blown at how incredible you were, and I had to work for you all."

"When did you know I was the singer of *Darkest Nights*," Lennon asks shrewdly as she chews a bite of her food.

Ah, Lavender, happily toasted, but dumb she will never be. I love how fast she latched on to this. I wondered the same.

"Honestly, I knew the first time I saw you play five years ago," he confesses. "My friends wanted to go see a concert, and it was during my team's off-season. I hadn't seen them in ages, so I Venmoed them money to pay for the tickets so we could all sit together. I flew into Denver for a couple of nights to see the show and some friends, and then left. I knew very little about *The Darkest Nights* or your music, but I wanted to hang out with my friends. I watched you all for a few minutes, and when the cameras on the band blew you up on screen... it hit me. I knew you were the little girl in school I never let up on and hated."

He looks up from his food and stares at her with tortured eyes. "I went to four more concerts, and then decided I had to be your social media manager when the position opened up. Fuck, this makes me a stalker doesn't it," he groans, rubbing his face.

Lennon has the oddest reaction and snorts. I chuckle looking over at her to see what's happening. She covers her face, and her shoulders tremble. I'm not sure if she's laughing, seizing, or crying right now.

Derek frowns hard, staring at her. "Fuck, guys, I think I broke her..."

Roark rolls his eyes, shaking his head. "I think she's processing," he rumbles. Ror doesn't sound like he's completely sure either.

She inhales and a laugh bursts out. Thank fuck, Lennon isn't broken.

"Oh my god, you're totally a stalker," she exclaims. "I mean not a creepy, weird stalker, more like the please push me up against the wall and fuck me kind..." Lennon dissolves into giggles again, holding her stomach as she squeals.

She's fucking beautiful as she just lets go. Derek leans back, staring at her. "So what you're saying is you want to fuck me," he says stoically.

I must be infected with the giggles because I guffaw, too. "Derek, of fucking course that's all you hear," I laugh.

The man shrugs. "I just want to know where I stand," he says seriously and Roark roars with laughter now.

We look insane as we lose it in this booth, and I wouldn't have it any other way.

25

ROARK

Derek, for as rough as his entrance in our lives has been, turns out he's good for us. The flirting, teasing, pushing us to open ourselves up to him, brings a new level to our relationship. Lennon and Turner are my everything, I did ask them to marry me after all, but Derek fits in with us as well.

We all have demons, and mine can get loud and mean, but Turner and Lenny always help quiet them. I don't remember the last time that we all laughed this hard and we weren't fucking.

We decided to walk after breakfast before choosing what we wanted to do next. There's shops, cool music stores in the area, and bars. Lenny's buzz is strong as she loops her arm through mine and smiles up at me.

"Hey beautiful, ya doing alright there?" I tease.

"Aye," she giggles. I love that this is something she's picked up from me over the years. I really want to take her to Ireland someday. Of all the places around the world that we've toured, we've yet to go there. I haven't the faintest idea why either. I should really ask Jordan if there is a reason.

"The last week or so has been kind of shitty," Lenny continues as she wrinkles her nose. "It's nice to do something carefree and fun instead, and we haven't been able to do this in ages."

My lips twist as I realize that we've not gotten lost in a city in over six months. Fuck, no wonder we've all been exhausted. It's finally started to burn us all out.

"I'm glad, sweet Lenny. We definitely needed some fun. Huh… that store looks interesting," I muse.

The shop looks to be a mix of music, books, and knick knacks. There's a few people walking around inside, and it couldn't hurt to pop in for a bit to look.

"Let's go in," Lennon gushes, already pulling me in that direction.

"Oye boys," I call over my shoulder to where Turner and Derek have wandered ahead. "We're gonna head in here for a bit."

Turner jerks his chin in my direction and heads my way, his arm easily around Derek's shoulders. I have to say they look fantastic together. An easy smile tips up on his lips as he walks with Turner, his fingers twitching.

I wonder why they are, does he want to wind his arm around Turner's waist, lean into him? Derek's a deep enigma that I'm excited to unravel… hopefully while fucking him.

Walking into the store, I smell lavender and sage and inhale deeply. My mother always had lavender and sage sachets around the house, so the scent brings me back to my childhood, before things went to shit.

Lennon feels me take a breath, and leans into me, giving me strength. A shiver at the repressed memories runs through my body, and while she's unaware of the full story, she knows enough. I haven't spoken to my mother in years, she chose to marry a rich fuck over me, and I never looked back when I left at eighteen. It's a wound that I don't care to open either, even though this entire fucking store smells like my mum. It should bother me that Turner calls Lennon "Lavender," but the color has never been a trigger for me.

"Shall we explore then, loves," I say to my crew with a forced smile and gritted teeth. I force back the feelings my mum makes me feel even after all of these years, because I will not be the downer in our day.

Lenny picks up my lead and pulls me towards a corner of the store. Turner chuckles darkly and pulls Derek in another direction. Divide and conquer always.

"So we shall," Turner drawls.

My body loosens a bit at his voice, my smile coming easier. The sound of his voice arouses me, even when he doesn't mean to. It's darkness and sin personified and delicious. I wonder now if Lenny will be up for a quickie against one of the many bookshelves.

"Are you thinking dirty thoughts, Ror," she teases me and I step behind her to curl around her body as we walk.

"I could be eighty, and my cock would still harden at the sight of you," I growl into her ear, palming her breast.

"Ror," my gorgeous Lenny pants. "Please play nice, you're destroying my panties."

I chuckle darkly. "I happen to know you're not wearing any under those adorable leggings today, so don't even try, my girl."

Lenny giggles and shrugs. She's such trouble. We walk lazily through the different aisles, and she picks up a book with a smile. We don't often buy much when we do go on our adventures, because there's only so much storage on our bus. Earrings or a bracelet to remind her where she's been is usually Lennon's go to.

Lennon frowns all of a sudden, dropping the book back on the shelf. Surprised, I follow as she darts around the corner.

"What the fuck," I whisper furtively. It's not a library, but some of the books are so old, it has the feel of one. "Lennon O'Reilly, what the hell is going on?!" I try again when she brushes me off again.

Deciding there must be a reason, I trail her down the aisles until she stops. On an old record player is the blasted song she keeps humming, and I finally place the name of the song. *She Moved through the Fair* is a song about a man whose love dies and returns to him as a ghost at night. The lyrics are haunting, and I have no idea how she would know of it.

"What's the name of this song," Lennon asks softly to the woman who is listening to the record. The older female glances up, dashing away tears left on her cheeks. Lennon cringes in embarrassment and sympathy, not having realized the woman was having a private moment. There's no way she could have known with the way her face was turned away. "I'm so sorry— " she begins to apologize.

"No, no sweet girl," the woman says, shaking her head. She has long dark hair, and looks like she's in her late sixties. "The song is called *She Moved through the Fair* and is a very sad Irish song about love and loss. I lost my husband and daughter at a young age, and I sometimes torture myself by listening to this song. The owner is very sweet, and I come in a couple of times a week to wander and pick up new books. I refuse to own a copy of this song because I'm not a complete masochist."

She shrugs as if to say she understands her need to listen to this song isn't healthy but she can't help it. I don't know what I would do if I lost Turner or Lennon forever. I would be a basket case I think, utterly broken. I imagine that soon I'll feel the same way about Derek as well. The Connolly boys love hard.

I smile softly at her, swallowing thickly. While I don't know her pain, I can stand in witness to it.

"My fiancée has had this song in her head for days now, so when she heard it, she had to follow it," I explain.

The sad, lonely woman nods as she focuses her light green eyes on Lennon. "I hope you never feel this pain. Enjoy every moment with those that you love. We aren't promised anything in life, nor are we meant to."

Lennon reaches out and squeezes the woman's hand. "I will," she whispers and we walk slowly away.

"God, that's so sad," she says softly, leaning into me.

"Aye, it is, baby girl," I murmur, running my fingers through her soft violet strands. Lennon is perfect, empathetic, and I know that woman is going to haunt her thoughts. It still bothers me that I don't know where she heard this damn song, because it's not something she would have heard on the radio.

It's going to rankle until I figure it out.

"Roark? Lennon? Where are you at?" I hear and know Turner and Derek are looking for us.

"Over here," I call out, tugging Lenny with me to cut through the bookcases. "Looks like our quickie in the stacks will have to happen another day," I tease Lennon.

Her face clears of the storm she's thinking of and she smirks up at me. "Game on, baby," she challenges with a more carefree smile.

"What are we betting on," Derek asks, rubbing his hands together. Oh shit, the man is competitive. That'll be fun.

"Nothing," Lennon rushes to say and I snort derisively.

"We were talking about making her come hidden in a bookstore another day," I respond honestly and wait to see what they say.

"Oh Len, you dirty girl," Derek says with a dark chuckle, pulling her over to him. "Anytime, anywhere, beautiful. The question is, can you stay quiet," he teases.

"Only with her mouth stuffed full of cock," Turner inserts

and I snicker, leaning in and kissing his neck as we leave the store.

It's already been a day filled with more ups than downs, and I will take that any day.

Derek

I feel lucky to be able to enjoy down time with Lennon, Roark, and Turner. They are uninhibited, free, and it's clearer than ever how much they needed this.

I thought that I'd feel like a fourth wheel with three people so obviously in sync with each other, but I don't. I'm always pulled back into their circle if I fall behind, included in conversations, and just loved on.

It's odd to say this, but it's true. A touch here, a kiss there, and it starts to feel more natural. I've never been someone comfortable with public displays of affection, or any kind of affection honestly. Mom was affectionate with me until my dad chased her away with his infidelity in middle school, and my dad was only interested in my next win. My mother made sure to send me encouraging texts, notes under my windshield wiper when she was in town in high school, but I can recognize that being home was difficult for her. I never really dated in high school, other than to get my dick wet, and I wasn't interested in relationships in college either.

I was invested in my future: first to finish college, then playing football through school, and finally playing professionally. I always had another goal in mind, and I told myself I was too busy for relationships. I also disliked the way girls had stars in their eyes when they talked to me, so I kept everything casual. The few times I made the mistake to hope after football failed miserably.

And then my dick became uninterested completely in

fucking indiscriminately. Funny enough, it stayed limp until Roark, Turner, and Lennon.

"Penny for your thoughts," comes an amused voice and I smirk, looking at the floor. My thoughts went a little off the rails there for a minute.

We found this free music festival happening, and walked over to lose ourselves in the bands playing. I didn't mean to also get lost in my head.

"I was just thinking," I tell Roark with a wince, because duh of course I was.

"Uh-huh," he says with a chuckle, jerking his head to the side in the universal sign to walk with him.

My head moves in a swivel to find Turner and Lennon listening to one of the bands playing. They start dancing and I relax, knowing they probably won't be moving any time soon.

"Look at you," he murmurs as he starts to walk with me. "You're already checking in and making sure your people are safe."

I bite my lip because I really am. It's funny how quickly it becomes normal to do this. Fuck, I'm already starting to get attached... which led me to my current thoughts.

"I was thinking that I don't do attachments," I explain, blowing out a breath. "I don't kiss on the lips, do public displays of affection, or date. First it was because I was too focused on my goals, later it was due to someone always wanting something from me. I made really good money, and girls wanted a piece of that. I decided a few times to see if a relationship was for me, but I felt fucking suffocated," I explain.

Roark nods sagely as he listens, his arms hanging loosely at his sides as we talk.

"So I stopped bothering and fucked around. There are women who are free with their bodies, enjoy sex, and the excitement of a one night stand. I was glad to fill those shoes, and then fucked off to the next city with the band I was working with. I took what I wanted and that was that. This worked great until— "

I sigh, frowning as I scuff my feet along the path as I walk.

"Yeah?" Roark prompts and my eyes rise up to his.

"My dick lost complete interest," I mumble.

His face pinches in amusement as he holds his laughter in. "Your cock decided it had had enough, huh? It hasn't had any problems with the three of us though," he points out.

Fuck, why can't he let sleeping dogs lie?

I rub the back of my neck, embarrassed. I shouldn't be after what we've already done sexually, and our previous misunderstandings, but how do you explain that they're the only ones you want? Is that considered needy after just a day of agreeing to see where your connection with each other goes?

Fuck, dating is already exhausting.

"You're kind of the only ones my cock or I have been interested in for the past two years," I say really fast so it all sounds like one word.

Roark must have superhuman hearing powers because he frowns hard to figure out what I said before the most gorgeous smile spreads over his face. He doesn't give me shit like Turner might, he just wobbles his head back and forth as he thinks. Throwing his arm around my shoulders, he says, "That's the best fucking compliment I've ever been given. Thanks mate."

My jaw drops and a hysterical little giggle escapes. "Seriously?!"

"Fuck yeah," he says excitedly, shrugging a shoulder in a way that makes his shirt tighten across his body. Damn, I could trace my tongue across every muscle on his body every day and never get bored. "Look. Turner, Lenny, and I... we don't fuck around. We've been committed to each other since the start. The tabloids and Prescott insinuate that we bring other people in to 'spice things up,' but we never have or needed to do that. Lenny and Turner are adventurous enough on their own with me. We want to date you to see where this goes because there's a connection between us and we want to explore it. We don't do casual, and I'm glad your cock doesn't either."

This man says this like it's the most natural thing in the world and I stare at him, forgetting I'm supposed to be watching where I'm going. Roark moves us against a huge tree and presses his body against mine.

"I have a feeling you're into all of that," he growls and I swear my eyes roll in pleasure as he presses his cock against mine.

"God, why do you have to be so damn perfect," I breathe.

Roark chuckles and it's so sinful, my cock twitches against him. "It's so fucking hot that you react to me like this. With Turner it's his tongue ring... did it feel good dragging around your thick cock?"

He doesn't wait for an answer before he nips my lips. I chase after them, wanting more, and then it's firmer pressure. A demanding kiss that asks for everything, refusing to back down, and I even love how his hands pull at my hair to change the angle.

"You taste delicious," he sighs and I can't do anything but groan as Roark kisses me again.

We come up for air, only to hear applause and cat calls. Looking around I realize it's not directed at the stage... but rather at us.

While I turn beet red, Roark just grins, inclining his head to our audience before grunting 'mine' into my ear. I think I could get used to being his... theirs.

Why doesn't that all scare me more?

Roark tugs me into motion, his fingers entwining through mine.

"Let's get a drink to cool down some," he teases me with a smile.

It's so nice to be in Los Angeles, where two men making out is more accepted, unlike back home.

Fuck... my dad. How long ago did I last talk to him? I can feel his deadline looming over my head. Thoughts of how open the City of Angels is only serves to remind me how conservative and immovable my father is. I feel lightheaded as I spiral, my head starting to throb a little. My ass buzzes as I sigh. Grant Williams has always had impeccable timing.

Roark glances at me as we walk, eyebrows raised in question. Pulling my phone out of my back pocket without releasing his hand, I open the message.

Dad the Ass: You are trying my patience, boy. Your plane ticket is set up for the day after tomorrow at eight in the morning I'm tired of waiting and don't want to wait any longer. Do not make me send someone for you; I promise the experience would be far from enjoyable for you.

Fuck! Fuck! Fuck.

"Something's wrong. You're squeezing my hand, and I normally wouldn't mind, but the look on your face is freaking me out. What the fuck, Derek?"

Taking a deep breath to ground myself, I let go of him and turn towards him. People move around us as if we aren't there, and I take another breath. I really don't want to go home.

"Just give me a second, I need to make sure I answer this," I tell him nervously. My father has never been very patient.

I'll be on that flight, Dad. Please make sure I have the information needed to ensure my arrival.

I have spoken formally to Grant Williams since he almost broke my nose after graduation. He told me I was now a man, and I needed to change my tone when I spoke to him. I didn't respond quickly enough, and I went to summer football camp right after I graduated. I didn't want to deal with lying again about a bruise.

> Dad the Ass: Good. I've emailed you the information, and look forward to your imminent return. We have some things to discuss.

I take a deeper breath as our conversation comes to an end. We're done for now, and there's no way for me to slip up and show him how I really feel.

Relaxing slightly, I look back at Roark. "My dad called me yesterday, and asked me to come home," I explain resignedly, crossing my arms with a sigh.

I was supposed to have an extra day, but of course he would pull the rug out from under me. I'm surprised he didn't tell me to get my ass on a plane tomorrow. Damnit, I still need to talk to Jordan.

"We aren't very close, but when my father calls, I am expected to follow his directive as soon as possible. While generally it wouldn't be a big deal to go home to see family, he's a mean son of a bitch," I explain with a sigh. Roark looks more worried by the second, and while I don't want to sugar coat it or lie to him, I don't want him to worry. "Either way, I have to go back because he told me that my mom is sick, and she didn't text me back when I messaged her. I just have this bad feeling about everything."

"A bad feeling because you don't feel safe in your da's home, or because of your mum?" Roark's voice is gruff, raspy, and sharp. Fuck, and his gorgeous accent is out in force.

I shift my weight, telling my body that now is *not* the time.

"I'm his only kid, so I'm safe enough," I counter, understanding that's a non-answer, but this is dangerous territory. "I don't talk about my home life. Not when my father used to hit me, and not as an adult who is now bigger than him. The man is still powerful, and would probably have hog tied me and had me thrown on a plane back to the Midwest. I'm more worried about how intent he is that I come home and how vague my dad was about my mom. I need to talk to Jordan, and I don't know how long I'll be in Kentucky—"

"Two days," Roark says, walking towards me. "That's all you get, or so help me, we'll come get you. I don't like this, but I'll respect this for now. Is that understood?"

I blink hard. "Holy shit," I whisper, staring at him.

"Words, Derek. Be good for me and follow directions, and I'll send you off with some fond memories," he teases.

Promised orgasms with this man would make me promise him the moon.

"Yeah," I rasp, nodding. "Got it, yes, you're the boss," I say rapidly and I'm rewarded with a smirk.

"You're fucking adorable," Roark says before kissing me languidly. Every kiss with him is amazing and I have no idea how. "Get in, get out, and come back. That's your only job."

I hope it's that easy, but I have no idea what my dad wants this time.

26

LENNON

Roark and Derek were gone for a while, but Turner and I were having so much fun dancing, it helped the time fly. Turner doesn't dance in public very often, so I love that he threw caution to the wind and said 'fuck it'.

A warm embrace from behind and Turner's answering smile when I look up, ensure it's Roark. Relaxing into his arms, I smile as he kisses up my neck.

"Hey beautiful," he murmurs in my ear.

"Hey Ror," I sigh in return.

"Have you been dancing this entire time," asks an amused Derek.

I reach out my hand towards him as if it's the most natural thing in the world and Derek grabs it as he walks into view. He looks slightly stiff and I wonder why. Did something happen?

"Easy there, Lenny. Just relax, your thoughts do not need to be going wild over this," Roark whispers at a level only I can hear.

I can't force my face to do what I want, and I can't smile at Derek because he'll know it's a lie so I just watch him.

Derek tugs me to him. "Are you thirsty, Len? You never answered me..."

"Give me the waters, Derek. I trust you, but I'm not taking any chances with bottles anymore," Turner says.

Derek hands over the waters and turns me in his arms to hug me to his chest. He sways me gently and I begin to relax. Whatever it is, Roark didn't seem concerned, so they'll tell me later. Roark doesn't keep secrets from me, and Derek will tell me his when he's ready to.

Turner pulls out little strips and I remember the time where he was obsessive about checking any liquids that weren't in his view at all times. A fan once drugged him and his band members and took advantage of Turner with her friends. He is adamant that this never happens again.

It's why he was so upset when I was drugged earlier this week. God, I can't believe it's been less than a week since that all happened. Time moves so quickly while on tour, while still moving at a snail's pace.

"What are you thinking about," Derek asks, sweetly kissing my cheek.

"How evil people are," I say. Derek stiffens slightly in surprise and I twist my head to look at him. "Turner shouldn't have to test our damn water at a music festival," I sigh. "He shouldn't have the trauma because someone once took advantage of him and his bandmates. It's just so unfair."

"You're such an incredible person," he says in awe. "Lennon, Turner checks things obsessively because he may have had his water fucked with, but you recently did too. The first place your brain went to was Turner and how he feels about having to do this, and not yourself."

"I'm fine though," I tell him in confusion. As far as I know, nothing happened to me. If I hadn't left the parking lot because I was disoriented and upset, the guys would have found me sooner. But... ultimately? The guys still found me in one piece, completely safe.

It could have been worse, but I live in the reality of today and not what ifs.

"You're fine today," Turner confirms, nodding when he finds the water to be clean. "Here Lavender, have a sip now that it's safe."

I smile as he hands it to me and take a deep sip. I lean into Derek's body as my head tilts back to drink, not having realized how thirsty I was until now.

"Mmmmm," I moan happily as I swallow. Looking back at Roark and Turner, I blush at the heat in their eyes as they watch me.

"You're so sexy even when you're doing something as simple as drinking water," Turner snickers as he takes a shallow sip of his own.

"They're thinking of other things in your mouth right now," Derek chuckles. "I know because I sure as hell am." He slowly grinds his cock into my ass and I whimper.

"So pretty when you're needy," Roark drawls, suddenly in front of me. I am so damn distracted by Derek, so close to writhing in his arms and ignoring how many people are around us right now that I didn't notice him move.

These men make me wild.

Roark drags his finger down my throat, under the cowl neck of my sweater, skirting around my already pebbling nipple.

"I think the responsible thing would be to go now, don't ya think," he grins as he stares down at me.

"Responsible," I sputter, confused as to where he's going with this.

"Yes, responsible. I wouldn't want to have to explain to Jordan why I had to break cameras because they caught me fucking you in public," he deadpans before kissing me.

I mewl into his mouth, so incredibly turned on. I can feel Turner's hand on my hip, hear his wicked chuckle, and fuck yes it's absolutely time to go home to the hotel.

Breaking from Roark's demanding kiss, I gasp out, "Time to go home!"

Derek barks out a laugh as Roark removes his fingers from under my neckline. The fucker tweaks my nipple on the way out and I yelp.

"God, it should be a crime how wet you all make me," I purr, knowing I can rile them up in my own way. "Who is calling the car? First one who does, gets to fuck me..."

Derek hurriedly shoots a text, and fuck... I didn't think he even had the number for our driver today.

"I win!" he crows and then pales. "Shit, the first time we have sex shouldn't be because I won a stupid bet. I'm just really competitive. Fuck me, I'm sorry— "

Roark snorts and shrugs. "I think it's adorable," he says as his arm pulls me into him to start walking. "I love how competitive you are, and I want to explore that one day. Like who can make Lennon cream on their face the fastest. Or who gets the honor of fucking Lenny... oh wait looks like you won that. Huh, funny how that worked out," he teases me and I can't help but giggle wildly.

Holy shit. Is this really happening?

"Oh my god, guys. Really?!" I hide my face in Roark's shoulder, my face flaming red.

Roark and Turner are competitive themselves, and we have played this game before. I passed out mid-orgasm, and woke up to them fucking like rabbits. These men broke me the last time we did this, but damn was it fun.

"Let's pretend I didn't win, god it feels awful to say that I 'won' when we have a really fucked up history already," Derek says.

The man is spiraling. I also, funnily enough, didn't think about the bet he made in high school with his friends for the first time in ages. Huh, maybe this is what healing looks like?

"Derek," I say, swallowing what I was going to say afterwards. It's natural to say 'love or honey' for me after I say the guys' names. I can't with Derek and my heart squeezes just a little. So I show him how much I already care about by breaking away from Roark to put my arms around Derek. "My head didn't go anywhere near there. I already think of you as mine, which means my body remembers the last time Roark had a competition like this with Turner."

"They had a competition to see who could have sex with you first," he asks disbelievingly.

I laugh, shaking my head. "Nope, they wanted to see how many orgasms it would take before I passed out."

"Oh shit," Derek breathes. "Dammit I wanna do that too," he whines in the next breath.

I smile up at him happily. It means a lot that he worried about my reaction to his winning a silly game. We have history that we are still working our way through, but I need to explain to him that this doesn't bother me.

"This is completely different from the previous bet when we were in high school," I begin, looking ahead of me as we walk to make sure I don't trip on anything. "First because I made the bet, and second because we were having fun. I want to feel you inside of me, feel your thick cock destroy me," I explain, stopping because I am now shivering with need. "Fuck, and now I'm completely turned on and not wearing panties."

Derek trips and I snicker, helping him find his balance.

"Called it," Roark crows. "I knew you weren't wearing any, little minx."

"You know me so well, Ror," I tease him back with a wink.

"Sweet, sweet Lavender... it seems you've gotten yourself into a pickle," Turner says as we step onto the sidewalk to walk to our pick up spot.

"I don't like pickles, so I would never find myself in one," I respond, being purposely obtuse.

Derek buries his face in my hair and I swear I hear him inhale. Did he just sniff mer?

I'm distracted by this as I feel his lips on my neck next. "You're adorable. I think Turner wants to know if I get to bury my cock in your pussy or his ass."

Turner protests, "I didn't know my ass was in this conversation... although I'm not against it. If you want to fuck me, you just have to let me know, Derek."

Derek almost trips again and I snort, unable to control myself. It seems we've both bitten off more than we can chew. An inappropriate giggle escapes and Roark rolls his eyes.

"Giggle bug get you, love?" He teases.

"Yep," I gasp, my hand clamping over my mouth. My mind is following the idea that it's ridiculous that Derek and I are teasing each other about having sex when just days ago we were at each other's throat, but here we are. Life has a mysterious way of giving you what you need.

The car pulls up as we walk closer and I struggle to sober up from my laughter. "So am I getting orgasms, Derek, or no?"

"Yes, you're most definitely getting orgasms, Len," he says with a sexy smile, eyes heated.

The driver opens the door, but Derek gives me his hand to help me in. Hello chivalry, you are not dead.

Getting into the car, I get comfortable, swallowing a yawn. Damn, if the guys see me starting to get sleepy, they may try to sweet talk me into a nap. I was up later than usual last night.

"I see you smothering that yawn, Lennon O'Reilly," Roark teases me. "You are not at all stealthy."

"Ugh, I know, but I don't want to nap. I feel like a toddler though whose batteries are starting to die," I say with a sigh.

Derek is sitting next to me, looking mischievous with his smirk. "Would you mind the nap as much if you had orgasms before it," he asked in a low voice, mindful of the driver in front of us.

We are sitting in the middle seat of this SUV, with Roark and Turner in the back.

"Bad influence," Turner murmurs. "You're both such brats, and I love it. You two are going to end up with red asses and keep us on our toes."

Derek blinks in surprise, then adjusts himself with a cough as he realizes what Turner means.

"I'm pretty sure I've only ever been like this for you and Roark," he says honestly. "It'll totally be worth it though," follows in the next breath and I giggle.

"God, I seriously love this," I gasp, shaking my head. "Yes, it would make it better. Roark's hand is huge though, I always suggest spankings from Turner... from one brat to another." I wink stealthily at Derek, while knowing nothing gets past my men.

Derek simply chuckles to himself, lost in thought as we head back to the hotel. Somehow I'm not worried about his thoughts though, because he goes from blushing to shaking his head with a snort.

Sounds like he's learning a bit about his own kinks himself. I can't wait to explore more of that with him.

Turner

I hang back with a smile as I watch Lennon, Roark, and Derek clamor into the elevator while talking. Starting to follow, I hear my name called. Turning, I see Layla and grin.

"Hey girl, I hear you're opening for us. We will be in the wings tonight," I tell her with a grin.

Layla is breathless and she smiles back. "I can hardly believe it, but I kind of need to talk to Lennon for a second."

Lennon pushes out from between Ror and Derek as she sees Layla. "Hey! Are you settling in okay? What's going on?"

"I just wanted to tell you thank you for offering up our name to replace your opening act. What happened to them really sucked," she says, chewing her bottom lip.

It feels like more is happening here if she chased us down to talk...

"Girl, please. I really feel like Jordan was just waiting for me to throw your name in. He didn't seem surprised when I said to call Velvet Escape."

"Yeah, there's kind of a reason he knows who I am..." Layla flushes and I still don't understand why she's being so weird.

"Are you okay? You seem really off right now," I start to say. Maybe if I push we'll get it out of her some time today.

No offense, but I have plans to watch my girl's eyes roll into the back of her head several times before our show. And also tire her enough for a group nap.

Layla blows out a breath, and I can see she's really struggling. What could be that bad?

Roark steps out of the elevator, forehead crinking. "Come up with us and let's talk?" He can be the nicer one out of the two of us when he gives a shit about the outcome.

Layla is important to Lavender, so he's invested in whatever tea she's about to spill.

"Yeah, okay," she says with a nod. "Derek, you're on the way up to?"

Derek nods, hitting the button to keep the doors open. "I am. We hung out today, and we were just headed to our rooms.

It seems like you're struggling to tell Len something, so come on up and chat."

"Damn," she murmurs, standing next to Lennon in the elevator as the doors slide closed. "It appears I missed some shit, Lennon."

Lennon blushes and I chuckle. Yeah, that girl gab session will be very interesting when they have it. I'm glad she has Layla, because she doesn't have any girlfriends. It's not a surprise, with how women in her past have treated her, but I hope it's not about to bite us in the ass.

Whatever she has to say better not hurt Lennon.

The walk to the hotel suite passes in a blur and then Layla is pacing. "Layla," Lennon says with a sigh. "Honey, just rip the bandaid off and tell us already."

Layla whirls around and stares at Lennon. "This isn't common knowledge, and honestly it rarely comes up. We aren't close, and last I heard, my dad doesn't talk very much to him. Jordan Miles is my uncle... I didn't want to not tell you and have you think I lied or that he set me up to get this gig because—"

This girl hasn't come up for air the entire time, and I'm worried she's gonna pass out.

"Layla!" Lennon interrupts, throwing her hands up to stop her. "I would never think that of you. It does explain why Jordan said he knew you and would get in touch with you, and I figured I'd ask you about it later. You seemed so weirded out when I called him by his first name and said he was my new manager, that I wouldn't have thought in a million years that he was your uncle."

Layla doesn't hear any anger in Lennon's voice and sags in relief. Lennon would never bite her head off for something like this.

"I don't know why I thought you'd be mad. I've been

working myself up this entire time, and the guys finally left the hotel because they couldn't deal with me," Layla says, rolling her eyes. I wasn't sure, but I definitely don't think she's sleeping with any of them, and if she is they're a bunch of dicks.

Who leaves their girlfriend when she's freaking out this much?

"So, my dad and Uncle Jordan had a falling out when I was five years old, and I haven't had much to do with him since. He's a huge mover and shaker in the music industry, and my dad works in a different area of Music Horde Records, so he doesn't have to interact much with him. Uncle Jordan is larger than life to me, and I haven't seen him since I was seven years old either, outside of press releases or the news that is. It is going to be really weird to be here, but I didn't want you to be upset that I didn't tell you right now. I wanted to earn my place as your opening act," she says passionately.

Layla is definitely riling herself up for no reason. Her voice is amazing, and she would have gotten this spot even without Jordan Miles being her uncle. I open my mouth to say something, but Lennon beats me to it.

"Layla, hold on. Stop. You have an incredible voice. You just spot on are amazing. Add on the band, and you deserve to be our opening act," Lennon says with a shrug. "I don't know the reasons for your dad and Jordan to not be talking anymore, but I don't want it to be awkward between you two either. He seemed to think of you fondly when I mentioned your name, so I think it may only be awkward if you let it be."

"So don't let it be," I finish lamely. Damn, Lennon really took the wind out of sails, but she looked so pretty doing it that I don't care.

"You're sure," Layla asks with a tired sigh. She pushes her hair out of her face, and I chuckle. Lennon isn't the only one that's about to need a nap.

Firecrackers would attract each other as friends it would seem.

"Positive. Now you've built this all up in your head, and you have to perform tonight. Ya know, show everyone what a badass you are," Lennon teases her. "We'll catch a drink at the hotel when the show is over, okay? You should definitely nap beforehand though. Do you need any help with your hair or makeup? I'm getting ready in the room if you do."

Lennon is the little engine that could, but I see the yawn creeping up on her before she does. There's definitely not going to be any sex before the show tonight. Maybe one tiny little orgasm though so she'll sleep better.

Layla yawns herself as Lennon walks her out, and I swear they're adorable together. They have some of the same mannerisms as well. Like they both rub their faces before they push their hair out of their eyes. Is this a normal thing for girls?

"Are you gonna nap beforehand," Layla asks, as if Lennon is, then she will.

I hide a smile behind my hand as they talk.

"Yeah, I think the boys are going to ask me to take a nap. Not in a domineering way—" Lennon starts to say.

Roark snorts. "No one could make you do anything you don't want to do, baby."

Lennon smirks as she looks over her shoulder at us. "Yeah, that," she explains as if it says it all.

"Hmm. A nap does sound good. The guys will be back before the show they said, so the suite will be quiet."

"Are you sure you're not dating any of them," Lennon asks, turning a bit so I can see her face. Her nose is a bit scrunched, and I can tell she has the same worries that I had.

"I'm sure. They all treat me like I'm the annoying younger sister," Layla says with a sigh, blowing her bangs out of her face.

I'd laugh if she wasn't so frustrated by it.

"Do you want them to treat you differently," Derek hazards.

"Ew, no," Layla says, wrinkling her button nose. "I just wish they didn't cock block me at every turn," she groans.

Roark snorts. "Layla, when are you planning to get dick when you have those two stalking your every move? Have you talked to them about it?"

"Ugh, I get lectures about condoms and how gross boys are when I tell them I want them to back off," Layla grouches.

I kind of love her. Maybe we should take her bar hopping one day. Wait...

"Layla, how old are you anyway?" I ask. Something is bugging me. She looks so young.

"Twenty, why? Are you going to tell me I'm too young to be on the road too?"

"Me?" I snort. "Nah, love, I would never. Lennon was eighteen when she joined us," I reveal and her eyes widen. "Her circumstances were a bit different, but music called us to this life. You have more in common with each other than you know. Leo and Albert are just protective because a lot of bad shit can happen on the road. If you want to have fun, come hang with us. And let Lennon buy you a vibrator. It comes with less STDs or assholes."

Layla sputters a surprised laugh and Lennon shrugs. "I know where the best vibrator websites and stores are," she confides.

"Oh my god, really?" Layla doesn't seem to know if we're serious or not.

"Yeah, we really like our sex toys," I tell her with a grin. Before she asks too many questions, and I'm inclined to answer and shatter her innocent mind, I need her to go.

"If you decide you want help with your hair and makeup, shoot me a text," Lennon says with a smile.

"Yeah," she says, relieved with a nod. "I'm going back to my room to nap. I really worked myself up earlier."

Layla covers another yawn and I chuckle. "Night," I tease her and she waves as she walks out.

"Ugh, does this mean I don't get orgasms," Lennon whines.

Derek walks over and tips her head up. "Do orgasms help you sleep," he teases her, dipping his head to kiss her.

They've been getting more and more comfortable with each other, and I'm glad for it. There's been a lot of wasted years due to their misunderstandings, but it also brought Lennon to us.

Life is a very odd thing.

"Yeah," Lennon breathes with a small smile. This girl already has Derek wrapped around her finger. "They really do."

Derek smiles and kisses her again. "Damn, why do I feel like I'm the one who just got played," he teases her. "Tasting you again is hardly a hardship, Len. Go strip, and I'll have you writhing and moaning my name soon enough."

My Lavender squeals happily and runs for the bedroom that we've been sharing. We could never deny her an orgasm, it's nice to see that Derek shares this trait.

Derek smiles as he watches her and then turns towards us. "Is this okay?" He bites his lip and I realize he's nervous. "Last time this happened, it was all of us involved, and I just wanted to make sure I wasn't overstepping."

Roark shakes his head with a smile. "You're not at all overstepping. I'm not tired, so I'm going to stay out here and hang out with Turner. I wanna hear her scream, so I can't help but have to gag Turner with my cock. Drive me wild with the sounds of her pleasure. Think ya can do that for me, Derek?"

Damn, they say I have a dirty mouth, but I'm hard as steel listening to Roark.

"Yeah, yeah I can," Derek says, his eyes hooded with desire.

"Good man. There are condoms in the side table in case things progress further. Go have fun with our girl."

That seems to be all the encouragement Derek needs because he nods and runs for the bedroom. I chuckle as I watch him.

"Holy shit, Ror," I murmured with a sigh, fingers pulling through my hair.

"Yeah," Roark agrees, lips twisting a bit. "Derek has some big news himself, so I'd rather they both distract themselves for a bit. I don't think they'll have sex tonight, even he isn't that big of an asshole. Honestly, he's been paying attention to her cues more and what she needs. It'll be nice for them to get some alone time together for a bit, and then Derek can hold her before he has to go home. It'll remind himself of what he needs to come back for."

"Back? Where the fuck is he going? You said he's going home," I sputter, realizing I missed something today.

"Yep. His father is quite the character apparently, which I feel like is code for King Of Dicks. He's pressuring Derek to go, and apparently his mother isn't well. So the guy pretty much has to leave, since they have a decent relationship," Roark says with a snort.

Yeah, because Roark's mother shouldn't be one to a litter of feral cats, much less him.

"It sounds like I missed a lot," I grouse. "Did anything fun happen at least when you guys left? I was hoping you'd fool around or something."

"Does making out against a tree count as fooling around," he says, turning and walking towards the kitchenette.

"Go on," I beg, following him.

"And we also had our own personal cheering section afterwards," Roark chuckles as he grabs a beer.

"Yes," I fist pump. "Do you think Derek is going to be safe seeing his dad? There's really no way around it?"

"No, there's not. The shite already booked his ticket home and threatened to send people for him. Honestly the man sounds like he's in the mafia more than the mayor of a sleepy town in Kentucky," Roark says as he offers me a beer as well.

I decline, knowing I'll be swallowing Roark's cock instead soon. I'm just waiting for the symphony of Lennon's cries to fill the air. I'm honestly starting to get impatient, even though it hasn't been very long.

Trailing Roark, I think about what he said as we settle on the couch.

"Has he talked to Jordan yet about a leave of absence? I get a vibe from Derek's dad if he's as bad as you're saying he is." I don't know why, but I don't want him to leave. I have a really bad feeling about it.

When did Derek become someone I'm protective over?

Roark nods, his body shuddering. I'm getting the impression he's reigning in his own protective feelings. "I told Derek he has two days to make his way back to us, or I'm coming for him. There are very few people who will fuck with me or mine," he rumbles. "Derek seemed really disturbed by this visit, and while I can't tell him what to do because his mom is involved in this, I can at least try to control the risk."

Roark takes a slow sip of his beer and I watch as his throat works as he swallows. Fuck, he's calm as can be as if he didn't just claim Derek. Damn.

A long moan sounds from bedroom Derek and Lennon are in and I smirk. I guess Roark and I aren't the only ones claiming Derek today.

"We'll make sure he stays safe," I tell Roark, biting my lip as my knees hit the carpet.

Roark looks down with a twitch of his lips. "So you want my cock now, baby?"

"Fuck yes," I purr as I open his jeans before reaching in so his pierced cock bobs free. "Yum. I was getting hungry for a snack anyway."

My tongue traces up the vein on the underside of his dick and his breath starts to hitch. Grabbing his bottle and setting it aside, I get to work to add Roark's groans to my gorgeous Lavender's cries. Looks like the group nap may be happening after all.

27

DEREK

I was nervous when I walked into the bedroom, and the feeling only intensified when I found Lennon naked in bed.

"Holy shit, you are absolutely gorgeous," I whisper reverently. It's almost as if I speak too loudly, she'll realize this is a mistake and kick me out. I want to deserve to be here, worshiping between her legs.

"And you are wearing entirely too many clothes," she breathes. "Come closer, let me help."

Lennon gets onto her knees, and I swear the sight of her spread wide nearly kills me. Her pussy is all I can see. "Fuck me," I groan, grabbing the back of my shirt and pulling it off one handed.

She smiles lazily, and I think about how she has to know how wild she's making me.

"I mean, that's the hope..."

This girl, and her wicked mouth. I kick off my shoes next and then drop my pants. I don't care how excited I look, or if it makes me desperate. I have zero chill when it comes to her.

Lennon and I have circled each other for years, missing opportunities, and I've terrorized her for my own stupid reasons. The time for posturing is over.

Lennon's eyes roam over my body, tongue peeking out to wet her lips as she finds that the last thing that I'm wearing are my boxers.

"Off," she demands, making grabby hands at me. "God, just watching you is getting me going. I swear, if you just touch me and I come, I'll be so embarrassed."

Fuck. I shove my boxers down, my cock bobbing proudly. The tip is red, angry, and already leaking. "We've both been teased today, haven't we, gorgeous?" Her eyes fly up to mine and she nods wildly as she bites her lip. "You are the most beautiful woman that I've ever seen, and no one else can ever compare," I growl as I push her back on the bed.

She gasps as she falls and I smirk as I stalk her onto the mattress. It's true. Even the people who looked like her, only acted as her stand in. I refuse to let memories of her dead mother follow me here so I kiss Lennon hard. Any time I need to ground myself, I drag my nose up her neck or smell her hair.

Is it creepy? Meh, I don't care. There's too much history for me to care about that. Her lavender and vanilla scent is so different from the magnolias that I keep smelling everywhere, haunting me. It helps to ground me and keeps away my nightmares.

Kissing down her neck, I allow myself to inhale, letting it chase all other thoughts from my head.

"Are you smelling me," Lennon asks with a gasp as I palm her breast.

"Yeah, Len, I am. I don't fucking care if it's weird. You smell absolutely delicious," I growl. "God, if I could bottle it and take it everywhere with me, I would."

Fuck, I don't want to tell her I'm leaving yet. Dragging my

tongue along her nipple, I suck hard.

"Ungh," she moans and I smirk. I plan to make sure she can't string words together for a while. "Wait," she pants. "Why would you want to go anywhere that isn't with me?"

Fuck me. Truth is, I don't want to be anywhere else. She must be really lost in how I'm making her feel to reveal what she did.

"I'm not going anywhere, Len. And if I did, it wouldn't be because I want to, okay?"

Hoping she's appeased for the moment, my fingers trail down her body until I'm dragging them along her wetness.

Lennon whines, arching her back for me, and I smile against the nipple that I'm currently torturing. I wonder if the guys can hear her.

"Please don't tease, Derek," she gasps. "Please."

"I love how you writhe underneath me though, Len. You beg so pretty too."

Her skin is so soft, and I drag my fingers down the colorful tattoos on her arm, my thumb caressing along it. I want to ask her about the music and roses that crawl up her skin, have her tell me her stories since she left Farrelsville. I suck and torture her, loving how dark her nipples get. Traveling down her body, I grab her hips, opening her legs. My fingers caress her and I freeze when I feel the rough skin on her hip that's covered in tattoos. I didn't really notice it last night, and must have been completely enthralled by how sweet her pussy is.

I kiss up her inner thigh, letting my fingers explore what I'm realizing may be scars from how they're raised. They also continue down the inside of her thigh, which is exactly how far down these tattoos go. *Did she do this to herself? Are they covered because someone did them to her?*

Forcing myself to relax, I suck hard on the tattoo that wraps around her thigh. The vine work is beautiful, the leafy greenery colorful and well done. There are also purple and red flowers in various forms of bloom branching off the vines. She'll tell me about this when she's ready, but I refuse to rush her. I just hope that if she is doing this to herself still, that Lennon will explain sooner rather than later.

Lennon's hair is spread across the pillow as she writhes. "Such a good girl, you didn't even beg for me to eat your pussy," I tease her.

Surprisingly, I'm able to call her a good girl, mean it, and not have it trigger me. I know how unequal it is, but I can't explain why this is.

"Fuck," Lennon says, her voice strained. "I swear if you're not eating my pussy and making me scream your name in the next ten seconds—"

I guess I'll never find out what she was going to threaten me with, because I bend her in half and suck her clit hard. She screams and I smirk as I eat her like my last damn meal. Lennon tastes like peaches to me, and I decide it's my new favorite treat. Grabbing her ankles in one hand, I shove her knees to her chest.

I enter her wet channel with two fingers, trusting she'll acclimate to them quickly. Sucking her tight little nub and fucking her with my fingers, I draw out her first orgasm. As she breathes hard, I swear I hear Roark groan. Fuck, yeah. I love knowing that they're getting off to hearing us.

"I'll never get tired of tasting you," I growl against her as she shivers.

"Derek," she breathes. "I need your cock right now."

I blink. I wasn't prepared for her to ask for this. Swallowing, I gently drop her legs, crawling back up her body to kiss her. Lennon moans as she tastes herself, wrapping her legs around my waist, causing my dick to slide through her folds.

"Oh my god, Len," I gasp in pain. I want her so badly, I

may die if I'm not inside of her soon, but it's not about me. "Are you sure, you can't be... Fuck, I was just going to give you a few orgasms and then fuck my hand later," I pant.

I'm talking way too much, but she's right fucking there and my brain isn't getting enough blood flow. Lennon thrusts up as she pushes against my ass with her feet and we both cry out as the head of my cock rocks against her nub.

"Baby, Len, Lenny, ah fuck a duck," I groan. I grab her hair firmly. "You're such a fucking brat," I growl before kissing her.

I've always controlled every sexual interaction, but with Lennon there's push, pull, teasing, and it makes it special. Somehow she flips us so she's on top and my jaw drops as she tosses her hair.

"How did you..."

"You're built like Roark," she says breathlessly. "Built like fucking tanks, but if I can get enough leverage and you're not squishing me with your full weight, I can manage a flip. Don't get used to it though. I only have enough energy left to ride your cock before I need a nap." Lennon winks and my hands wrap around her hips in awe.

A look passes through her gray eyes, turning them stormy as my thumbs caress the bumps on her hips. It passes quickly as I rock her along my hard length and her breath hitches.

"Come again, just rocking on me like this, and I'll think about letting you fuck me," I tease her with a smirk.

I've wanted to be doing this most of my life... there's no way I'd ever deny her.

"Are you saying you like it when I use you," Lennon asks, her hips starting to swivel and glide along me.

I definitely didn't think this through.

Her breath quickens as her eyelashes flutter, having closed without her realizing. Fuck yes, I want her to use me, but I need her to be looking at me as she comes.

Crack.

Crying out after I spank her ass, her body shudders as Lennon's eyes fly open. "Do you want me to watch you or something, Derek," she asks, voice raspy and low.

Lennon's pussy is dripping, and I can hear the moisture as she slides forward on my cock, shuddering.

"You feel so good," she whimpers, and my control shreds.

I want to line my cock to her needy hole and fuck her until we're both sated. But I had to give her terms, and now I have to stick to it. Damnit. *What a time to be a decent guy.*

My hands tighten on her hips and my breath quickens as I watch her. I'm impossibly hard, but I'll hold the course. I will be inside her when I come, or not at all.

"Len," I groan. "Are you gonna come all over my cock? Get me nice and wet to fuck you?"

"I thought," she cries out, throwing herself forward to grab my forearms as she shudders. Poor girl is struggling, riding the edge between pleasure and pain. So damn close, yet miles away from oblivion. "I thought you didn't want to fuck me," she says, eyes rolling as she grinds her clit on my dick.

"Motherfuck, goddamn, Len you're gonna kill me," I roar in frustration. I never said I *didn't want* to fuck her. I need to fix that right now. I move to flip her and her thighs clamp down and she pushes my arms over my head, all the while using me as her personal toy. I freeze, eyes wide. I didn't expect her to do that.

"Tell me to get off and I will," she whispers in my ear.

I inhale her sweet scent and relax. "No, sweet girl, because you're perfect just where you are. Mmm keep moving," I grunt, thrusting up at her, smirking as she cries out. I'm hitting her needy little bundle of nerves just right, and I know it.

"Derek," she whimpers as her eyes roll. "Fuck, I'm so damn close."

Lennon sounds so frustrated and I want to help. "Len, baby, fuck me," I gasp. I can't even string words together. "Len, do you want to come," I groan.

"God please, yes," she pants.

Taking this as consent to do whatever the fuck I want, I pull my arms away from her, lift her up and drop her on my face. She yelps as her knees catch her weight on either side of me. Wrapping my arm around her waist, I pull her onto my face, shoving my tongue inside of her as the pad of my thumb rubs her clit.

The creak of the headboard sounds as Lennon holds on for dear life, and I'd smile if I wasn't so busy. Lennon quickly loses the ability to speak as she moans and gasps.

"Please, ugh, fuck, yes," she cries as she comes on my tongue.

I lap at her slit, moaning happily. Lennon pushes back and looks down at me. "Holy shit, I can't believe you did that," she pants.

I grin up at her without a single regret. "Ready for a nap," I tease her.

Lennon scoots back and drags the pad of her finger along my slit. My back arches as I gasp. "Holy shit balls, Lennon," I half whine, half moan.

"I want to ride your cock, the only question I have is whether or not I need a condom," she says with a smile.

"Lennon, you're the only person I've even thought about sleeping with in the past two years. I have a clean bill of health so if you— "

Lennon has heard everything she needs to know because she lines me up and drops onto my cock. We both groan as I slowly stretch her tight, wet channel. No matter how many orgasms she had, she's still insanely tight. Slowly rocking, she sighs, her head thrown back as she rides me. To watch her, you'd swear this was a religious experience, and she's so beautiful as she enjoys fucking me.

My hands move up her thighs as I watch her head drop back again as she's lost to sensation. Squeezing her hips, I lift her a little and then drop her back down onto my cock. Lennon's whimpers and shivers tell me she's close to coming again. Her gray eyes are tortured as they move to meet mine, yet filled with pleasure. She just came, but it's clear she is needy again.

"Derek," she breathes, grabbing my forearms as she rocks and bounces. I know Lennon has great balance, but it's more like she craves the connection, and needs to be touching me. Sitting up, I take her gorgeous, darkened nipple into my mouth and suck on it. Lennon keens as she grinds on my abs.

The change in position takes me even further inside of her and I groan. "Fuck, yes," I breathe as I get on my knees. "Len, I want you to use me, fuck me, grind on me. Show me what you like."

Lennon's fingers tangle in my hair as her other hand continues to hold onto my forearm. She rocks, grinds, and lifts and drops her in a rhythm only she knows. All I know is my balls are drawing up, and I growl.

"Lennon," I whine. "Fuck, I'm going to paint your pussy so pretty with my cum. I'll push it back inside of you, knowing I filled you. I made you come. My cock is yours— "

"Oh my god," she moans, shuddering as she lets go.

I feel the wetness as it covers my thighs, and take over. My hands encircle her tiny waist as I lift her and fuck her from underneath. Lennon's gorgeous tits bounce, her walls pulse around my dick as she explodes, and it triggers my release as I pound into her. Grunting, I do exactly as I said, painting her perfect pussy walls with my cum.

Lennon collapses on me and I chuckle weakly as I drop onto the bed.

"I think I'm broken," she whispers and I chuckle.

"If you are, then I definitely am with your superhuman tight pussy," I murmur.

"Ugh," she chuckles. "It's just a normal vagina, but your dick is fucking magic," Lennon sighs with a smile.

I love sleepy, happy, sated Lennon. I've never seen her this open and happy, and I know I'll do anything that I can to keep her this way.

Still sprawled on my chest, her eyes drift close and her breath starts to even out. Lennon inhales sharply all of a sudden, her eyes flying open. Surprised, I glance down at her.

"Derek, did you notice anything off about my body," she asks self-consciously. "I mean, other than my super human vagina."

I rub her back and shake my head. "You're perfect, Lennon. All I felt was your body, and how fucking strong you are," I murmur.

It's true, whatever the story is, my girl is a damn warrior.

Lennon's eyes fill with tears, and funny enough, I'm not scared of her emotions.

"I just want you to know, I don't do that anymore. Cut, I mean," she whispers. "I did at home when things were really bad. The whispers, the bullying, I could take all of that. I couldn't handle feeling unsafe all of the time, and this helped when the pressure became too much."

My eyes filled with tears as I feel the full weight of how hard her life was. I have to go home to a place that was her literal hell too, and I don't know how I'm going to do that. For now, I kiss her forehead.

"Did Roark and Turner help?" I ask, wanting to know more but not wanting to push too far.

"Yeah," she whispered. "I stopped cutting once I was out, but I had all of these little white and red scars. I explained that they were from cutting, but never what led up to it, and they made me promise to talk to them if my emotions became too overwhelming. I also had music by then too, and they were always on hand for a jam session or to bounce ideas off of. Mav and Atlas have seen the scars when I wear a bathing suit or tiny pajama shorts, but they never judged me for it. Five years ago, I started getting tattoos, and I noticed that Roark and Turner both have vines in theirs. Vines are special to us, they show how strong and fucking stubborn we are," she says with a chuckle.

"So that's why you have the vines. They're gorgeous, and they suit you," I tell her, pushing the hair out of her face.

She smiles, looking happier and more relaxed. "Thank you," she sighs.

"Snuggle me and nap," I ask with a small smile. "I need to hold you, know that you're safe and with me. It feels like this is a dream."

Lennon burrows into me and I cover us with a blanket. "If this is a dream, I never want to wake up," she says as she drifts off to sleep.

Me either, sweet Len.

"She sounds happy," Turner says from the doorway.

I look up and blush. I don't know how the guys are going to feel about us having sex. They seemed okay with it, but it also wasn't planned.

"Yeah, she is," I murmur, looking back down at Lennon to see her breath has already evened out and she's sleeping. "Wow, that was fast."

Turner walks into the room, followed by Roark. I swear they both are so quiet when they move. I wonder if they practice...

Roark clears his throat gently and I smirk. I must be tired

myself, because staying on topic is difficult.

"Did you know she was cutting herself," I blurt out, keeping my eyes on Lennon as I enjoy her weight on my body.

Turner sighs and I look at him as he collapses into a chair next to the bed.

"You found the scars, did you? She doesn't usually let anyone close enough to her to usually see or touch them outside of us and Mav and Atlas. We're the only ones to have ever seen her in a bathing suit, and she doesn't do any advertisement photo shoots where she has to show her hips or inner thighs up close," he confesses.

Roark gives a small growl as he looks down at us and then shakes his head. "The label knows she won't do these, and we had it written into our contracts so they don't even ask. Fuck, I kind of wish we had prepped you for it. What was happening when you noticed?"

I wince, and stormy looks roll over their faces. "No, nothing bad happened. I was so invested in what was going on that I didn't notice last night," I sigh. "I had time to just savor her today, you know? So my hands were roaming over her, and I noticed the multiple raised spots. I investigated in the guise of kissing up her leg, and I found how far up they spread. I didn't want to get into it while I was teasing her, her eyes rolling as I sucked along her body..." I trail off with a shiver as I remember, my cock hardening again.

Roark and Turner smirk. "She's fucking delicious, isn't she," Turner says knowingly.

"God, she really is. She fucking tastes like peaches and smells incredible," I tell them, kissing her forehead.

Roark chuckles. "That's kind of funny actually. I always say she tastes like vanilla cream and Turner always says Lennon tastes like— "

"Strawberries... and juicy as fuck," he chuckles with a grin.

"Wow," I snort softly as I shake my head. "She's gorgeous in every way, and the scars don't bother me because they're a part of her. But at the same time... I worry about Lennon. Fuck, her past is so damn dark, and it reminds me I'm part of that reason."

"You can't think like that," Roark rumbles as he lays next to us on the bed and looks up at the ceiling. "You created the monsters, sure, but I'm coming to terms with the fact that you're not responsible for what they did. We all live with the memories of our monsters and trauma, Derek. Turner and I, we do just as much as Lenny here. Lennon is our light in that darkness. Even when she's sad, falling apart, and losing herself to it all, this woman finds a way to channel it into something beautiful."

Turner leans forward, his forearms on his knees. I'm lost for a moment in the vines and purple flowers and wonder if they all got their tattoos at the same time or different. He flexes his muscles and I lick my lips as I watch. "Derek, I feel like you're waiting to pounce when you look at me like that," Turner teases me.

My eyes look up to meet his amused pale ones that are staring back at me.

"Trust me, that's not a complaint," Roark says. "He'd be disappointed if you didn't look at him like that."

Turner shrugs with a grin, completely unabashed. These men are gonna kill me.

"To get back to the matter at hand," Roark laments, his nose scrunching. "Lenny was really skittish when we met her. She had nightmares often, and she did quit cutting the day she left home. Except she threw herself into work instead of facing what happened. I'm not here to ever judge her for it, drugs, alcohol, and the next adrenaline high was what I lived for before I met Turner."

My eyebrows raise. "You're usually so zen," I sputter.

Turner snorts, shaking his head. "Nah, my man is anything but zen naturally. He works at it, sure, but he has a hair trigger just like I do. The girl in your arms is the key to his trigger. Lennon can take care of herself for the most part, but I have no problems being her back up."

I wince, remembering how often her knee and I have met. "She's way stronger than she looks too. Len managed to flip us when she had enough of me teasing her." I grin as I remember how surprised I was. "So that's how we ended up having sex. I seriously wasn't planning to, but fuck me is she hard to say no to."

Roark and Turner stare at me for a long while and I can't help squirming. The only thing that may save me from being beaten up is Lennon on top of me.

"You're an idiot," Turner confirms, shaking his head. "We didn't tell you to say no to her, but rather let things happen. I had a pretty good idea that you weren't going to pressure her," I shake my head hard at him and he nods. "See, you're already smarter than most of the men on this planet. If she flipped you over and practically made you stick your dick in her, then she wanted you. Fuck, Roark and I were going wild listening to you two in here. Our girl was very satisfied tonight."

I relax, knowing I won't be beaten up today. *Shit, they may still beat me.* "We didn't use a condom," I blurt out. "Lennon said she'd only been with you two and I haven't had sex in two years. It happened fast, but we had enough of a conversation about it before she dropped herself on my dick," I confess.

Roark and Turner roar with laughter and I worry they'll wake Lennon up.

"Don't worry about our Lenny, Derek," Roark says, wiping tears from his eyes. "She'll be out for a few hours, especially with the quality fuck you gave her. We should probably all take a nap before the show anyway, and then I'll make us dinner.

We should see if Layla wants to eat with us too when we get up. Her band members can fend for themselves," he grumbles.

He's not wrong, I'm not particularly happy with them after this afternoon either.

"Fuck yeah, family nap," Turner says excitedly as he strips his clothes off and gets in bed next to me.

Lennon and I are officially a Roark and Turner sandwich. Holy shit... and he called me *family*. Damn. I blink my eyes rapidly at the prick behind them. Today feels like it's been the best and most confusing rollercoaster of my life.

"Don't think too hard, Derek," Turner whispers in my ear. "Let a guy come in for a cuddle."

Roark smirks as he snuggles in on the other side, his huge hand settling on Lennon's hip. "Careful there with Turner, it all starts out with snuggling, and then he's balls deep inside of you."

I lift my arm and Turner uses my chest as his own personal pillow before I wrap my arm around him. Lennon's right, I am built a bit like Roark from all of my years of football and then maintaining even while on the road.

"It was one time," Turner groans. "Don't let him put crazy ideas in your head. I already said you'd have to beg for my cock."

"Jesus, guys," I sigh. "I'm never going to be able to fall asleep if you keep talking like this."

Turner grins against my skin. "Try. Tonight will be busy, and then I plan to reward you for making Lennon scream like your own personal porn star."

Shivering I nod even as a yawn tears out of me. Damn, I must really be tired. The sounds of Turner and Roark's deepening breaths lull me quickly to sleep. I really could get used to this.

28

LENNON

"Where is she," I ask with a sigh.

Layla was supposed to come up for dinner and she's twenty minutes late. She's usually so earnest and excited to hang out together, I'm just surprised.

Roark rolls his eyes and pulls out his phone. The sounds of ringing can be heard just outside our suite and I smirk, relieved.

"I'm here," Layla exclaims, knocking on our door at the same time that she answers. *"I got caught up leaving, and then the damn elevator was really fucking slow."*

I think I can count three times that I've ever heard her curse and snicker. Opening the door, she's in ripped jeans with fishnets underneath them and an off the shoulder gray shirt. High heeled boots with a large buckle finish off the outfit. There's also zero hint of a bra and my grin widens.

"Well hello there bombshell!" I holler and she blushes.

"Is this too much," she asks. "I wanted to look the part a bit tonight. Ugh, I look like I'm playing dress up, don't I?"

"What's going on then? Who's playing at something?" Roark asks, looking around me to see Layla. The line is still open, but neither of them have bothered to disconnect the call. "Nah, Layla, you look like a musician coming into her own. You look beautiful, little love."

Roark and Turner warmed quickly to Layla after my debacle on stage. Layla is a force, and she has zero problems making people stop and listen to her when she needs it.

"Thank goodness. I escaped before the guys saw me. I don't want to deal with their crap today, and I didn't want to have to change."

"Lay, honey, we aren't your parents, and I would only make you change if your outfit *really* didn't work," I tell her pushing against Ror so he'll move. He's blocking me from stepping back.

Dropping a kiss on my neck, he chuckles and steps back. I open the door the rest of the way and let Layla in.

"Ror made dinner, so I figured we could eat and then I can do your hair?"

Her eyebrows go up as she walks in. "Wait, he actually made dinner?"

"Yes, I did, and we don't want it to go cold so move your arse," he teases.

She jumps and hurries over to our kitchenette. I shake my head because the man can be imposing when he wants to be. Or, maybe it's just that he stopped being scary to me a long time ago.

Closing the door, I follow Layla over. Roark made a big Greek salad and chicken skewers with rice. The oven here is bigger than the one on our bus, so he's currently in heaven.

"This looks amazing," she breathes. "I'm so used to eating on the road, this is incredible. Do you cook like this often?"

"Whenever he can," Turner says proudly with a smile as he sits down. "I've never seen anyone able to do so much with so little. Our kitchen on the bus is tiny, but I swear we'll eat like kings and a queen. You're welcome any time by the way," he continues with a shrug at her widened eyes. "There's certain things that are hard to come by on the road, and you and Lavender hit it off quickly."

"Aye," Roark says as he starts serving. He starts with Derek and goes around the table. Derek was so excited for food that he was already sitting when I answered the door. "There's always a place at our table for an extra mouth or three," he shrugs.

I melt a little because I know he truly means it.

Digging in, I sigh happily. I can admit to myself that I am starving, and was impatient because the hanger was looming over me.

"Lenny, I think your hanger was about to rear its scary head," Roark snorts as he takes a bite.

Shrugging, I don't respond except to take a bite of rice and smile sweetly at him.

"Len, your hanger is kind of scary," Derek murmurs. "How long have you been a gremlin waiting to happen?" He sniggers after delivering that in a serious tone.

Rolling my eyes, I sigh. My eyes cut over to Layla and I chew my lip. I really didn't want to get into anything serious tonight.

Quickly noticing my shift in mood, Derek shakes his head. "You don't have to answer if you don't want to. I really was only teasing, but now I'm realizing it may have been in bad taste."

I mean, there's no way that he'd know...

"What am I missing, Lennon," Layla asks, eyes narrowing at me.

Ah, fuck me. Damn, why does she have to notice everything.

I growl under my breath and take a sip of water. "I got kind of funny about food once I started getting enough to eat again. It's like my body refused to go hungry, so it makes me really cranky when I am."

"And why exactly were you not eating," Layla asks, her voice dark and angry.

I bite my lip as I stare at her. We haven't talked about our past very much and I sigh. "So, this is that shitty past I mentioned. My mom became really unstable when I hit middle school, so I was on my own a lot. I pretty much raised myself from there on out as much as possible, except I had no access to money until I started tutoring in high school."

I take another bite of chicken and wait.

"How... what... but how did you eat?! Who kept the lights on? I need more here," Layla growls.

I guess it sounds crazy from the outside, but it was just my reality.

"My mom was bipolar, and would just disappear. Sometimes I was lucky enough that she had grocery shopped beforehand, and other times I wasn't. A neighbor noticed my mom wasn't home when he came by to ask me something, and his wife started dropping off a covered casserole dish once a day. I just made sure to make it last."

Layla is still staring at me, her food forgotten. "Where's your dad in this picture? Why didn't child services get involved? I'm sorry, this just seems really bizarre to me."

I glance over at Derek and he grimaces. "We lived in a really small town," he explains. "Lennon's mom was a bit of an outcast, and as nosy as people usually are, they ignored little Lennon O'Reilly."

"Yeah," Layla drawls. "I have been getting this feeling that y'all have history, but I've been too nice to say anything. Are you moving in on my friend? Have you been a douche canoe to her in the past?"

Derek chokes on the water he's drinking and Turner helpfully pats his back as he rolls his lips in to hold back his smile. Layla isn't holding back though, and Turner finds it amusing.

"Erm, can I say it's super complicated?" Derek asks, voice rough from coughing.

"It's complicated is a Facebook status, not an explanation," Layla replies. The girl is a spitfire and I love it, but it really is too much to explain over dinner.

"Derek was my next door neighbor growing up," I cut in. "My dad left when I was seven and I never saw him again, but someone had to have been paying our bills, so I assume it was him. My mom couldn't hold a job to save her life," I explain, my tone without emotion. Dammit, I was having a really good day, and I can feel it's about to go downhill. I take a shuddering breath as I continue. "My teenage years were just something I had to survive, so I could enjoy my life afterwards," I shrug, expecting that to be the end of it.

Ror and Turner stare at me thoughtfully, Derek looks horrified, and Layla angry.

I push away from the table with a sad smile. "Excuse me," I murmur, standing up. I'm tired of my past coming back to haunt me. I'm not normal, and I never will be. My feelings are bubbling up, and the mask is starting to crumble. There's too much that's happened, too many scars my life has left on me, both on my skin and under.

"Lennon, wait," Layla says, standing up too. "I didn't mean to pry, but there's so much that doesn't add up when it comes to you. If I don't ask, chances are you'll never tell me. You're so incredibly private, and now some of that makes sense. We don't know each other well yet, but I really want to." She crosses her arms, staring at me. I can tell she feels bad for pushing, and it's not her fault I have a fucked up past.

Pushing my hand through my hair, I pull to feel the bite of pain to ground myself. It's not the release of cutting, but I've gone too long without it to go back.

I also realize I was caught up in my head, and Layla's eyes

are now glossy with unshed tears. Damn. I release my hair, letting it tumble around me.

"It's not your fault," I say, blowing the purple strands out of my face. It's something Layla and I have in common, it always seems to be in our face. "Derek and I have our own kind of twisted past, but we're finding out there were things we didn't know about the situation or each other back then. It's still kind of fucked, but we're figuring it out," I explain. "I don't talk about my past because none of it is pretty. My mother was very selfish, and her illness took its part in making her that way. I couldn't change any of that, even if I wanted to."

Layla nods, chewing on her lip as she stares at me. I tilt my head watching her, wondering what she wants.

"One more question," she says, raising her finger, and Layla reminds me of the kids who say this. Lips twitching, I nod that she can continue. "Where is your mom now? Because I kind of want to kick her ass."

"She's been dead for a long while," I state. I bare my teeth, because I don't feel at all charitable towards my mother right now. "Apparently she died on the side of the road in an accident when she left town. I was seventeen, and still in high school when she left. One day, I randomly got a letter from someone that had been traveling with her," I say as I purse my lips and remember the feel of the paper the letter was written on.

"I saw it as the out I needed. I was waiting for a sign that I could leave, so I called the water and electricity companies, canceled them, and sold the house. I donated most of the items in the house, and hitchhiked out of that godforsaken town."

"Fuck, I didn't know all that," Turner says softly, brows furrowed.

Roark shakes his head too, because I just don't *talk* about it. It lives in the past, so I can live in the present.

"I honestly forgot some of it until I have to think about it," I murmur. "And it's been a long fucking time since I've thought of that day. I found the first person who didn't know me, and begged for a ride. I had just turned eighteen, graduated high school, and my present to myself was to get free."

I shrug as I look over at Derek. His eyes carry banked anger over everything. "You weren't home anymore, having done the same thing I did, except you went to college. I don't know how they even agreed to let me sell the house when it wasn't in my name, but the manager of *Farrelsville United Bank* was probably just glad to be rid of the O'Reilly's. I sold the house to the bank, and then got the fuck out within three days of finding out my mother was dead and gone."

This woman was supposed to protect me, and she was my greatest disappointment. It's honestly up there with my dad who abandoned us both. I shudder and I feel tears start to prick behind my eyes. "God, it's like it just creeps up on me," I rasp, shaking my head. "I have to get ready for this show and I don't have time for this. Thanks for dinner, Ror," I whisper and walk away.

I ignore the shouts and Layla's apologies, just like I ignore the hot tears sliding down my cheeks. I close the door with finality and lock it, knowing it won't keep the boys out if they really want to get in.

Taking off my clothes, I let them drop haphazardly as I walk to the bathroom. I'll pick them up after my shower. My nails dig into my hands as I walk across the cold floor. With my luck, I'll need to play my guitar tonight, so I can't mess up my hands. Breathing deeply, I relax my hands as I exhale and shake them.

I open the shower door and turn on the water before stepping in. Hissing at the frigid water, I let the temperature bring me back to the present. I'm safe, I'm okay, and the ghosts of my past can't physically hurt me anymore. But fuck if they don't beat my soul even now.

There's a knock and raised voices on the bedroom door and I roll my eyes. "Can't a girl get some privacy," I mutter. I know better though. Tour life doesn't lend to privacy, and neither do protective lovers. Or, apparently, a friend who threw herself in my path before she even knew me at all.

I wonder if she's rethinking that decision after hearing my confessions. I snort, shaking my head as I think about how that's just the cusp of it. My tears run faster, mixing with the cold water as I think of all the fucked up things that have happened to me in my hometown.

God, what a legacy to have.

The door is unlatched, and I can see it bang open from here. I didn't bother to close the bathroom door, since the bedroom was locked. Oh well.

Grabbing my lavender scented shampoo, I start to wash my hair.

"Lennon, I need to talk to you," Layla says as she stalks into the bathroom.

"Well, it's not like I can go anywhere," I drawl as I lather my hair.

"Ummm, yeah. Crap," she turns and faces away only to face the mirror, and meets my eyes in it. "I don't think I thought this through," she murmurs as she flushes with embarrassment.

"It's just skin," I shrug with a smirk. "We both have the same parts, and it's really not that serious. You're here now, so what did you want to talk about?"

I don't want to enjoy her embarrassment, but she broke into my room and followed me in. The shower door is completely clear, so there's nothing to cover me. My scars aren't visible to her with the water and the steam, so my nudity doesn't bother me.

Tilting my head back to rinse my hair, I wait her out.

"I wanted to apologize for pushing. I'm angry that this was your childhood, and that you didn't have people to protect you. I didn't understand, and I'm still having trouble wrapping my mind around a childhood where you don't have a loving parent." She presses her hands on the granite counter and sighs. "I know that makes me sound really sheltered and stupid—"

"Pshh. Don't call yourself that around me. There's nothing wrong with being well-loved and protected. I'm happy you had that," I tell her as I start to condition my hair. I'm not even a little jealous of it either, because parents should love, cherish, and adore their children. It just isn't the hand I was dealt. "My mom was a decent enough parent to me until I turned eleven or twelve years old, and that's what I try to remember. My past doesn't affect me until someone asks and it becomes glaringly apparent how not normal I am. Most girls aren't worried about getting raped repeatedly over a dumb bet in high school either, but that was my reality. My childhood mostly sucked so I channel that into my music. It's a place I don't have to explain it, but I can push that pain into," I explain.

Finishing my shower, I turn off the water and grab a towel sitting just outside the stall.

Layla is staring at me, tears streaming down her flushed cheeks and I sigh. This is why I don't talk about my past. I don't have a filter because it's just there. I can't change my life, my mother, or the bullying that made everything spiral.

"Lay," I murmur, water dripping down my body as I stand there. "I have very little tact when it comes to what happened, because I don't know how to feel sorry for that little girl. I can't go there, because my entire life up until I joined the band has been a struggle." I wrap my towel around me, aware of the droplets along my skin. Oh well, I'll mostly air dry I guess. "I don't talk about it, and with Derek here, he's just taking the top off my tightly boxed memories. I didn't mean to make you cry," I lament gently.

"It's just not fair," she whispers harshly, wiping her eyes. "You're so nice and amazing and you had to deal with all of this bullshit!"

I'm apparently a really bad influence too. Ugh.

"Just because I have a shitty past doesn't mean I have to be a shitty human," I tell her, stepping out of the shower. I dry my body the best I can without completely flashing her and decide to finish drying off in the closet as I dress. I had a barrier between her and I in the shower, so it feels different now being so exposed. I'm weird about being naked in front of people who tend to see too much. My tattoos do a great job of covering my scars, but I still always worry someone will see and ask.

They remind me of a time of shame and sadness.

"Len," says a voice and I startle when I see Derek is standing in the doorway. "Do you not realize what you just said? How many people use their past to dictate being a bad person? The phrase,'hurt people, hurt people,' means exactly what it says it does."

I shrug, pushing past him to dress. I refuse to look like shit on stage. "I'm aware, it just doesn't mean I need to punish the people around me for it. I can be a good human being in spite of it."

Roark leans against the wall as I come out. "Lenny, stop for a minute, beautiful and give me a hug."

I wrinkle my nose. I want to be annoyed and I was really working myself up, but I can't do that if he hugs me. Ror knows this. Dammit. Sighing, I walk over and let him envelop me in his arms.

"You're being a brat, baby. You don't want to be mad, so stop working yourself up. Lenny, you're one of the best people any of us know, because you refuse to hurt even though others have. Do you know how rare that is? You're just a good person, who leans on her people when you need to, and pours out her pain in a constructive manner. You've found coping mechanisms that work for you," he murmurs, kissing my forehead. "Take the fooking compliment, baby, and go get dressed."

Roark turns and pushes me towards the closet, making sure to swat me on the ass.

"Ow, holy fuck balls, Ror," I whine, rubbing my butt. "See," I wink at Derek, "this is why you should only be spanked by Turner."

"Lennon O'Reilly, you're gonna give me a complex," Turner roars and I squeal and run for the closet to get dressed.

Layla laughs and shakes her head. "So you're all together then? Even you, Derek? I get the feeling you were a shithead to her. I swear Turner almost beat you with his bat and there was an awful lot of heat and hostility in that bus the first night," she says with a smirk. I can see her in the half opened door as I pull on a thong and a leather skirt.

Stepping out half-naked, but the more important parts covered, I hold out two tops. "Which one?" I ask.

Layla stares, giving me a long blink in surprise. "You really are comfortable with nudity, aren't you?"

"Eh, for the most part. It really is a serious question though," I laugh.

She glances at the shirts and chooses the black cropped corset with gold thread running through it.

"Yay, that's what I was thinking too," I say with a grin. Putting it on, I turn my back towards Turner. He's the best at buttoning up my clasps. Without skipping a beat, he sidles behind me, to start closing them up.

"To answer your question, yes Derek and I have some fucked up history, but we are working through it," I tell her. Layla arches her eyebrow and I know it sounds like I'm making excuses. I'm not, though. "Think of the game telephone," I begin, pursing my lips in thought. "Sometimes what you think you heard isn't, so a lot of what happened between us was due to some miscommunication and misunderstanding. It doesn't make it right, but I'm choosing to see the good."

"Derek, I swear if you fuck this up, I will ask Turner for permission to use his bat on you," Layla says, pointing at Derek.

Derek sputters while I snort in amusement.

"Turner, what's the name of your bat? I kind of feel like it has a name," Layla muses, crossing her arms. She's trying to look dangerous, but doesn't quite hit the mark. Layla is just too dainty for it.

"Sally. Her name is Sally. She's very special to me, but I promise that if Derek fucks up, you can get a few licks in," Turner says. I glance over my shoulder and he bares his teeth at me. Mmm, now Turner does dangerous so very well.

"My hero," I murmur, with a dark and sultry smirk.

"Ewww," Layla says and I snicker. Oh my god, I have no filter when it comes to these men. "Why do I feel like you're the most dicked down woman on the planet with these three. This is definitely a harem, right?"

"Something like that," I say just as Roark shrugs and says, "I mean I did propose."

"You what?!" Layla shrieks and I wince. I didn't tell her about that. "Is there a ring? Who did you propose to?"

"Uhhh," I blush. "Really early Thursday morning when we were in Seattle, after a really shitty night, Roark proposed to Turner and I. He said he'd feed and caffeinate me for the rest of his life, and that we were his everything. It was spontaneous and amazing," I remember with a smile.

"You didn't think you should mention I was dating three people engaged to be married," Derek growls.

Um, oops?

"It doesn't change anything between us, Derek," Ror drawls, his brogue in full force. "As things progress, if things work out between us, we may very well end up having a large group wedding. Thursday night was shitty, and I thought I had lost my girl, so I needed to tell her how I felt."

Derek blows out a breath and nods. "Yeah that was a crazy, fucked up night."

"Ahem, explain for the newbie," Layla insists, waving. "You're all starting to worry me with your codes and secret glances."

I swear she's going to stomp her foot at any moment.

Making sure my clasps are all done up, I step away from Turner. "I swear, I need a drink for this," I mutter.

"Lenny, I'm sure a glass of whiskey won't be a problem, as long as you eat a little more while you get dressed," Roark counters.

I grin and relax. *Yeah, I can totally do that.* "Have I mentioned how much I love you today," I ask him with a smile. I bounce over to him and kiss him hard.

"Mmm, I'm sure you have at some point, but I will absolutely take the extra kisses and love, beautiful girl," Roark rumbles.

I smile brightly at him and Roark hums happily to himself as he walks out of the room.

"Lennon, I need words," Layla growls and I roll my eyes.

"I was kind of drugged in Seattle after my set," I tell her, turning towards her. Damn, I'm just ripping off the bandaid on everything tonight it seems. "I was lost for a few hours because I was a bit out of my mind and ran out of the parking lot." I decide to gloss over a lot of the details because I'm safe, and Layla would beat Derek with a bat.

God, that glass of whiskey is sounding really good. Why is my life so complicated?

Layla's eyes are getting wider and wider and I swear her head may pop off at any moment. "I think a roadie drugged my water bottle," I explain. I need her to know not to take anything from the staff, unless it comes from a band member or Jordan. I don't want this to happen to her either. "Please don't take anything from a staff member right now, because we don't know who drugged me, okay? I only really trust my guys, your band members, and Jordan."

Turner nods as he listens. "I don't want you getting hurt, and I'm testing all of our drinks from now on. It sounds like overkill but—"

"No, it's not. You're being protective and smart, and I appreciate it," Layla says. Her mercurial moods may give me whiplash. I give her an amused glance and she shrugs. "You've had a busy week it looks like, and it may feel insane that I'm this protective of you. It's hard to explain, but the second I saw you, I knew that we had to be friends. I just felt like we needed each other."

I think about it, and it's true. I felt drawn to her when she sang, but I thought it was her talent speaking to me. Layla may be right, and it was more than I thought it was.

"Alright, if that's everything, I need to finish getting us ready. I also," I smirk as I take the glass from Roark, "don't believe in wasting good alcohol, so I'll be drinking this, since we won't be having anymore of this heavy conversation."

Layla nods so quickly she resembles a bobble head and I snicker. "Yep, I'm done for now. Can you do something fun with my hair?"

"Hell yeah, how do you feel about braids to hold your hair up and off your face for the top part? While the rest is left free down your back in loose curls? It would be totally different from normal, and will complete your badass outfit."

I grab my phone and pull up a photo of what I'm thinking

and her eyes light up. "Yeah, oh my god I would never have thought to do this. How are you so good at this?"

Roark's lips twitch as he watches Layla flip out. "We will leave you to it, ladies. Lenny, do not neglect your dinner, please. You know my hand hasn't finished twitching since you're still being such a brat."

Fuck. "Yes, Sir," I say innocently and he snorts. Nothing about me is wholesome.

As Turner walks out the door he comments, "You should have Layla see your sketches of hairstyles."

"Wait, can I see those, please?!"

Thanks, Turner. I swear he stirs the pot just to see what will happen. I started those in between song writing to help me plan my hairstyles for shows, and to do something other than music with my hands. They're not very good.

"Yeah, but they're on the bus. Maybe on the way over you can ride with us?"

Layla gives me a blinding smile, and I decide I really like having a girlfriend.

THE NEXT HOUR and a half was a whirlwind, and then we're hustling to a new venue on the bus with Atlas and Mav meeting us outside our hotel door with wild grins. It's obvious they had a great day today. I need to grill them about what they did, and if they managed to get laid or not. Those smiles are filled with tales of fuckery.

There are so many great venues in Los Angeles, so each show is at a different one. I love being able to experience the different stadiums and theaters, and tonight we are at the Microsoft Theatre. We've never played here before, and I'm excited. Our driver navigated traffic well, and we arrived with plenty of time to spare.

Jordan is waiting for us as we get off the bus, and I glance over at him, surprised. I didn't expect him to be this hands-on as a manager.

"Hey guys, I wanted to catch you before you went inside to chat. Oh, hi, Layla, lovely to see you," Jordan says with a wider smile. I wonder what the reason was for his estrangement with his brother, especially when it's obvious to me that he's been watching Layla from afar. "I thought you'd ride in with Leo and Albert, but what I have to say isn't a big deal. In the past, *The Darkest Nights* always had different drivers with the bus service, but I wanted you to have a trusted face, so Larsen is going to be your driver from now on. Is that alright?"

I glance over my shoulder at the driver, and I hate to say that while I'm polite towards all our drivers, their faces meld together after so many stops. I stopped making an effort to learn their names because I knew they would be gone the next day. It'll be really nice to have another pillar of stability during the tour.

"It'll be nice to have a friendly face driving us," I say to Larsen with a smile. "It's great to have you on the tour."

Larsen smiles tightly and nods. Huh. Maybe he'll take a bit to warm up to us? Please God, don't let him be like Prescott and not so secretly hate rockstars.

The rest of the band all welcome him, and he's a bit warmer to them. Maybe there's hope there.

Jordan doesn't see anything wrong because he tilts his head towards the stadium to tell us to walk with him.

"Is everything satisfactory with your rooms?" he begins as we follow him.

"The suite is amazing," Turner gushes dreamily. I chuckle

because I know he's loving the huge king bed and our shower. I've been loving it too.

"Everything has been amazing, thank you," I tell him. "I know Turner is loving the larger showers."

I end there because Jordan Miles doesn't need to know everything that has happened in said shower. Roark hides his own smile behind his hand and I blush. Mav chuckles darkly, muttering, "I'll bet the man is having a wonderful time with that larger shower."

Jordan looks over his shoulder at me almost knowingly, and I swear I just need the ground to swallow me up. My face is officially flaming.

"Well, I'm glad. You all needed the rest, and Derek I'm glad you're spending more time with the band members. Did you get any good photos today?" he asks.

"I actually did," Derek jumps in with a nod. "I'm going to upload some once we get inside before the concert starts to give them a peek at the band's day."

I reach out and squeeze his hand quickly, and he grins as he squeezes it back. I'm glad things have been looking up for us lately. There's no way I can go back to all out war now that I've experienced the softer side of Derek.

"—that brings me to my next topic of business," Jordan continues and I realize I missed part of what he said. Shit, I hope it wasn't anything important.

"You mean the fact that they work so much, Uncle?" Apparently Layla is pulling off the kid gloves now that I know he's related to her.

"Uh, yes, Layla. I didn't know you wanted to be known as my niece," he says, walking backwards to face her with an arched eyebrow.

She shrugs, wrapping her arms around her waist. Jordan takes his time watching her, glancing over his shoulder just in time to turn and open the stadium doors. The guard checks our credentials, and we continue on through the stadium.

"I mean, I've never been against it, but you and Dad are so cold to each other, it was easier to ignore the fact that we are related. It keeps the peace with Dad, and I can't miss what I don't remember," she explains.

My heart clenches for her and I throw my arm around her waist in support. Derek comes up behind me, along with Turner and Roark. I find it interesting how quickly Layla was adopted by the guys. I've never had a female friend, and Roark and Turner wholeheartedly supported it once they saw how fiercely protective she was. Even now, she's going toe to toe to fight for *The Darkest Nights* and our sanity essentially. Burnout is real for musicians, especially at the pace we've set. Layla deserves the same kind of backup.

Jordan stops abruptly and Roark pulls Layla and I to a stop so we don't plow into him. I gasp at what could have become a collision.

"Wait, what did your dad say about our argument?" Jordan asks, his brows pinched and lips pressed together in the beginnings of anger. I have the feeling the man is explosive when he really gets going, and I don't want it anywhere near Layla.

"That's the problem," Layla rolls her eyes, not in the least bit concerned that her uncle is stewing. "I don't know a damn thing. Dad shuts me down every time we talk about it, and tells me he'll tell me 'one day.' I'm twenty years old now, so when is it a good time to understand why you're so estranged that you tend to walk the other way when you see me? I don't know how I'm even on this tour right now. This is already really fucking awkward," she sighs.

"No," Jordan shakes his head. "I've been watching you for years. I know everywhere you've ever played over the last two years, and people send me videos of your shows. I have never ignored you, I just couldn't put you in a position to choose." Jordan blows out a breath that's so reminiscent of Layla, it's surprising anyone would be able to not know they're related.

"Wait, really? You've heard me play," Layla asks, tears slowly crawling into her voice and I bite my lip. Her hands are curled into fists, and I have no doubt there will be fingernail prints embedded into her skin. Our similarities are already uncanny.

I had a feeling Jordan knew her work since he was so open to having *Velvet Escape* as our headliner for the next two days. I also have the feeling he hasn't been staying as far away as it seemed. My soul warms a little for the man with such a big heart, even though he's inadvertently currently breaking my friend's.

"Layla you haven't truly heard someone play until they do it live and in color for you. So let's make sure you do that tonight, okay?" Jordan smiles gently at her, seeing she's feeling overwhelmed, and this isn't the time to have this conversation.

Layla takes a shuddering breath and nods, quickly dashing away the errant tear that had escaped. "You're right. But I want answers soon. What are you going to do about *The Darkest Nights* and this ridiculous pace they've been playing at?" she asks, refusing to walk forward.

She really is a dog with a bone, and I kind of love it. We can fight our own battles, but it's so nice to know someone is in our corner. Mav and Atlas stop giving us space at this point, and stand guard behind us. We are a united front, and a pieced together family of our own making.

Jordan stares at his fierce little niece and then at us. "*The Darkest Nights* are coming in to reevaluate their contract tomorrow at the label. I know you don't want to remove tour dates," he rushes to say as I scowl and open my mouth to complain, "but we need to put in the stipulations we discussed about time off into your contract. I don't know how long I'll remain your manager, and we need to get you all protected."

I wrinkle my nose at this. "Are you sure you can't be our manager forever? Everything is already so much easier with you in charge."

Jordan barks out a laugh at this. "I don't put up with mediocrity or bullshit, so no one dares to let me see it. Everyone pulls their weight, and have started telling me what wasn't working or needs tweaking. We are a committed unit to ensure you all have a smooth tour. Speaking of," he clears his throat, rubbing his neck. "Derek, you and I are going to need to have a conversation tomorrow."

Oh fuck. Did someone say something about the bullying? Shit. I look over my shoulder and see Derek pale under his tan. He gives a curt nod. "Yes, sir. I need to speak to you about something as well."

Jordan stares at him for a moment longer, and I hope he can see Derek isn't acting like a dick any longer. Shit, I really don't want to rehash all of this shit with someone else. Can't my demons stay buried for a bit?

Jordan smiles tightly and nods. "Let's get backstage then and get ready. Layla, I hate to break it to you, but you're going to have to fix your makeup. Our conversation definitely played havoc with it. I'm sorry about that."

Layla shrugs. "Lennon do you—"

"I always have emergency makeup placed in a dressing room," I assure her and then freeze. I don't want to explain to anyone at this moment why I need emergency makeup. Sometimes Roark or Turner like to make me gag on their cocks before a show and then I have to fix the aftermath. "I'll tell you why later," I mutter and Jordan snorts.

"I'm well aware of your proclivities and healthy sexual relationships," he tells me. "I've heard more than I wanted to in fact," Jordan mutters, and I hide my face in Derek's chest.

Breathing him in helps my embarrassment and helps ground me. Derek smells like the shaving cream he used earlier to clear his face of his five o'clock shadow and cedar. Humming in contentment, I let Derek pull me into his side.

"Well that's an interesting development," Jordan says with a furrowed brow.

"Whatever you may have heard on this tour, some things may have happened to change what you think," I tell him, standing taller next to Derek.

Jordan nods, contemplating the two of us. "I can see that. I'll take that into consideration when he and I talk. Now we really have to move."

And then the man digs into his pocket and pulls out a packet of gummy bears before tossing them to me.

"Yay," I squeak happily, opening them.

"Zoom, zoom," Atlas coughs into his hand.

"Hush," I say as I bend my head back to stick my tongue out at him.

"Save that for someone who wants it," Atlas sasses back and I almost choke on my candy.

"Oh my God," I laugh, shaking my head.

Jordan rolls his eyes as he starts to walk. "Come along children."

I glance at Roark and he smiles evilly. Altogether, *The Darkest Nights* chorus, "Yes Daddy!"

Jordan snickers, refusing to look at us and I grin. Tonight is going to be amazing. I can already tell.

29

DEREK

I'm equally scared shitless to face the music and sad for Layla as I go to my makeshift workspace backstage to start working on *The Darkest Nights'* social media posts. As I drop teasers and photos on different platforms, my stomach is in knots as I think about how I could be fired in the next few hours.

I was willing to walk away just yesterday from Lennon, but today made me realize how much I am also attracted to Roark and Turner. I shouldn't have been jealous of Roark proposing to them, but I don't want to be left behind as my feelings develop. I've been anti-relationships for so long, and now I'm worried I'm about to be fired if I can't convince Jordan that I am an asset to the team. It was stupid of me to let my anger take the lead and bully Lennon before. She is the priority for the label, as she should be.

I sigh heavily as I start to schedule another post for tomorrow. I have been working for *The Darkest Nights* for less than a week, but I want to stay. I'm prepared to do whatever it takes, even beg. Whatever this fragile thing is between Roark, Turner, Lennon and I won't survive if I have to leave. Proximity is one of the reasons it's moving so fast, our attraction is hot, and we are seeing each other day in and day out. Long-distance is difficult enough...

I want to stake my claim on the three of them, even if it makes me selfish when so much is up in the air.

I scowl as I stew. It's the same reason I have to come back after my trip to see my father. I can't let him pull me into whatever bullshit plans he has for me. I tap on my keyboard harder than needed as I continue to think. Roark was probably right in saying he may have to come get me, I just didn't have the heart to worry him. My mom is a priority of mine though, even if she's been more distant lately. Surviving Grant Williams is a full time job.

My mind wanders to Layla and I wonder how she's doing. I'm a right bastard and typically only worry about myself and those closest to me, but I'm trying to be less of a dick. Layla is sweet and innocent, and in some ways makes me think of Lennon if she had grown up differently. Layla is fierce, protective, and is good to have in Lennon's corner. I have zero doubts if I ever hurt Len again, that Layla will break my knee caps with Sally.

I know all about dysfunctional families, and I could feel her confusion and hurt at Jordan seemingly ignoring her for years. The man is sneaky though, and I'm glad he hasn't been as distant as she thought he was. I've also seen him interact with Lennon and the guys and he seems like a really good guy. It still has to be really confusing for Layla though, and I don't envy her.

"You doing alright there, Derek? Why does it look like your computer's offended you?" asks Roark, amused.

I glance up in surprise and force a weak smile. "No, no. I'm just trying to get this done before you all play tonight. I'm almost finished, but I need to snag some photos of *Velvet Escape* headlining tonight too. I really want to hype them up on our socials."

I turn away, figuring he was just coming to check on me, ready to get back to work.

"I don't think so," Roark says with an unamused laugh. A large hand grabs my neck and turns my face.

I blink in surprise as I stare up at him. "Newsflash, Derek. You're ours. You don't get to fooking ignore us. The next time you do, you won't like the consequences."

I open my mouth to respond and then he's abusing it with his lips. I moan into his mouth, my fingers plunging into his brown hair, forgetting he needs to be on stage. I couldn't give two shits that I'm fucking it up right now though. Roark's lips are firm, his tongue rough as it swipes along mine. Kissing him is all-encompassing, and I forget all about professionalism as he forcefully plunders my mouth.

"You're delicious," he growls against my lips. "Don't distance yourself from us. You may be just joining us, but I am all fucking in, and we protect our people. Don't think I didn't see your face when Jordan said he wanted to talk to you," Roark smirks knowingly as he stands up. "Think he wants to talk about how you were treating Lenny?"

I blow out a breath, my head still spinning from that damn kiss. I swear he sucked out my damn soul and rearranged it. "Yeah, I'm pretty sure that's what he wants to talk about. If I can't figure out how to convince him that I deserve to stay on this tour, he'll fire me without a second thought and that'll be it." I lean back in my chair and cross my arms. "I did this shit to myself, I have to face the music."

Roark grimaces. "So fatalistic, damn." I idly wonder if he's on drugs or had his dick sucked by Turner or Lennon because he's way too chill about this. "Look, you may have to face what you've done, but Jordan is also extremely fair. There's no way he'll kick you off if you explain things."

"No," I negate, shaking my head. "Telling him why I was being a shithead will get me a one way ticket out of here. The old man may even punch me as well. Jordan took great pleasure in firing Prescott, and she honestly deserved it. But, really, what I did was worse. I'm still surprised that you let me anywhere near Lennon after I told you the truth."

Well some of it. How do you tell someone you used to fuck their mother? God, how did I fuck my life up so much?

Roark purses his lips as he crouches down by my chair, squeezing my knee. My dick twitches at the small contact and I tell it to be quiet. It seems to be the reason for many of my problems.

"There are no easy answers here, and I have to tell Jordan I also need a few days off to deal with my father. Everything is so damn complicated right now."

"Tell Jordan that you and Lenny had a misunderstanding, and explain as little as possible. Lennon will back you up if you ask her to," Roark says softly as I look away. "Everyone fucks up, and while not everyone deserves a second chance, we are giving you one. So will Jordan Miles. The man is ridiculously fair."

Nodding, I sigh as I look back at his caramel eyes. "I didn't realize how much being here meant to me until he said something today. I almost quit yesterday before you tackled me to the ground." Roark snorts, cheeks coloring. It's adorable. "I'm honestly glad you did though, even though my face still hurts a bit."

"I need to doctor you up a bit more when we get back to the hotel to make sure nothing scars that pretty face," Roark grins.

"Is doctoring also code for sucking my dick after," I tease.

The words 'if I'm a good boy' ghost through my mind, but with Roark it doesn't give me the cold sweats. It's nice to know that bitch hasn't permanently scarred me.

"Layla and the guys are heading on stage," Lennon says, popping her head into the little room.

Roark looks over his shoulder at her and nods. "Be right there, Lenny. Derek is joining us in watching them play to take some photos."

Lennon smiles and walks away.

"Wait, is she by herself—" I start to say, leaning forward to keep her in sight, when I see tattooed fingers trail along her waist. I relax knowing that Turner is with her and lean back.

Roark looks bemused as he watches me. "See, you're one of us," he says with a shrug. "You've changed over the last week, realizing our Valkyrie wasn't who you thought she was. Lennon is fucking fearless, has lived through horrors, and is stronger than when you left her ten years ago."

I wince as I think about that. "She is so fucking strong, but Jesus do I wish she didn't have to be. I want to go back and change so many things," I lament. I blink and shake my head.

"Hey," he murmurs as he pushes my face to look at him with a single finger along my cheek. *Fuck, why was that so hot?* "I honestly shudder to think if things had gone differently. She wouldn't have left the second her mom died, and Lennon may not be here with us, sharing her words. She gives people hope, Derek. You can't take that away from them or her."

Winking at me, he stands up and holds out his hand to me. My heart pounds as I stare up at him, hearing the truth in his words. *Holy shit.* Everything Lennon went though has shaped her: good and bad. It's fucked up, but true. I can't protect her from her past, but I can help her in other ways.

Grabbing my camera, I grab Roark's hand and let him haul me up.

"Let's get to work," I murmur with a small smile.

Roark throws his arm around my shoulders, not giving a shit who may see and nods.

Let's see what the night brings.

WATCHING *Velvet Escape* perform is like watching people step into the role they were always born for. I watched Layla perform in San Francisco, and she was amazing, but there's a confidence now that wasn't there previously.

Layla takes command of the stage, her contralto voice making you want to get closer so you don't miss a word.

"I'm going to go jump into the crowd for just a little. I need video of them," I yell into Lennon's ear.

Surprised, she nods with a smile as I take off. I flash my badge at security before running down the stairs and pushing through the crowd. This is a smaller venue with a capacity for seven-thousand people. That's still a lot of people to piss off. I yell excuse me left and right, garnering dirty looks. I couldn't give two shits if people hate me if I can just get the goddamn video I need.

Finally I'm front and center and go live on TikTok with the subject line: **Support New Artists. Check out *The Darkest Nights'* headliner!**

Comments go wild, while I take video and photos with my camera. It's a miracle I'm not jostled more, but I get a little bubble of space around me as I work. I make sure I can take photos of the crowd going wild as well around me, thanking my height as I do. As the band ends, I mutter, "Thank fuck," after I end the TikTok live.

I decide to stay in the crowd since I need to be here for our main act, Lennon and the guys. One of the guys next to me stares at me as I let myself relax, stretching my neck.

"You're that ex-football player, aren't you?" he asks, leaning in to talk to me.

It's been a long time since I've been recognized as I stay behind the scenes when I work with bands. I smile and nod because I'm in a good mood for the moment. I know my videos were good, pictures solid, and it'll be the promo that *Velvet Escape* needs to get noticed.

"Yeah man, I am. I'm the social media manager for *The Darkest Nights* now."

The man grins. "That's awesome, is it true that they're chill as fuck? Everyone always says that the band is good people and real tight knit."

My grin widens because that's exactly the band's vibe. "That is all true. They're some of the best people."

"Cool. I'm Rory," he says, sticking his hand out.

I shake it, my camera hanging from my neck. "Great to meet you, Rory."

The stage darkens and I glance up, turning to watch the stage. I'm as mesmerized by the ritual Turner has with Lennon now as I was when I first saw it. His hand is on her back, leading her to her mic. I get the feeling she forgets to close her eyes as the lights go off and ends up semi blind. You'd think being a performer for this long that she'd get used to it, but I think it makes her human in my eyes.

Lennon is a rockstar to so many, it's nice to simply know her as Len. She's the girl who loves gummy bears, bounces when she's high on sugar, and apparently is a great artist. I caught a peek at her sketches and they're beautiful. There's so much more to Lennon than she shows to the world, and I want to know all of her.

I'm not in a hurry though, I'll learn it all. I refuse to leave this tour... I just have to figure out a way to make that happen.

Lennon

The crowd tonight is amazing, and the more intimate setting is a different experience. I've missed singing in smaller venues, and it makes me feel nostalgic for our beginning years. I did sing and play tonight with my guitar, which doesn't always happen, but I had a feeling it would tonight.

Turning, I wink at Turner. Striding towards me, he leans into me as he throws his arm over my shoulder.

"You rang, Lavender," he drawls and I swear it takes everything in me not to swoon.

"I'm feeling a bit nostalgic," I tell him with a smile. "Want to sing *Love Notes from an Addict* with me?"

Roark helped me write this song in the early hours of the morning one day six years ago. He was having a bad day, feeling twitchy, and I asked him for his words. He stared at me for a full minute before agreeing. There are few songs where he drives the lyrics, but when he does, Roark Connolly tears at my heart strings and destroys my panties. He fucked me the rest of the day after we wrote this song, and we broke three pieces of furniture on our bus.

Oops.

Turner doesn't skip a beat and inclines his head. "You're getting a song that we haven't sung together live in a long while, but is incredibly powerful. Are you ready, Los Angeles?"

The venue explodes in cheers and noise and I grin. I feel energized tonight, my blood on fire with the promise of excited fans, and my soul settled, because I'm doing what I've always been meant to do.

Turner and I face each other as we sing, Roark giving us a

punishing beat on the drums. Thankfully, Roark was able to give up drugs early on, but the day we wrote this song, he was itching for an outlet. His mother had texted him out of the blue, and Roark was insanely angry.

I'm not the only one with mommy issues in our band. While we haven't sung the song live in ages, Mav and Atlas pick it up as if it was rehearsed. We really should make a set list, but damn that just sounds boring. Turner and Roark agree that being spontaneous helps concerts from becoming monotonous, and if anyone has an idea for what we need to sing, we speak up.

Our words are important to each other, even in front of seven-thousand people.

The rest of our time with our fans flies by, and then Roark is walking me off the stage with a grin. Nuzzling my neck, he snuggles around me.

"You were perfection as usual," Roark growls.

I swear my pussy clenches and I swallow a whimper. Fuck, would anyone notice if I slipped away for a quickie? Damn, they totally would, wouldn't they?

"Whatever you're thinking about, I can assure you that you don't have time for it," Jordan says smoothly as he walks over to us.

I blush and he chuckles. "Young love," Jordan says wistfully with a smile. "The three of you are adorable but not at all subtle, Lennon." Yes my face is indeed on fire. I don't usually care who sees how affectionate we all are, but Jordan teasing me causes all of the blood in my body to rush to my cheeks.

Roark kisses my forehead with a smirk.

Jordan holds up a bucket with ice cold waters in his hand and then his clipboard. "Please hydrate and then head over to the third door on the left for our VIP group in the next twenty minutes. Is everyone feeling well tonight?" His eyes land heavily on me and I smile back, ignoring how warm my face still feels.

"Yes, very thank you. The break today really helped and I feel energized tonight," I tell him.

"Excellent. Turner, I assume you'll be taking the waters from me to test?" Turner looks surprised as he steps forward and retrieves the bucket. "Once I am on a tour, there's very little I don't know," he admonishes lightly. "I wish you'd have told me you had a problem with your drinks, Lennon, in Seattle," Jordan says with a small sigh. I bite my lip as I nod. I had vented about it on the phone when I told him about Prescott, but didn't go into details. "From now on, I'll collect your water bottles and Turner can check them. I am still conducting a full investigation on everyone on the tour, and then making decisions on who will stay." Jordan's eyes wander over to Derek as he enters the backstage since he'd stayed in the audience during our set to work. "I will start making those decisions by the end of week in some instances."

I chew my lip, wondering how I can help Derek. I don't want him to leave us. "Have I mentioned that Derek and I have known each other since we were kids?" I ask Jordan, needing to get this out quickly. I don't want Derek to know that I'm sticking my nose where it may not belong. Regardless, I'll do my best to protect him, even if I wouldn't have done this even a day or two ago.

Jordan's eyebrows raise so high, it's a miracle they stay on his face. He crosses his arms and shakes his head. "Please continue," he murmurs.

"Derek was my neighbor when we were kids, and to be fair my entire town disliked my mother and I. Derek and I have a pretty tumultuous past for various reasons. So whatever intel you gather or think you know, please take into account that it's easy for the past to become twisted."

Jordan stares hard at me. "Are all of you in agreement with this? I have heard some alarming things from the roadies about how Lennon has been treated. There are eyes everywhere on a tour, but you're right. Sometimes what is seen and what is actually happening are two different things." He shifts his weight from side to side as he thinks and I wonder if he's thinking about Layla. "I will take it into consideration when I speak to him," he promises.

I smile gratefully, bouncing on the balls of my feet to expel some of the anxiety I was feeling about asking him. "That's all I'm asking for."

Derek catches up to us excitedly. "Great show, guys. The crowd adored you tonight, and I got some great footage of *Velvet Escape* too." Jordan looks over surprised at Derek and he shrugs. "I had this feeling that their show would feel different than it did in San Francisco, so I wanted to highlight their performance on our socials. They were fucking amazing," he gushes, "and if you don't need me for the VIP meet and greet, I'll happily be editing it all."

Jordan appraises Derek, and I get the feeling he's seeing him in a new way.

"God, tonight felt really good," Layla says happily as she bounces up to us. "Is that how it feels every time you play?"

"Like your words are making a difference and people are connecting to your music," Turner asks with a smirk. We all watched her set and it was incredible.

Layla nods, eyes wide as she waits for confirmation. "Aye, little love, it does," Roark says with a knowing grin. "And between you and me, it just gets better. Especially when they start singing your songs back to you."

Jordan chews on his lip nervously as he watches Layla. "Would you mind sending me some of the highlights of tonight's show, Derek? But make sure to include *Velvet*

Escape. If you caught any crowd reactions, send me those too."

Derek rocks back on his feet as he appraises Jordan. "I can do that. Can I ask why?"

Jordan's forehead furrows as he thinks. "Layla, your stage presence was incredible tonight, and I feel like the audience felt that. I am also wondering how you'd feel about a contract with *Music Hoarde* to be *The Darkest Nights'* headliner for the rest of the tour."

Layla's eyes widen and she screams. "Are you fucking kidding me right now?!" Yep, I definitely have ruined her for life. She's gonna have a truck driver's mouth for life. I wonder if I should apologize to her parents, whoever they are. Layla's jumping up and down and hugging me and I laugh as I squeeze her back.

"Oh my god, yes," I shriek and Jordan winces. Meh, he's in the business of managing and launching the careers of rock stars and performers. He can deal with girlie screaming. "Holy shit, it would be amazing if you were touring with us all of the time, Layla. Will Leo and Albert go for it though?"

Layla shrugs as she brings her trembling hands to her face to push back hair that's no longer there since I braided it. I get the feeling it's a nervous gesture.

"Leo and Albert are in the band and each have *Only Fans* accounts," she divulges. "They both have a decent following apparently, but I refuse to look." She gags, shuddering, and I giggle. I was worried she was dealing with some unrequited attraction, but they just live to cock block her.

I'm definitely going to work on getting Layla laid if that's what she wants.

"What do you do for work?" Jordan asks delicately and Layla gives an unladylike snort.

"I do not have an *Only Fans* if that's what you're worried

about," she says. Jordan sighs in relief and then pales as if he's worried Layla will think he's judging her. "I live off the money I make doing gigs and work short-term jobs in corporate offices. My life is pretty normal and boring."

Albert and Leo walk up behind us as she says this and roll their eyes. "You are kind of boring, but boring is safe," Leo says with a shrug. "Our apartment isn't in the best area, so I'm just glad you're not bartending in some shitty bar."

Trust me, I'm happy she's not too. It sucked.

"Would it be boring to tour as *The Darkest Nights'* headliner?" Layla asks with a grin as Turner finally decides all the bottles are safe after testing them and hands them out.

Albert's jaw drops. "You're kidding me, Layla. Don't toy with my heart, girl."

Layla rolls her eyes. "I don't want to toy with anything, you big lug. Uncle Jordan just asked if we would be interested in the job.

Albert and Leo don't seem to be surprised by the relation, but look wary as they stare at her. I'm glad they're worried now, but they really should have checked on her earlier today when she was freaking the fuck out.

I don't realize I'm grumbling under my breath until Layla hip checks me. I shrug because I really can't help myself. Jordan looks amused as I open my water bottle and take a small sip. I really hope Jordan can back up his invitation for Layla and *Velvet Escape* to tour with us.

"I am most certainly serious, Albert," Jordan says as he sticks his hand in his pocket and smirks when he pulls out a small bag of candy.

My eyes light up when he tosses it to me and I see they're gummy bears.

"Here come the Lenny zoomies," Roark mutters.

"Zoomies? What on earth are zoomies?" Jordan asks, confused.

I moan happily as I open the bag and bite off the head of a gummy bear. "They're when adrenaline and sugar have a baby," I tell him with an evil grin. "Apparently I get really annoying, and the only thing that stops it is, uh nevermind," I tell him, flushing again. I am never going to be able to tell him that the only thing that stops my zoomies is being railed repeatedly after a show. Nope.

Turner has no such issues as he says, "Lavender just needs multiple orgasms to come down from her zoomies. We got it handled," he says with a wink and Jordan snorts, shaking his head.

"I'm so glad you have this all well in hand," he says and then thinks about what he says and chuckles. "Thank god my niece isn't involved with her bandmates. I clearly am not cool enough to handle that," he grumbles and I release a very inappropriate giggle. Jordan gives me a mock glare as I take another sip of water, and I spit it out as I guffaw. Roark barks out a large laugh and Jordan rolls his eyes.

"As director of this circus, let's go talk to your fans. Layla, Albert, and Leo, I'd like for you to join us in this tonight. I would also like for you all to come with us to the label's office tomorrow to present joining the tour to some of the executive board to make this official. Everyone on board?"

"Aye," Roark, Turner and I say together and I press my face into Turner's chest because now I have the zoomies and the giggles. Fuck my life.

"It is kind of funny," Turner murmurs as he kisses my forehead. "Come be a good girl and I'll give you orgasms with Derek and Roark after."

My eyes grow hooded as I look up at him, glad Jordan is

already walking away with the group. "Promise? I can be a very good girl."

"Prove it," he growls as he turns and pushes me away.

Smack.

I squeal, rubbing my ass as I hurry to follow Jordan. Fuck, now I'm all turned on. I can already feel that I'm wet from his promises and well timed spank. I hope the rest of the night goes quickly, because I definitely need orgasms.

30

LENNON

Our fans were incredible as usual, and I quickly got lost in the excitement of talking to them. We took photos, signed autographs, and my high from the adrenaline and sugar carried me through easily. I had a blast and was kind of glad Derek was working on photos because I can be a bit over the top when I have the zoomies.

The Darkest Nights fans love it though. I figure it's better than being tired after a show.

Velvet Escape had a special treat as well. Layla and the guys were shocked to find that they had fans of theirs in the room too. I'm super excited to see this grow, and I would love a recording deal to be negotiated for them.

I'm thinking about this as we walk out to our bus.

"Lennon, you're thinking awfully hard," Jordan says with a smirk. He insisted on walking us out, and was going over reminders of what to expect for tomorrow.

It's amazing how different Jordan and Prescott are, it really is like night and day. I release the lip that I'm torturing with a start. "I guess," I sigh.

"Out with it," he laughs.

Layla and the guys are ahead of us, so I'm not worried they'll overhear me.

"I was just wondering if this would lead to a record deal for *Velvet Escape*, because they're already building a following and they're amazing," I explain. I'm aware I'm gushing over them, but I knew there was something special about them the moment I heard them perform.

Jordan nods as he thinks about it. "Has anyone ever told you how amazing you are today?" he asks and I blink, surprised by the change in conversation.

"I don't know what you mean," I ask, my voice showing my confusion.

"Well someone needs to," he grumbles and I wonder what age people go senile. "To answer your question, if *Velvet Escape* does well on the rest of the tour, we'll offer them a record deal. It's possible it'll happen sooner rather than later if Derek's posts gain traction. I took a peek at your socials, and fans are losing it over both of your performances tonight. His photos and videos were amazing."

I squeal in excitement. "I'm so happy Derek thought of going into the audience during their performance. He said he had a feeling about tonight, and his intuition was right. I just want all the good things for them," I tell him with a happy sigh.

"That!" he yells, pointing at me, and I jump in surprise. "You want good things for other people, and in this industry, it's a trait that is hard to find. You're so insanely giving, and it humbles me at times to be in your presence, Lennon. Do me a favor and make sure you refill your own cup, because it's so easy to give too much, okay?"

Stunned, I nod. I didn't think about it. I replay Albert's reaction when I clapped for them as they walked off stage, and how surprised he was, and realize he's right. I've never wanted to be like everyone else, and I know exactly how important it is to be kind to others.

"I promise," I murmur with a smile. "I haven't had the easiest life, and I guess I've always wanted the best for others. Well the best for good people," I snort. "There are some people who don't deserve good things."

Jordan opens his mouth to ask questions and Roark looks over his shoulder and shouts for me. I happily skip ahead and jump into his arms. He catches me easily with a bark of laughter and carries me to the bus. I am sure at some point I'll end up spilling my guts to Jordan, he is persistent and he has the kind of personality that makes you want to tell him things.

Today is not that day though! I have a feeling it'll be soon though because he's very observant.

"I'LL SEE YOU TOMORROW," Layla says happily with a grin as we say goodnight on her floor.

The guys are having a drink downstairs, and she's rightfully tired. I would invite her over to our room if it wasn't for the fact that Roark or Turner kept slipping their hand under my skirt to tease me when no one was looking. I need to be fucked in the next five minutes or I'm going to combust.

"Goodnight!" we chorus as the doors close behind her.

"Little Valkyrie," Roark teases me. I bite my lip as I look up at him.

Mav chuckles as he shakes his head. "You're in so much trouble, Lennon. Don't think I haven't watched Roark and Turner tease you the whole way back to the bus, or that I hadn't noticed Turner not-no-discreetly grab the go-bag of sex toys from the bus."

"God, you always notice everything," I complain as I blush.

Atlas grins as he watches me. "You've all been fucking on every surface possible in your room, haven't you?"

A giggle releases as I cover my mouth. The last thing I need is to be horny and giggly.

"There are still places we haven't christened yet," Turner defends with a wicked chuckle, as he shifts the full bag on his shoulder. "We need to change that. You up for it, Derek?"

Derek grins as he watches us all. "Yeah, I'm absolutely up for it," he says. His eyes meet mine and I bite my lip as my hand drops from my face. "Scale from one to ten, how much have they been teasing you?"

God, why is that smile destroying what's left of my panties. "I should probably give up the ghost when it comes to wearing panties around the three of you," I mutter.

Atlas and Mav roar with laughter as we arrive on our floor. Following them out, Derek picks me up and throws me over his shoulder. My eyes widen and I spank his ass.

"Ya know, I didn't think I was into that until just now," Derek says with a shiver and Roark and Turner share a glance that I just catch as I push my hair out of my face.

"Have fun, love bugs," Mav says as he disappears down the hall with Atlas catcalling.

"So are you going to destroy my pussy when we get inside, because I don't think I can accept anything less than that," I sass and they walk towards our room.

My body swings with each movement, and my skirt begins to ride up. His hand isn't helping as he strokes my ass slowly before moving up to drag his thumb across my drenched panties.

"Fuck," I pant.

I struggle not to whimper as I shift in Derek's arms. He's not making things easy for me and I'm ready to combust. Derek spanks my ass and I shudder.

"Oh God, Derek," I groan.

Derek shivers and mutters to himself as he walks faster.

Turner chuckles. "We really have been teasing her the whole way back. She's gotta be dripping wet right now," he says.

"Fuck me, I can feel it," Derek groans as I bounce from the pace he's keeping.

"No, please fuck me," I argue.

Derek swings me up and onto my feet and pushes me against our door to kiss me hard.

"I need to tell you something," he murmurs against my lips.

I struggle to pull myself from the haze of arousal I'm in. Derek can fucking kiss.

"Yeah," I ask, blinking.

"Baby, you're so horny right now," Roark says, rolling his lips in to hold in his smile as he pulls me to him.

"Yes, I really am, and I feel like I'm about to explode," I mutter, goosebumps rising with need as my panties pull against my clit as I move. Derek's rubbing against my thong managed to push them into a now uncomfortable position. I am never wearing panties again.

Turner opens the door to our suite and the fog of lust slowly starts to rise as I remember Derek saying he needed to talk to me.

"Derek, before I decide to make this a party of one on that huge bed with my toys to get me off, I need you to tell me what you need to tell me. If you don't, I promise to be really loud when I come," I tease evilly as I walk into our rooms.

Roark adjusts himself at that thought as he walks ahead of me and I grin. It is not the first time that I've done this.

Derek groans. "Please, the Gods can not be so mean. Okay," he sighs. "I have to go out of town the day after tomorrow because my mom isn't well. I promise to be back as soon as possible though, and I wasn't trying to keep it from you."

I turn to face him, my brows furrowing. "Oh shit," I murmur. I'm trying to remember his mother, but it's a struggle. I remember she was always well spoken of and sigh. I wasn't good enough to witness any moments between them, and I'm younger than him. I probably missed a lot of their special ones.

I walk over and hug him. "Give us updates on how she is? I don't know how serious it is, but you obviously have to go see her."

Derek sighs, staring at me. "I adore you, in case I haven't told you," he says.

I stare at him, hearing everything he isn't saying in that statement. "Ditto," I breathe. It's not a proclamation of adoration, but it'll do because he grins and picks me up.

"I do believe I owe you orgasms, beautiful girl," he growls.

I squeal, laughing as he throws me over his shoulder again as he walks to our shared bedroom. I'm never going to say no to this.

I spot Roark and Turner's boots following and I grin. Fuck yes, I can't wait to see where this goes.

Derek

I had to tell her I was leaving before I told Jordan. I felt like this was hanging over us, and as much as I wanted to lose myself in Lennon and the guys, there are only so many secrets that I can stomach right now.

My large hand squeezes Len's luscious thigh and I bite my lip as I imagine them around my face. I'm desperate to taste her, fuck her, and maybe even get fucked. I hear Roark and Turner's steps behind me, and know that's a possibility.

Vaguely, I smirk as I realize I can only hear either of them walking because they want me to. I carefully pick Lennon up around the waist off my shoulder and toss her at the bed. I chuckle as she squeals when she bounces twice on the mattress.

Grabbing my shirt by the back of my neck, I'll pull it off.

"Fuck me, I swear your muscles have muscles," Turner says as I throw my shirt to the side. He grabs my neck and arm, turning me to face him before he begins to kiss me.

My hands automatically roam along his body. Turner is lean, with sinewy muscles covering him. He rocks his body against me, perfectly lining the outlines of our cocks against each other and my eyes roll in pleasure.

"Fuck yes," I gasp against his mouth.

"Think you're game for some fun," Turner murmurs as he kisses down my neck, his hands making quick work of unbuttoning my pants.

"Yes," I tell him, because I can't fucking think when he's kissing me.

Warm arms hug me from behind as Roark grinds his cock against my ass. "Don't you want to know what he has in mind," he teases me as he pushes my pants down my hips.

I kick off my shoes and ask myself if I want to know. Meh, I probably need to know or I'll end up being pegged by Lennon in the ass. *I need to ask her if that's an option.*

"What are you thinking about," Turner asks, pulling away as he smirks. "You went a little pale, yet maybe intrigued? What do you think I'm proposing?"

"Little early to propose," I counter and Roark snorts as he drops to his knees and pulls down my boxers. My breath hitches as he drags his tongue down the dimples of my ass.

"Fuck, your ass is delicious," he groans.

"Before we continue," Turner snorts with laughter, "spill and tell us what you were thinking about."

I shiver as Roark scrapes his teeth up my hips and bites

down. "Fuck," I gasp. "I was thinking I should probably ask what I should be game for, or I may end up with Lennon pegging me," I continue in a rushed, breathy voice.

"Ooh. Is that an option? Because I'm always down to fuck your sweet ass, Derek," Lennon says.

My eyes widen and I look over my shoulder at her. She's naked, going through toys and pulling things out to play with.

"Seriously?! I didn't even know that was a thing."

Turner grabs my face and turns me back to him. Licking his lips, my eyes center on his lips and the flash of his tongue ring. He bites his lip and smiles, and my eyes fly up to his eyes. His pale blue gaze sparkles and darkens with lust as he says, "Don't knock it till you try it. She tops with the best of them. Lavender's a switch, so she is down to be a good little submissive some days, and others she needs to call the shots."

I think back to when she flipped us so that she was on top, and nod. "Okay, yeah I've noticed that. Maybe one day that would be something I'd be down to explore, but," my breath hitches as Roark spreads my ass cheeks. Someone is getting impatient as he nips and sucks... and Jesus he just licked my asshole. My dick jumps ready to go and I groan as my eyes roll back. "Holy fuck," I gasp.

"Words," Turner commands with a dark chuckle as he licks up my neck.

The buzzing sound fills the room and I wonder what it is until I hear wet sucking sounds and a moan. I look over my shoulder and see Lennon playing with a toy, legs spread open as she watches us.

"Poor sweet girl, we got you all excited, and now you're done waiting," Turner says and Lennon's breath saws as she works her perfect pussy.

"Oh fuck," I groan. "Words are hard," I whine and Roark barks out a laugh as he kisses the small of my back.

"Go join our girl before I have to punish her for making herself come without us. Are you up for Turner getting you ready for his cock while you eat Lenny's sweet pussy like it's your last damn meal?" Roark asks.

Eyes wide, I can't see him because of how his hands hold my hips still. The filthy fucking mouth on this man. "Yes please," I breathe instead and Roark gets up, letting me go.

"I wanna hear her scream before I fuck you both into the mattress," Turner growls and I shiver. *Holy shit, I may die tonight between the three of them.*

"Damn," I whisper, walking quickly to the bed. Stalking Lennon, I crawl up and cover her body.

"You're gonna get us both spanked and not fucked if you keep using that toy, little bit," I tell her with a grin. Her eyes widen as she stares at me, and I'm determined to make her remember me fondly instead of as the asshole I treated her as. When I arrived on the tour, I fucking hated her still so much, for all the wrong reasons. Her mother's actions had nothing to do with her. She was just a sweet kid back then.

Chasing those thoughts away, I kiss her as I reach between her legs and toss her toy away.

"He told you, Lennon," Turner teases as he climbs onto the bed with Roark.

I grab a bullet type toy and turn it on, running it through her folds. As if electrocuted, her body bows and her nails dig into my biceps. "That's it," I praise her as she moans, "show me how much you want to come."

"Derek," she whimpers as she tries to chase the toy so it'll hit her clit. *Absolutely fucking not.* She'll come all over my face or not at all.

"Shhh," I whisper as I kiss her hard. I slide the toy closer to her clit, allowing it to bump against her and then move away.

"Derek," she screams in frustration. "Please, please let me come, I swear I'll be a good girl."

"You're a fucking brat, darlin', don't lie," Turner says as he strips his clothes off. His hand finds his dick once he's bare and slowly corkscrews around it and his head falls back with a sigh.

"Make yourself feel good," Roark murmurs as he comes up behind Turner, also naked.

Lennon's head turns and I continue to tease and kiss her neck as I watch Roark plaster his front to Turner's back and cover his hand. They fuck his cock together and I groan. They are porn personified.

"They're so hot to watch," Lennon moans with a smile.

"That they are. Watch them while I make you come. It's time I stop playing with you, and enjoy my damn meal."

I kiss, lick, and suck down her body, loving her noises. My hands hold her down as she writhes, pinching her gorgeous plum-colored nipples. My teeth scrape and suck along her hip bones until I can smell her. Damn, all I smell is peaches as I kneel, grab her legs and spread her open wider. "Fuck yeah," I mutter as I lick her from ass to clit.

Lennon squeals and I grin. She's fucking adorable. I'm so consumed by her that I stop watching Roark and Turner. Last I glanced, Roark was languidly sucking Turner's dick as he told him to get it wet for my ass. Fuck, what does it say that I can't wait?

Lennon is dripping and tastes amazing. Slipping two fingers into her wet channel she gasps as she takes them.

"Such a good fucking slut, taking my fingers," I purr.

I pick up the toy that I had dropped as I worshiped her body and rub it against her little nub.

"Derek," she screams, shuddering.

"She's our perfect little slut," Turner says as he kisses my back. "Aren't you, beautiful?"

Lennon claws at the sheets as she barrels towards her orgasm. I push another finger into her pussy and she whimpers.

Concerned, I go slower, watching her face. "You good, Len? Can you take it all for me?"

"Yes, god it feels so good. So close, argh," she mewls.

"Make her go out of her mind. Keep edging her and she'll squirt like the pretty little whore she is for us," Turner grins as he kisses my shoulder.

Somehow, it doesn't seem like an insult when we use it together. She's perfect, so close to coming, and begging for it.

"Hands and knees while you eat her pretty pussy," Turner commands, smacking my ass, and I move automatically while still stretching her walls with my fingers.

I alternate between using the toy on her and sucking and nipping on her clit. Her head thrashes on the pillows and she sobs. She's so damn beautiful. I'll let her come at some point... maybe.

Roark pulls her shoulder so her head hangs off the bed, pumping his cock twice. "Lenny, I need you to be screaming around my cock when you come," he growls before pushing it between her lips. Opening wide, she sucks him down and I curse under my breath. She's our ideal woman.

Roark fucks her mouth as he grabs her legs, pulling them towards him. Now she's completely splayed open for me.

"Give me something pretty to look at," he teases me as his head drops back in pleasure.

I roll her nub between my fingers and her hips buck.

I feel a cool wetness drizzle between my ass cheeks and I gasp.

"Sorry, it's always cold," Turner murmurs. "Relax and push back."

He inserts one of his long fingers into me and I groan. I feel a slight burning sensation at the stretch and gasp. "That's so good," he says approvingly.

Another finger is inserted quickly after and I shout as he also plays and tugs on my balls. I lay my head on Lennon's thigh, knowing it's going to increase the stretch she's feeling, but I need the support. It is starting to feel really good and I whimper as my dick jumps. Fuck, is it possible to come just from ass play?

I am done teasing Lennon, needing her to come all over my face. I am loving how damn tight she is. Grinding the toy against her clit in little circles as I amp up the power, she screams around Roark's cock as she comes. It's fucking gorgeous as she gushes and I focus on her as Turner pushes a third finger into my ass. My eyes roll and I swear my eyesight darkens and makes me shudder.

Fuck, I pant as he pumps in and out, fucking me gently at first. I push my hips back towards him and Turner hums in approval. "So fucking good for me," he groans. "Are you gonna take it all for me like a good little cum slut?"

Holy fucking shit. I bite the inside of Lennon's thigh and she comes again. Ah, she likes a little pain, I had forgotten about that as I was being dickmatized over this man's fucking mouth. I'm hungry for his cock, and whimper as he slowly draws his fingers out of me.

"Fuck our girl, while Turner fucks you," Roark moans as he slowly draws his dick out of Lennon's mouth and drops her legs.

A thread of saliva follows off the tip of Lennon's tongue and she looks incredible.

"You're a fucking goddess," I tell her as I move into position to enter her. I coat my cock in her arousal before pushing inside.

"Oh fuck, yes," she gasps. "I can't wait to feel you all."

How could we ever deny her anything?

Unable to wait anymore, I thrust my hips, pushing my way inside her. Lennon writhes as she gets used to my size.

"Lean over her so I can fuck you into her," Turner rasps into my ear.

I shiver as I bend over, his hand smoothing down my back.

"You're so strong, and damn your ass has a fucking dimple. I need to spend hours one day exploring your body," he sighs happily.

"Mmmm. We need a Derek sandwich," Roark says appreciatively as he looks down at me. "Just imagine: Turner can suck your dick, I can take your ass after eating it so you're ready, and Lenny can straddle your face with a nice fat plug in her ass."

Lennon's eyes grow huge, but she can't say anything because Roark is stuffing her mouth with said cock. I lick my lips, trying not to drool, and then I'm promptly distracted by the feel of Turner's dick against my own tight hole.

"Breathe for me, mister," he whispers into my ear as he cages my body with his. "I need to know, do you want me to use a condom? I totally can go grab one." Turner kisses my neck and I relax as I think. "No," I shake my head as I decide. "I want you to fill me with your cum, and I want to feel everything," I tell him. Turner smiles against my neck as he nods. "You're about to get everything you ever wanted," he growls as he stretches my hole.

"Oh fuck," I breathe.

"Tell me if you need to stop, but I swear once I'm all the way in, it'll get better," he groans.

Roark watches greedily as he groans between the real life porn and Lennon's hot, wet mouth.

Turner is careful as he slides slowly back and forth, working his way in. Every single nerve ending fires, creating starbursts of color behind my eyelids that have mysteriously closed, and I bury my face into Len's tits. *Fuck, I never knew it would ever feel this good, and now I may be addicted to it.*

"So fucking good, you just took my cock like a damn pro," he praises me and I clench around him on reflex. "Oh my god," Turner whimpers, "fuck you're so damn tight, I'm not gonna last."

I don't know why, but bringing this smug, confident man to his knees really does it for me. I struggle to relax and he sighs. Turner slides out, dragging me with him before slamming forward, rubbing a place deep inside that makes me pant for more. We are literally fucking Lennon into the damn mattress. Her fingers pull at my hair as she moans, unable to do anything else but hold on for dear life.

Turner is firmly in control as he fucks us, and when he grabs my balls and tugs and rolls them, I mewl. "Holy fuck, I need to come. Len, come with me, baby," I gasp.

She taps my shoulder and I raise up on my elbows just enough for her to grab her little vibe and push it between us. Her increased cries cut off as Roark gags her with his cock, breathing hard.

"Fuck, I'm close too," he says as his eyes flutter. This man is riding the edge between pain and pleasure as he struggles to hold back.

Lennon's walls flutter as she rubs her clit, her feet flat on the mattress as she lifts her hips every time Turner and I thrust into her to push deeper inside of her. I shudder as Turner grips me tighter, and groan.

"Turner, I'm never gonna be able to touch my balls again without thinking about you," I grind out from between my teeth. Fuck, I'm about to reach my breaking point.

Turner sucks on my neck, tongue flicking out to lave at the skin. "I hope you think of me every time your hand fucks your cock while you're gone, so you come home that much faster. We are fucking going to ruin your ass, cock, and mouth for anyone else."

Holy hell, I whimper as Lennon's body bows as she comes. Thank fuck. I bury my face in her tits as Turner fucks us deeper into her and I yell as I come harder than I ever have in my life. Roark pulls out of Len's mouth and blows his load all over her open mouth as she moans and shakes from her after shocks. I never knew women could have mini orgasms after an epic orgasm until Lennon.

I must not have been trying hard enough, or Lennon's a damn unicorn. Turner grunts as he starts to come inside of me before pulling out to mark my back and ass thoroughly with his cum. I shiver at the sheer possessiveness as he ruts between my ass to cover me before collapsing next to us.

"Oh my God," Lennon gasps as she shifts so her head is on the bed.

"Len, honey, you've got a little something right here," I tease before I lick up her cheek.

Lennon giggles as I do and Roark mutters, "Fooking hell, that's hot."

Snuggling Lennon, I look up and smile cheekily at him.

"You're so not ready for the can of worms you're tryin' to open up, Derek," Roark rumbles.

I have never giggled in my life and I hide my face in Lennon's neck as I do.

Lennon hugs me to her happily, kissing my forehead.

"I think this calls for a group shower," Roark chuckles as he drags his finger down my back.

I peek up at him as he sucks his finger after. God, these three really are going to ruin me.

"Come on now, hop to," he says before he smacks my ass hard. I gasp, shuddering as my dick goes from beginning to soften to full mast. "I'll help you shower and suck your cock," Roark promises and I scramble up while helping Lennon.

She smiles at me, and I pick her up because I don't want her to fall. It's the gentlemanly thing to do after all, since her face is still covered in Roark's cum.

31

ROARK

I yawn as I snuggle in with the person next to me. There's a warm back that isn't Turner or Lenny and I smile. My eyes open slowly, finding Derek laying on his side. Turner stole Lennon away for cuddles in the middle of the night, so my nose found Derek's neck to keep me warm, and I threw my leg over his.

However, I'm now awake and so is my dick. Wincing, I pull my hips away from the perfect crease in his back and ass. Fuck, I really want to grind into him and wake him up by playing with his cock, but I don't want to scare him. Consent is important to me, and he can't consent while he's asleep.

I wouldn't think twice to wake Turner or Lennon this way, but I don't feel like we're there yet. Instead I kiss up Derek's neck and let my hands explore the divots and ridges of his muscles. He sighs, arching to give me access to more skin to kiss. I'm fairly certain he's still sleeping, so I'm going to be patient and explore what I can.

"Roark?" Derek asks sleepily, his voice deep and throaty. Fuck, hearing my name on his lips makes my cock jump.

My mouth opens and I frown as I think about what I'll say. I drag my tongue up his neck, reminding myself not to call him baby boy. Fuck is it hard though when I'm holding him and he's so warm and cuddly.

"Aye," I rumble because it's safe. "Is this okay?"

"Yes, God," he sighs.

Turning he smiles sleepily at me. Derek's curly brown hair flops a bit into his eyes and I push it gently out of his face.

"Did you—" I never finish because Derek kisses me. It's gentle and probing and my breath hitches. This sweet, broken boy is going to fucking kill me.

I slowly open my mouth to his closed kiss and Derek whimpers as he follows suit. His tongue gently slides against mine and I groan. My right arm curves around him and my other hand gently fists his hair. This kiss is fucking everything.

Derek hugs me to him, his strong leg thrown over my hip. Carefully, I thrust my hips against him and our cocks brush.

"More please," he gasps into my mouth.

My control is going to fucking snap if he keeps begging like such a good fucking boy. Damn. I kiss him back harder, shifting a bit so our cocks rub against each other. Derek's not small, but thick, with a slight curve. I watched as he filled Lennon up perfectly last night as he fucked her. His head drops back a bit as my piercings slide against him.

"Oh my God," he sighs.

"So fucking good," I growl, my voice hoarse as I hold back.

"Roark," Derek says as his hips thrust against me. We are so entangled, we would be on top of each other to get any closer.

"Yeah, what do you need?" I ask as my teeth scrape against his neck as I kiss and nip.

"Fuck, I really love that," he moans. "I'm not made of glass, and I can feel you holding back," he says as he fists my hair to pull my head back.

"Oh can you," I smirk as my eyes hood. "There's so many things I want to fucking do to you that I don't know if you're ready for. I want to suck your cock, I want to fuck your sweet tight hole while Lenny sucks your cock, God I just want to keep you in bed all damn day, Derek."

Derek grins at me and I swear this man's smile lights up a room. He needs to grace us with it a whole fucking lot more.

"I have a voice, let me use it. If it's too much, I promise to squeeze your wrist or something," he assures me.

Oh sweet summer child. You can't do any of that if you're tied up.

"How do you feel about restraints," I ask him as I turn him over and straddle him.

Grabbing my dick, I slap it on his and his eyes roll at the contact. My length is heavy, and I know I'm big. I would probably agree to him fucking me before fucking his tight ass. I slide my precum along his and then ask myself how far the lube is. Glancing at Lenny and Turner, they're both completely asleep, and I don't feel like moving too far.

Fuck it. "Sorry about this," I chuckle and spit on our dicks. The slide is much better. I lean over him and grind against him.

"Oh fuck that is better," he mutters and I grin. Glad that didn't gross him out. "As for restraints, I can get weird about those. We may have to work up to that, Ror."

I love my nickname on his lips just as much as my given one. My fingers dive into his hair as I kiss him, my other hand grabbing his leg to hitch it around my waist. Derek whines softly as he thrusts against me.

"Fuck, yes. Right there," I breathe against his lips.

His eyes are blown wide, the muscles straining as he holds me against him. Derek is fucking gorgeous right before he's going to come. I'm so damn close, my balls are drawing up on me, and I feel like a teen. I'm always pent up in the morning no matter what, but fuck Derek's noises are driving me wild.

"ARE you gonna blow your load all over me," I growl in his ear as I grab his luscious bubble butt to grind on him harder.

"Fuck," he pants. "I'm gonna paint you with my cream, and then clean you with my tongue."

Dirty boy, but I adore it. My back tingles as my cock piercings drag along Derek's warm length. He's so hard, I whimper as my tip rubs against his.

"It feels too good," he cries out as my eyes roll. I know if Lenny and Turner weren't awake, they have to be now. I don't want to look over, my attention completely devoured by this man that I haven't spent enough time with between the sheets.

I reach between us, grabbing his balls to tug and massage. He gasps, shuddering before I feel wetness covering my abs.

"Thank fuck," I praise before burying my face in his neck. "Such a good little slut, using me as his personal toy to fuck against."

My words draw me higher and I shudder as I come with a roar. I have never been quiet when I finish, outside of a quickie with Lennon backstage after a show.

Breathing hard, I enjoy Derek's arms as he holds me. Something tells me that outside of our group, he's not very affectionate.

"That was a wonderful performance," Lennon says, amusement clear in her voice.

I still can't form words, but I huff a laugh out as I kiss Derek's neck.

"Mmmm it looked like a fantastic good morning too," Turner says and I can't help it, I fucking giggle.

I trigger Derek to laugh and the two of us are very soon

laughing uncontrollably. Picking up my head I grin down at him. "Good morning," I murmur, still breathless.

"It's a great morning," Derek grins back. "Do you want me to clean you with my mouth in or outside of the shower," he sasses and I shake my head in wonder. Lennon has met her match in sassy attitude.

"Shower," Turner says, making an executive decision.

I glance over at him as he stands, tugging Lennon after him.

"We have to meet Jordan in an hour downstairs to head to the label," he smirks. "Shower and play while you're in there, but don't make me have to come in after you."

"Oh no, please don't do that," I sass and his eyes widen. I've become really playful in the last couple of days, and it's surprising Turner in the best of ways. I'm only thirty-eight, but it's easy to fall into the "daddy" mode where I have to be more serious than I need to be.

Turner's eyes heat as he grins. "Your spankings may hurt more, but I'm no slouch, and I have better endurance."

Those are fighting words!

"Oh no you fucking didn't, you brat," I jump up and run after him and the fucker squeals as he runs.

"Looks like we're showering together instead," Lennon laughs. "They're probably going to hate fuck it out."

"See you in the kitchen to grab something to eat in thirty," I yell over my shoulder as I jump over an ottoman and follow him into the next room before I tackle Turner. I make sure to roll so my back hits the soft carpet before I twist to straddle him.

"Old man, huh?" I grin.

"Punish me, Daddy," he yells and I burst into laughter before kissing him hard.

God, I fucking love my life.

Derek

I grin, remembering our fun beginning this morning as I ride down the elevator. The last thing I expected was to be woken up like that by Roark, but I'm glad he did. There are times where both Roark and Turner treat me like spun glass, and I understand why because I'm the same way with Lennon.

Now I can see why it irritates her.

"Is anyone else nervous about today," Lennon asks, biting her lip.

I don't know what she could possibly be nervous about since she's not in trouble. However, I refuse to be a shithead this early in the day so I nod. "Yeah, I am," I tell her.

She smiles tightly at me and gives me a quick hug. "I am pretty positive you'll be okay, Derek. Jordan is really fair."

When you deserve it. Part of me wonders if I'm going to have to open up old wounds to be able to get him to understand. No one ever deserves the bullying I unleashed on Lennon, especially not an entire town's worth.

The doors open to the lobby floor and I sigh. We are splitting up between several cars instead of the buses because it's easier to park at the label that way. I just know I won't feel better until I know where I stand.

I fucked up and I'm prepared to do anything I can to make amends.

As a unit, we step off the elevator and I'm hit with a wave of magnolia scent. I wrinkle my nose, feeling dizzy. Glancing around to see if there are bouquets in the lobby, I don't see any. Lennon doesn't notice I'm spiraling as she skips ahead to talk to Layla, though I'm not surprised since I am struggling to keep an unaffected mask.

"Hey," Roark says, throwing his arm around me. I can't help but startle, gasping at the contact. My body is rigid, and I know he'll notice. Roark tends to wrap himself around you when he hugs you and it's usually my favorite thing. "Hey, you okay? What's got you so tense?"

Roark squeezes me and it makes me realize I'm kind of starved for affection. I've spent a long time keeping people at arms length. Taking a deep breath, I shudder. I need to tell him something.

"I was once with a woman who wore too much magnolia perfume," I confess. "She was a fucking nightmare, and I still have bad memories surrounding her scent."

Roark takes a deep breath and nods. "Yeah, I can smell a hint of it. If you have bad memories of it, I can see why it's stronger for you. Turner says that I smell like caramel to him, so come snuggle with me," he says like it's the most natural thing in the world.

I am not too proud to wrap my arm around his waist and stick my face between his shoulder and neck. Taking a deep breath, I shudder in relief. I wouldn't be surprised if I dream of the bitch soon, because I've been finding more reminders of Carrie lately. It may be better that I am going to Kentucky because I won't be the best company. I also don't want to have to answer questions about my nightmares.

It's harder to keep secrets about your monsters when people who care about you are always around.

"You do smell amazing," I moan happily, my body already starting to relax.

"I will now remember never to buy magnolias when I buy you flowers," Roark says, kissing the top of my head.

We are just about the same height, so walking while hugging isn't difficult.

"Why would you buy me flowers?" I ask, confused.

Roark chuckles softly. "Has no one ever bought you flowers before? Fuck, now I really want to," he mutters. "Even though we're touring, I'll occasionally buy Turner or Lenny flowers just because they're pretty. It's an added bonus that it makes them smile."

I look up with a grin, his scent firmly surrounding me. He smells incredible: like caramel and sin. I can feel the panic leech away and it makes me even more grateful for Roark Connolly's presence in my life.

"You're kind of amazing," I tell him. "... and a romantic."

"You sound surprised," he teases me as we continue walking out to the cars.

I feel naked since I don't have my camera. It helps me hide, shine a light on others, and stay in the background where I'm most comfortable these days. Roark's eyes see too much as he stares at me.

"I guess I am. You're this bear of a man with a heart of gold."

Roark shrugs. "I'm kind of irritated that I can't kiss you right now," he mutters.

As soon as we get closer to the cars, we separate from our entangled position. I'm on thin ice with the label as it is, and I still can't remember if there's a no fraternizing clause in my contract. Today is gonna be a long fucking day.

"I completely agree with that," I murmur.

Roark squeezes my shoulder as he gets in the car with Len and Turner, and I move to a car with staff heading over to the label. All I can do is hope for the best.

Lennon

I haven't walked into the label offices in over a year. We travel so much, I haven't been back to Los Angeles in that long. I'm glad we are able to play a few days here because I get to reconnect with this amazing city.

Our identification is taken, and it's nice to be treated like a normal person. My ID is so rarely asked for, I usually forget to take it with me. Layla links arms with me as we walk through the lobby.

"I grew up coming here," she confides with a grin. "My dad used to take meetings and I would color at my own desk. I know some people would have been bored, but I was always so mesmerized by it. My dad scouts new bands, closes their deals, and then travels all over the country to find new talent. I don't get to see him as often as I'd like now, but when I texted him last night he said he would be in his office today."

I can hear the wistfulness in her voice and squeeze her arm gently. I also hear the happy memories from getting to spend time with her father. It's been so many years since I saw my dad, I don't remember what he looks like at all outside of his hair color and that he smelled like cloves. Maybe he was a smoker? The only memory that really stands out to me is the day he left, and I can only see him clearly in my dreams. Otherwise he's this wispy memory I can't hold on to.

My mom also had a giant bonfire of everything she could find that belonged to him when I was seven, right after he left. I sat there wide-eyed as she burned everything that reminded her of him.

Sighing, I walk into the elevator with Layla and all the guys. I'm hopeful this meeting will find Layla and *Velvet Escape* permanently on the tour, and an addition to our contract to get more downtime. I'm only twenty-eight, I don't want to burn-out. I love music too much.

The elevator music is relaxing, and I smile as I hear Atlas grumble about how he skipped breakfast and is hungry.

"If you had come by our room, Roark would have fed you," I tease him as the bell rings, announcing our arrival on the twelfth floor.

"God, you all ate?! Fucking hell, that's just rude to tell me now," he growses as I giggle.

"Good morning boys and girls," Jordan says, amused outside the door as we step off the elevator.

"Good morning," we all chorus back and he snorts.

"Did I hear someone was hungry?" Jordan asks as he turns and directs us to follow.

"Yeah, but I'll survive," Altas groans.

"For real though, are you offering to feed us," Leo asks and Layla rolls her eyes. Turner had handed her a bagel sandwich earlier that Roark had packed up for her. I love how they immediately adopted her when we became friends.

Making sure I don't get left behind, I follow Jordan with everyone.

"I'll make sure breakfast is delivered to the boardrooms that you're all in," Jordan says with a grin.

"Best manager Daddy ever," Turner says approvingly and the guys snicker.

I cover my mouth to hold in my giggle, but can't when I meet Layla's horrified eyes.

"Oh my God," I choke as I sputter out a laugh.

"It's Daddy Jordan to you, Turner," Jordan says as he takes a turn, winking over his shoulder.

"Touché old man," he laughs, snorting out a laugh.

"There's so much laughter filling these halls today," says a booming voice.

Layla's eyes light up as Jordan rolls his.

"Daddy!" she squeals and I see a man with her light brown hair and blue eyes grin and open his arms to her.

"Layla, honey, it's so good to see you," he says as he catches her and hugs her to him. "You never did tell me why you were coming in today."

Jordan stops as he surveys the two of them. "James," he murmurs and Layla's dad glances over him.

"Jordan," James says cooly.

Yeah, this isn't gonna be awkward at all.

Layla is starting to look uncomfortable in her father's arms and I decide fuck that.

"Boys, play nice," I tell them, walking forward. I don't give two shits that Layla's dad doesn't know who I am. "Layla and *Velvet Escape* are joining my band and I on tour as our headliner because they're incredible. We just wanted to make it official."

James' eyes move over to stare at me before recognition lights in his eyes. "*The Darkest Nights*, right? I don't keep up with all of our bands, since that's my brother's forte, but you I recognize. It's Lenny, right?"

Roark growls and James looks surprised. No one calls me Lenny but Ror. I don't want to go into it, and also don't want to be late, so I don't correct him. You'd think he'd know my name since he works for the label, but mistakes happen.

"Sure," I agree, very much a non-answer, but I'm being a big girl and not rocking the boat today. My eyes meet his blue ones and he frowns a bit.

"Your eyes are very distinctive," he says. "They're a really beautiful color."

My eyes widen, and I have to ask myself if he's hitting on me right now. Ew. The color of my eyes have always been a sore spot for me, because they're such a startling color. I've been teased growing up for them too. The gray shade is also one of the reasons I go night blind so easily when too little or too much light enters them. Turner is a sweetheart for just leading me where I need to go when this happens.

"Thank you," I murmur, refusing to say anything else about

this. "It was great to meet you, but I think we have somewhere to be?"

I glance at Jordan and he's looking at me oddly.

"Yep, we have a full morning of meetings. Contracts to change, sign, and new *Music Hoarde* family members to welcome," he says, forcing a smile.

The smile doesn't reach his eyes, and I wonder if it's just the stress of talking to his brother.

James flinches, looking at his brother. "What do you mean by new?"

"Layla and her band members are joining the tour, and I want to open up talks with our executives about a recording contract for *Velvet Escape*," Jordan says slowly as if he's speaking to a toddler.

My lips roll in and my fingertips touch them. I've never experienced sibling drama so closely, and I'm amused.

"Oh," James says with a surprised huff, staring down at Layla as she peeks up at him. "This is wonderful news, darling. Can I see the contract when it happens? I'm sure you're in good hands with your uncle, but you know I'm your dad and I want to be sure everything is above board."

Layla nods with a large smile as her dad looks at her dotingly. I'm not jealous, but I wish I had parents who weren't as damaged or absent as mine were.

"I'll have Layla come find you later so you two can have lunch or something," Jordan says, head jerking in the direction he wants us to continue to travel in.

"Of course, please do, Layla. I want to know all about it, and how you came to start touring with *The Darkest Nights*." James' stare feels heavy on me and I struggle not to shiver. He must also be done interacting with his brother, because he's ignoring him.

This feels like more than just fatherly worry, but I don't

know how to explain it. *Does he know me from somewhere else?* He's behaving like someone who can't place someone and it's irritating him. Oh well, maybe I just have one of those faces?

"Bye, Daddy," Layla breathes, feeling how uncomfortable the air is starting to feel. "We'll catch up later. I promise, I'm in really good hands too."

She eases out of his arms and links arms with me again as if taking a firm stand. Layla smiles brightly at her father, ignoring his startled expression, and tugs me with her to walk with.

The dynamics of this family are really odd to me.

We drop *Velvet Escape* off at a boardroom and then continue on with the guys to our own meeting.

I had almost forgotten that Derek had his own appointment when Jordan tapped him on the shoulder to follow him. I stare after him for a second, hoping he'll look back.

"Lenny, he'll be fine," Roark says from the table. "Come on in and we'll catch up with him after.

Sighing I feel like it may not be that simple, but I walk into the room anyway, letting the door shut behind me.

32

DEREK

I feel like a doomsday soundtrack is playing in the background as I trudge to Jordan's office. I'm terrified of what I'll have to divulge to him to be able to stay employed. I'm convinced that if I'm asked to leave, that'll be the end of everything I've been building.

Blowing out a breath, I walk in, waiting for the man in charge to tell me where to sit. I wouldn't dare without permission in my dad's office, and I revert to that logic here. My mask is teetering, and it's all Lennon O'Reilly's fucking fault. I can't even bring myself to be upset about it because she's also brought so much light into my life too.

My mind is a really confusing place right now.

"Please take a seat, Derek," Jordan says. "I've never stood on formalities, and I'm not into power plays. They've never been my thing."

Nodding, I sit down. I didn't think they were either. My dad always needs to be the biggest swinging dick in the room, and it's not something I look forward to when I go home tomorrow. The man is exhausting.

"Alright then, Derek," Jordan frowns as he sits behind his desk. "I've had several people come forward about how you've been manhandling Lennon. Another person said you shoved her in a closet with you, and yet another told me about some concerning language. The language is enough that I have to remind you that Lennon is a person, and not a fuck toy."

I wince because he's not wrong. I was an absolute fuckwit and a dick. "I wish I could deny these things, but I can't. As I said, Lennon and I have known each other for a long time, and when I started this job I thought she was someone that she's not. She's an extension of a nightmare for me, and I wanted to make her pay for that."

Well, it looks like honesty is my only option here, and the one I'm going with. I've never talked about any of this outside of my head.

Jordan sits back in his chair as he stares at me, and I swear his blue eyes can see through me.

"Lennon is a sweet girl, Derek. Who the fuck did you think she was?"

"Her mother," I blurt out and then groan. "None of this makes sense. Honestly, in hindsight, I'm a complete dick, and there's no excuse for anything that I've ever done to that girl."

A stormy look rolls over his face. "So there's more that you've done to her... I feel like I need the whole story. Start from the beginning. I was just gonna fire you and be done with it, but Lennon asked me to take a second look. Understand I'm only doing this for her."

Sucking in a breath, I nod quickly. "I completely understand. Thank you for this, no matter what you decide. I have been Lennon's neighbor since I was twelve years old. I never paid her much attention aside from how beautiful she was: all that white hair and gray eyes. She's been incredible her entire life. Lennon also used to be somewhat happy... until me in some respects. I found out recently that her mother was negligent, and would disappear without feeding her. This meant leaving her alone without adult supervision for days on end so Lennon would have to walk miles by herself to school." I shake my head because I still struggle with knowing Carrie did this to her own daughter. "I didn't know she did this before, but I don't know if it would have changed my behavior back then."

I stare at my hands as I think about what a piece of shit I really am.

"Lennon and her mom weren't very well liked in our town. We're from a really small town in Farrelsville, Kentucky, and Len's mom was kind of erratic. Once I found her swimming naked in our pond when I was twelve and had just moved in, and Lennon had to fish her out. I told her that crazy was catching and to watch herself."

A fist slams on the desk and I jump, my eyes flying up to meet his. I swear they're darker than they were a moment ago, and my breath grows erratic as I watch him.

"You fucking told her she could catch crazy? How old was she anyway?" Jordan seethes.

I think back on it, and wince. "She was ten years old fishing her naked mother out of my pond. I'm pretty sure it's not the worst thing that's happened to her when it comes to her mother either."

"Fuck, that's a pretty low moment, Derek. So is her mom actually mentally unstable, or is something else happening?"

"She was unstable. Lennon said her mom died when she was eighteen. She took off and left town without her, and died in a car accident a little while after when traveling with others. She received a letter from someone that was apparently with her, stating Carrie was dead. Her mom had bipolar with mania, and while I've seen the effects of that, I don't know enough about the symptoms."

Jordan is nodding, but now he's also taking notes and muttering to himself.

"Where was her dad during all of this?" he asks, forehead furrowing.

"He left when Lennon was really little. Six? Seven? I can't remember exactly, but that's my ballpark idea."

"Okay," Jordan murmurs. "So what was this terrible thing Lennon did to make you hate her so much?"

"Her mother fucked my very married father, and I walked in and saw it all when I was fourteen."

I don't mince words because there's no other way for me to say it and Jordan blinks slowly at me. "Fucking hell, Derek. You do realize, that as shitty as that is, Lennon didn't fuck your dad. She was a little girl."

"Yeah... I can admit that now, but I wasn't seeing things all that clearly back then. I saw someone I wanted to hurt, and since I couldn't hurt her, I decided to hurt her daughter. Lennon looked so much like her mom back then it was like looking into a goddamn mirror most days, and it just killed me every time I saw her."

"So what did you do? From the way you're looking at me, I can tell you did something to her."

What I wouldn't give for a damn drink...

"I bullied her, and I recruited classmates to help me. I pushed her books out of her hand, stole her lunch whenever she brought it—"

Jesus, I stole her lunch.

"Holy fuck," I breathe, leaning forward as I brace my elbows on my thighs. "Her mom started disappearing on her right around this time, and I just realized I stole her lunch during a time period that she probably wasn't eating much anyway. Her mom started disappearing for days at a time, and

Lennon went hungry. God I want to kick my own fucking ass right now," I groan.

Self-reflection is an asshole.

"It's obvious you didn't know that," Jordan says, waving his hand, his eyes sparking. "Keep talking," he insists.

I don't know why he wants this information, but I'm a roll so why not? In for a penny, in for a pound.

"Things got worse when I got into high school. I'm two years older than Lennon, but since we are in a small town, all grades are in the same school, but in different hallways. I went out of my way to fuck with her, but when I turned fifteen, something happened. I was outside my house, taking a breather after a fight with my dad, and Carrie Fucking O'Reilly walks by practically naked..."

Jordan looks more and more horrified as I continue my story, and at one point he stands up to sit on the edge of his desk closer to me. He's also chewing his lip in a way I've only ever really seen Len do. I get the feeling he doesn't typically let all of his defenses down like he is now. I appreciate that the great Jordan Miles is just letting himself sit with the information I haven't told anyone... ever.

"I never told anyone how I lost my virginity. It felt wrong, and I lied and said I lost it to a college girl one night at a party. I sometimes would visit my aunt and go to parties there, so no one thought to call me out on the lie. I fucked around with a few other girls in high school at parties, and I made sure Lennon walked in on me getting my cock sucked by a cheerleader in the stairwell. Look," I sigh as I see his face as he grimaces in distaste, "I was and am a dick. I had a certain image to keep up in high school, so I did. But no matter what I did, Carrie always managed to find me over the next couple of years."

I rub my face as I sigh. I feel really ashamed as I think about

Carrie and how fucked up it was that she insisted on fucking both my dad and me over the years. It colored every interaction I've ever had with a woman after that.

"Carrie O'Reilly loved games. To this day I can't handle nicknames, being tied up, or the damn scent of magnolias. She climbed into my window one night when I had just turned seventeen, and when I woke up she was bouncing on my cock and my hands were tied to my bed frame. She shoved her panties in my mouth and told me to keep quiet and fuck her. I couldn't punish her because she was untouchable... so it was my mission to fuck with Lennon instead. Only... things went really wrong and I just found out stuff I never knew, which is the only reason that girl doesn't hate me."

I feel tears finally prick my eyelids as I cry for Len and not myself. I'm already beyond redemption, unless it comes from her, but I can feel so much more for the innocent girl who just had the misfortune of being born to Carrie Fucking O'Reilly and left to her tender ministrations.

"Holy fuck," Jordan mutters as I finish telling him about the bet in high school and how I even came to work for this company when I realized Lennon was the face of *The Darkest Nights*.

"Lennon is also aware of all of this except her mom. I don't know how to even tell her or the guys. It's all so fucked up," I tell him, wiping my face quickly.

"You're not responsible for what that woman did, but you are responsible for your actions now," Jordan says, blowing out a breath. "I feel like I need to tell you something, but you can't tell Lennon yet. I know that won't sit well with you after so many secrets but—"

"How long do I have to keep the secret for," I blurt out. I need to know how fucked I'm going to be for making a deal with this blue eyed devil. There's a reason he's considered such a force in the music industry, and it's because he's ruthless. However, he's also one of the nicest men I've personally met in this field too, so the dichotomy between them is a mind fuck.

"Not long, but you have to promise to go on your trip sooner than planned because you'll have a hard time keeping this secret. I know there's some kind of relationship between you and Lennon and possibly Turner and Roark. I'm not blind, and she looked panicked every time I mentioned our meeting. So I'll have her be the deciding factor on whether you're able to stay on this tour or not." Jordan stands, worrying at his lip, and I want to tell him he's going to end up without one if he continues. He holds my entire future in his hands though, so I'm going to leave it alone.

Starting to pace, he tugs at his hair. "There are a few things that aren't adding up for me in my head, and I need you to help me out. Do you happen to know Lennon's middle name at all? Her mother's name and your town sound so familiar and I can't figure out why."

Do I know this? I stare into space as I think. Lennon won an award once in school when she was fifteen, and it was announced at a school assembly. School tradition dictated that the student's full name be used when presenting the award, but I also remember how uncomfortable she looked when she went on stage.

Forcing myself to push that all aside, I struggle to remember. Lennon...

"Campbell O'Reilly! " I exclaim.

"Fuck me," Jordan groans. "I never put it together before because I never knew..."

Jordan looks ten years older as he beats himself up. *What the fuck is happening?!*

"Jordan, I'm a little lost. What are you talking about?"

Jordan collapses onto the couch next to me and pulls a

bottle of whiskey from the hidden compartment in its arm. *So it's that kind of conversation, is it?* Jordan unscrews the top from the bottle and takes a healthy swig.

"You're gonna need some of that, lad for this conversation," he says, wincing as it goes down.

Whatever he's got to tell me is clearly really bad. Taking his advice, I take a sip. *Fuck, that's strong.* Handing back the bottle, I sit back to hear what he has to say.

"Campbell is my mother's maiden name, and James and I are both O'Reilly's. When my brother was twenty-two, he got married to a woman named Carrie and moved to this tiny town in Kentucky. He was a musician then and traveled for work in the band we were in. When he had a kid with her, he got really secretive. James never talked about either of them much, and I never knew its name. James always called the kid Peanut, so that's what I called the baby." Jordan stares at his hands as he says this.

Holy fucking shit. How am I supposed to keep this from Lennon?!

"Jordan," I whisper, my voice cracking regardless, wanting him to stop. I don't need the burden of this secret, I don't want to be forced to keep it. *Shit.*

"Jordan, he looked right fucking at her! How did he not realize? How many Lennons are there in the world?"

Jordan's eyes are red from unshed tears as he looks over at me. "He called her Lenny, and I don't know why. James travels a lot and is in charge of scouting new talent, but follow up isn't his gig. That's my job, and that of those in upper management. James gets in and out and doesn't have any attachments outside of Layla. This is why this is so fucked up. He kept staring at her like he knew her, and Lennon does things that remind me so much of Layla or myself. Fuck me and they're friends and sisters. Goddamn it!"

The usually unflappable man throws the bottle at the wall and it shatters. I hope the office has decent sound proofing or people are going to come to investigate. I don't think he's known for throwing things in his office or yelling and breaking shit. Jordan Miles is known for being mild-mannered and keeping his head in stressful situations. This just hits too close to home.

"I asked him when he came back to Los Angeles without a wife or child what had happened. I didn't even know if he had a girl or a boy. Fucking Peanut is what he'd call the kid, and when I saw him he showed me a photo once of a kid that could have been a girl or boy with white blonde hair crawling. I should have pushed harder, but we were both establishing our careers, on the road and busy. Fuck, I'm such a prick," he sighs. "He told me that the marriage didn't work out, he was getting a divorce, and he was paying her bills. James said Carrie was crazy, and he didn't ever want her to find him, so he changed his name from O'Reilly to Campbell, and that was that."

"Layla said that you and James were on the outs, did that have anything to do with Lennon?" I have no right to ask, but I may never get answers for Lennon if I don't push now.

"Yeah, poor Layla ended up in the middle of that a bit and I never meant for her to. James always shut her down and told her it was sibling rivalry and to thank her lucky stars that she didn't have any. Fucking dick," Jordan curses. "Dammit, I may beat the shit out of him for this and not tell him why. I'm too old to be getting in a fist fight these days—"

"Turner would beat the shit out of him, with almost no questions asked," I volunteer with a shrug. "He adores Layla, and Turner and Roark really clicked with her too."

"I'm glad, because Layla and Lennon are both going to need support, and I'm sure you saw her shithead bandmates aren't going to be it. They're good kids but—"

"They're insensitive dicks," I finish. "Layla tracked down Lennon freaking out because she wanted to tell her about how you were her uncle before you did. She explained how she didn't see you very often but didn't know why."

"I always had eyes and ears on that girl," Jordan says wistfully, "but James is petty. When Layla turned seven, I went to their house and told him he needed to remember his other kid. James' been playing house with Layla and her mom all of this time, and he didn't want to be reminded of that child. He told me to mind my own business or to fuck off. I told him I would find her no matter what because that child was my blood too, and the fucker beat the shit out of me. I didn't even have a chance, the punches kept coming." Jordan wrinkles his nose as he thinks about the past. "Layla's mom and James divorced when she was ten, and he gained full custody somehow. Layla spent a lot of time here or with a nanny growing up, but she didn't seem to mind."

"Nope, I overheard her telling Len about it, and it seemed like she has good memories about this place. This is so much worse than I thought your secret was going to be," I mutter in disbelief.

"It really hit me when you said Carrie's name and that you lived in a small town in Kentucky. James told me he lived in the sticks and he was over living in a house with a white picket fence when he left. I was prepared to look for Lennon, but I didn't even know if she was a boy or a girl, or what her name was. And she still managed to walk into my life as this shy girl who was scared of her own shadow, but sure as fuck wasn't scared of me. Well," Jordan growls,"maybe blood really is thicker than water."

"It's such a fucking mess," we say at the same time and Jordan snorts.

"I would say we should drink to that, but it appears I've destroyed our alcohol."

I shrug, unaffected by it, because I'll need my wits about me if I'm going home early.

"I need to change my flight then," I say, grabbing my phone from my pocket.

"I got it," he says with a shrug, rounding his desk to sit at his computer. Jordan taps on his keyboard for a minute before nodding in satisfaction. "You're leaving in the next three hours, which will give you time to grab your things from the hotel and travel straight to the airport. I canceled your ticket and rebooked you."

Who the hell is this man? "How on earth," I ask.

Jordan shrugs. "I hacked into your email and pulled your ticket information. You really need a better password than Farrel300," he says smugly.

For fuck's sake. "Alright then. You're a fucking ninja, good to know."

"I've always been good with computers," he says mildly. "I put out fires for the label, so it's important to know which fires need to be extinguished."

Never get on this man's bad side.

"I'm expected to be back in two, no, three days," I explain. I'm leaving sooner, so I'll give myself the extra day. "If I'm not back, Mr. Fire Extinguisher," I say with a smirk, "Roark said he was coming after me."

Jordan stands straight up, frowning. "What are the odds you won't make that deadline?"

"I don't know why my dad wants me home, but he is getting me on this plane because my mother is sick. Other than that, I don't know why he wants me. I know he wants to run for governor next term, and the great Grant Williams told his son he's depending on him to help." I roll my eyes because it sounds stupid even to me.

"Two days," Jordan barks. "I didn't know this before I dropped my own secrets on you, and I won't have you suffer for them. You have two days to be back, is that understood?"

I think the old man may actually have a soft spot for me. I press my lips together to hide my smile. "Yes, Sir. That's understood. My new flight information is...?"

"In your email, of course. I'm a damn professional."

The statement breaks the damn on my laughter and I snicker. "Of course you are, Sir," I gasp, trying to rein back in my laughter. I blame the stress of the last few hours. "I'm gonna head out."

Jordan looks slightly amused as he watches me rush out of the office. I'm so glad he didn't call me out on my inappropriate laughter because there's no way I'd be able to explain it without laughing.

"Hold the elevator please," I call as I rush to make it as the doors start to close. I don't want to be languishing in the hallways waiting for an elevator and run into someone I know.

Someone hits the button and the doors open. Sighing in relief, I rush in, hoping the flight home goes smoothly.

33

LENNON

I spent an hour and a half talking with the head executives about how the tour is going. Mav made a point of stating that while we love touring, the pace of also interviewing on days we perform is exhausting.

"Lenny almost passed out after both recording and then doing a show," Roark reports as evidence that the pace is too much for us and I hold in a sigh.

I guess we're gonna milk this.

"Wait, you recorded and then did a show the same day, who the hell approved that?" Allen, a gentleman I don't often speak to, but I know to be one of the top execs, asks.

"Prescott," we chorus, a man groans. *Oops.*

"She's becoming a bit of a problem, Laurence," Allen says with a sigh.

"I need to know everything else that's happened with her before I make a final decision. I know Jordan is on a witch hunt to fire my daughter," he responds.

"It's not a witch hunt if it's true," I mutter and his green eyes snap over to me. They're so cold and clear, I shiver.

Turner's hand finds my thigh without apology and squeezes.

"Tell me everything," Laurence insists and we dish. The name calling, overbooking of our time, not giving us our schedule ahead of time, etc. It all comes out like word vomit and Laurence looks more displeased with each word.

It's not our fault she's a twatapotamus.

Jordan comes in at one point to join the meeting with paperwork, and he looks tired. Gone is the normally peppy man, and his eyes look slightly bloodshot. *I wonder what happened.*

"Lady and gentlemen," he says with a small, tight smile. "I trust you have all been getting along well. We are here today because *The Darkest Nights* is going to burn out if something doesn't change. This band is incredibly talented, which is shown in the new songs they recorded while on the road. I for one," Jordan insists, "want to ensure a long and happy relationship with these young people."

Jordan can't be more than his early fifties, but he always reminds us of our age. The group he is speaking to doesn't take this to mean we are immature, but rather that we are people they should nurture and take care of. The sly fox definitely knows what he's doing.

"You're of course correct, Jordan," Laurence agreed. I doubt anyone wants to go toe to toe with our manager and expects to win.

"In my hands are new contracts for *The Darkest Nights*. It states the revision of recording dates built into their schedule, unless there's a burst of creativity that needs to be handled immediately. The contract calls for flexibility in this case," Jordan states as he stands at the head of the table. This position had remained suspiciously vacant, and now I know why. "The revision also states that they will not have a show on the same day they record or have heavy interviewing or photo shoots. *The Darkest Nights* has been working a breakneck schedule, and sucked it up, thinking this is what was expected of them with the upgrade of their bus," he explains disapprovingly.

"Absolutely not. We discussed you'd have more tour dates this year, but no one expects you to work yourselves into the ground," Laurence explodes.

As Prescott's father, he's amazingly level-headed. I wasn't expecting that. I guess sometimes people have blinders on for the ones they love, but mine were ripped off long ago.

"Prescott pushed us to do more, often scheduling our day out by telling us it's what was expected," I explain with a shrug.

He needs to know that we weren't responsible for the pace that was set.

Laurence wrinkles his nose disapprovingly. "Yes, well, I can assure you she'll be handled accordingly. I find her behavior despicable, and not up to par with our standards at our label." He sighs, shaking his head. "I had no idea any of this was happening."

"I swear, you spoil that child," mutters another executive and I can't bring myself to disagree with him.

"Anyone disagree with the changes to *The Darkest Nights'* contract?" Jordan asks. There's an edge in his voice, as if daring someone to disagree.

I shift my weight in my seat, wondering how his meeting with Derek went. Am I going to leave this room and find out that he's been fired? God I hope not.

The executives shake their heads and Jordan explains to us where we need to sign. I'm starving, and my hand shakes a bit as I sign.

"Lenny, are you doing okay," Roark asks, glancing at me as he signs.

"I'm fine, but I'm getting hungry. Trying to power through," I murmur.

"Nope," says Atlas, and I have no idea how he heard me. "I think I saw crackers somewhere."

"Atlas," I laugh as he gets up.

"Is our tiny Valkyrie hungry?" Mav asks, amused as Atlas comes back with crackers.

"Is this okay?" Atlas asks as he puts them on a plate.

I chuckle, amused because the boys are terrified of my hanger. I swear it's not that bad.

"Do you have a low blood sugar issue," asks Allen, looking on in amusement.

Taking a bite of a cracker, I shake my head. "I don't think so? I apparently get really mean when I'm hungry, so the boys live in terror of it."

Another exec snorts, picking up the phone. I only remember his last name... Walsh? I think it is.

"A woman who is hungry is more than enough reason to live in terror," he says with a grin. "I'll order food for us all. How do we feel about Greek?"

My stomach makes an embarrassing sound and I wince. He barks out a laugh and makes the call.

"We tend to go on and on," Allen says with a shrug, "and sometimes the only way to shut us up is for someone's stomach to growl."

I giggle, still embarrassed, but happy no one is holding it against me. Popping another cracker into my mouth, I finish signing the amended contract.

Jordan watches on in amusement as he checks things on his phone.

Food arrives quickly, and we all just chat as we eat.

"I've listened to your music," Mr. Walsh says with a smile as he takes a sip of water. "I love the message it all has, and my granddaughter says I get cool points since I 'know' who you are."

I roll my lips inwards, knowing exactly how snarky teens can be. "Jordan, I'm sure we have *The Darkest Nights* swag somewhere in this building, right? I feel like I need to up Mr. Walsh's cool points for him by signing some with the boys."

Jordan grins. "Teresa will never stop talking about this, and drive Walsh crazy. I'll be right back." He gets up, throughly tickled by it all. I'm glad he's back to what I consider his normal now, because I hate seeing him upset.

"It's just Walsh, Lennon, no mister," he says, nose wrinkling. "My father was Mr. Walsh, and I just can't do it. I also never admit to being a fan, but—"

"I love that you did," I tell him, happiness coloring my words. "Music allows the guys and I to connect to people, and it makes me happy knowing you enjoy our music."

"We also aren't assholes about signing merch," Mav says with a shrug. "Knowing it's gonna make someone happy their grandfather thought of them, and it'll create a happy memory, we're always gonna be in for that, Walsh."

"I can see why Jordan has always had a soft spot for you all," Allen says with a grin, "and why your fans love you. You're just all really genuine."

Turner shrugs. "We have our asshole moments, but it usually surrounds our girl. Be mean to her, and see how quickly we'll burn it all down."

Laurence shrugs like this is normal. "I'd do the same for my wife, so I don't blame you for it. We also don't need the reminder either," he smirks. "It is in all of our best interests to keep you happy and healthy."

On that note, Jordan comes back into the room and we spend some time signing merch for Walsh's granddaughter.

"Send me a photo if you remember when you give it to her," I tell Walsh, grinning happily as we finish up.

"You got it," he says with a nod. "She's going to lose it in the best way."

Standing from the table, I stretch. I'm sore from sitting for so long, and need to walk.

"Ready to go, beautiful," Roark asks with a smile.

"Yes please. I need to stretch my legs and then take a nap," I laugh.

"Always a pleasure," Allen calls out as I turn and let Roark pull me into his arms.

"Same, thank you guys," I call over my shoulder. I know I'm being pretty informal for talking to the top executives of my label, but it's obvious none of them stand on formalities while in this room.

Jordan rocks on his heels as he waits for us outside of the room. "I think that went very well, don't you?" he murmurs as we move down the hall.

"Aye," we confirm as a group and he chuckles.

"Sooo, I'm gonna call out the elephant in the room to just be done with it," Turner drawls and I shiver in anticipation.

Roark squeezes me gently, and I remind myself I need to see what Jordan has to say for himself.

"Ah, not pulling any punches today, are we Turner?"

"Nope," he says, popping the 'p.' "What decision was made about Derek today, if any?"

God, I just love this man.

"We decided he'll stay on as your photographer, with the agreement that you're comfortable with it. We had a nice long talk, and I feel like there were some extenuating circumstances that will allow him to stay on if you want him to."

"I do," I hurry to say. "I'd like for him to stay."

"I have no doubts as well that if he ever fucks up again he'll be well handled," Mav says with an evil grin. I'm glad he's one of those people who can let shit go when warranted, but will also be the first to stand up and call a person out. I am their girl after all, and no one fucks with me.

Never again.

"As you wish," Jordan says with a nod as we walk down the hall. I suddenly have an urge to watch *Princess Diaries*, and wonder if I can get the guys to watch it with me tonight with pizza after our concert. "I do need to mention that Derek had to leave earlier than planned to return home, and he said he'd be back in the allotted time you all agreed on. I believe it was three days?"

"Two," Roark grunts as my heart sinks.

"He's gone?" I breathe. "He didn't text anyone did he?" I look up at Roark and he shakes his head.

"Negative," Turner mutters. "Was there a pressing reason for him leaving early?"

"I don't know, he simply asked me to change his flight," Jordan says, "and he said you all knew how to contact him if necessary. I don't think he wanted you all to worry," he soothes. Jordan looks over his shoulder as he turns the corner as we follow closely and there's worry in his eyes.

We were all gonna fucking worry.

Pulling my phone out of my back pocket, I'm glad I put on cute pants today because of the pockets. Hoping for a missed message, I open the phone and see nothing. Growling under my breath, I open a text to message Derek. He made sure we all had his number last night, and I wonder if it's because he thought he may be fired.

Hey, stay safe and please let me know if you need anything. I'm a little disappointed I didn't get to say goodbye.

Derek must have his phone in his hand and not be in the air yet because his response is immediate.

> DEREK: I'm sorry, Len. I promise I'll make it up to you. I didn't have a choice. I had to leave early. We'll talk when I get back?

Huh, okay I'm not as upset now. I wonder if his dad threatened him again, but don't want to ask in a text. Chewing on my lip, I glance up to make sure I don't run into anything as I walk. Where are we going anyway?

> Yes we can. Be safe. You have two days and then we're coming to pull your ass out of Kentucky. I hate that damn town so don't make me have to come.

Sighing, I tuck my phone away as we come to a stop in front of a room.

James Campbell says the name. Awesome, we are probably grabbing Layla before we leave. I don't know what it is, but I get this weird feeling around Layla's dad. I'm sure he's a perfectly nice man, and Layla has kind words to say about him, but the way he stares at me creeps me out. I also think it's unprofessional that he couldn't even remember my name. I've been with *Music Hoarde* for nine and a half years.

Huffing in annoyance, I settle as Turner hugs me from beyond.

"You and I are gonna have words later, darlin'," he whispers in my ear so only I can hear.

I barely nod and he kisses my ear. These men know me so well, and they know I'm whipping myself up into a mood.

Jordan knocks on the door and James yells for him to come in.

Opening the door, I'm surprised to see his office is done in cool blues and grays, and that there's a wall covered in Layla photos as she grew up. My heart softens a little as I see how well-loved my friend is.

"Time to go?" Layla jumps up with a smile.

"Yep, we're all done here for today, and I think Lennon wants to take a nap before the show," Jordan says with a smirk.

Unbidden, I yawn and cover my mouth as I roll my eyes. "Dude, it's like you knew," I complain and Jordan laughs.

"I also heard the guys like to con you into napping before you perform," he teases me.

"Orgasms," Layla grins. "I'm sure orgasms will be more than welcome to help you nap too."

Jordan looks a cross between horrified and amused and it just makes him look constipated which makes me sputter out a laugh.

"I volunteer as tribute," Roark and Turner chorus. I shrug and decide to go with it. May as well.

"I will say yes to that sandwich any damn day, boys," I tell them, letting Roark pull me into his arms with a smile.

"Wait, so both of them," James asks, looking confused and a bit angry. He stalks across the desk and crosses his arms.

I swear, he better not give us shit for this. It's bad enough that the rest of the world does. I swear that having a harem isn't contagious, so it's not like I can corrupt Layla.

"Dad, relax. Lennon has her own harem, and I'm kind of jealous. Okay, love you bye!"

Well, so much for that logic. Layla gives her dad a side hug before turning to face us and mouthing '*run*.' Spinning, I look up at Roark and squish my nose at him because this entire interaction has been really fucking weird.

"Lovely to see you again, James," Roark says with a polite smile. "We'll be sure to take great care of Layla."

Oh no no no...

"What the fuck does that mean?!" he roars.

"Fook... now we run," Roark mutters and we all rush out of the office like the fires of hell are following us as we giggle.

"They're just friends, James, chill," Jordan says as he closes the door behind himself and walks quickly behind us. "I swear, it's never boring with you all. We are all on your father's shit list, Layla," he mutters.

Layla shrugs. "It wouldn't be my dad if he didn't get his blood pressure up about something," she giggles.

Well, I guess all families have their quirks.

Derek

I rented a car from the airport to get to my dad's house because I refuse to be stranded in Farrelsville. I need an escape plan if needed.

I smirk as I think about Len's text to me : ***I'll come and pull your ass out***. I know it took a lot for her to say that because this town has a lot of fucked up memories for her. There are a lot for me as well... but I have to go back.

I need to know what's going on with my mom.

I press the gas pedal a little harder, sighing as I scrub my hair with the palm of my hand. It's about a two hour drive to his house, and now that I'm coming up on signs signaling that I'm close, I'm getting nervous.

I'm sick to my stomach about this huge secret that I'm holding onto for Jordan. How did this even happen?! My dad is a dick, but building an entire life without their kid in it takes the damn cake.

Disappearing and changing your name makes me think he knew exactly how negligent and dangerous Carrie O'Reilly was.

My blood boils and my heart aches for the little girl who

was left behind. Maybe Lennon's life would have been different, for the better, if James had thought to take her with him. Or maybe not, because she wouldn't have Roark or Turner, and I have no doubts that they are the reason she's still here with us today.

If one thing changed in her life, her entire path would have too.

I turn on the radio impatiently, smiling as a song by *The Darkest Nights* comes on. Fuck, I thought I'd be able to dip out and then go back to them without an issue, but I really miss them. I leave the song on, hoping the sooner I arrive is the sooner I get the fuck out of Farrelsville.

The scenery of greenery blurs until it's replaced by office buildings and neighborhoods as I drive into Farrelsville. People stare at the unknown car curiously, and I roll my eyes. I wonder if I'm going to be put on parade by my father and have to make the rounds to see people, or if he plans to try to use me as his personal punching bag. No, you know what fuck that. He needs to learn to keep his hands to his damn self, since I'm a damn sight larger than he is now.

Too soon and not soon enough, I see the huge willow tree that stands in front of my childhood home. Blowing out a breath, I turn into the driveway and shut off the engine. There's still some light in the sky, but shadows are starting to encroach in. I almost expect Carrie to walk out towards me as I get out of the car and shiver. Damn, that woman's gonna haunt me even in death.

Slamming my car door shut, I grab my duffle bag from the back seat and throw it over my shoulder. *Okay, now or never.*

Shutting the back door quieter, I walk across the front yard towards the house. It doesn't look like it's changed at all, the huge lake looks idyllic, and the house gleaming white with blue trim. At least my father keeps up appearances in all respects as the mayor. You'd think he'd move into town to be part of things, but he likes the quiet, and in some respects I don't blame him.

Knocking on the front door, I twist the knob and push in, almost surprised it opens. Honestly though, my father rarely locks the door out here, and neither do half the residents of Farrelsville.

"Who's there?" I hear my dad call out and I stand straighter.

"It's Derek, Dad. I decided to fly in a little sooner. I hope that's okay?"

I bite my tongue hard after I say this, not wanting to give too much away as I shut the door behind me. I don't want to seem overly eager either, since I was so hesitant to come home at all.

I just want to know what's happening with my mom, what he wants and expects from me, and then to get the hell out of here.

"I'm glad you're taking me seriously, come back to my office, and let's have a chat," my dad says and I grind my teeth together.

Forcing myself to relax my jaw and don my mask of cool indifference, I walk to his office. The house looks the same as always, but it feels cold, as if no one's lived here for a while. I know that's not true, but this house just doesn't feel like a home.

Fuck, I need to know what's going on with my mom. While she hasn't lived here in years, my mother has kept up pretenses well, since my father has people over for work. So there's always been flowers in a vase when you walk in, and everything smells amazing. The air smells stale, as if it needs to be aired out.

Holding back a shiver, I knock gently on the open office

door. Grant Williams looks up from his desk with a smile, but it's not warm, instead it's calculating.

"Come in son, and sit down. There are some things we need to talk about."

Nodding and murmuring,"Yes, Sir," I walk over and sit down. This meeting feels very different from the one I was just in, but no less uncomfortable.

"I want to make the move from mayor of this small town to governor, son. I'm sure this isn't a surprise to you, as I've been talking about doing this for the past few years. I have the backing from powerful key players, but I can no longer fall back on what was my platform before: family."

Blinking, I frown. "Why would that be, Dad?" I ask.

Breathing deeply, he nods at my question. I usually wouldn't interrupt him to ask questions, but this is slowly killing me. Usually he'd smack me for asking before he's ready to tell me. My dad seems to agree that leading questions are what we are doing today, because he continues.

"Your mother hasn't been feeling well, so she's taking a small vacation to Hidden Hills for a little bit. Marian has been complaining of headaches, and her sister told me she's worried about her. Marian hasn't been wanting to get out of bed, and she seemed erratic our last few conversations," he confides.

Erratic is not something I would ever call my mom. Where have I heard the name Hidden Hills before... it definitely doesn't seem like a spa. My breath hitches as he drones on about how my mother has been saying things she doesn't mean, and he's afraid she may hurt herself. *Holy fuck.*

"Hidden Hills is a psychiatric facility isn't it?" I ask, struggling to keep the growl out of my voice. I don't completely manage it, because my dad's eye twitches.

"Psychiatric facility isn't exactly what I would call it. It's a healing mental health clinic meant to help her get back on track. Marian had delusions of wanting to divorce her loving husband, and you understand why I couldn't have that happen, right?" I taste bile and swallow hard.

Who the hell is this person?!

"I suppose not," I murmur. My father is running for governor, of fucking course he can't have his wife trying to divorce him. This man has clearly lost the plot, and is so much more evil than I remember.

"So here's what is going to happen. Instead, I'm going to run a campaign on improving mental health in Kentucky. It's a growing concern in our state, and it's important that I take steps to help with this. We've seen firsthand how mental health can spiral out of control with our own poor sweet neighbor. Your mother will be kept comfortable for as long as you're willing to play along. I expect you to be available when I need you, is that understood?"

I flinch as he mentions Carrie. I don't know how to get out of this conversation because there's no way I will allow him to hurt my mother. She's innocent in all of this and one of the only people he can leverage over me. My father is the damn devil.

"Of course, Sir. How will it look when I also quit my job? Your campaign is also focused on hard work isn't it?" I'm assuming a hell of a lot by asking this, but he's never liked my job.

"I never said you had to quit your job," my dad muses. "But you're right. I can't have anyone saying my son is lazy, because you aren't. I may not approve of what you do, but everyone always speaks well of your work. I've been watching, you know."

I didn't, but I'm not at all surprised.

"I didn't know, but I appreciate that you're aware of my work ethic," I tell him.

"Of course, of course. Now, I expect you to make the

rounds, say hello to people in town, and be seen. Starting with a run. You still look like a linebacker, there's no reason for you to get fat while you're here, Derek," my father says derisively.

I hold back a snort. Yeah, okay. There's no way I would let myself go. God, I hate this man.

"I'll change and head out now for that run," I say instead. "Can I ask where Hidden Hills is located, and if I can see Mom?"

"Of course, of course," he says distractedly, already having dismissed me in his head now that he's getting what he wanted. "Hidden Hills is in northern Kentucky, I'll arrange a visit if you do everything I ask."

Awesome. That's just great. He's such a prick, but I shouldn't be surprised. He knows exactly how to control me still.

"Alright, I'll be back later then," I tell him and walk out. Grabbing my bag that I had dropped at the door, I walk to my room. If I had stayed any longer, I wouldn't have been able to keep it together.

I have no doubts my mom is drugged out of her mind right now in that place, and it's gonna piss me off. Dammit.

Changing quickly, I shove my feet into my running shoes and tie them up. I need to get out of here. I knew I would need to run while I was here, because I knew my father's expectations would require it, and I'd need the release. Strapping my phone to my arm and grabbing my Air Pods, I walk to the kitchen for a bottle of water from the fridge. I'm honestly surprised anything is in it since my father doesn't cook.

Striding across the house, I slip out of the house and walk as far as possible into the yard before beginning to stretch for my run. I can't wait to feel the whistle of wind blowing across my body as I run until I'm too tired to think. Today has been a major mind fuck in all respects.

34

ROARK

I look out into the crowd of faces as I play the drums and wish Derek was with them, watching us play. He hasn't been with us for very long, and much of it I've hated his guts for being a fuckwit, but he's grown on me.

I'm drawn out of my thoughts as Lenny walks towards me with a smile. The woman dressed to pull herself out of her own funk tonight. A blue lace corset pushes up her tits, black shorts skim her ass, and she has fishnet stockings under them to finish the outfit with high heeled combat boots. My mouth feels dry as my mouth falls open at the sight of her.

"Close your mouth, Daddy, or you'll catch flies," she whispers in my ear.

"You're such a brat," I growl.

"I know," is all she says, then kisses me hard before skipping back, beginning to sing. The crowd loves Lennon, and shaking my head, I pick up the beat on the drum.

It'll be fun spanking that gorgeous bubble butt and then choking her with my cock. Maybe that's exactly what I need tonight.

These thoughts carry me through, and I am able to lose myself to the music. We are celebrating *The Velvet Escape* tonight, because the board agreed to open talk of a recording contract with them. They'll continue to play as our headlining act as long as it works for them.

I have a feeling they'll be with us a while since Layla and Lennon are determined to be inseparable. They automatically clicked, and the guys and I feel very protective towards Layla as well. I'm not exactly sure what to think of her father, and because I won't need to see him for a bit, I am tabling my feelings on him.

He kept looking at Lennon in the oddest way, and I could tell she was skeeved out by it. She was uncomfortable by the attention, and that's coming from someone who has no problems performing in front of five-thousand people. We are in an outdoor stadium today, and while the air is chilly, being under the stadium lights always keeps us warm.

Our VIP meet and greet is taking place at a bar that Music Horde Records rented out for the night. Los Angeles is having a burst of cooler weather, and talking to people while your teeth chatter is never comfortable. After the hour and a half meet and greet, we are going to a late dinner with Layla and the guys. I've realized that everything should be celebrated in life, and we wanted to teach *Velvet Escape* to do the same.

No time like the present.

Feeling a rush of adrenaline as I always do at the end of our performance, Turner and I sandwich Lennon between us to kiss her. Lenny basks in the glow of our attention before saying goodbye to our fans.

"Thank you for having us, Los Angeles! Tonight is our last night here, and you've been amazing," Lennon says, laughter coloring her voice.

The crowd goes wild, and we walk off stage together, Mav

and Atlas flanking around us. As much as possible, we act as a unit, even when we don't agree on everything. Disagreements happen behind closed doors only, otherwise people start freaking out that we're going to break up.

Such drama queens. This is why I kind of hate the paparazzi and social media. It's easier to spin our own stories so they don't go looking for other ones.

Jordan smiles as he waits for us backstage. "Let's walk and talk, guys. Layla and the guys are on your bus already, and I expect you'll be getting cold soon, Lennon."

Lennon grins at him with a shrug. "You can only feel warm from adrenaline for so long," she says.

Tugging Lenny to me, I wrap my arm around her. At least I run warm, and can lend her some of it as we walk. Sighing happily, she snuggles into my side.

"Lennon," Jordan chuckles, shaking his head as we walk together to the bus. "It's really cold tonight for... the lack of clothing that you're wearing. I know you all have plans to go out after the meet and greet, maybe you should think about changing beforehand?"

I roll my lips inwards, because Jordan looks like he just wants to demand she change. Lennon is damn stubborn, and I hope he holds this instinct he seems to be fighting within, because she'll just wear this outfit all night and freeze otherwise. Lennon does what she pleases.

"Are you telling me to change?" Lennon asks sweetly and I shoot a look over to Turner. His eyes grow wide and he mouths, "oh shit".

I can't wait to see how this will end up. She's already channeling her inner brat tonight. Dammit.

"Never," Jordan says firmly, shaking his head. "It's extremely difficult to be happy and have a good time when you're freezing your ass off, unless you're drinking a shit ton. If you're going to go with the second option, that's fine, but I may invite myself along or send you with a bodyguard. Just in case, you know, so Turner doesn't have to beat anyone who touches what isn't theirs."

Bravo, old man. He actually diffused that really well.

"Ugh, I hate bodyguards," Lennon groans with a sigh and I stifle my laugh.

"The ball is entirely in your court, Lennon."

"I don't like to drink when I'm out," she explains. "I'm either on the bus, in a place I feel completely safe, or I'll keep it to one beverage."

I nod because it's true. "We also won't have more than a couple beers if we have a show the next day."

"This I knew," Jordan says. "However, tomorrow is a traveling day, and you don't have a show." He looks smug and I don't even bother to hold it in, I laugh because he looks so clever.

"I always forget when we have days off," Lennon murmurs. "The days start to run together, and I forget to check the schedule unless I need to. I have clothes on the bus, I'll change because it's fucking frigid tonight."

I agree, for late September, LA is definitely not usually this chilly. Just our luck to have our last day be cold weather. As we head into the later part of the year, the label makes sure that our venues are all indoors.

Jordan nods as if this was clearly all her idea and I hide my snigger behind a cough. He clearly has experience with women or children, because he handled that really well. Climbing the stairs of the bus, Lennon says hello to the driver and he grunts at her. If he's going to be our permanent driver, he really needs to loosen up. He always appears to be sucking on a lemon.

Lennon continues on to the back, grabbing Layla to go change.

"That was masterful," Turner murmurs to Jordan as we sit down.

Jordan hides his smile by touching the corner of his mouth with his finger. "I haven't the faintest idea what you mean."

I snort in amusement. "Keep your secrets old man, because if you had treated that any differently, she'd have taken it as a challenge to wear that outfit the entire night. Lenny is gonna find herself with a red ass later, she's really gone all in on being a brat."

Jordan takes a second to process what I just said and flushes. "Damn," he mutters, shaking his head. "I have no response to that."

I giggle and Turner bumps my shoulder with a smile. "I never thought I'd see the day that Jordan Miles would blush over something we said."

Miracles do happen. I was pretty mild in what I said too.

Turner

The bar we are doing our meet and greet at is a small, intimate spot. It has black and white wallpaper, a black granite bar, and plenty of seating. Lavender grabs a bottle of water and cracks the seal. Glancing over at me, I smile and nod. I am only going to be crazy protective over water given to us at a venue we play at or when it's not in our sight.

The label is paying for drinks tonight, as it's our last show in Los Angeles, and they planned to do something fun for our last day. People are more excited to chat with us all than drink, so I don't see it being a problem. It's also nice to be inside tonight after our outside venue.

Lavender pushes away from the bar, walking to the first group she sees with a smile. She chose to change into a pair of thick lavender stockings, a gray sweater dress, and fun unicorn crawler earrings. This ensemble is uniquely her and Jordan couldn't help but smile when he saw it.

Taking my cue from her, I head towards the other end of the room. Roark is with the group next to her and Layla is with the group she's speaking to now, so I feel comfortable that there are enough eyes on her. Lennon can take care of herself, and there's nothing saying there's any danger here tonight, but I will never be too careful when it comes to her.

Lennon gets that and I love that she just goes with the flow most of the time. She also doesn't let me get away with anything if I go too far. I smirk as I think of how many times I've wanted to kick Derek's ass. He's still a dick, but he's a hot dick with a tight ass now.

Fuck, I may miss him, just a little.

I need to make sure I check in with him to make sure everything is okay. I'll also ask Roark what he thinks, as he's the one that Derek talked to more about his home situation.

There's a dad in this group that I'm talking to that's exactly what you'd hope a father would be. He brought his sixteen year old son to our show because he really connected with our music.

"My son has been going through a rough period with bullying, and he really found your music helpful," Harry says.

His son nods with a shrug. "Kids kind of suck at my school, and don't like how I look. I like dark clothes, my hair is longer, and I usually have AirPods in my ears as I walk to classes. For the most part, I can ignore it, but—"

Harry shakes his head, lips pursed. "They beat the shit out of him a year ago and put him in the hospital. The kids also wrote nasty slurs all over his body while he was passed out and then dumped him in front of our house. It was the most terrifying thing as a parent that I've ever witnessed. I was driving home and saw this black limp bundle being pushed out of their car."

Holy fucking shit. "Can I ask what the slurs were?" I breathe, almost afraid to hear. I feel like this is about more than just him wearing dark clothes and ignoring the outside world.

Harry's son, Zayne takes a deep breath, wincing. "Homophobic slurs. God, I can't even say some of the things they wrote on my skin."

"Fuck," I mutter. "I had a feeling that's what this was about. You can't help who you like, love, or even have a crush on. Attraction to any gender is normal and healthy. It's also something that can take people by surprise at any age, and the right person just clicks with you," I explain with a shrug. "I hate to be the person that uses a bumper sticker saying that says, 'love is love' but I really do feel it's true."

Zayne chews on his lip, thinking. "I started talking to this guy in my class who likes the same things I do, and we really clicked. I mean, I thought we did. But once people started gossiping that we were 'gay for each other,' that was it. The guy ended up telling them I hit on him, pushing unwarranted attention at him."

I blink, wishing I had something strong to drink right now. *What the fuck is wrong with people.* "Did he hurt you? Did he think it was really so terrible to like you that he had to start bullying you?"

"Yeah. I live in a really small town in Georgia, and I've never seen someone turn on another person so quickly. I don't know if Ian was scared of his feelings or what people thought, but it was awful. He tried to ignore it, but when he started getting shoved and the slurs started being shouted as he walked home, he was out. Ian texted me that night saying he wanted me to come see him, and they all jumped me outside of his house. They freaking curb stomped me on the sidewalk, beat me with bats, and someone got too excited and stabbed me. That's when they all panicked."

Everyone in our group has tears in their eyes at this young man who had to live through this. I know this can happen anywhere, but damn these small towns seem to be the biggest keepers of these secrets.

Swiping under my eyes, I force a smile. "Not everyone is strong enough to accept their attraction at this or any age, and it can very quickly lead to hate. Roark and Lennon are my loves, did you know that?"

Zayne frowns as he thinks. "You both kissed her tonight, but I wasn't sure if you and Roark were together too."

There are a lot of photos of us together, but sometimes people don't realize we are committed to each other. Derek was a surprise none of us expected, but I want to ease into being with us before exposing him to the public eye. That's a conversation to have when he's back.

"I want you to chat with the three of us for a little bit. Harry, is it okay with you if I steal him away? I promise to bring him back," I joke.

Harry looks relieved, shaking his head that he doesn't mind. Poor man has been through hell with his son, and I'm glad he trusts me enough to go talk to him.

"I want Zayne to see how a not quite traditional relationship looks like," I explain to his dad. "I grew up in South Carolina, and while bigotry was rampant there as well, there were people that were open minded. My friend, Red, is in a relationship with three men, and two of them are also involved with each other. We have big hearts, and there is someone or multiple someones that are just going to accept you for who you are. They'll love your music, this fun emo-nerd vibe you have going on, and everything you have to offer. I can see you haven't let this break you, and I'm glad we could have had a small part in helping you."

Zayne nods, tears welling in his eyes. Damn, I didn't mean to make him cry, but his story really spoke to me. Bullying, bigotry, and a hate crime. I couldn't stand by and not say something when he bared his soul to tell me his story. Harry doesn't seem upset at all about what I've said, and I think he's one of those parents that just wants his kid to be genuinely happy.

"You're really brave for telling me your story," I tell him. "And I value every word. Now let's go find my people, shall we?"

I throw my arm around his shoulder as he discreetly wipes his eyes. I squeeze his bicep to show I'm here, and steer us towards Lennon and Roark.

"Hey guys, have a couple of minutes to come hang with us for a bit? This is Zayne, and I think this young man needs to hear some truths about how much people can unfortunately suck and how to deal with it," I tell them.

Zayne sighs. "I know exactly how much they can suck," he sasses.

Good, good. I like the sass.

Lennon stares at him for a moment and purses her lips. "You probably do, but chat with us anyway. There's a reason Turner dragged you over to meet us, and it's more than just because you're a fan."

"I mean, I'm still a fan," he laughs. "It's why I'm here, but y'all helped me through some fucked up shit without even knowing it."

Ah, he doesn't curse around his father. Good to know.

I steer him towards a booth, and wave my arm at Jordan so he knows where we are. He nods with a small smile, and I know he'll cover for us. We won't be long.

"Okay, then..." Lennon says. "Tell me everything? I feel

like you may need to talk about things. We're a safe space, and maybe your story can help others. Bullying is the worst kind of abuse, because it's psychological, physical, and mental. Our peers aren't supposed to be twat waffles, and their opinions tend to matter to us, especially in high school."

Zayne sighs. "There was really only one person who mattered to me, and he beat the shit out of me while calling me a fag. He accused me of 'turning him gay,' as if he hadn't been the one to kiss me the night before."

Lennon's eyes widen. "Fuckwit," she mutters and he grins.

"You're kind of the coolest adult I've ever met," he says, shaking his head.

Lennon smirks back at him. "Trust me, I often ask myself if I am an adult on a daily basis. I didn't have the best childhood, and had bullies for no other reason than I was pretty and different. Oh, and my mom was a bit off her rocker. Ridiculous, right? People dislike what they can't explain, are different, or are scared of. Welcome to the club, Zayne," she says with a wink.

Zayne gives her a small smile. "Weirdest club ever. I almost want to stay home and do online schooling for the rest of the year. Is that giving in to them?"

Lennon purses her lips in thought, shaking her head. "You're in danger at school, your classmates beat the shit out of you, what's to say this won't happen at school too? If I had had the chance, and things were a bit different for me, I would have chosen online schooling. Then get the fuck out of that small town and live your life. There are home school communities online that you connect with people who aren't homophobic and decent people too so you're not isolated. It's worth a shot?"

"Yeah? I didn't think of looking for friends outside of my town... this is a good idea. I didn't really hang out with anyone really before Ian... so it's not like I'll miss friends at school."

Zayne breathes a sigh of relief, and it's so deep, I expect it's the first in a long while.

"There's a tribe for everyone," Roark rumbles. "I've realized that few people escape unscathed from their childhood, and there's always something. You could hate these people, or chosen to give up, but it doesn't look like you have."

Roark's a big man, but very quiet, so it's easy to forget he's there. Zayne startles a little, eyes wide as he looks at him.

"I'm not proud of it, but I considered it," he says, meeting Roark's eye's unflinchingly. "It was a little after I got out of the hospital, and my dad had helped me change my bandages. He left a sharp pair of scissors without thinking about it when he went to dump out the trash." Zayne's eyes well with tears as he thinks about a low point in his life. "I even had them in my hands, and I thought about how easy it could be to say fuck it all. And then as I heard my dad opening drawers and talking to himself... I couldn't do it. I decided fuck that. I threw the scissors across the room and cried. I cried for the stupid, innocent guy who just wanted to enjoy his first crush, and this broken *person* that I was now. My dad came in while I lost it and just hugged me. He didn't ask questions I'd have to lie to give him answers to, Dad just was there for me."

"Your dad seems like a really good man," I murmur.

He nods as he wipes his face. Lennon gives him a gentle hug and Zayne leans into it. "He's the best. This past year and a half have been the hardest of my life, and I just want to move past it. I'm sure if I ask him about finishing school virtually or even finishing early, he'll be fine with it. He hasn't been exactly excited about my going back to school. Medically, I am supposed to go back next week now that I'm cleared for everything, but I've been feeling anxious about it."

"Choosing to have a different kind of education isn't giving up," Lennon says, sitting back as she thinks. "You can even find interests outside of what your school is able to offer. Music was my outlet once I got out of high school, but anything that channels your attention is healthy."

Zayne frowns as he thinks. "I really like video games and drawing. Maybe I can find some classes at the local college that I can use as dual enrollment online or talk to my dad about?"

Lennon grins at him and he blinks at her. I swear, even gay teens are mesmerized by her. She just glows when she smiles.

"Plans are good," she encourages with a smile. "Look, life sometimes has a way of kicking us in the ass, but the people who stand back up and tell it to fuck off are the ones who make it. You have this really amazing spark, and I want to see what you do with it in life, okay?"

"Thanks for talking with me," Zayne says with a smile. "And Turner... thank you for showing me there is more to life than what people tell me there is."

With that, he slips out of the booth with a smile, and I smirk as I watch him.

"What was that about," Lennon asks as I stand up and hold my hand out for her to get up. We really need to keep making the rounds.

"I told the kid that the three of us are in a relationship together, and that sexuality can be fluid. Who you love is who you love, and there's no right or wrong to it. You can also love more than one person too," I explain.

"What did his dad say to that," Roark asks as he follows.

"Honestly, not much, and he didn't seem that surprised. If he follows on social media at all, I'm sure he's seen photos of us together, and we both kissed Lennon tonight."

"Zayne is going to have some hard times ahead, only because people are close minded, but I'm hoping getting out of his town will help. God, I wish I could have ten fucking minutes with that little asshole that set him up," Lennon growls.

Damn, that's sexy as fuck. It makes me wonder what she'll be like with our own kids and I lick my lips in surprise. We've talked about kids, but I haven't thought about them outside of as a possibility. Our girl would be a truly amazing mom.

I'm harder than stone now, and all I can think about is fucking my Lavender. Here's to hoping Layla and the guys don't want to be out too late.

35

DEREK

Breathing hard, I stare at my childhood home. I didn't expect to run as hard as I did tonight, but I hate feeling helpless. My father is holding my mother's safety over my head so I'll play ball with him for now. While he hasn't loved her in years, it's still hard for me to believe he'd check her into an institution against her will.

Shady is a name that's synonymous with my father. I hadn't realized when he started making such strides to become governor that it would mean selling out his wife too.

Shaking my head, I trudge towards the house. The scent of magnolias pricks at my nose and I wrinkle it in annoyance. They always remind me of Carrie, and just being in this damned town, heading into my father's house, is enough to do that anyway.

Thank god my father remodeled the kitchen to a granite counter for the island while I was away in college, so I don't have to stare at the butcher block and remember seeing them together.

Shaking my head at the audacity of someone who fucks his

mistress where his son eats, I open the front door. Toeing out of my shoes, I leave them outside. It had sprinkled lightly while I was running, and dirt and dead leaves cover them at the moment. I'll have to clean them in the morning, but don't want to track dirt into the house. That's the last thing I want to fight with my dad about.

Shutting the door softly, I start to walk towards the kitchen for a snack when I hear my father's voice. Frowning, I try to remember where every creak in the floorboards are as I change directions to listen in. He rarely forgets to close the door to his office, and it's open just enough for me to be able to hear everything.

"Yes, Mr. Xav, my son is on board with helping me campaign," my father says in a low voice. "I want to contribute to our plans to have more private facilities in Kentucky as a haven for those who need to immobilize family members that become a problem for them... for a price, of course," he chuckles nervously. "I think that the state will be so on board with affordable mental health opportunities for the public, that they'll ignore these private mental health facilities as they are built. They'll look like private country clubs with all the amenities from the outside, but those housed within won't be able to take advantage of any of it. It'll be the perfect vacation for them, and easily explained away by their families. 'Oh Suz went on a vacation so she could get away from the stress'," he parrots and I pale.

God, I can already hear him telling people this about my mother.

"I appreciate your help in my campaign and your contributions, Sir," my father continues. "I also want to thank you for helping with the distasteful job of getting a psychiatrist's agreement that Marian needed to be hospitalized. I really needed that in order to be able to continue to run for governor. I won't forget any of this."

I startle as I hear another voice, realizing the asshole is on speaker phone.

"Of course, Grant. The rich need a place to put those that oppose them: their gay son, cheating wife, sister that's opposing a will. I know that you'll keep my involvement to the forefront of your mind while not breathing a word of it to anyone. It is imperative that I remain a ghost," Mr. Xav states. I notice his voice is deep and hoarse. I wonder if he's an older man? *"I only ask that you allow me entrance to your facilities for my own form of experimentation? If I can get my people in to practice conversion therapy or mind control on people that are forgotten by society, it'll allow me to expand it to other areas once it's perfected,"* the man says.

My jaw drops. Holy fuck, who is my dad working with?! This breaks so many laws and human rights, my head is spinning. My blood also chills as I think about what he said... their '*gay son*'. This is so fucked up. I am very quickly falling for Roark and Turner and would never want to be forced to forget them. My heart hurts as I realize how much I miss them already and it's only been a few hours.

My father doesn't have the best of morals, but I hear him swallow thickly at what he's being asked to do. It's a mighty fall from grace to go from being a shady politician to agreeing to torture and abuse. *How did he get to this place? How did he even meet this person?*

Grant Williams has always had morally gray values as he's smiled and talked to people on business trips. I never knew how he made his money, since I doubt being mayor of this podunk town is very profitable, but somehow we've always been well-off. I regret turning a blind eye now. The man I call my father is a monster.

Realizing I've already been standing here too long, I turn and walk back to the door on silent feet. My father needs to think I just came home. I have so many questions, I'm even more terrified for my mother now, and know I can't possibly be a part of whatever he's planning. There's no fucking way.

I open the door silently, thanking all of the gods that the hinges are well oiled and shut it loudly.

"Sir, I have to go as my son is back, but we'll be in touch," my father says quickly, and hangs up. "Derek?" he calls out and I roll my eyes.

Our home isn't Grand Central Station, who the fuck else would it be?

"Yes Dad, I'm back. I'm gonna catch a shower and then go to bed if that's alright?"

I am usually starving after a run, but I've lost my appetite after what I just heard. My mind is spinning, and I have a feeling it's just the tip of the iceberg. I wonder how powerful this Mr. Xav is, and how far his operation extends. "Experiments" sounds very 'mad scientist' to me, but Mr. Xav seemed very sane on the phone.

I've always known there was evil in the world, but to be related to someone capable of this is a mind fuck all of its own.

Please don't want to speak to me. I'm not above praying right now, as I don't know if I can keep my face from saying everything that I'm currently thinking.

"Night," my father says. "We'll be having breakfast in town, so be prepared to make the rounds. You've been gone for too long, and I've been asked often about how you are or what you're doing."

God, this town is filled with busybodies. "I'll be ready," I promise. I'm sitting on the edge of civility. I need to end this conversation now. "Eight in the morning, then?"

"Yep, that's the prime time everyone is sitting down to breakfast at the diner," my father responds.

"I'll be ready, Sir. Good night."

I high-tail it down to my room in the basement. My father converted the basement to give me more 'freedom' my junior year of high school, but it was also a way to keep me out of his way. It helped for the most part, but there were days he just wanted to pick a fight with me.

I was also desperate to get away from easy access windows after Carrie tied me to my bed. The woman climbed through my window when I fell asleep with it open. It's one of the reasons I need so much control during sex, or meaningless hookups.

Sighing, I wonder how the fuck this is my life as I walk through the weight room I set up while I was in school. The equipment all looks well maintained, and I walk toward it. I won't be able to sleep unless I'm about to fall over. My mind is racing, and it isn't going to get any better.

Turning on my workout playlist, *Nicotine* from Panic! At the Disco begins. I need to get out of my head for a while, and this is the perfect distraction.

~

I'M IN BED, *with a gorgeous woman riding my cock. She has lavender hair, gray eyes, and beautiful vine tattoos scrolling up her thigh. I move my hands to encircle her waist, feel her soft skin, when I realize I can't.*

"Shhh, baby boy, I'll take care of you," her throaty voice croons and it feels wrong.

"Len," I whimper, my body arching in discomfort. I instantly recognize this woman, now that I'm not ruled just by my dick. How did she get here?

She knows I don't like being called 'baby boy'. Why is this happening? Lennon knows I can't be restrained either...

My body erupts in a light sheen of sweat, which she ignores as she rolls her nipples between her fingers and she grinds her little nub on me. I feel a tingle in my balls as I feel her drench my cock with her arousal, but I don't want to come. I don't want to feel pleasure while she's ignoring my trauma.

"Lennon please stop," I croak, writhing to knock her off of me. My legs are tightly bound to the bed as well, so I can't get away.

"Such a good, strong boy at my mercy. It's just how I like you, don't you remember sweet boy?" Lennon's skin starts to shimmer and her lavender hair becomes a silver-blonde, gray eyes becoming piercing blue.

"Carrie," I gasp, struggling harder and yanking on my restrained arms. Breaking my wrists to get out of these cuffs seems like a better alternative than having this viper on my cock.

Fuck, when she died, she was supposed to stay dead. Even in my dreams.

I can't calm my panic, even knowing this can't possibly be real. I never got over her breaking into my room to fuck me, and I just need this to end. Why did my subconscious choose this to fuck with me?

"You have so many more muscles than when you were younger," Carrie whispers as she kisses down my neck, traveling to bite my nipple.

"Please get off of me, Carrie," I beg her.

She shakes her head as she smiles down at me. How can someone look so angelic while being so evil? "Silly little boy, no matter how grown up you get, you're still mine."

Screaming, I wake myself up, my legs kicking off the bed sheets. Breathing hard, trying to get my lungs to fill as I panic, I sit up and all I can smell is magnolias. My stomach lurches and

I run for the attached bathroom. I barely make it to the toilet, dropping to my knees, before my stomach betrays me, expelling the little I've eaten today.

I'm so fucking broken.

How can I start something with Lennon, Roark, and Turner when I'm still having nightmares about her mom? I knew being home would trigger me, being in my dad's house where she had basically assaulted me as she did in my dreams.

Shuddering, I drop my head back on the cool wall behind me. The basement isn't heated, but I've never minded since I'm rarely here when it snows. We have another month or so before winter really hits.

My thoughts drift as my eye catches the sight of my phone buzzing in my bedroom. The light is flashing as a call comes in and I sigh. Wrinkling my nose at the noxious fumes, I haul myself up, praying the scent of magnolias was an olfactory hallucination.

Flushing the toilet, I shuffle over to the sink to brush my teeth. My face looks pale in the mirror, my eyes haunted. There's no better representation of what I'm feeling than this. I feel shaken, but for once in my miserable life, I don't want to strike out at Lennon for her mother's mistakes.

Thank god. I don't know if I could handle reverting back to that single minded asshole, I think as I scrub my teeth and my tongue. I feel really gross, my skin clammy and covered in goosebumps. I would take a shower if my phone wasn't ringing for the third time.

Who the hell is calling me?!

Spitting, I wash my mouth out before grabbing a towel to wipe my face as I stride to the nightstand to pick up the phone.

"Hello," I answer gruffly.

"Fooking finally," Roark exclaims.

Frowning, I realize he was worried about me. Sighing, I sit

on the edge of the bed, grateful there's only a slight scent of magnolia left in the air, not enough to trigger me.

Maybe Dad's new maid is using a new air freshener?

"I'm sorry, Roark," I murmur. "Today's been a really shitty day, is everything okay over there?"

Roark grunts, and I can tell he's trying to calm himself. He was spitting nails when I picked up. Checking the time, I realize it's two in the morning. They must have had a late night.

Laying down, I yawn as I wait to see how everyone is.

A beep sounds on my phone, and glancing down I see he's video calling me.

"Ror, I'm fine—"

"I need to see you. Just hit accept, Derek. Please?" There's so much vulnerability in that one word, that I hit accept and hold the phone away from me so I can see him.

"See? I'm in one piece, and totally fine." I may be in one piece, but I'm more than a little rattled by the events of today.

"Derek, if this is your idea of 'fine,' we need to work on your definition of it. You look like shit. Are you sick or something?" Roark worries at his lip as his eyes bounce over my face, looking for the culprit of why I'm so pale.

"I'm not sick, just had a nightmare. It was so vivid, I puked over it. I hate this fucking town, and it just triggers me I guess." I let my head drop back in the pillows as I close my eyes. I have a headache starting to build right behind my eyes.

"Can I ask about the nightmare?" Roark's voice is soft, comforting, and I relax as I listen. It's easier if I don't have to look at him, he's larger than life, and just seeing him on the video is making me miss him even more.

Breathing deeply, I think about it and what I can tell him. "When I was in high school, I was involved with an older woman. She was really possessive, and climbed in my window when I was asleep. I'm a very deep sleeper, especially after a football practice or exercising hard, and she took advantage of this," I shudder as I think about what Carrie did. The terror of being tied to my own bed, and the betrayal of my own body. My cock was rock hard, totally fine being inside Carrie's warm, tight pussy.

"Derek," Roark breathes. I'm sure they had a feeling it was bad, but how do you explain that you were fucked against your own will?

Carrie was strong, and somehow also really good at tying off knots. I was completely helpless. Some people would have said '*Poor Derek, forced to fuck a gorgeous woman,*' but I asked her to stop repeatedly.

I open my eyes, daring myself to be brave, and meet Roark's beautiful caramel-colored gaze. They're usually warm and caring, but at the moment they're murderous. It honestly gives me the strength to continue, even if I can't tell him the complete truth. I don't believe that burden should lie with anyone, except apparently Jordan who pushed me into it.

Anyone who tells you sharing is caring, is full of shit. I'm carrying more secrets than I could ever want.

"When I woke up, I was tied to my bed, wrists and forearms tightly bound to the headboard, and my ankles and lower legs tied down to the foot of the bed. I don't know how I slept through this, but I remember it was after a rough away game out of town. I was exhausted and it was a Friday, so I had school that day too. I was startled awake because she was fucking me. I must have been asleep once she started and she got bored because she dropped herself on it, and I woke up gasping for air." My heart starts to beat faster as I think about it and I clench my hand in anger. Anger at how helpless I felt and still feel at times, even though she's long dead.

I am lost to my memories as I think about it before I look back at the phone. "For the record, I asked her to let me go. I fucking begged her," my voice breaks as I explain. "She laughed at me and called me her good fucking boy and told me I had to make her come first. She got tired of hearing me yell at her, so she shoved her panties in my mouth to gag me. I had to be her human toy, and she had had a rough day and needed the release, she told me. My father was out of town—"

Fuck, I almost told him my dad was out of town, so she figured she'd take her aggression on me instead.

"...so no one heard me yelling for help," I finish instead.

"No restraints, no nicknames," Roark growls, as if restating my hard limits and I nod.

"I'm noticing sometimes it's different if said by a man and not a woman," I sigh. "The whole thing is a minefield for me of trauma, and I don't always know what will trigger me. Lennon had my wrists in her hands when she was on top the other day, and I was weirdly okay with that for the most part. She said "tell me to let go and I will," and I immediately relaxed. Consent is important to what I can or can't handle," I explain.

"Consent is really important for the three of us as well," Roark says with a nod. *"Even when one person is in charge, we've known each other for so long, we know each other's limits now. But Lennon and Turner know their safe words, and if they can't talk for whatever reason, they know to tap out. Turner's arms were restrained last week on the bus,"* Roark explains and my eyes widen in surprise. He'd asked me about restraints, but didn't know this was a regular part of play for them. *"There are hidden restraints and hidey holes with toys or snacks throughout the bus,"* he chuckles. *"You already have experienced how Lenny is about food. But, all Turner had to do was close his fist, and he'd be untied if his mouth was gagged or something."*

"Wow," I murmur. *I'm apparently pretty vanilla in comparison, but I know sex with them will always be fun.*

"Derek, you know we'll never force you to do anything you

don't want to do," he admonishes. *"You're always in the driver's seat, regardless of what we're doing."*

I blush, thinking about how I wished he wouldn't treat me like glass. It's completely inappropriate for me to be thinking about this after my nightmare, but it's helping my heart to stop racing.

"What are you thinking about," Roark asks with a smirk. They all have a way of pushing past my defenses, or maybe I'm tired of clinging so tightly to my masks.

"When we were messing around together before we went to the label, I remember wishing you weren't quite so careful with me," I confess with a sigh. "I understand why you are, and I do it with Lennon too, but—"

"But it pisses Lenny right off," he grins, throwing up one of his hands.

Now that I'm not talking about my dream, I focus on Roark. He's shirtless, laying on the couch in boxers. Roark pushes his hand through his slightly disheveled chestnut curls and my fingers itch to touch it.

"I really miss you," I murmur quietly as I watch him. "I fucking hate it here, and my father is batshit crazy. I'll have to tell you all when I get home."

"Home, I like that," Roark grins lazily as he rubs his chest.

Lord save me, this man is beautiful.

"I don't know how it'll all work, but yes. Jordan isn't firing me, and he decided to give Len final say on if I get to stay."

"You're staying," he says adamantly. *"Lenny already told Jordan as much. I really don't fooking like that you're in that damned town. It's not good for you. Is your mother involved in whatever fuckery your dad is up to?"*

"Kind of? She wants a divorce, and my father insists on keeping his image intact. They were at an impasse, so Grant Williams neutralized her," I tell him. His eyes widen and I shake my head. "My mother is alive," I sigh, "but he's hiding her from me unless I do whatever he wants. Except... I can't. It's too fucked up."

"Derek," Roark rumbles. *"I know you're talking in code, but you're confusing the fuck out of me and scaring me. How soon until you can get out of there?"*

"He wants me to go into town later today to have breakfast, shake hands and kiss babies. I'm the all-American son in town for a visit to see his old man," I explain, frowning in annoyance. "It's part of his stipulations for being able to see my mother. I may be able to leave the following day as long as he doesn't have anything planned. My father made it clear that I'm expected to keep working my job, and I have to be on the road with you all in order to be able to do it."

"I already hate this man," Roark grumbles.

"Same, and I'm related to him."

Roark stares at me thoughtfully. *"Set your phone where I can see you, and we'll chat until you fall asleep. Turner and Lennon are asleep after we all went out celebrating with Layla and Velvet Escape. They're officially joining the tour as our headliners, and it's a big deal."*

"Fuck yes it is," I say as I swallow a yawn. My bedroom door is slightly ajar, but my father never comes down here. Turning onto my side, I prop up my phone against a pillow. I miss the warmth of Lennon and the guys, so I burrow in my blankets, imagining that it's them. "I'm really happy for them..."

My eyes grow heavier as Roark chats randomly about things, and I hum at the important parts. I've never fallen asleep talking to someone before, as I've never had anyone that I cared enough to stay on the phone with.

As my breath evens out, and my eyes close for the final time as I drift off to sleep, I swear I hear, *"Hurry back to us, Derek... we all miss you too."*

36

LENNON

We're so late. We managed to all sleep in this morning, and now we're packing up in a hurry. Roark fell asleep on the couch last night talking to Derek and his phone died. Unfortunately, he's also our alarm clock, so no one woke up on time.

My phone rings as I'm grabbing our toiletries, and I answer on the second ring.

"Hello," I answer as I pack my makeup up.

"Is everything okay over there," Jordan asks, amusement in his voice.

"I'm so sorry," I rush out. "We didn't mean to all sleep in. Roark's phone died and he usually turns the alarm on it. We're almost packed up, I swear."

"Lennon, you're fine. I assume you haven't had time for breakfast yet?" he asks.

Is he offering? Because that would be amazing.

"No, not at all. I'm starving, but I don't want anyone to be forced to wait on us." I explain as I grab the rest of the packed items from the bathroom and drop it into my bag.

As I'm closing my luggage up, Turner walks into the bedroom we've all shared.

"I'll take those, Lavender. Man, I'm gonna miss this place," he says wistfully.

"There will be other hotel rooms, Turner," Jordan says sardonically.

Turner snorts. "Good morning, Jordan," he says, rubbing the back of his neck as it turns red. "How much trouble are we in?"

Jordan hums over the phone as if thinking about it and I roll my eyes. *Drama queen.*

"None. I'm going to go pick up some bagel sandwiches at a cafe on the corner I saw, if that's okay with everyone?"

"Aye, please save us from the Lenny monster," Roark calls out as he braces his weight against the doorframe.

"I'm not that bad," I grouse just as my stomach growls and I wince.

"I'll walk a little faster, and call it in. Bye guys!" Jordan hangs up and I shake my head as I laugh in disbelief.

"Alright guys, let's head out," I tell them, making sure I have my phone and the last bag on the bed.

"I'll take that Lenny," Roark offers with a smile.

"Such a gentleman," I grin. "You're all so good to me."

"Ha, that we are, but I don't need you becoming even hungrier. I'm conserving your energy, little Valkyrie," he teases, dancing out of reach as I try to swat him.

"Ugh. I'm truly not that bad," I whine. I am starving though. Dammit all.

Sometimes I hate how well they know me. Turner throws his arm around my waist as he pulls the luggage behind him. Thank goodness for rolling bags. Within minutes we've left behind our room and are on the elevator. Somehow, leaving our room where we really connected for the first time with Derek, makes me miss him more.

"How was he, Roark? Derek, when you talked to him, was he okay?" I ask, looking up at him.

Roark bites his lip as he looks down at me. "There's something about that town that's just fooking evil, baby. Derek's doing the best he can right now, but I'm worried. He had a wicked nightmare before I called him. Apparently he's spending today schmoozing with his father and the town's residents."

I wrinkle my nose. *Sounds super fun. Not.* "His dad's been the mayor of Farrelsville for a long time, and I remember seeing murmurs that he wanted to run for governor in one of the local online newspapers. Sometimes I can't help myself," I admit, "and I look up news of the area."

Roark kisses me hard and smiles at me. "There's nothing wrong with that. You turned your back on that town for good reasons, but it's natural to be curious."

Biting my lip as I look up at him, I ask myself if a quickie is at all possible. He's looking delicious right now.

"No, you can't eat, Roark," Turner chuckles darkly behind me and I shiver, rubbing my legs together. "Interesting, you've made our girl horny right now. We'll have to see how we're going to handle our bus situation until Layla gets her own, or we're all going to suffer from blue balls and bean," he reminds me and I groan.

Please decide to bunk at least at night with Atlas and Mav. A girl needs to get laid.

The bell rings as we arrive at the lobby, and the doors open. Striding out, I grin as I see Jordan is standing outside the hotel, directing people like an air traffic controller. This man has efficiency down.

"Perfect timing!" he exclaims. "We'll have a bus meeting us for Layla, Leo, and Albert once we get to Albuquerque. You don't have a performance until tomorrow night, so we are going to take it easy as we drive over, okay? Do we need to stop for snacks?"

"Yes please," Layla and Leo chorus and I smirk.

"We should be set," Roark rumbles from my side. "I sent a grocery list out last night, so the bus should be stocked."

Mav and Altas nod. "We did the same, so we're well-stocked now too. Layla knows that Roark makes the best food, so maybe we should crash their bus around dinner time, and you can hang out with us part of the drive?" Atlas asks.

"Yep, we haven't had enough time to hang out yet," Mav agrees. "We can have a jam session, watch movies, and most importantly snack."

Atlas meets my eyes over Layla's head and winks at me with a sly smile. Well, looks like my dreams of fucking out my worries are going to be fulfilled today. Hell yes.

I can't do anything for Derek right now, but I can keep myself from making everyone else crazy as I spiral.

"—Lennon?" I blink as I glance over at Jordan. *Damn I missed what he was saying to me.*

"I'm sorry?" I ask, confused and really hungry. *God, this is embarrassing.* I blush as I realize it's really noticeable that I wasn't paying attention. I totally feel like when I was in school and caught daydreaming.

"I just wanted to give you your food before you pass out on me," Jordan teases me, handing me a wrapped bagel with a grin.

Squealing, I leap for it before unwrapping and taking a bite. "Mmm," I sigh happily.

"We averted the gremlin, good looking out, boss," Mav says, squeezing Jordan's shoulder.

Rolling my eyes, I flick him off but he still sees me as Mav starts walking towards his bus. "Back at ya, little Valkyrie. Be sure to eat all your food so you don't get confused later and bite off Roark's cock!"

I inhale as I laugh and end up choking on my own spit and I'm sure some food. Jordan shakes his head and hands me an unopened bottle of water.

"Lennon, that bottle came from the cafe on the corner, so it's safe," Jordan explains and I nod gratefully as I take a sip.

"Oye, why's it gotta be my dick," Roark complains.

"It's pierced, maybe she'll get confused since it's so sparkly?" Atlas jumps in to tease him and Jordan's eyes widen. *God, these men.*

I don't know why he's been super weird about the guys' conversations around sex lately, but this is tame for these boys.

Clearing my throat as I struggle to breathe after my coughing fit, I shrug. "There shall be no Dick McMeals thanks to Jordan. Crisis averted. Thank you for protecting the sanctity of his cock," I grin.

Jordan was in the middle of his own drink of water, which he promptly spits out. Layla cackles as she walks by, rubbing his back. I have no problems wolfing down my breakfast sandwich as she teases him. Ultimate tag team.

"I'm gonna be so corrupted on this tour, Uncle Jordan. Maybe I'll even lose my virginity," she says cheerfully.

"Wait, what?" he whines, and I giggle. Jordan may not survive this tour.

Shrugging, I walk over to our open bus door as Roark and Turner demand Layla dish about how she's made it to twenty years old as a virgin. Smirking, I climb the stairs. They must have forgotten that I was a virgin around then too.

Our driver isn't there as I walk in and I frown. *Aren't we leaving soon? I'd think he'd be ready to go.*

Telling myself I'm just being silly, I keep walking. He could have ended up having to use the restroom. It's going to be a long day of driving.

"Lennon," Turner yells as he runs after me, his arms wrapping around my waist.

"Hey baby," I sigh happily.

"The driver is getting all of our bags and bringing them up. He insisted on helping. Roark's coming up now, we seriously need inside your sweet pussy," he growls as he kisses up my neck.

Well that explains that. Why do I get such an odd feeling around him?

"Someone's a little tightly wound I think," Roark says, smirking.

"I can't help it," I sigh. "I miss him, and it feels wrong for Derek to be away from us."

"You're right, it does," he agrees as we walk deeper into the bus.

Turner flicks open the button on my pants, pushing his hand into the opening.

"Turner," I moan as he sucks and kisses my neck.

"We both miss him, but we have to trust that he knows what he's doing. If he's not on his way back to us tomorrow or doesn't call with an update, we'll make a plan for extraction, okay?" Turner pushes aside my panties, pushing his long tattooed finger along my folds.

I smirk, trying to keep the thread of conversation. "Are we secret agents now," I tease him, gasping as he pushes two fingers into my hole.

"No, but I may have met one a long time ago," he breathes.

Before I can ask him any questions he wraps my hair in his hand and pulls it back to kiss me. That's the last coherent thought that I have for the next few hours as the guys help me keep my mind off of anything, but my next orgasm.

Derek

My eyes threaten to glaze over as I listen to Mrs. Rystek tell me about the state of her zinnias. I've seen at least twelve photos and had to comment about each one.

Focus. Pinching the inside of my elbow hard, the pain helps to clear the cobwebs that are building. I despise small talk, and that's all I've been doing today. My father left me to meet with someone, and told me to walk down Main Street and stop and chat with whoever stopped me.

Fucking kill me. Just stab me with a rusty nail please.

"Derek!" I hear my name called and I turn. I smooth out the frown starting to form when I see it's someone who was on the football team.

Reciting the names in my head of everyone who hurt Len back in high school, I relax further as I realize Orion Kingston was a year older than me and never messed with her.

Turning back to Mrs. Rystek, I give her an apologetic smile. "It's been so nice to chat with you, ma'am, but it appears I'm being called elsewhere," I explain to her, in case she didn't hear him yell.

Nodding, she pats my arms. "You're sweet for entertaining an old woman like me," she says with a smile.

In reality, Mrs. Rystek is a very nice woman, but her children have all moved away and only visit on holidays. I'm short on patience because I've talked to so many people today. Since I'm out of practice with small-town gossip and small-talk, I'm ready to throw in the towel now that it's four in the afternoon.

God, I've been at this all fucking day.

Forcing a smile, I say goodbye to her and cross the street. *Please don't let this conversation be painful.*

"Hey man, what have you been up to these days?" he asks with a smile and I know my prayers will be unanswered.

"I'm in town visiting, but I am on tour with *The Darkest Nights* as their photographer and social media manager," I explain and wait for him to tell me he has no idea who that is.

"Are you freaking serious?! They're amazing, and the new songs are incredible." Orion gushes.

We spend the next few minutes talking about music, how much fun tour life is, and I allow myself to enjoy the conversation. It wasn't nearly as painful as I expected it to be.

"I'm glad you two seem to have connected while walking about town," says a voice that ruins the easy conversation. Grant Williams has a way of doing that, and I can feel my hackles going up.

"Hello, Mr. Williams," Orions says politely, and I turn to face my father.

"Hello yourself," my father says warmly. "Derek, Orion's father and I are working closely together as we begin my campaign for governor. We believe our platforms for family and health will be the key to our and Kentucky's future," he explains.

I watch Orion closely as I congratulate my father on their partnership. Really, my mouth fills with bile and my skin feels clammy. I'm disgusted by their 'work' and wonder how much Orion knows about it. As he colors and shifts his eyes away from me, my heart sinks.

How far does this thing go?

Thankfully the conversation is brief, and then my father and I begin to stroll back towards his car. My dad left it in the diner parking lot since the town is small and he had business to attend to. Swallowing, I decide to see if I can get any more information from him.

"Was your meeting productive?" I ask carefully. If I push too much, things could go south for me.

"It was, I was meeting with Orion's dad. He's very smart, and since they moved away after Orion graduated high school, he's started working with some very powerful people. He's the perfect ally. You were a great help today, Derek, and I know you didn't want to come back this week," my father says. *No shit.*

"I didn't. It was nice to catch up with everyone though," I lie.

My father snorts and rolls his eyes. "Don't bullshit a bullshitter, my boy. I know you dislike people on a good day, but they appreciated your efforts, and now they'll stop asking to see you for a bit. You're free to go tomorrow." He frowns, as if doesn't want to let me go, but has no choice. "I'll arrange for a short visit with your mother as well within the next few weeks. Please understand that she's been heavily sedated for her own protection, so doctors have to gradually bring her out so you'll be able to talk to her. I'd hate for her to be a vegetable."

I've never wanted to kill my father more than right now. I feel flushed with anger, but I button it up tight. My mask is already slipping, and I need to keep it together for just a little longer.

"I understand," I murmur. I hope that if I keep my voice low enough that it'll hide the beginnings of a growl that's setting in. "Just let me know the date and time, and I'll make it happen."

"This is your best asset and greatest downfall," my sperm donor laughs. I'm having a hard time calling him my father at the moment. "You'll drop everything for the people you care about, and it's exploitable. It's a good thing you only care about one person in your miserable life, which is why I've kept her alive."

My father can never know about Lennon, Roark, and Turner. If I had any doubts before, they've disappeared with those words. I am not living in the closet for fear of what he'll do to me, but what he would do to *them.*

"I'm glad we understand each other now, Derek," he says, patting my back roughly before sliding into the front seat of his car.

I was so engrossed in our conversation that I hadn't realized we were back at the diner.

I really need to get out of this damn town. I wonder if I can leave tonight and catch a red eye.

Clenching and then releasing my fists, I walk around the car to get into the passenger seat and negotiate my release.

Grant is scrolling through his phone absently as I strap into my seat.

"You really are the best that label has, aren't you," he muses as he watches his phone.

"I know their fans have been enjoying my content," I hedge. "Why do you ask?"

"You've been gone about twenty-four hours, and nothing of value has been posted on their feeds for that band. You didn't leave them any material in your absence?"

This could go one of two ways...

"Yes, I left them completed material, but it takes a lot of time to post the right material to different platforms. I usually stream live from the audience as well, and without me, they don't have anyone to fill that position," I explain.

Nodding, he sighs. "You should go now, then. I don't want their inability to fill your shoes to reflect badly on you. I want you to pack up and get the next flight to where they are performing next, is that understood?"

I thank every benevolent God in existence for this gift.

"I absolutely understand, thank you, Sir," I murmur. I hate seeming so subservient to him, but until I know where my mother is and how to get her out safely, my father is a menace.

The drive home is silent, and I'm grateful for this too. I won't take a deep breath of relief until this damn town is in my rear view mirror though.

I struggle to take measured steps when we arrive, even though I want to run into the house and pack my shit. This house is one of literal nightmares, and I'll still wake up and find that I'm inside of one.

My steps take me in the house, down the stairs, and into the basement. My breath starts to come out harsher, not because of the exertion of going downstairs, but the stress. I can't relax yet.

Throwing my clothes into the bag, I check the bathroom to make sure I have everything. Zipping it up, I blow out a breath.

"Fuck it, if I leave anything, I'll just replace it," I mutter, turning to leave.

Calm your shit down.

As if it's been ingrained in me, because it has, I stop in my tracks and close my eyes.

In one... two... three. Out... one... two... three.

My heart rate slows, my amenable, respectful mask is firmly in place. The last thing I need is for something to fuck up my leaving here. I don't want to waste anymore time, or have him come to see what's taking me so long.

My father prides efficiency, and being able to pack in minutes is something he taught me early on. Keeping my things where I'll remember where they are, taking pride in my appearance, and being neat. While these are probably important things, being taught them at the age of five was a little excessive.

Needless to say, I was never allowed to make a mistake...

The beatings for it started later in my childhood than the lessons.

Shaking my head, I will my feet to keep an even pace as I move. Once on the main floor, I look around to see where my father is.

Does he expect me to say goodbye?

His office door is shut and I shrug. *Out of sight, out of mind.* Out the front door is my goal, and no one is stopping me, so I go for it. Opening the door, I walk out, quietly close it behind me, and I don't stop until I'm in my car. Even steps, measured breaths, it's a carefully choreographed dance. I feel a heavy stare bearing into my back, but I refuse to look over my shoulder.

I still can't relax. I need to make sure the car will turn over.

It may seem pessimistic, but this trip out here has been a mindfuck for me. Hand slightly shaking, I push the button, teeth clenched. The car turns on and I almost black out from the stress.

Bye bitches.

I throw the car in reverse, backing out of the driveway, and forcing myself to drive slowly. The last damn thing I need is to be pulled over.

Am I allowed to make a call while driving in this state?

Deciding to risk it, I call Lennon. I need to know everyone is okay. Logically, I know my father doesn't know about my budding relationship with them, but I'm feeling really paranoid. The stress is giving me a headache, and I just need to hear her voice.

"*Hello,*" I hear on the other line and I blow out a breath.

I've fucking missed her voice. I revel in just that single word, until she sounds annoyed.

"*Derek, are you okay?*" she asks.

"Yeah, baby, I'm doing a hell of a lot better now that I'm

talking to you," I tell her, taking my first full breath since I left the house. "I'm driving now, and I don't even care where I'm driving to, as long as it's the fuck out of here."

"*I was so worried,*" she sighs. "*We're headed to Albuquerque now, so we'll get Jordan to get you a plane ticket there.*"

"I could do it myself, but that man is magical when it comes to scheduling and booking things." I remember his skill with the computer and shake my head.

Damn, there's so much I need to tell her, and I know Jordan said soon...

When is it *soon*? I sound like a child asking, 'is it time yet', but it's hard to help myself.

"*I'll get it sorted. I can't wait to see you. I don't mean to sound needy...*"

"If you are, I am. I will call myself out every day of the week for you. I miss the hell out of the three of you," I confess.

"*Who's that, Lenny?*" Roark rumbles and I smile.

"Hey Roark," I murmur. The affection is clear in my voice, but I really can't wait to see them all again.

"*Derek! Are we rescuing you or are you on your way home?*" he asks, amusement masking his worry.

"I just left, and I'm headed towards the airport. It's gonna be a long fucking trip, but I didn't want to spend anymore time in that damned house. I was half worried something would stop me from leaving. I have a lot to tell you all..." I trail off, because my story feels so far-fetched. *How do you explain that your father is fucking evil?*

"*Tell us when you can, we just can't wait to see you,*" Roark says.

"*We're keeping Lennon well-fucked in the meantime,*" Turner pops in and I laugh in surprise.

"*I get grumpy when I'm upset, and when I'm worried, I sometimes spiral,*" Lennon says, dejectedly.

"I can understand that completely. I'm sorry I worried you, I just couldn't get out of this trip."

"Don't be sorry, I know you had to go back. Is your mother okay?" Lennon asks.

"She's... I don't know. My father is hiding her away for being what he considers to be a nuisance. She wanted a divorce, and he basically drugged her. I don't understand how this is real life right now," I groan.

"Your father has always liked control," Lennon snarls. *"I remember the black eyes you passed off as football injuries. Except they weren't from football at all, were they?"*

"No, Len, they weren't. My sperm donor's a dick, and I can't even claim him as my father right now. I'm so disgusted and disappointed in him."

Grant Williams was never the ideal father, but he's really lowered the bar when it comes to being a good fucking human.

"You're not your father in any shape or form," Turner growls. *"I thank God for that, because under your tough exterior, is a really good man."*

Blinking rapidly, I nod, even though they can't see me. "I think I really needed to hear that," I tell them.

"We'll tell you this as many times as you need to hear it, Derek. Now, please concentrate on driving and I'll have Jordan email your new flight itinerary."

I smile genuinely for the first time in over twenty-four hours. "You're perfect, Len. Thank you for the help."

I could do it myself, but I've never been able to lean on someone else, and I have to say that I'm enjoying the experience.

We chorus our goodbyes, and I hang up the phone. Glancing at my speedometer, I slow even further as I cruise through the town. I adopt an easy smile as I wave goodbye to people as I pass. Fuck, I will keep this pasted smile on the whole way if it means I get back to the tour faster.

It feels as if I'm crawling along as I drive, but I know it's my anxiety. As soon as the town is in my rear view mirror, I turn on some music and force myself to relax.

PLEASE LET *it be smooth sailing back. I deserve some good luck today.*

37

TURNER

Thursday, the following day, three in the morning

DEREK TOOK AN OVERNIGHT FLIGHT, but he still won't be here for hours. Getting back into our routine on the bus wasn't difficult, even with more people on tour. We had a family dinner last night, and having *Velvet Escape* with us was amazing. Lennon even made sure to invite Jordan.

He's been staring at her more often, and I'm unsure why. It's almost wistful. I don't like it, not because Jordan would ever be inappropriate to Lennon, but I feel like I'm missing something.

I hate being out of the loop.

I need to corner him and ask him why he's being odd. Lennon hasn't noticed for the most part, and she's this incredible light. Layla is coming out of her shell just by being around her, and I am excited to see how she transforms.

It's obvious to me that the men in Velvet Escape *keep her sheltered.*

"You're thinking so loudly I can hear you from here," Roark mutters sleepily.

He can always tell when I'm unsettled.

"I'm just thinking, and I am going to be annoying. I don't care," I mutter with a sigh. "I am excited for Derek to get his perky ass back here, and to hear how his trip went. His father is obviously a bastard, but holding Derek's mom over his head is just a shithead power move."

"You're right," he murmurs, tugging me away from Lennon and into his arms. "I love that you care, baby. We went from plotting where to hide his body to missing him when he's gone. Derek's important to us, and I don't see this changing. He fits."

I listen to Ror's heartbeat, rubbing his pec. "He does fit. Derek's broken, but mending. I see how he speaks to Lennon, how he holds her as if she's precious. Lennon doesn't need it, but it's nice to know someone adores you like that, you know?" I ask.

"Mmhmm," Roark rumbles. "He told me I sometimes treat him too carefully, but I reminded him that we're still getting to know each other. I don't know when to push or pull back, so I'm going to pace myself."

"I'm glad you told him that. I know it drives Lennon crazy, but with their history, it's normal for Derek to feel the need to be sure she consents. We are feeling each other out, and you said he had a nightmare where he was tied to his own bed. Fuck, as a teen that has to be scary, and to relive it again... I don't hit women, but I want to punish the woman who stole his ability to trust," I growl.

"I have a feeling there's more to it," Roark says. I look up into his beautiful eyes, only to find that they're pinched.

"Derek is holding back part of his nightmare and past, and it's not my place to push—"

"...He'll come to us when he's ready," I grumble. Have I mentioned how much I hate waiting? I'll do it because it's what he needs, but damn do I want to help him, heal him, and fuck him back together.

"You're thinking about something naughty," Roark chuckles, his large hand wrapping around my neck.

"Maybe," I rasp. "Why don't you make me tell you?"

Flipping us, he kisses me as he grinds his cock into mine. "Were you thinking about Derek," Roark teases me as he sucks on my neck.

My back bows as I moan, but I can't go very far when he's pinning me. "Yes," I gasp, wanting to know what he thinks of that.

"You were thinking of his tight ass weren't you," Roark growls and the sound makes me shiver in anticipation.

"Yeah, I wish he was here already so I could show him how much I missed him, and how important he already is to us. I want to fuck his tight little hole as he whimpers—" I grunt as Roark roughly shoves my boxers down and my cock bobs up.

"He really loves his tight little ass filled by you," he growls as he shucks off his own boxers.

"The noises he makes are delicious," I agree with a happy sigh.

Roark grabs lube off the nightstand and grins as he kisses me.

"Get on your hands and knees for me, baby," he grunts as he leans back so I'll have room to move.

I'm down for whatever Roark has planned, always. Licking my lip, my piercing makes me shiver in anticipation. I need to get out of my head too, my thoughts are racing a mile a minute right now, and time with Roark will help.

Scrambling, I get into position, looking over my shoulder. Roark kisses my shoulder as he massages lube into my needy hole. Moaning, my eyes close as he pushes two fingers deep inside of me. The feeling of the cold lube and sting of his fingers entering me help to ground me in the present.

"Fuck, you're gonna kill me," I gasp. His fingers are thick, and my nerve endings are tingling as he works me over. My breath quickens as my head drops to the mattress as I force myself to accept everything that he's giving me.

"Deep breath for me, baby boy," he rumbles, and I shiver in anticipation as I inhale deeply for him. "Such a good pet," he whispers, and I whimper as I feel a third thick digit enter my ass.

"So full, Ror," I moan.

Roark's in control and not holding back as he rocks his fingers to hit my prostrate. *I don't know how, but he knows my body now as if it's his own.*

Every stroke is perfection, and I find myself pushing into his tender ministrations. Roark slowly removes his fingers, and I groan.

"Don't stop," I complain and Roark spanks my ass for being a whiny brat.

"Give me your wrists," he murmurs, and I thrust them up to him without a second thought. My face has been pushed into the mattress, so I don't notice when he grabs a coil of soft rope. Quickly and efficiently, he creates cuffs from the soft binding for me to slip my hands into. Before I know it, Roark tightens them and secures my now bound wrists to the hook on the headboard.

Grabbing my thighs, he pulls them back so I'm off balance. My wrists are above my head, keeping the top of my body suspended, while my ass is perfectly presented to my love.

"Such a perfect little hole," Roark praises, and my dick

jumps. Fuck, his mouth is something else. "I can't wait to fill you so full with my cum, I'll have to wake up Lennon to clean up my cream. Or," he muses as he spanks my ass hard enough to rock me forward, "maybe I'll plug you so you have to sleep in it. So many delicious options."

I'm about to beg him to fuck me when he's pushing into me. Each piercing on his cock sparkes my nerve endings. It feels so fucking good.

"Fuck yeah, Ror, no more teasing," I groan.

"No more teasing," he promises. "Now you're gonna take my fat cock till I fill you like a cream donut, aren't you?"

Fuck, this man's mouth.

Roark's powerful thrusts force my hips to the mattress, and the friction of the sheets bow my body as I mewl.

"Fuck, it feels too good. I'm not going to last," I cry out as he fucks me. The soft sheets are providing delicious torture as it glides against my dick. I want to grind harder on them, but can't because Roark is in charge of my movements as he fucks me.

"Aye, that's good. Make a goddamn mess and I'll make you lick it up like a good little cum slut," Roark says, his voice strained as he wraps an arm under me. His other hand is holding tightly to my side as his hips piston and swivel.

"Roark," I gasp. I'm unsure if I'm begging or praying for help as he fucks me into the mattress.

He's filling up every inch of me, and it always feels like the first time. The stretch is delicious and unbearable, and I know I'll feel empty when he's no longer filling me. Roark's hand glides down my body until he grabs my balls. I'm searching for more friction, sweat starting to build. I whine as he rolls my balls tightly, and the pain feels amazing.

"More, just like that," I gasp as he squeezes and plays. The edge of pain will allow me to last just a little longer but it feels so damn good.

"My good little pain slut," Roark grunts as his grabs my cock, jerking it roughly as he fucks me.

My eyes roll as I get the perfect amount of friction and pain, and Roark is pounding perfectly into my ass. I feel a tingling at the base of my spine begin to build, and I know I'm going to come. Neither of us are bothering to be quiet, and I know Lennon is probably enjoying the view of me tied up and properly fucked. There's always the edge of playfulness, violence, and pain between Roark and I.

We both crave it.

I shudder as he squeezes and strokes my cock once more before I come.

"Good fucking boy, so gorgeous and messy," Roark growls before he pulls almost all the way out before slamming into me twice more. I cry out because it feels so damn good before he empties inside of me..

The rough sounds of our breath fills the room as our chests saw.

"Our boy is a bit messy isn't he?"

Roark and I look over at Lennon who is grinning at us, her fingers deep in her pretty little cunt.

"He is," Roark says with a grin. "Wanna come clean him up?"

Roark unhooks my hands before flipping me onto my back, replacing them back above my head. I gasp as I land, grinning over at Lennon.

"Clean him up, greedy girl," Roark chuckles.

Grinning, Lennon crawls over to me. You could say this is definitely keeping my mind off things for a while.

Derek

It's been a long damn day already, and it's barely ten in the morning. I spent all night either driving or at the airport waiting for my flight. Thank God for Jordan because he had my itinerary emailed to me by the time I arrived at the airport. Dragging my hand over my face, I can say it's worth it, even if I am exhausted.

I feel relieved to be back in the same city as the tour again. I didn't realize how attached I already am to this job, Lennon, and the boys until I had to leave. I'm finally in a rideshare headed to the stadium in Albuquerque. I just wanted to get back, even if Lennon and the guys are still resting.

I have so much work to catch up on, and keep my mind occupied with. I just want to ignore this shit show that is my life. Secrets may as well be my middle name right now, because I feel like an asshole filled with them. My eyes feel gritty like sandpaper because I don't sleep well on planes, and I wish I'd had the forethought to grab some shut eye while I was in the airport.

My phone buzzes in my pocket and I tense. I don't want to deal with my father's bullshit, but there's really no reason that he'd call me right now. Digging it out from my pants pocket, I glance at the phone. It's Jordan.

Frowning, I answer it. "Hey Jordan, I'm almost to the stadium where they're playing tonight, is everything okay?"

"Yes, everything is good on this front. I was actually just checking on how you're doing. Your trip concluded sooner than expected?" Jordan asks.

I never expected the old man to just call me to check on me. *Weird.* However, it's also not, because that's just who he is.

"Thank God for that, but yes I finished sooner than expected. I actually persuaded my father to release me from my obligations earlier so I could get the hell out of there," I confess. "I hate that fucking town, and my father with a passion. I'm convinced both are evil."

"Huh. This isn't the normal feelings a son has after seeing his dad, Derek," Jordan muses. *"Are things really that bad right now? How's your mom?"*

God, why does he have to give a shit.

"Jordan, I can't really talk about it right now," I sigh. "Let's just say that he's involved in a lot of shady shit and my mom's alone and confused in a mental institution. Mom wanted a divorce, and his response was to neutralize her."

I'm not worried about our driver listening to our conversation because he has a pair of AirPods in and is humming to the music. Is it safe? No. But I just need to make it in one piece.

"Derek," Jordan sighs. *"You're the keeper of so many secrets, don't you think you should confide in someone? I feel bad now that I sent you into hell earlier than you had planned with new secrets."*

Wrinkling my nose, I lean back into my seat. "Speaking of those secrets, Jordan, I need to tell her. 'Soon' is going to have to be after their performance. It's eating at me. Len is so damn strong, she'll be able to handle this, and she'll be gaining so many amazing things from this. You and Layla for example. Her mother was a bitch that never deserved to be one, but it's the only good thing she's ever done."

I can hear Jordan grinding his teeth and he groans. *"You're right. I want to tell her with you, but if for some reason I'm caught up in something, you can tell her. Let's hope today goes smoothly otherwise."*

A shiver runs down my spine and I crack my neck. Fuck, I hope he hasn't just jinxed us.

"Absolutely, Sir. I want to get work done when I get there. It appears the band's socials have been a little quiet while I've been gone, and I want to set up some official *Music Hoarde* socials for *Velvet Escape...*" I trail off as I realize I'm getting ahead of myself. "Unless you already have someone working on their stuff, or they're planning on working on their own? Either way, it's totally fine—"

"*Derek,*" Jordan interrupts me with a laugh. "*I don't think we could hire anyone better for the job, so it's all yours. I'll increase your salary accordingly too. Layla, Leo, and Albert have told me they despise social media and talking about themselves, so I'm sure they'll be happy to hand it over to you.*"

Relaxing, I nod before I realize that he can't see me. *I'm an idiot and fucking tired.* "Thanks, Jordan. It looks like I'll be there soon."

"*You sound like you're about to crash. Why don't you take a nap on the roadies' bus? No one will care,*" Jordan says. "*You still have a bunk there anyway.*"

Biting my lip, I realize he probably knows about my relationship with Lennon, if not also the guys. Rolling my eyes, I decide if he isn't going to fire me over it, that it's fine. He won't blab to the press about it and it won't get back to father if Jordan knows.

"Yeah, that may not be a bad idea. I'm dead on my feet," I agree.

"*Take it easy today, get some work done, and then come have dinner with us all. Roark said he'd make it. I don't know how he cooks on that tiny stove, but he makes it work,*" he chuckles.

"That all sounds amazing. I'm gonna go crash then and I'll meet up with you all after."

We hang up, and ten minutes later, we're entering the stadium. Showing my badge, the security guard waves us through. Opening the door, I push myself to stand. Weaving slightly, I close my eyes to center myself. A nap is exactly what

I need. My body is starting to rebel after the long night and morning.

Grabbing my bag, I thank the driver. I already paid the fare from my app, and I am beyond done with today. Walking to the roadie bus, I swear I hear my name. Looking over my shoulder, I can't see anyone from the glare of the sun. It's sweltering here too, and I shuck off my jacket.

Shrugging, I climb the stairs and walk to the bunk I've been using since I started working here. I need sleep, to get some work done, and then some snuggles from my people. As long as I'm near them, I'm happy. As my eyes close, I think about how much my life has changed in the last couple of weeks, and how grateful I am to have them.

Lennon

Smiling, I snuggle into Turner's arms as Roark cooks dinner for us all. I love that we are instituting "Family Dinner" now. Turner and Roark are no longer participating in their pre-show rituals, instead preferring to hang out with me. After being drugged in Seattle, I'm still a little leery about being alone lately.

Who knows what they wanted from me? Or why I was the only one drugged?

"Lavender, what are you thinking about," Turner asks, turning my head to kiss my lips.

Sighing, I wrinkle my nose. "I was thinking about how we never found out who drugged me or why. I don't want to borrow trouble either, but—"

"You're wondering why they haven't tried again?" Turner asks.

"Yeah," I say gratefully. I'm so glad he just knew what I meant.

"I've thought about that too," Roark murmurs as he checks on his roast chicken. The oven is actually the perfect size for him, even though he dwarfs our kitchen. "They haven't tried anything, but you're always with someone now, too. I want to circle the wagons, so to speak. That's why I'm doing family dinner, and why Turner and I aren't leaving you anymore. We are perfectly fine using you as our ritual to find our center," he teases me.

They may have been fucking my center most of the day...

Roark chuckles at the flush of my face, leaning against the counter to watch me.

"I think as you stay close to us, it'll be okay," he says, slowly sobering. "And we'll try to figure out what's going on as well. You're important to us, and our priority."

Nodding, I sigh. "I love you guys," I murmur.

"I love you most," the guys chorus and I snort in amusement.

"Remember when you said you needed a ring," Roark asks and my eyes narrow.

"I said no such thing," I begin and Turner chuckles into my hair.

"Aye, you didn't, but I saw something when I ran out for a snack for us the day before yesterday," Roark says with a grin. "It's just so you. I know you don't need anything fancy, but it's just very us."

My heart melts a little because he knows that. "Okay, but Derek got a little weird when we were talking about the engagement. I don't want him to feel uncomfortable," I explain and Roark nods with a smile.

He covers the space between us in two steps and kisses me. Turner picks me up and puts me in his lap, and I can feel his hard length against my ass. Writhing, I whimper. Skirting up the inside of my thigh, Roark palms my panty clad pussy underneath my dress.

"Can I still show it to you," he breathes against my lips.

"If he wants to show you his thick, pierced cock, I'm in," says a snarky voice and I glance over and grin when I see Derek.

"The driver let me up, is that okay?" he asks, shifting on his feet.

"Yes!" I scramble up, my eyes drinking him in. Derek looks tired. "Are you okay? We missed you..."

He smiles and nods, opening his arms to me. Thank God. Running for him, I leap into his arms. He catches me with a grin and I wind my legs around his waist.

"It's good to see you, little spider monkey," Derek grins against my throat.

"She is a little spider monkey," Turner says with a smirk as he stands up. "We were worried, and we did miss you. Are you okay?"

Derek's hands roam along my skin as if to convince himself he's really with us. Inhaling deeply, I know he's breathing me in. "I don't think I can use that word for what I'm feeling. I have a lot to tell you after your show tonight, none of which is good news. Right now, I'm just happy to be back. I was really worried my father wouldn't let me go, and I just felt really odd the entire time I was home. Len, my dad is fucking unhinged," he tells me as he wraps his arms around me tighter and squeezes.

Derek reminds me of a man who's been off to war instead of going to see his father, and I wonder what kind of shit his dad is into. Frowning, I squeeze him back.

"Did you catch a nap at all," Roark asks. Derek nods and I lean back slightly so I can see his face.

Rubbing the line on his forehead, I purse my lips. "What put this here?" I ask.

"A lot," he sighs unhappily. "At the moment, it's that there's not a lot more hugging happening."

Roark rolls his eyes. "Fucking brat," he mutters as Derek laughs.

If he can brat to us, then he's moderately okay. Roark and Turner move in and I'm engulfed in their arms with Derek. Humming happily, I lay my head on his shoulder.

"I'm still wondering if Roark was going to show you his dick or not." Derek mumbles and I snicker.

Roark grabs his hair and tugs his head back. "It sounds like your bratty mouth needs to be filled with my cock instead, to remind you what it looks like after so long," he teases.

Derek's eyes heat, the hands that are now on my ass, clenching in need. I whimper, unable to move. Roark kisses him, their tongues dueling together.

Turner pushes my panties to the side, sliding through my wet folds. Roark and Derek break away as I moan.

"You're so fucking beautiful, Len," he says, drinking me in.

I have a feeling that whatever happened in Farrelsville, Kentucky, made Derek appreciate the things in his life a lot more.

"I want the three of you," he says, greedily drinking me in as Turner pushes two, long fingers into my pussy. "That's it, beautiful, he's gonna take good care of our girl, isn't he?" My head drops back onto Turner's shoulder as I writhe.

I don't think he's ever claimed me with them before. If he has... it just feels so much more potent now as I'm surrounded by the three of them.

Roark opens the buttons of my dress, pulling on my bra so they'll spill out.

"I'm like a rabid dog once I latch onto something," Derek

warns. I'm not following the conversation as he sucks on my nipple.

Turner circles my clit and I shudder. Roark walks behind Derek, flicking open the button of his pants.

"You really want to know what I wanted to give our little Valkyrie," Roark teases as he pulls down his zipper. Pushing his tight jeans down his hips just enough so his cock bobs out, Roark's large hand circling it perfectly. Derek hisses and Roark just kisses and nips down his throat, lips twisted in amusement.

"God, do I get to come if I push for this," Derek groans.

Poor Derek. Even in my nerve fueled mind, I know the answer to that.

"Fuck around and find out," Roark says, squeezing the base of his cock.

Turner pulls me back just a little so I can watch Roark torture Derek.

"Fuck... fuck... fuck," Derek groans.

Roark slowly moves his hand up Derek's cock to drag it through his weeping slit.

"I want you in my mouth while Lennon rides your face and Turner fucks Lenny's tight pussy, Derek," Roark rasps with need. "You can suck on his balls while you eat her out, because you're so fucking good at that."

Whimpering, his eyes roll, and Derek still struggles to follow a conversation. Turner grins pulling me away completely to place my feet on the ground. I groan annoyed as his fingers slip away to pull my dress over my head and rip my panties off me. *Damn, I kind of liked that pair.*

"I'll order you more," Turner growls, pushing me over the sofa arm so my ass is high in the air. Derek gets an eye full as Turner eats my pussy like his last damn meal.

I don't know how long we have before people start coming

over, but god this feels too good to stop. "God, yes... more!" I demand as his piercing flicks at my needy nub.

"Fuck they look so good," Derek groans.

Pushing my hair out my face, I watch as Derek writhes in Ror's arms. I think at this point he's only holding out to be a brat.

"What about you," Derek gasps brokenly as Roark cups his balls and starts rolling and tugging at them with his other hand.

"What about me, baby," Roark chuckles, kissing him and nipping at his lips.

Turner pumps his fingers inside of me and hits my G spot at this angle and I keen.

"Fuck, Len you're so fucking beautiful," Derek sighs. "You should get to come too, Roark. So what about you? Who gets to make you come?"

Turner chuckles as he realizes why Derek was so worried. "Roark never has a problem getting off, Derek. One time won't hurt him..."

He noisily slurps at my juices and I gasp. "Turner, fuck I'm so close. God, I want your cock so bad."

"Come for me baby, get Derek to stop overthinking everything, and you'll get my cock."

"Derek," I breathe as Turner lazily fucks me with his fingers, twisting them deep inside of me. My toes start to curl and I whine. "Please, please... if you shut up and let me have Turner's cock, I'm sure Roark will fuck you after the show."

"Really?" There's so much surprise and hope, the three of us laugh in some way. I didn't know for sure until now that this is what he'd been wanting.

"Aye, you can have my cock tonight. We have another thirty-five minutes of cooking time before people start showing up, so this is gonna be quick," Roark explains, never stopping his rhythm on Derek's cock. "You deserve for the first time I fuck you to be right and proper and without haste, okay?"

I moan because it's hot and romantic and...Turner groans as I gush on his fingers and I shudder.

"Fuck yes. I think Lavender thinks that's a great idea," Turner chuckles as he sucks on his fingers.

All I can do is twitch, still in the throes of my fantasies and orgasm.

"I'm in," Derek says, removing his shirt and toeing off his shoes.

"Thank fuck," Roark says with a grin. He stays dressed as Derek strips.

Derek carefully gathers me in his arms, kissing me. Sighing happily as he showers me with love, I straddle him, grinding on him as I kiss him.

"Len," he groans as I kiss down his neck.

"Yessss?"

"I need you to sit on my face and drown me in your greedy wet pussy, or I'm not gonna last, baby," he growls.

"Mmm. There he is," Roark teases with a smile.

Laying on the couch, Derek rotates me so I'm facing his feet before pulling me onto his face. I give an unladylike screech as he moves me. Turner pulls my hair, painting my lips with his precum with a smile.

"So pretty when you wear me," he says with a smile.

Moving behind me Turner pushes me slightly forward before kneeling behind me on the couch. From my position, I can look down and watch as Turner drags his dick through my wet folds. Derek sucks along the bottom of his cock and Turner moans, dropping his head back.

"Fuck, you're gonna be so much fun," he moans.

Derek meets my eyes and smirks before licking my clit, teasing me until I'm gasping. Derek shouts and I look up, only to find Roark swallowing him down whole. Sucking, licking, Derek is Roark's personal dessert of choice. Turner slides into my pussy pushing me forward and I cry out. Derek grabs me around the waist so I'm tightly bound to him... and the suction he begins on my clit.

"Oh fuck," I scream, shuddering as Turner pounds into me.

"She's fucking strangling my dick," he groans. "You're so tight, so damn wet, you're my fucking dream come true, Lennon."

Derek groans against me and my vision whitens out along the edges. Whimpering, my nerve endings are overloaded, and it feels so damn good. Blinking, I watch as Roark sucks Derek's dick, and grin as Derek grabs his hair and pulls him down to his base. Derek fucks his face and I mewl, clenching down on Turner.

Turner's hands squeeze tightly on my hips as he owns my pussy. I am wrecked by these men and I never want to be put back together again. Shuddering, I give in, squirting all over Derek's face as he moans.

Collapsing onto Derek's chest, I have front row seats as Roark swallows him down as he comes.

"Lavender, fuck. I'm gonna come," Turner gasps, and I can feel his cock twitch as he explodes and I moan, shivering as I clamp down on him again. I rarely come twice in such a short time, but I'm so turned on, I'm helpless to the sensations overwhelming me.

"Argh," I gasp as my body twitches.

Turner carefully pulls out and I whimper. "Shh, I've got you," he says as he picks me up into his arms. "Roark, how much time do we have?"

Ror glances at the clock with a wry smile. "Ten minutes. I'll air out the bus, you all clean up."

Derek grabs his clothes, dressing. "God, I have to wash my face," he laughs. "As much as I'd rather not..."

As he trails off, Derek stares at me heatedly and I bite my lip.

"You need to shower, beautiful," Turner laughs, changing direction to the bathroom.

I take the quickest shower ever, keeping my hair dry. Slipping out, Derek kisses me as I pass him and I moan.

"To be continued, beautiful," he growls, letting me go to wash his face.

I throw on leggings, an off the shoulder shirt and throw my hair into a messy bun. I'll have time to get ready for our performance after dinner, so I'm not worried. Walking back into our kitchenette, I sniff quickly, relaxing when I find that it doesn't smell like sex. Instead, the windows are open and a dry breeze blows through.

It feels really nice after how cold Los Angeles was recently.

"Is everyone dressed," Mav yells, as he climbs onto the bus.

I roll my eyes and hug him as he grins. "We are now," I giggle and he rolls his eyes.

"I had a feeling," he teases me.

Soon the bus is filled, and it's really nice to sit down to dinner with people that I care about. I've always had Mav, Roark, Atlas, and Turner... but our little family is growing, and it feels amazing.

38

LENNON

The Velvet Escape performed tonight as they officially opened as our headliner, and now it's time for us to play.

"Lenny, I grabbed some gummy bears from your dressing room, need any before we go on stage?" Roark pops one in his mouth and I grin.

"Gimmie!" I open my mouth and he pops a few in. Humming happily, I chew with a smile.

"Uh oh, I knew you were missing something," Atlas teases me and I roll my eyes.

"We all have our small indulgences, and mine is sugar."

"Are we ready, everyone," Jordan asks with a smirk, watching as Layla and the guys wave to the audience as they walk off stage.

Derek is in the audience, doing his thing, and I know he caught *Velvet Escape* as they played. Layla was on fucking fire tonight. I give her a huge hug as she walks off stage.

"You were so fucking good tonight," I tell her with a huge smile.

"God, is that how it feels every night? It feels like I could fly," she laughs. "I've played other nights for you, but tonight feels different."

"It looked even better," Turner grins as the lights are turned down. "Lennon, grab my hand, beautiful."

"See you later," I tell the band with a smile as I step forward to grab Turner's hand. I swear it's even darker at this venue than usual. Turner must agree, because his free hand wraps around my waist. Walking confidently, he walks me out onto the stage. The audience screams as they see movement, even if they can't see us yet. I grin, excited to sing tonight.

Turner drops me off in front of my mic, kissing my forehead. "Kill it, gorgeous," he whispers before he's gone.

I love his extra touches, how careful he is with me, and how protective. It makes me know exactly what song I'll start with, too. This song is about how harsh the reality of love can be, and when to push back when it's worth it.

"How are we doing tonight, Albuquerque!" I yell out. "This is actually the first time we are performing here, and I have to say it's nice to not be cold tonight. I want to start the night off by singing *The Lost One*. Let's do it!"

I look over at Turner and he grins, grabbing a guitar and bringing it to me. This is a duet, and one we wrote together last year.

"*WHAT'S it like when opposites attract?*
How do you go on when every step takes you back?
Love isn't a fairytale, and can tell you pretty lies...
Hidden disguises beneath a blue sky.
I thought you were perfect, but that wasn't the case.
So now it's time to put you in your place.

. . .

TURNER and I play a battle together, and the words push and pull. This is a song that I love to play live, because it's playful at times, and intense at others. Mav, Atlas, and Roark sound like they are choosing sides as they play and it's reminiscent of a friends group supporting the couple in hard times.

The show moves at a whirlwind, and there's just something about this venue that makes everything... better. Layla wasn't wrong when she said tonight felt different.

Smiling, we say goodnight to the audience, then walk off stage. Roark wraps his arm around my waist, kissing me from behind. My back bows in my black corset and skirt.

"You're gonna pop out of that outfit, Little Valkyrie," Mav chuckles.

Standing upright, I glance down and adjust myself. *Oops.* That was close.

"We have our VIP meet and greet in a half an hour, guys," Jordan says with a smile. *He's so great at keeping us in check.*

"Perfect," I smile, bouncing on the balls of my feet. "I need more gummy bears, so I'm going to pop into my dressing room."

"I'll walk you, love," Roark murmurs.

"I'll come with you," Derek says quickly. "I want to talk to you first before you start making the rounds with your fans."

"Derek..." Jordan says, almost in warning. Derek shakes his head at him and Jordan sighs. *What in the world?* Now I'm curious as to what's going on. "Yeah, okay," Jordan mutters with a sigh. "Don't be too long."

Derek nods, and we walk ahead. "Everything okay?" I ask as I step into the room.

I wrinkle my nose as the sting of magnolias fills my nose. Someone I once knew loved the scent, but it's not my favorite. Too many memories, good and bad surround it. Shrugging, I head to the jar of gummy bears that's placed in every dressing room that I play.

Pulling a few out, I pop one in my mouth as Roark follows me in.

"Who bathed in magnolias," Roark chuckles as he walks into the room.

"Thank God it's not just me who smells it this time," Derek mutters and I wonder what he meant by that.

"No man, you're not hallucinating," Roark teases. "Lenny, did you change your body wash or something?"

Derek pulls me into his arms, running his nose up my neck and I moan softly.

"You smell like lavender and vanilla," Derek growls. "It's definitely not you. I wonder if it's one of the managers on the tour."

Derek runs his hands up my legs, stopping when his hand touches the knife strapped to my upper thigh. I don't *have* to wear it when I'm surrounded by my guys, but we still haven't figured out who tried to drug me, and I don't want to take any chances. I don't comment as he rubs the leather of the holster absently.

Roark shrugs and I pop another gummy in my mouth and chew thoughtfully. Somehow, these taste even better than the ones I had earlier. It's weird, because Roark came in here for the candy he brought me earlier.

"It's possible. Jordan said someone new would be joining the tour today as his assistant. She apparently loves our music, and is excited to start. I haven't seen her yet though," I explain with a shrug.

I'm sure I'll be introduced eventually.

Derek's lips twist in thought and I turn to kiss him. Moaning, he kisses me harder.

"Y'all are adorable, but we have to get going soon," Roark chuckles.

Derek sighs, nodding. "Bring your treats and come chat

with me, yeah? I missed you and need to tell you about a few things. Just me and you."

Figuring it has to do with his dad, I agree. Grabbing a few more gummy bears to deal with whatever bullshit he's about to tell me, I follow him out of the dressing room, blowing Roark a kiss as I pass by him.

We walk further backstage by an exit, and I stare up at him with a small smile as I bite the head off a gummy bear.

"You're feral when you eat those," he smirks as I chew.

Shrugging, I ask, "What did you want to talk about? How was your trip with your dad?"

Sighing he stares at me. "Len, this is gonna be really hard to tell you, and I need you to keep an open mind, okay? Jordan promised to swing by too, but I want to start by telling you I'm sorry I didn't tell you as soon as I found out..."

"Wait... this isn't about your dad?" My voice is slightly shrill as I stare at him. "I thought we were past keeping things from each other? I thought things were different now."

"They *are.*" Derek drags his hand through his hair and fists it, frustrated. "Will you please just listen? Jordan asked me to wait to tell you. He and I talked right before I left, and he had me by the balls, Len. It wasn't fair, but I had to agree."

I struggle to understand what he means, dropping the rest of my candy. Rubbing my temples, I frown. "So he's blackmailing you so you can stay on the tour? This doesn't sound like Jordan, though."

"Lennon," Jordan whispers softly, and I whirl to face him. "Honey, I shouldn't have made him promise to wait, but I really needed to process a few things."

My lips twist, annoyed. *He's supposed to be a good man.* "Process what?"

"I'm going to tell you a story," he says with a sad smile. "It may not all make sense in the beginning, but you're a bright girl. I know you'll understand and put the pieces together sooner than I did." Jordan stares at me, his eyes starting to water slightly. Blinking quickly he says, "My brother once married a woman when he was in his early twenties. It was a shotgun wedding, because she was pregnant and he wanted to do the right thing. James traveled a lot, so he was rarely home, but apparently the girl was impulsive... kind of unstable at times."

I nod, feeling ill but not understanding why. "What happened to the baby?" I ask. I know first hand how children of these relationships get the short end of the stick.

"My brother was really cagey about the baby. He called it Peanut, and rarely would answer questions when I asked how his home life was. This was during a time that we were developing the company, scouting new talent, so I was a little preoccupied." Jordan frowns as he stares at me. "I should have pushed harder for answers about my niece or nephew's welfare, and I'll never forgive myself. Lennon, it took me a while to figure this out, but apparently he was living in a small town in Kentucky. When Derek was talking to me about his childhood with you, he mentioned your mom's name was Carrie, and things started to click for me. God, how do I explain this..."

My breath starts to hitch as I watch him blow out a breath and wring his hands. "Lennon, James and Carrie didn't have an easy marriage when he was home, and when they had a huge fight eighteen years ago, he packed his shit up and left. James changed his name, determined to disappear from his crazy ex. Remember that fight that Layla told you I had with James?"

My mind travels disjointedly as I remember and nod. "Yeah, Layla said she was like seven when you had that fight?"

"It took me a while to stand up to him. I did my best to look for that child on my own, but couldn't. I am decent at computers and finding information, as you may have noticed, but I couldn't find you." Jordan flinches as I stare at him dumbfounded.

"Me?" I breathe. *This can't be happening...*

"What's your middle name, Lennon?" Jordan's eyes beg me to understand, but I'm spiraling. My heart races faster as I stare back at him.

"Campbell," I respond softly. "I always thought it was such an odd name. My mom could never explain why this was my middle name when I asked her. She just said it was one of the only things my father left me with. Mom burned everything the day he went away... when I was seven." I stare at him, my brain screaming at me to *think*, but the room is starting to spin.

I don't feel great. I don't want to believe what he's telling me.

Jordan doesn't notice, pushing on. "The child in the photo my brother showed me had gorgeous white-blonde hair, but I never saw its eyes. My brother refused to tell me if the baby was a boy or a girl. *I knew nothing about you.*" Jordan rubs his face tiredly, clearly disgusted with his brother. "James changed his name to our mother's maiden name when he got a divorce, which was Campbell. He wanted to disappear completely. Lennon, our last name is O'Reilly." Tears start to build in his eyes in frustration. "I changed my name to a stage name, because I was young and dumb. I thought it would be better to reinvent myself." Jordan winces as he realizes this is also what James did.

I shiver, feeling like a bucket of cold water has been thrown over me.

"James didn't recognize me though," I whisper, finally starting to understand what he's trying to tell me. "He can't be my father because he didn't fucking recognize me!" My voice gets louder with each word until I'm screaming.

Jordan looks at me with pity, shaking his head. "He didn't,

but he recognized something in you. That's why he kept staring."

"He erased me," I spit out angrily. "If he's my father, he's the worst kind of bastard. He left me alone with *her*. My life was shit, Jordan." I shake my head, unable to wrap my brain around the fact that I'm apparently speaking to my uncle. "James threw me away and kept the other daughter."

"Lennon?" *Fuck, fuck, fuck.*

I feel as if in a dream where everything that can go wrong does. Turning, I see Layla staring at me with wide eyes, tears sliding down her face.

"Did you know?" I demand, brushing off similar tears on my own cheeks. I don't know how much she heard, but it was probably enough. "Did you know he threw me away? Is that why you were nice to me?"

Layla shakes her head. "*No.* I would never lie to you, Lennon. I swear on my life that I had no idea." She blows out her breath the way that I've seen Jordan do. The way *I do* when I'm frustrated. "Dad acted really weird at the office while we were there, but I didn't know why." I flinch as she easily claims him as her father... Something I can never do.

"I can't do this. It's too much," I whisper. My feet start to move, and I feel like I'm not in charge of them. I just need to go.

"Lennon, you promised," Derek says, taking a step to follow me.

"I didn't agree to listen to you tell me I had an entire family that's just been laughing at me. Poor fucking Lennon with the crazy mother," I yell at him.

I know I'm not being fair, but I can't keep the word vomit back. My life was *hell*. I turn and run, needing to be away from this conversation. I need space. I need to not hurt my little sister, who I thought was just my best friend. I'm a ball of destruction right now, and I just need to scream it out.

Crashing through the exit, I just need to get away. Slipping on the gravel, I catch myself on my palms before pushing myself up to keep going.

Memories of my childhood flash in my mind, alongside the happy memories that Layla told me about. I don't want to be jealous, but damn it's a mindfuck to realize how different my life could have been.

Dropping my head back, I scream in frustration.

"Dammit Lennon," Derek grouses as he follows after me. "Could you just wait? You're going to break an ankle in those heels."

Several feet away from him, I turn. This parking lot isn't well lit and the stress of the last few minutes must be getting to me. Weaving on my feet, I stare at him. For some reason, there's two of him, and I squint hard.

"How do you expect me to feel? This was a really big secret, Derek," I rasp. I've expended so much energy that I feel weak and tired now. "You know what my life was like. How do you expect me to feel to know it could have all been different? What am I supposed to do with that?"

Taking a step towards me, he holds out his hand. "We'll figure it out together, baby. Please? This isn't going to have a perfect answer. I refuse to lie to you and tell you I can wave a magic wand to fix it, because I can't. I don't want you out here by yourself though, and Roark would kill me if something happened to you."

The sound of clapping begins and I hear a giggle that I haven't heard in years. Goosebumps pebble along my body as a woman steps out of the shadows. She has silver-blonde hair and piercing blue eyes.

The woman is wearing heels, a demure pencil skirt and blouse. I'm pretty sure I've never seen her wear anything like it while she was alive.

"Mom?" I ask, eyes wide.

"Carrie?!" Derek breathes.

"Poor little Lennon. You're so damn pretty, even with all this terrible lavender hair," my mom murmurs, lips twisting. She reaches out and barely touches it, wrinkling her nose in disgust.

Chest heaving, I'm assaulted with the scent of magnolias. "You're supposed to be dead," I sob, shaking my head.

I feel like *I'm* the one losing my mind. People can't just come back from the dead. That shit doesn't happen.

"Oh darling, you never bothered to look for the body, and I needed to disappear for a bit. You understand, don't you? You did, after all, reinvent yourself. I just had to die to do it." My mother looks exactly the same somehow, and it's a mindfuck. She watches me carefully, as if I'm a science experiment.

Shaking my head, darkness starts to cloud my vision and she smiles. "It'll all be clear soon, but it appears those drugs are starting to work right on schedule."

"You stupid bitch, what the fuck did you do?" Derek roars.

Smiling, Mom clicks her tongue in amusement, waving her hand at Derek. "Fucking the mother and daughter I see? Lennon, I never thought I'd have to worry about you picking up my scraps. It's adorable that you couldn't get your own man, isn't that right, baby boy?"

Baby boy...

No, no, no. I remember Derek saying that he dated someone who was abusive and I can see the truth in my mother's possessive smirk.

"You always had such a sweet tooth, Lennon. I'm surprised you have any teeth left as it is. You're looking a little chunky, now that I'm thinking about it. In this case, it just made it a lot easier to gain access to you, so I'm grateful for it. I was so close last time with your water."

Blinking, I lose my balance and fall on my ass. It's all starting to make sense. My mother was behind everything. I don't know what she wants with me now after so many years, but it can't be good.

"Mom, please don't do this," I slur.

Derek shakes off his shock, face turning bright red with anger as he stalks towards me.

"You're not fucking getting away with this," Derek growls. "Lennon is mine, and you can't hurt us anymore. You can't have her, and you should have stayed dead."

He reaches out to pick me up when he jerks in surprise. Derek falls onto his side, jerking. There are wires sticking out of him, and as if I was underwater, I slowly follow them to the woman I call my mother. Smiling evilly, she's holding a stun gun.

"For now, I'll just knock you out. I'll decide what to do with you later," she muses. "You're still fucking gorgeous. Maybe you'll see things clearer when you wake up. The night is still young."

I whimper as I fall onto my back. The knife I didn't think I'd need is just out of reach. I can't move, and I have no idea what she gave me. It also doesn't help when the person who is kidnapping you is supposed to be dead, and the one you promised never to leave. Instead she left you behind.

"Lennon, you aren't going to be needing that foul weapon where you're going," my mother growls as she removes the knife from its holster. My skirt rode up when I fell back, my legs bare now. I hiss as she shoves a syringe into my upper thigh, pushing down the plunger. "Larsen, be a doll and load these two up for me into our car, would you?" my mom asks sweetly, her tone completely at odds with the one she used with me.

Larsen's face comes into view, and I realize he's the bus

driver Jordan hired for us. The darkness is creeping in, and I'm completely paralyzed. Larsen grunts as he picks me up and starts walking. My head flops back, and all I can see is Derek's still form.

If only he hadn't followed me. If only I hadn't gotten so upset. If only...

EPILOGUE
CARRIE

Glancing over my shoulder in the van, I grin at the sight of my daughter and Derek gagged and tied up on the floor. If I remember correct, Derek always enjoyed when I fucked him while he was restrained.

"Ma'am, what's the plan?" Larsen asks as he drives.

Pouting, I turn away from my captives. Larsen is Grant's man, and he hasn't realized yet that Derek is the good mayor's son. Grant gave him to me to help with my dirty work.

Lennon is integral to our plans, and unfortunately so is Derek. As much as I want to keep him as my sex slave, I can't.

"We'll drive farther out into the desert," I muse. "I don't want it to be easy for the boy to get back, so we'll take his phone and dump him on the side of the road without his clothes. I'll let him find his way from there. The girl, we're taking with us as planned."

Larsen nods, content with the plan. I don't plan to tell him who Derek really is because he'll balk at my orders. This boy is the apple of his father's eye, even though he's hard on him. I fucked up a little when I revealed myself to Derek, but if he's gone for awhile, Lennon's guard dogs will hopefully think he had something to do with her disappearance.

A girl can hope, right?

Looking out at the dark landscape, I hum an Irish song that I learned from my grandmother.

AFTERWORD

Ummm...did you see it coming? Does anyone want to come find me and shake me? No? Honestly, Lennon's life was always going to explode, but the ending took even me by surprise.

Okay cool. The Sweetest Note is next up, and I have to say this series will be a ride. Hang on tight!

If I made you cry, laugh, and curse me out...please consider leaving a review.

Listen to the playlist for The Darkest Chord On Spotify!

ACKNOWLEDGMENTS

Oh my goodness y'all. They say new adventures take a village and this is so true. Thank you A.K. Graves for telling a tiny pixie that her words would be fun to read! I literally started writing a few weeks later. Thank you Amber Nicole for telling me that I could do this, being my sounding board when I felt like I was stuck, and telling me to keep going. Thank you for editing my books and making sure everything works. Thank you Sarah Klinger PA for kidnapping me, and then kicking me out of the baby author nest. You are such an amazing cheerleader.

Thank you to my stabby alpha/betas: Kate, Cindy, Danielle, Asheley, Terra, Cheryl, and Oriane. I love how so many of you voice and messaged to yell at me about the cliffhanger in this book. They have all licked Derek by the way. The yelling helps my evil muse.

Thank you Antonette for bringing life to this cover. It's everything I dreamed I wanted.

Thank you to you, my readers, who continue to take the leap with me and trust me to fix things by the end.

ALSO BY JENN BULLARD

Living Words, The Unwritten Truths Duet Book One

http://Books2read.com/livingwords

Taking Chances, The Unwritten Truths Duet Book Two

https://books2read.com/Takingchances2

The Darkest Chord, Darkest Nights Book One

https://books2read.com/Thedarkestchord

The Sweetest Note, Darkest Nights Book Two

Coming 2023

https://books2read.com/TheSweetestNote

ABOUT THE AUTHOR

Jenn Bullard is a tiny pixie author that loves to read. She has three daughters and is married to her cinnamon roll— her Griffin. She is a stay at home mom with a healthy appreciation for things that vibrate. Most of the time, Jenn is ruled by her characters: they drive, she just tells their story. If Jenn could tell her readers anything: it's to follow your dreams. She wouldn't be writing if she hadn't.

Made in the USA
Columbia, SC
11 March 2024

33000878R00357